MADE
for
ME

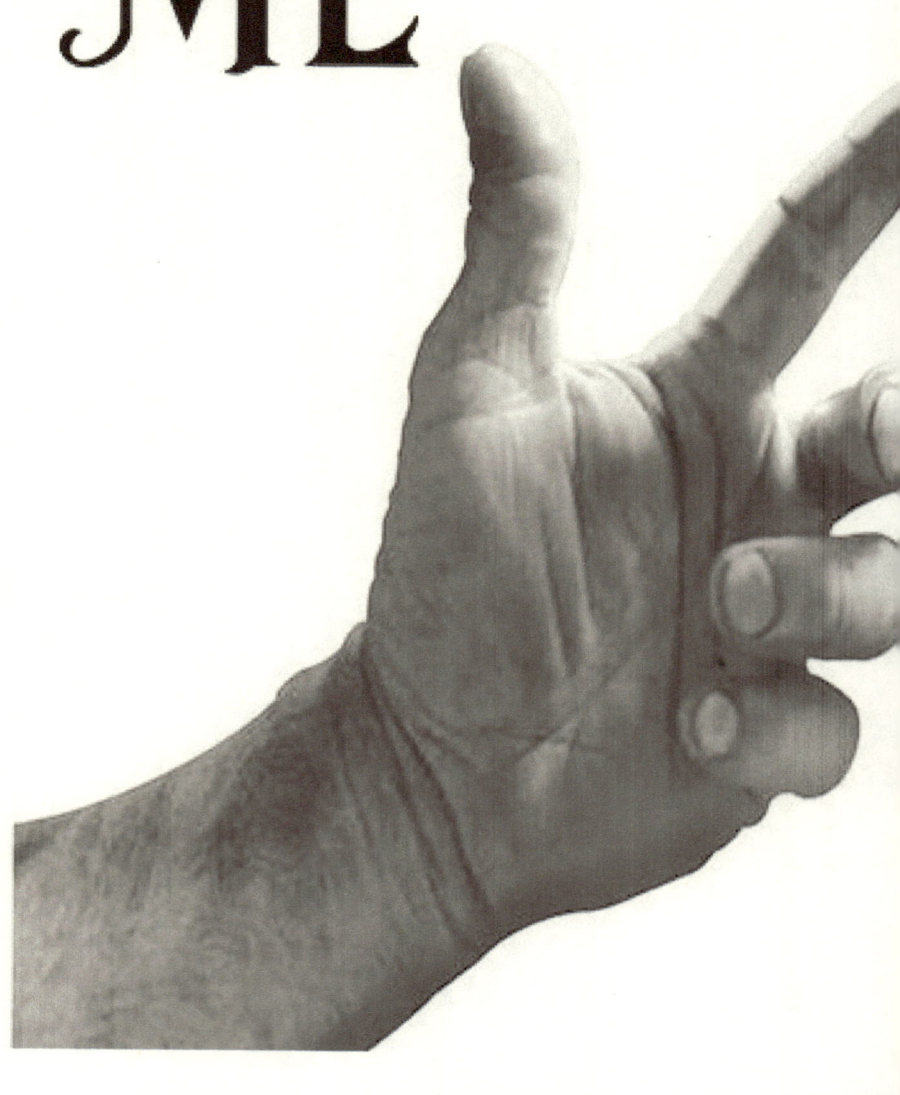

By
Laura Ranger

Foundations Book Publishing
4209 Lakeland Drive, #398, Flowood, MS 39232
www.FoundationsBooks.net

Made for Me

ISBN: 978-1-64583-152-5

Copyright © 2025 by Laura Ranger
Book Formatting by Bella Roccaforte
Artwork by Laura Fleming Summa

Published in the United States of America
Worldwide Electronic & Digital Rights
Worldwide English Language Print Rights

Contents

Dedicated to Alan Jude Summa and Glenn A Boyd for a storyline concept that was a blast to develop. And to all the teens who have felt like they never fit in. Embrace your individual uniqueness. There's only one of you, make it the best you can be and ignore the ones who don't get you. You'll grow into your own!

One

S andi swung her legs over the side of the bed and scrubbed her
face with her hands. *Another miserable school day,* she thought.
She just wanted to be grown and on her own. She was sick of all
the childish games and nasty students she had to deal with. Too many
mean teachers as well. But sitting here wishing for something different
wasn't going to make it happen.

She groaned as she lifted her small frame from her bed and padded
toward her bathroom. As she passed her dresser mirror, she stopped and
took a good look at herself. She didn't understand why no one liked her.
She knew plenty of people who were a lot less attractive than she was.
She might not be considered beautiful, but she was far from ugly.

In the bathroom, she brushed through her mousy-brown, shoulder-
length hair. *Okay,* she thought to herself, *I could try to do something with
my hair, but it's too much trouble, and who would notice anyway?* It was
fine just pulled up in a ponytail—a lot of girls did that. She had never
mastered the messy bun so many girls pulled off. She washed her face,
noticing her good, clear complexion. She was luckier than most,
especially given her age. She briefly thought about using a bit of
makeup, but it felt like more bother than it was worth. No one had ever

taught her how to apply makeup. One of the disadvantages of growing up without a mother. And she had never had girlfriends to learn from.

She spoke to her reflection, "Besides, I always end up looking like a clown. I get teased enough as it is. I don't need to give them material to torment me with." Instead, she just quickly applied a coral shade of lipstick.

Sandi believed her form was no form at all. She had a small, delicate bone structure. Her body was lean with knobby knees and stick legs. She regularly worked out in their home gym, but it did no good. Her chest was so small she could usually get away without wearing a bra. She might as well have been born a male—although a boy with her 5'3" height and 102-pound body would have been beaten up all the time. "What's the use?" she grumbled.

Sandi heard her father call from downstairs that her breakfast was ready, so she hurried to finish up. She never put any thought into what to wear. She always wore jeans and a T-shirt. Fashion was another thing lost on her. She simply dressed for comfort.

She bounded down the stairs and was greeted with the nasty orange drink her father insisted she ingest every day of her life. "Do I have to? Daddy, you know I'm sick of this stuff. What difference does it make? Is there *any* other flavor? I'm to a point I don't care for anything orange."

He hugged her to him. "You're the healthiest teen out there," he said with a grin. "Drink up. I made pancakes."

"Why can't I just have coffee in the morning?"

"You're welcome to a cup of coffee...with your pancakes."

She groaned, handed her father her empty glass, and slid into her chair at the breakfast table.

"What have you got going on at school today?" her father asked. "Anything exciting?"

"It's high school. There's never anything exciting."

"I know science is your favorite subject. Any interesting experiments you're involved with?"

"Here, always. School rarely. The experiments and observations they have us do in school are elementary at best. Can't I just test out, graduate early, and go to college?"

"I don't feel that's wise. You need the full high school experience to succeed in life."

"Oh please, I have no high school experience. I have no friends. I don't do any extra-curricular activities. I've learned everything I can from those imbeciles. I'm ready to learn without a ceiling. No one there is smart enough to teach me anything worthwhile."

"There's a time for everything. Right now, it's your time for high school. College will come soon enough. Just be patient, sweetheart."

"But I'm not, you know this. I just want to get on with my life."

Sandi came from a long line of scientists and fully intended to become one herself. It was the only time she felt passion for anything. They had an extensive lab in their basement. She came to life the moment she got home from school. Her whole day was spent in anticipation of working in her space in the cellar. She would often lose track of time until her father reminded her to go to bed.

Her favorite days were the weekends when she could spend most of her time in the lab. They weren't churchgoers. Her father always said there was no God. He knew men and women of science who created astounding things, and therefore believed God was just made up by those not intelligent enough to invent.

Sandi was dragging her feet but knew she needed to be in her seat by 7:30 a.m. She was pushing it. She scraped what she couldn't eat down the disposal, stuck her dishes in the dishwasher, kissed her father on the cheek, and grabbed her backpack on her way out the door. She hollered over her shoulder before the door slammed shut, "I love you, Daddy. Thanks for breakfast."

Sandi paid for an assigned parking space, so she never had to waste time hunting for a place to park. She grabbed her school bag and hit her key fob to lock her doors while running over the grass to clear the front door. Just as she crossed the threshold of her homeroom, the bell rang. Phew, she had cut this one too close.

As she slid into her seat, Jana Proctor, one of the mean girls, said, "Nice of you to join us, Slimy."

"It's Sandi, you moron. You can't even learn *that* in three years? Are you sure you shouldn't be in Special Ed?"

"Oh, shut up."

"Didn't your mother ever teach you that's not nice? But then again, you're not nice. Never mind."

The teacher interrupted their daily banter by taking roll call. The bell rang and Sandi started to stand, but Jana pushed her back in her seat as she passed her. "Just stay down, Maggot."

"How original. Did you work all night to think that up in your little pea brain? Don't tax yourself."

Jana flipped her long blonde hair over her shoulder on her way out the door.

Sandi really didn't like it here. She took a deep breath, stood, picked up her bag, squared her shoulders, and headed for the door.

Sandi took her seat in English class. As she pulled her books out, she felt a hard yank on her ponytail, her head snapped back. "Ow! What are you, five? Grow up, Jackson."

"You first," he replied.

"Do it again and I'll waste no time slipping you a dose of a strong sexually transmitted disease."

"Ooh, I'm so scared."

"You'll be more than scared when you feel like you're dying."

Mrs. Jansen, the teacher said, "If you two are quite through, may I begin class?"

Sandi turned and faced the front.

Her next class was Social Studies. There was no class she despised more—well, it ran a close second to PE. She was sure Mr. Collins hated her. She had no idea why. She always did her work, got good grades, and was never disruptive in his class. There was just never making this man happy. She'd stopped trying. He always talked to her like she was stupid. Nothing bothered her more than someone talking down to her. She could think around him and his small mentality any day.

At lunch, she had turned from the line with her tray when Betty the Beast plowed into her. Sandi fell on her stomach with her arms splayed over her head while her tray and lunch flew out in front of her. The whole place erupted with laughter. She was mortified to hear the kids heckling her: "Sandi can't even manage to stay on her own two feet!"

"She is such a klutz." "It's no wonder she doesn't have any friends; they all run for their lives."

Sandi picked herself up off the floor. With her head low, she walked out. She could hear Betty calling after her, "Hey, klutzy, clean up your mess!"

She just kept walking.

Sandi sat at a picnic table in the courtyard by herself. The fresh air would clear her head. She laid her head on her crossed arms on the table. There had to be a better way than this. Somewhere in this big world, there had to be nice people. They weren't here.

Down in the yard, a couple was alone on a bench, facing each other with their foreheads together. What could they be talking about so intimately? She believed it happened. She just couldn't imagine it for herself. Of course, she'd never even kissed a boy, so she was clueless on many levels. Sandi closed her eyes and imagined herself with a cute boy who was that attentive to her. Immediately, Houston MacAvoy filled her mind. He was the only boy she had ever been interested in, but he didn't even know she existed. She sat next to him in Physics. They only exchanged pleasantries. She had never seen him with a girlfriend. He was too smart and attractive not to be dating someone. She figured that whoever his girl was, she went to a different school.

He was tall, dark, and handsome with high intelligence, and he appeared to be strong. He was well-liked by everyone. All the girls fawned over him. He just didn't seem to notice.

She imagined Houston as her boyfriend. He'd carry her backpack for her, pick her up in his car for school, and keep her safe from bullies. Everyone would look at her differently and treat her with respect. She would never have an episode like she'd just experienced in front of the whole school again.

Sandi must have dozed off because she awoke to the end-of-period bell. She didn't want to be at school. If she had her way, she would live in her home lab and study on her own. She was working on creating a single-cell organism, which thrilled her. Once she had that aspect down, she was moving to a multi-cell organism. After that, who knew? She had to figure out a way to engage her father in this. She knew he had done similar experiments in the past. Instead of treating her as a child, she needed him to see her as an equal, teach her, and see how far she could go. She guessed she wouldn't be able to take it as far as her imagination was dreaming up, or else he would have more information on developing beings. Now, she figured, she was just thinking crazy. *Focus on creating a single-cell organism before you go making "beings"*, she thought to herself.

Sandi pulled into the garage, turned the car off, and thought for a bit. She wasn't finding the same enthusiasm she usually felt. She was just elevating one experiment to another. She'd done that so many times in the past. Was it due to her father no longer working with her in the lab? She grabbed her bag from the back seat and headed for the basement.

She stood staring at her table. Her father had suggested she introduce heat. She had been considering what heat source to use all day. She considered the various kinds and their impact on such a small entity. That's what research was for.

Sandi started pulling books from the shelf, spreading them on the table. Now the table also held a laptop and a small printer. But most of the time, like her dad, she preferred to use paper and pen. Sometimes, when she just needed quick information and didn't need to work anything out, she'd print a page or two to take to her workstation. With books, the laptop, her pen, and some paper, she was comfortable and ready to pore through everything she could.

She was wrapped up in all her reading when her father put his hand on her shoulder, startling her so she jumped. "Oh! Daddy, you scared the life out of me."

"What are you so engrossed in?"

"Well, I've been working with molecules, like I said last night. When you mentioned heat, I wondered what the best heat source would be, so I don't damage it. Do you know? I'll use all the knowledge you can share."

"I do have experience in this area. What do you ultimately intend to do with it?"

"Do with it? I have no idea. My main goal is to create just a multi-cell organism. How far did your research and experimentation get you?"

"Actually, pretty far. I created a full being."

"What? Are you serious? What happened to it? Do you still have it? Can I see it?"

"No."

"Where is it? What kind of being was it? Did it have features like we do? What did it do? What'd it look like? Did you have to feed it?"

"Enough with the questions. Just know it can be done, has been done, doesn't need to be done again."

"But I really want to try. I want to see how far I could go."

"For what purpose, princess? What is it you want to accomplish?"

"Nothing in particular. I just think it would be so cool to create life. Wasn't it that way for you?"

"I guess. Mine was just a lark. Once I proved to myself it could be done, I moved on."

"What could be more exciting than creating something like that? Did it have a face, hair, teeth, arms, legs—"

"That's enough. It's over with. You should move on."

"No, Daddy, I really want to see what happens. I really want to do this. Can't you just be supportive?"

"Oh, sweet pea, I am supportive of everything you do."

"It doesn't feel like it. Weren't you excited when you did yours? I just want you to be excited about mine. Please, don't throw a wet blanket on this for me."

"I'm sorry. That's not what I meant to do. I just don't want you to have any pain with the loss when it's over."

"You always say I need to make my own mistakes, to learn my own lessons. Can't this be one of them?"

"Yes, it can, and I'm sure it will if you insist on proceeding. I didn't mean to make you feel that way. I'll leave you to it. I have a lot of reading to get done tonight. Are you up for Chinese for dinner?"

"That sounds great. Just call me when it's here, and I'll be up."

As her father walked away from her, she stared after him, watching his form ascend the stairs. She thought, *How is a full body created? How does it grow and form?* She needed to tackle a single cell right now. She guessed she'd have to leave the full body-making to whatever creator did all that. It was a bit out of her reach. But it sure would be cool if she could make a person. She would make herself the man of her dreams.

Well, at least a boyfriend good enough to make the kids at school stop looking at her like a loser.

Her father called down the stairs, so she set her pen down and got up. She'd get back at it as soon as she had a bite to eat.

At the dinner table, her father tried to engage her in different conversations, but she couldn't pull her thoughts from the idea of creating. It made her feel powerful.

Two

S andi cleaned the kitchen quickly, so she could return to the basement and begin implementing her concept of heating molecules to see if they would transform. She put a petri dish over a Bunsen burner. Within seconds the whole thing fell flat. Well... that proved to be too much heat too fast. After an evening filled with multiple attempts in various ways, she considered asking her father, but she knew how stubborn he was. She'd figure this out on her own. It was getting late, and she was tired. She needed rest.

Sandi wrapped the dish in a piece of thermal fabric for the night, hoping it would retain at least some of the heat she had introduced.

As Sandi got ready for bed, she couldn't help but wonder about all the components it would take to create something as intricate as a body. Creating plant life would be simple enough, but a living, breathing being was so much more exciting. How would one add such things as breath, blood flow, heartbeat, and brain activity? As much as she enjoyed a good challenge to her mind, her brain was on overload, and she couldn't wrap it around all the variables.

She slipped between her sheets but found it difficult to turn her brain off. She grabbed her latest pleasure read, a romance. She might be a science nerd, but she longed for love. She believed her father loved her, but she wanted more. He might not have wanted another wife, but she didn't want to be alone for the rest of her life.

It was a typical paperback romance: boy meets girl, tension, conflict, then resolution, with a happily ever after. Just the way she saw her future.

In the morning, Sandi was anxious to begin her day where she left off the night before. She showered, dressed, and met her father in the kitchen. "Morning, Daddy!"

"Hey, sugar, what big plans do you have today?" He gave her a warm hug.

"I'm still working on introducing heat to my molecules."

Her father's face clouded, and she wondered why. What was his problem? No matter, she wasn't going to let his mood change her direction. She had her mind made up. With his dissatisfaction came more resolve for her. Funny how that worked.

She poured a cup of coffee and sat down at the table.

"Forgetting something?" her father asked.

"Oh, come on. What is the big deal? It's Saturday."

"I'll make you some toast with peanut butter, you get your juice."

"Never mind, I'll make it myself. Honestly, you're obsessed."

She dropped a couple of pieces of wheat bread in the toaster and pulled out a knife, the butter, and peanut butter. There was no use fighting it; she knew she'd lose. Sandi poured herself a glass of her father's nasty concoction. She threw it back like medicine and chased it with her coffee to get rid of the taste.

She sat down with her breakfast. "So, with the being you created, were you able to add breath and blood flow? Is a heart and a brain required, or did you not go that far?

He remained silent, just looking at her.

"I have no intention of letting this go. Either you can help me, or I'll just figure it out on my own. I'd prefer to learn from your experience, but if you don't want to share, I'll do it all without you. Your choice."

They sat in silence. Her father continued to study her.

"What?" she asked. "You know me well enough to know I'm going to do it anyway. You can make it more difficult on me or tell me what I need to know."

When he said nothing, she got up and cleaned the kitchen. They had an agreement: her father did all the cooking or ordering depending on his desire, and she did all the cleanup. When she was done, she headed for the lab.

Sandi carefully unwrapped her experiment. When she observed positive molecular changes, her excitement rocketed . She now knew she was heading in the right direction. She was going to make this happen. Her father could keep his knowledge to himself. She was just as intelligent as he was. It might take some time, but she would never give up and eventually figure it out. She figured this apple hadn't fallen far from the tree, and she was even more stubborn than her father.

She worked throughout the day and lost track of time. She was making great strides and had managed to create a multi-cell organism. In theory, it just meant exponentially increasing that to form a being. It occurred to her that maybe her father didn't want to share his knowledge because his being was a failure. He was prideful. She realized he never did answer her question about what he had done with his creation.

Her father called down the stairs that dinner was ready. She hated to stop now but knew her father didn't tolerate a meal getting cold. "Be right there," she called out.

Her father said nothing to her for an uncomfortably long time before he spoke. "Princess, I'm sorry for not appearing supportive in your endeavor. You just don't know what you're messing with."

"Then why don't you tell me?"

He took a deep breath and said slowly, "What if you begin creating and produce a living, breathing organism, and it dies? I'm afraid you'll be devastated. I don't want to see you heartbroken."

"You're breaking my heart more now than an experiment could."

He looked as though she had just slapped him. The twinge of pain that flew across his face in a split second made her realize she'd hit the mark.

"I'm sorry, Daddy. It's how I feel. I didn't mean to hurt you. Can't you do this with me?"

"I'd prefer not to. I can see you're determined, so I'll give you some of my notes. You can glean what I learned from there, okay?"

She jumped from her seat, threw her arms around his neck, and hugged him tightly.

"I take that as a yes?" he said.

"Yes! That would be fantastic. After dinner?"

"I'll dig them out for you."

Sandi couldn't clean up the kitchen fast enough. She really hoped her work to date wasn't too far off and she could figure out how to continue from where she was.

She heard her father descending the stairs and her heart leaped in her chest.

As he handed Sandi his stack of notebooks, he said, "Here you go. If you can't decipher my formulas or chicken scratch, just ask."

"Oh, thank you, Daddy! Are you sure you won't work with me?"

"No. I'd rather not." He went back up the stairs.

She didn't understand his choice, but it was his to make. Sadly, she carried them to the table and started from the one titled *Multi-celled Organisms Book One*. There was no telling how old his notebooks were. The edges of the pages had yellowed. As she read through, she realized she was right on track with what her father had done, who knew how many years ago. When she finished his first notebook, she noticed how she had arrived at the same place with about half the number of pages used in her notebook. Each of his steps seemed to hold much more detailed observations, but she didn't see that his notes had anything that would significantly change where she was.

Sandi continued with the second book. This was getting into the things her mind had already jumped to. She read the whole thing and went on to read all the notebooks he'd given her. When she got to the end of book seven, she wondered where the rest was. She found it hard to believe he just stopped there. What happened? He was on the right track. He had even gone as far as introducing his DNA to his being. That was brilliant. She went upstairs to find her father in his office. She took the chair in front of his desk. He removed his glasses.

"Why didn't you finish?" Sandi asked.

"There was no need."

"Of course there was! You could have actually made a human, not just a simple multi-cell organism. Why didn't you?"

"Do you remember what I said at dinner about being heartbroken?"

"Oh, yes. I'm so sorry. Did it die on you? What went wrong? What should I do differently?"

"I just walked away and never looked back. I really wish you would as well."

"I can't. I have to do this."

"Why? We're not the creators of the universe. There are some things better left alone."

"This can't be one of them. Besides, what if we, or ones like us, *actually are* the creators of the universe?"

"Point well taken. Well, you have the advantage of my work. Good luck, baby girl."

Over the next week, Sandi implemented each successful piece as her father had. It was at the point she was about to add her own DNA that she felt ethically torn. Was it infringing too much on creation? She tried reconciling that in her mind. She wasn't God. However, she believed He had given her her knowledge and abilities.

Her secret desire was to make herself a boyfriend. It felt a bit incestuous to make a boyfriend with her own DNA. She wondered whose DNA her father had used. She wanted to ask him but didn't want him to shut her down if she asked too many questions. As thorough as his notes were, he hadn't said where he got that from. She checked every morning and every night, and nothing was happening, either positive or negative. Unless and until it went in one direction or the other, she would just continue the observations of her subject.

Sandi sat in her miserable Social Studies class doodling, trying to work out what to do to advance her experiment. She began jotting her name with a boyfriend's name. Every name she came up with reminded her of some boy in her school who she didn't like. No! She'd scribble it out. She wanted a beau with a unique name that didn't make her cringe every time she said it. There was one name she'd have loved to write but didn't dare. She tried name after name, acronym after acronym and nothing was working.

Then she came up with MAX. That was it! It stood for Made-up Artificial eXperiment. She liked it. Sandi and Max. Max and Sandi. It had a good ring to it.

Unbeknownst to her, her arch nemesis, Kristy, was standing over her shoulder and said, "Who's Max, loser? I don't know any Max."

"It's nunya. Now, go away."

"I'm sure, if there really is a Max, he's just as big a plague to society as you are."

"Those are big words for such an ignoramus."

"Bite me."

"Now, that's more your mentality."

The bell rang. Sandi gathered her things and left. She was mortified Kristy had seen her doodles. Now she felt obligated to create a Max for a boyfriend.

Sandi had to see if she could test out of this hellhole without her father's permission. Maybe if she tested high enough, the school would back her and get her father to sign off. She had to get away from all the juvenile mentality that permeated this place. How was she expected to thrive in this environment? She couldn't. Therefore, she needed a change of influence. A university would provide more intelligence and give her a more level playing field.

During her lunch and remaining classes, Sandi finished her homework. She didn't want anything interrupting her nighttime work. Her classes were dumbed down enough for her to keep up with the lectures and work on her other classwork on the sly.

It was the end of another wretched day at school. Sandi felt she couldn't get out of this building fast enough. Dodging and weaving through all the bodies in the hallway, she saw an opening with a straight shot toward the front door. She took it. Suddenly, she felt herself propelled through the air, landing spread-eagled across the floor. She felt her books fly over her head. She always left the top of her book bag unzipped throughout the day, so she could easily slip books and notebooks in and out. She always zipped it up at the end of her last class. Today, she could only focus on getting out and had neglected that part. She lay there face down while everyone laughed and took jabs at her. Some even kicked her on their way by. There had to be a special place in Hell for these people.

Then she heard a familiar voice say, "I've got your books. Come on, let me help you up." She looked up into the beautiful blue eyes of Houston MacAvoy.

Houston was the only one in this place she liked. He was perfect. He was kind, considerate, and about the only one who could carry on an intelligent conversation with her. It didn't hurt that he was so attractive. He was much taller than her. He had thick, wavy, brown hair that he kept short on the sides and back and just a bit longer on top. He had the cutest dimples, a cleft chin, and a strong, chiseled jawline with high cheekbones. He was friendly with everyone but didn't seem to be close to anyone. She wondered if his friends were outside of school. There was no way this gorgeous boy wasn't taken. He was intellectual, witty, and seemed to be a good conversationalist, from the few times they'd been able to talk. He sat next to her in Physics, but they usually didn't have time to chat, though Sandi did try to engage him every chance she got.

She wanted to invite him for coffee after school one day, where they could sit and chat. She just hadn't worked up the nerve yet. She wasn't sure she wanted to give the time to something meaningless that wouldn't lead anywhere. Yes, she'd love to have a full, uninterrupted conversation with him, but she knew, if it ever happened, it wouldn't lead anywhere, and it would therefore be a pointless encounter.

Houston slid her books into her backpack, and she heard the zipper close. Sandi took his outstretched hand. She felt a shock go through her body at his touch. Did he feel that? As she rose, he put an arm around her waist to help lift her. She felt the ripple of muscles in his strong arms and abs beneath his shirt. *Holy momma,* she thought. Now she had even more to admire him for. She wasn't aware of any sport he participated in, but those muscles suggested otherwise. She would love to see him shirtless!

He snapped her out of her wayward thoughts. "You okay?"

Sandi nodded.

"I'm sorry. People can be so mean. You have a great night. I've gotta run. See you tomorrow."

Oh, she certainly hoped so. She looked down at her feet. There was Houston's gray hoodie he often wore. He must have dropped it while helping her. Sandi snatched it up and ran for the door he had just exited. Her eyes scanned the grounds, parking lot, and bus lane. He was nowhere to be seen. She didn't know if he drove and, if so, what his vehicle looked like. She didn't know where she should be looking. She would just bring it to him the next day.

She was mad at whoever had pushed her, but glad Houston was there to help her. A sucky day had ended with a big bright spot. When she got in her car, she did what she was dying to do since picking up the garment: she held it to her nose and inhaled deeply. It really did smell like him. For now, she would have a piece of him. Maybe one day, he could become her boyfriend, and she would have more than just a hoodie.

Once she was in the protection of her own home, she slipped the sweatshirt on. It was way too big on her small frame, so she rolled up the sleeves. It felt like a hug. His hug. She had never stolen anything, but she was strongly considering not giving this back.

Sandi ran upstairs, took the hoodie off, and hung it in her closet. She didn't want anything to happen to it in the lab. As she descended the stairs, she experienced a sense of loss at the distance away from this small piece of Houston she now possessed. No, she wouldn't be able to give it back right away. Maybe just an extra day and then she would return it.

In the lab, she worked methodically. She couldn't keep her focus. She was consumed with thoughts of her crush. She could still feel his touch. It made her body tingle. While taking notes, she realized she'd written her first name with his last. "Oh, come on, girl! Stop this silly teenage nonsense." She just wanted to consider what it would be like to be part of a true couple. She had her daydreams of one day introducing Max as her boyfriend when she started down this road.

Of course, she never had tolerance for any of the foolish boys around her age. The girls weren't much better, and she wasn't inclined that way anyhow. She left the idiots to entertain each other. She certainly had noticed Houston MacAvoy and wished he could be hers. But she really needed to shake herself away from all this now. There was no way she would ever have Houston, so it was pointless to dwell on it.

Three

S andi had a few setbacks with her experiment, but it was all coming along nicely. She was still determined to take it further than her father's work. As she researched, it dawned on her that she'd forgotten how necessary oxygen was to creation. All living things needed oxygen. Her father should have been able to figure that out. So, where was that in his notes? No matter; she would try slowly adding the O element to bring her experiment fully to life.

She started off very slowly. It would be a long time catching up to this point if she had to start all over. After carefully observing her experiment for a long while, she saw her organism appear to become animated and grow. She jumped up and down, spinning in circles. She'd done it! Now what? Back to the books.

One thing puzzling her was the whole form part. How was he to have ears, a face, limbs, a brain... how was he to be male, when it came right down to it? The more her mind worked and she researched, the more she found herself going in circles and down rabbit holes.

"Stop!" she shouted out loud. She was too close to everything. She needed to step back and look at it in a scientific way: from a distance, not so close and intimately. She thought, *What if someone was needing this information and wanted my knowledge to shine a light on some dilemma this work would help?*

Sandi pushed away from the table and paced the floor, wondering what suggestions she would give an outsider asking for advice. She had to think this through. What did she know? *Go back to the basics, Sandi,* she thought.

She could add some of her DNA, as her father had, but she wanted to be certain this being would be male. Every human had twenty-two pairs of like chromosomes. What made the difference in male and female was the twenty-third pair, also called the sex chromosome. In the twenty-third pair, females had two X chromosomes, where the male had one X and one Y. Her DNA alone wasn't going to work, or would it? She had it! She could add stem cells from a male. That would help with the formation of various parts.

She went back to the books on the table, then pulled up the internet and typed in "How to harvest stem cells." The answer returned with bone marrow. She typed in "How to get bone marrow." It came back with the six best bones to take marrow from. She also noted it would take about two quarts of marrow.

Just great, where am I going to get two quarts of bone marrow from a man? she wondered. It wasn't like she could put in an order and go pick it up.

She continued to hunt. She discovered that sometimes marrow was taken from the bones of cadavers. That she could see being able to accomplish. If the temperature of the bones could be maintained at zero degrees Celsius, they would be viable for up to four days. That was astounding.

As she considered all this, her father called down the stairs that dinner was ready. Maybe talking it through with her father would bring clarity about the direction she needed to go in. Or maybe it would entice him to work with her going forward, since she had accomplished so much already.

Sandi took the stairs two at a time, excitedly rounded the corner into the kitchen, kissed her father on the cheek, and said, "Hi, Daddy! How was your day? Dinner smells great."

"What's up, buttercup? It's nice to see you so happy."

"I'm really excited about how my experiment is coming along. I was able to successfully introduce oxygen and now have a living entity."

"You have what?"

"Well, I wanted to bounce a few things off you and see if you could help me. Or maybe you'd want to work with me on this."

"Whatcha got?" he asked reluctantly.

"I need male stem cells. I can get that from bone marrow. I just found out that I could actually use the marrow from the bones of a cadaver."

Her father's jaw dropped right along with his fork. He stared at her.

"What? What's wrong? Say something."

"Absolutely not, young lady!"

"Why not? It's not like I'm looking to take it from a live human. If they've already died, they don't need it. It won't hurt them. Why can't I use it?"

"You are not playing God. End of discussion."

"So, you won't even work with me on this?"

"No. There's a reason my research ends where it did. You've had your fun, now it's over."

"No! I won't end it. It's living. Ending it would kill it."

"Correct, and that's exactly what you will do. I told you it would come to this if you insisted on going forward. If you don't destroy it, I will."

"You can't."

"I can and I will. You put an end to this now! Have I made myself clear?"

"Crystal."

She got up from the table with her plate, scraped off her dinner into the trash, rinsed her dishes and silverware, put them in the dishwasher, and went downstairs without another word.

He had to be out of his mind if he thought for one second she was going to terminate her greatest experiment to date. Fine. If he didn't want to work with her or help her, she'd figure it out on her own. There were other ways around this issue.

Sandi sat in her chair and stared at her treasure. She would one day turn it into a living male, her very own boyfriend. He would be smart,

19

witty, and good-looking. She had to figure out a way to continue without her father finding out she was disobeying him. How was she supposed to hide a full-grown human in the same house? She didn't have time to figure it out right now. She was disenchanted with her father's hard line. She needed to sleep on it and approach him in the morning with a more logical stance—one he would be able to get behind and understand her feelings.

Sandi wrapped it up for the night and left it under the heat lamps. She wasn't going to lose it now while she reasoned with her father. She had come too far and was so close.

She turned out the lights and went upstairs to bed. Her father must have heard her in the hall and called out, "Sandi, did you destroy your experiment?"

"No."

"If it's not gone by the time I get home tomorrow night, I'll do it myself."

"You're not God!"

"Neither are you."

She stepped around into the living room. "At least I believe in God, you never have."

"I'm a realist."

"How can you look at all the complexities of this world and not know there is a higher power?"

"Who put these crazy ideas in your head?"

"I've read the Bible."

"That's just a collection of old stories people used to tell each other to keep others inline."

"Have you read it? Did nothing in it stir anything in you?"

"No. It's just a storybook. An antiquated one at that. Those of us who have the brains to understand and create know we are the designers of life. There is no 'higher power', as you call it. We are the highest power."

"You're impossible."

"Enough of this talk. One way or another, your experiment ends by tomorrow. By your hand or mine. Good night."

She didn't even respond, she went to her room and got ready for bed. He was being unreasonable. Another day would allow her to think of how to talk sense into him. She was tired and needed sleep.

The next morning when she got to the kitchen her father was standing holding out her glass of gross juice. "Good morning, princess. About last night..."

She didn't respond. She didn't even look at him. He attempted to hug her as he did every morning, but instead, she snatched the glass from his hand and turned away. She was mad at him for robbing her of her dreams, while he apparently had taken his as far as he desired. It was so unfair.

"I understand your ambition. I also understand you're playing in a realm you have no business in. I didn't mean to sound so harsh, but you need to stop this now."

She downed the juice, set the empty on the table, grabbed her backpack, and walked out.

She heard her father calling after her. "Get back here this instant. You haven't eaten anything yet."

She left for school.

Throughout the day, Sandi doodled and scribbled trying to figure out what to do to keep her experiment but keep it hidden from her father. In Study Hall at the end of the day, she thought of a way to throw her father off. With more time, she knew she would come up with a more permanent solution. Now she was anxious to get home and carry out her plan. She'd have to work fast to have it completed by the time her father got home. She knew him well enough to know he was a man of his word and would follow through with his threat. She had no intention of interacting with her dad in any manner right now.

When she got home, she grabbed a pack of peanut butter crackers. She dropped them off in her room with a bottle of water and her backpack. She quickly ran to the lab. The whole right side of the basement was behind heavy drapes. They stored all their supplies and backups on that side of those curtains. Sandi parted them and stepped through. Down both sides were floor-to-ceiling shelves, most with short extensions perpendicular to the wall, creating mini aisles. She knew her father kept most of his things to the right, so she went to the left. She could easily hide this on the last aisle at the end. She set it up with the heat lamp.

Now she had to figure out how to make it appear she had done as she was told. She made up a similar mixture to the appearance of her Max, blew into the bag and tied it up to create some condensation on the inside, and set it in the trash can to the left of her lab table. She put away all the books and notebooks that had been left open around the room for so many days, shut down the laptop, wiped everything down, and stood at the foot of the stairs. It all looked very sterile. She turned out the light with a sharp pang of regret that her dad refused to work with her on this.

Her father wasn't home yet, so she ran up the two flights of stairs to her bedroom and locked the door behind her. Her bathroom connected with the guest bedroom next to hers. She locked the door from the bathroom to the spare room.

Sandi heard the garage door going up and knew what that meant. She stopped doing the assigned class readings to listen for any possible reaction from her father. She heard nothing. Then she heard the distinct footfalls she had grown to recognize ascending the stairs. She held her breath. She noticed they stopped outside her door. She quietly controlled her breathing. Maybe he would believe she was asleep. He knocked softly on her door. She didn't make a sound. After a moment he continued to his room. She waited. Listening. Shortly after, she heard him go down the stairs.

He hollered up the stairs a little later, "Sandi, dinner's ready."

She didn't move and said nothing.

After a while, he came to her door, knocked, and told her again that dinner was ready. She lay perfectly still. He knocked again, then tried the locked door. He said, "Are you coming down to eat? I've got dinner on the table. Come on before it gets cold."

She said nothing. He could talk until he was blue, but it wouldn't make her respond to him. She was mad. Too mad to even look at him, let alone share a meal with him.

After a few minutes, he retreated. She breathed a huge sigh of relief.

She ate her crackers and drank her water. She took her shower and got ready for bed. She wouldn't have time in the morning, because she was going to make sure she was out of the house before her father even got up. She wasn't ready to face him. She set her alarm for thirty minutes before her father's would go off. She slept with her earbuds in, so when her alarm went off, he wouldn't hear it. Getting up before dawn wouldn't be an issue since she was going to sleep so early.

The next morning, she quietly got ready and crept down the stairs. She paused in the kitchen wondering if she should drink her juice. She chose not to. The juice police weren't here forcing her. Missing a day wasn't going to hurt anything. She didn't care if the garage door opening woke her father. By the time he got down the stairs, she'd be gone.

As soon as she rounded the corner of their street, her cell phone rang. She knew it. It was her father. He was so predictable. She hit the button to send the call to voicemail. He called again. She repeated the action. When he called a third time, she turned her phone off. Now he could call as much as he liked, but it wasn't going to bother her.

She needed something to eat. She was tempted to buy donuts but knew they wouldn't sustain her long. There'd be no thinking on all those empty carbs. She went through a drive-through and bought a bagel with chicken and cheese. For a brief second, she considered getting an orange juice but decided against it and went for just coffee instead.

Sandi drove to the park to eat and listen to the birds wake up the day. She got to watch the sun rise. Beautiful! After wasting enough time, she drove on to school to trudge through this last day of the week. What a miserable weekend she was in for.

Four

S andi debated going home at all but knew if she didn't, it would
spark a manhunt by her father. She wanted as little interaction
with him as possible. She would get home before him and
sequester herself in her room again. If she stayed out, she wouldn't have
the opportunity to check on her Max. That was her priority.

She again ran her backpack to her room, this time with food to get
her through the weekend. She stashed her food supplies in the bottom
drawer of her dresser. That should get her through the weekend without
coming out for anything. She planned to check on Max once her father
went to bed at night. She ran to the lab to check on Max before her
father got home.

At the bottom of the stairs, she saw the trash bag was gone, replaced
with a new one. She hoped she'd convinced her father she'd done as he
said.

"Hey, Max! I'm here. How are you doing?" Her insides were a ball
of nerves. She hoped it hadn't been discovered and he was safe. The last
thing she wanted was for all this to be in vain. She raced around the
corner and down the aisle. She threw back the gray fabric covering the
shelf and gently uncovered her Max. He was still growing. He did
appear to have some kind of life. She wondered if all this wasn't a happy

25

accident. He was secure and stable. Maybe he would flourish more in the current surroundings. She ran her tests on him. She was happy with his temperature, oxygen levels, and growth rate. Right now, he was just a tiny, squishy, pale white blob that resembled a two-fisted stress ball. She started to daydream about when he was grown and fully human.

Snap out of it, she mentally berated herself. If she didn't hurry, she'd be caught in a compromising position. She lovingly rewrapped him and gently placed him back in the container. She slid the box back under the lamp, covered the shelf back up, turned out the lights, ran up to her room, and barricaded herself in for the weekend.

Sandi pulled her phone from her pocket, turned it back on, and was hit with numerous calls, voicemails, texts, and emails from her father throughout the day. He was obsessed! She deleted them all without listening, reading, or responding.

Right on time, she heard the garage door open and braced herself. This time she chose to work on her laptop with her earbuds in and her music loud enough to drown out anything her father had to say.

It had been a long time since she had taken any time to play computer games. She would make this a great weekend. It would be nice to have a break from her dad, regardless of the fact that it was self-imposed. She logged into one of her favorites. It didn't take long to re-acclimate herself with the rules and how to play. She was fully involved when the pounding on her door was enough to shake things in her room. Looked like her father was irritated. *Oh well,* she mused. She turned her music up louder.

Before going to sleep, she set an alarm for 3 a.m. Her father would be asleep allowing her to slip downstairs to check on Max since she wouldn't be able to throughout the day.

In the middle of the night, she stealthily checked the hallway before descending the stairs. She felt her heart racing at the thought of being caught. All was right with Max, so she hurried back to her room as quietly as she could and re-locked her door against her father's intrusion when she refused to join him in the morning.

The next morning, she jumped out of bed. She was so routine. She needed to stop and remember she wouldn't be leaving her room. She took her shower and got dressed instead.

Shortly after 11 a.m. her father knocked on her door. "Sandi? Aren't you coming out at all? You at least need to drink your juice. I have it here for you."

She didn't answer and stayed still.

"Fine. I'll leave it here outside your door. Please drink it. It's too important."

She heard him leave. It didn't matter to her what he wanted. She wasn't drinking that nasty stuff. What was the worst that could happen? She'd get a cold? Big whoop! She had bigger things to think about. She had to figure out where she could get bone marrow from.

As Sandi's mind kept wandering back to the juice sitting outside her door, she realized if she left it as it was, she would have a bigger fight on her hands. She took the juice to the bathroom and poured the contents down the drain. She was going to rinse it out but thought better of it. She set the dirty cup on the floor outside her door and locked herself back in.

She was enjoying this time of seclusion. She was used to being alone for the most part. There was so much she could be doing with her Max. She would have to make up for it by working throughout the night while her father slept. She figured she should use this time to take a nap. She could sleep all through the day tomorrow. *Why was he making this so difficult? Wasn't her win his win also?* she mulled in her head.

Sandi climbed back into her cozy bed, put some classical music on her TV, and drifted off to sleep.

～

"SANDI, WAIT UP!" Ciara called to her.

Sandi stopped but refused to turn around.

Ciara caught up to her. "Didn't you hear me calling you? I've been chasing you since just outside Study Hall."

Sandi said nothing.

"I have something to ask you."

Still Sandi said nothing.

"Look, a bunch of us are having a party and we wanted you to come. Are you free Saturday night?"

Sandi slowly turned her head to stare at Ciara.

"What's that look for? It's no wonder you don't have any friends. What is wrong with you?"

"The likes of you. What is it you really want?"

"I told you. We want you to come to the party."

"Why?"

"What do you mean, 'Why?' We want to be nice. What kind of question is that?"

"So, why me? Why now?"

"I'm beginning to think this just is not worth all this. Just come."

"What are you planning on doing to me?"

"Nothing, you paranoid freak. Come or don't, it's at Kristy's house at 9 p.m. We were just hoping you would grace us with your presence."

Ciara turned on her heels and headed back for the school. Sandi stood for a long moment pondering why they would invite her. She wasn't even close to being one of the 'populars'. That was more than double the total number of words Ciara had ever said to or about her. The word that kept playing over and over in her mind was, *Why?* She snapped out of her deep thoughts and walked to her car.

As the week went on, more and more girls were saying, "Hope to see you Saturday night, Sandi." She didn't understand what was going on, but all she could think was the prom scene from the movie *Carrie*. She had no interest in being the school's laughingstock even more. She was *not* going to be there for whatever they had planned.

The more she thought about it, the more she began to change her mind. She had never been to a party and always wondered what went on. What was the worst that could happen? They could make fun of her, like they did in school. The good thing about this was, unlike school, she wasn't required to stay. She would have her own wheels and no obligation. She could just leave. They could slip her something, so she just wouldn't eat or drink anything they offered. She went everywhere with her thermal water bottle. She would just bring her own and thwart any attempts to drug her. They could tie her up, but eventually an adult would have to come home. She knew her father. If she wasn't home by midnight, he would be pounding at their door. No, she couldn't see anything they could do to her that they hadn't already tried at school. All the other girls she knew had at least gone to each other's slumber parties. Not her. She had never been invited. Yes, she would at least show up to see what all the fuss was about.

Often on Monday mornings, the school was abuzz about the party of the weekend. Whenever Sandi had attempted to eavesdrop just to learn what went on at these deals, she was always shut out rudely. She would go find out for herself.

The week was hard. One minute she was excited to be going to her first party. She'd never even been invited to birthday parties. Her childhood was pitiful. The next minute Sandi was filled with apprehension and fear of what they were going to do to her. Saturday, she spent the day changing clothes, adding makeup, taking it off, fussing with her hair only to brush it all back out. In the late afternoon she took another shower just to feel like she was starting back with a clean slate. She was a wreck. She never let anything get to her. She needed to get over this. If it was a setup, she would end up even more disappointed. If it wasn't, she didn't want to ruin the experience because she'd gotten herself so worked up that she made herself sick.

Sandi lay down across her bed with a cold wet cloth across her forehead. She took full, deep, cleansing breaths. She knew it would alter her physiology, and that's what she needed right now.

On her way to Kristy's house, her stomach felt like a kickboxing championship was going on in there. She pulled off the road, got out of the car, and paced in the grass. *Get it together!* she mentally reprimanded herself. This was crazy. It wasn't worth all of this. She should just turn around and go home. She shouldn't have ever believed they would really want her as a guest at their party. She got back in her car but just sat there. "Oh, what the hell. I'm just going to go. I may regret it later, but I'll regret it more if I don't even try."

Sandi pulled up as close to Kristy's house as she could get. There were cars lined up on both sides of the street for blocks. She really hoped nothing bad happened. This would be a long way to run to get away. As she got to the front yard, her steps slowed to a crawl. Actually, being here, she had to really think about it. It wasn't too late to leave. She waited and listened to see if it was anything she'd be interested in. There was loud music. She could see a lot of people through the windows.

Every once in a while, the crowd would erupt in laughter. She took a deep breath and walked up the front steps. She paused on the porch. She didn't know what protocol dictated. Should she ring the bell or just walk in? She couldn't imagine herself just walking into anyone's home. She rang the bell and waited. Kristy opened the door, looked past Sandi, and bobbed and weaved her head like there was a crowd behind Sandi and Kristy was trying to spot a celebrity.

"Who are you looking for?" Sandi asked. She looked behind herself. There was no one out there.

Just then Sandi saw one of the school football linebackers sail through the air and crash down on the coffee table, breaking it to splinters. Kristy called out over her shoulder to the crowd, "It's just the loser. No one's with her. She's just a liar. It was a joke to think she really has a boyfriend."

SANDI WOKE with a start and sat straight up in bed. It was then she realized her father must have been knocking on her door. She gripped her chest with one hand while she pulled the headphones from her ears. It was just a dream. It felt so real! One side of her was relieved, while the other had a twinge of disappointment. She flopped back on the bed and lay there staring at the ceiling. Eventually, her father stopped his relentless beating on her door for her to come out for dinner. Not on his life!

She went to her food stash and pulled out a protein bar and a banana. Sandi pulled up a movie to keep herself occupied until her father finally went to bed and she could check on her experiment. She was pleasantly surprised that her father had left her alone as much as he had. One day, she would be on her own and not have to hide from him like this. One day.

Sandi dozed off at the end of the movie. When she awoke, the house was silent, and night had long since settled in. She reprimanded herself. She should have stayed awake, so she would know if and when her father had gone to bed. Crap! Now what should she do? She really wanted to get down to the lab, but the last thing she wanted was to go creeping down to the basement and run into her father along the way. She had better wait until 3 a.m. again, when she *knew* he'd be in bed.

She went to the door with her ear against the crack and listened hard. She heard nothing. She quietly opened the door just a bit, listened some more, and pulled it open enough to stick her head out. She still heard nothing and didn't see a glow from down the stairs or up the hall from under his door. She slipped out, gently closed the door behind her, and scurried down the stairs. When she opened the cellar door, she opened, slipped in, then closed it very slowly. It was creaky and she had no intention of alerting her father that she was outside her room. Not until the door was closed behind her did she turn on the lights. She ran to see how Max was.

She felt a bit odd calling it that, but Sandi found it more and more difficult to think of it as an inanimate object. It was a living entity. Maybe not much of anything at this moment, but still a being. When she slipped the container from the shelf, she was shocked to discover Max had doubled in size. If it continued to grow at this rate there would be no hiding it from her father. She had to get some bone marrow and fast. She would have to pay strict attention to its rate of growth. Sandi really hoped it wasn't a matter of doubling every day. Then the thought occurred to her, *What do I do to stop the growth when he reaches full human male size?* She had a lot of work to do. She wished she didn't have to do all of this in secret. It was a lot more work taking it out and putting it back to remain hidden, than if she could just wrap it up, turn out the lights, and go upstairs until the next day.

She went through her battery of tests to try to gauge the rate of development. She took copious notes and continued her research. She left Max sitting out on the table beside her while she learned how to get in line to be a recipient of cadaver bone marrow. That was going to be impossible. There were too many people to answer to for a simple donation. She had to think of another alternative. But what? Even if she did use some of her own, how would she introduce one less x and one additional y chromosome?

What *did* she know? She knew with the given conditions, Max would probably continue to increase in size. There was no telling if or when its growth would stop. Sandi strongly believed the introduction of stem cells from bone marrow was the only way to form this entity into a human. It wasn't as if she had a stem cell research lab. Wait! She knew someone who did. How could she make that happen? She stood and paced.

If she asked specifically for stem cells, it would get back to her father and there was no telling what he would do. However, she also knew that sometimes love will transcend customary boundaries.

All she could do was try.

Sandi had grown up in opulence. Her family was extremely wealthy. Although she preferred simplicity, she had never wanted for anything. There were never any monetary limits put on her. She often wondered if that made her the hated target she was. She never flaunted it; she just didn't think much about it. There were a lot of advantages to coming from so much money. She had freedom that most grown adults didn't. Still, she really hoped this didn't end in disaster.

Sandi returned Max to his shelf with the heat lamp on and went back to her room. She packed an overnight bag and took her backpack. She would stay at a hotel and go to school from there.

Five

After loading her playlists and stashing her things in her trunk, Sandi took off for what she knew would be a four-hour drive. Road trip!

She arrived on the enormous campus of one of the largest science and technology centers in the world. She drove up to the entrance and passed the guard her license. Moments later, he passed it back and opened the gate. Although it was a complex maze of roads and buildings, Sandi knew her way well. She pulled into a reserved space facing the huge glass front of the largest building. It towered over all the others with its soaring thirty-four stories. She sat for a minute to run over one more time what she would say, took a deep breath, and got out of her car.

When she entered the lobby, the silence was deafening. The only people there were two guards at the front desk, who looked surprised.

"Is he here?" she asked.

They nodded in unison. "Is he expecting you?" the older guard asked.

She shook her head *no*.

"Do you want me to let him know you're here?"

Again, she shook her head. "I've got this, but thanks anyway."

There was the loud sound of a buzzer, and large, ornate double doors opened to her. She stepped through to the bank of elevators and went to the one on the end with no buttons. She swiped a card with a chip over a keypad. The doors opened, she stepped in and swiftly rose to the top floor. The doors opened and she stepped inside an elaborate penthouse with marble floors and an eclectic mix of modern and antique furnishings. She made her way through the foyer and the living room, down a long hallway to an open door on the left. She stopped just outside, took another deep breath, and rounded into the stately office.

"Well, Sandi! What a pleasant surprise. Do you have any idea what time it is? Don't tell me you just drove here. Is everything all right?"

"Hello, Granddad. Yes, everything is fine." She knew that even though she had told the guards not to announce her, they would have notified him anyway. Her grandfather, Pete—she wasn't sure if it was short for Peter, but she'd only ever heard him referred to as Pete—was getting up there in age, but always maintained a youthful appearance. He was distinguished-looking with just a touch of gray at the temples of a head full of hair. His body was long and lean, and his clothes were always tailored to perfection.

He smiled as he crossed the floor and greeted her with one of his cold, formal embraces. "Come, sit with me."

He led her to a pair of leather wingback chairs. Although she was sure they were created for the appearance of warmth and comfort, instead they came off the same as her grandfather: stiff and rigid. She sat, and almost immediately, an elderly woman entered with a tray. She set it on the small coffee table in front of the chairs, poured two cups, added cream to both, stirred, and handed them one at a time to her grandfather, who passed Sandi one.

"That will be all, Mildred."

"As you wish, sir." She left the room.

"Another new one, Granddad?"

"You just can't find good help these days."

Sandi chose not to speak her mind. Her grandfather was a difficult and rigid man who could be cruel, causing his personal staff to turn over quickly. She knew he tried to make up for it by paying handsomely, but money wasn't always enough.

After discussing the frivolities, her grandfather said, "So, out with it. What brings you here?"

"I'm working on something. It could change the world. I just need a little help."

"I know it's not money, so what could you possibly need my assistance with?"

"I've been working a lot in the lab."

"On what?"

"It began in a petri dish, as everything usually does."

"Stop stalling. I don't have time to beat around the bush."

"I've made a discovery, and I just need an element I'm not able to acquire. I was hoping you would let me have some from one of the facilities."

"What sort of element?"

"I need stem cells. Actually, is there any way I could get some bone marrow?"

Her grandfather cast a glance her way as he sipped his coffee. "Exactly what kind of experiment is this you're doing? What on Earth could you possibly need stem cells for? Are you sick?"

"No, I'm not sick, and neither is anyone I know. Dad's fine."

His eyes became slits as he glared at her. "Does your father know you're here?"

"No."

"Shall I call him?"

"No."

"Then what are you up to?"

"I've created a living being that I've been able to sustain and grow over time. I want to introduce stem cells to try to form it—"

He cut her off. "Into a human?" he said coolly.

"Well, that was the idea."

"What does your father say?"

"He doesn't want to help me."

"Why would I help you with something like that? Do you have any idea how many people I employ? If it could be done, don't you think I'd have done it by now? You're just a kid."

"I just want to try, to give it a fair shot. What if I'm onto something? Shouldn't I be allowed to see it through to a conclusion? If it works, I can share my findings with whomever you wish on your staff."

"Not. On. Your. Life." He said so low and deliberately that Sandi could hardly hear him. She recognized that as his angry voice. "Enough of this nonsense. I don't want to hear another word about this."

They sat in silence for a long time. She held back the tears that threatened to spill over. She would never give him that satisfaction. She had flashes from her childhood of his glee at another's demise. The harder and further he witnessed another person fall, the more joy he showed. She knew him to be cold and heartless.

Eventually, he said, "If that was all, I must get back to work. So nice to see you, my dear. Do tell your father I said hello. You may show yourself out." He patted her shoulder and returned to his massive, intricately carved mahogany desk.

She carefully set the china cup on the tray and crossed the room to the door. She stopped and without turning to look back said, "I hope we can keep this between us."

"Of course," came the clipped response.

Sandi walked numbly to her car with no acknowledgment of anyone she passed. She fought to hold it all together as she drove back to the guard shack. She stopped at the gate until the exit arm rose, allowing her to drive away with the same empty feeling she always had when she left her grandfather. She pulled off the side of the road, laid her forehead on the steering wheel, and cried. She hadn't really believed he would give her what she'd come for, but she wished that at least once, she could leave him and not feel stripped bare like thrown-away trash.

As she pulled herself together, she thought, *I need to figure out option two. Number one certainly got me into hot water.* She knew her grandfather would never keep her visit to himself.

So, back to cadavers. That would be more difficult than just asking for stem cells. She had no one to help her. Right now would be a great time to have friends, even one friend. Since she didn't, she had to figure this out on her own.

36

Thirty minutes from her hometown, she stopped to get a hotel room. She needed some sleep. It was long before check-in, but she knew what cash would do. She parked, tossed her bags over her shoulder, and walked inside. She was right: slipping the desk clerk some extra green got her right in. She had no interest in more than a simple room with a comfortable bed, a TV, internet, and a hot shower. Additionally, she wanted to stay below the radar.

Sandi dropped her bags on the bed, went down the hall for ice, put the Do Not Disturb card in the key slot to her door, and drew a hot bath. She needed time to think. Time to figure out the best way to get her hands on bone marrow. A live donation was out of the question, which just left the deceased kind. How? It couldn't be too old and would have to be kept frozen to be viable. The time was so limited: It could not be more than four hours, and that was only if it was quickly put on ice. How was she going to attempt to pull this one off? It would take more thought than her tired brain could concoct at this time.

After a long soak in the tub, with all sorts of thoughts running through her head, she had a granola bar, an apple, and a bottle of water. She climbed into bed to sleep through the day.

When Sandi awoke, she checked her phone. Sure enough, her father had blown it up with text messages. She just deleted the conversation. He had called over twenty times before she had reached her grandfather and not at all after she left him. He knew. She just hoped he hadn't discovered Max. If he did, she'd start over. Yes, it would take a lot of effort, but she'd done it once, and she could do it again. Now, she needed to find something to eat. She was starving.

On the outskirts of town was a hole-in-the-wall diner with great food. They were always open into the morning hours. It was a popular late-night eatery for the drinking crowd. By the time she got there, she had missed the dinner rush and was way ahead of the drunks.

A middle-aged woman in a short skirt, plunging neckline, white, starched apron, and jet-black hair straight out of a bottle called out, "Sit anywhere, honey. I'll be with you in a minute."

Sandi took a booth in the farthest corner from the door and pulled a menu from the rack on the table. Right about now, everything looked good.

"What'll ya have, darlin'?" said the woman, as she pulled a pencil from behind her ear and drew a pad from her apron pocket.

On closer inspection, Sandi saw too many cracks and crevices etched on this woman's face, neck, and chest for her to be even middle-aged. Sandi felt a twinge of sadness that she was obviously trying to be a young woman again. That ship had long since sailed.

"I'll have a cheeseburger, just catsup, onion rings, a Coke—oh, and could I get a salad with ranch dressing?"

"Sure, honey. Be right back."

The bell on the door chimed and a young couple walked in. The waitress sang out, "Sit anywhere. I'll be right with ya." Sandi wasn't sure they heard her. They were draped all over each other, oblivious to the rest of the world. They slid into a booth, both sitting on the same side, and started making out like they were behind closed doors. Sandi was repulsed by their public display of affection, but jealous she didn't have someone so attentive to her. When she had her Max, they would never be so shameless in public. They would be much more demure, less affectionate and more loving. There was a difference between lust and love. This pair was recognizably in lust. She and Max would be in love.

The waitress set the drink and salad down in front of Sandi, plunked a bottle of catsup on the table, and headed for the couple. "What'll ya have?"

Sandi's mind wandered as she studied the pair, imagining what her life would be like once she had a boyfriend to validate her being on the planet. To show all those stuck-ups at school she had value. Someone who loved her but was off limits to them. She imagined them sitting in the library, heads together, whispering about theories and inventions they would make together. On the weekends, they would take long walks and go on picnic lunches. They would stay up late cuddled on the couch, watching some cheesy horror flick and pointing out all the flaws. They would study together, do experiments together, go to the movies, the museums, and the mall. They would wander hand-in-hand and sneak the occasional kiss but never be so blatant as the couple across the diner. They would be classy, not trashy. Those two were disgusting. That would never be Max and her. The whole world would know they were in love, not just lusting after one another. No, it would be real, lasting.

She was yanked from her daydream when Ms. Wish I Was a Kid Again spun her plate of burger and rings on the table. "Anything else?" she asked as she was turning from the table.

Sandi said, "No, thanks," to the woman's back.

Sandi pulled a notebook from her purse to make a list as she ate. She wasn't one for list-building, but she couldn't afford any mistakes. She intended to just get marrow from one cadaver but wanted to make sure she was prepared if she needed more. She would need a few hollow needles, some tubing, and several PVC IV bags to collect the marrow as it was extracted. She'd rather have too many and not need them than not enough. She had a collapsible cooler she could sneak in but would have to figure out how to get it back out without notice, once she had it filled and fully expanded. She had to remember ice packs for the cooler. It was imperative to keep it as cold as possible until she could get it to the freezer. Ideally, she would have several in order to layer between each bag, but conditions would be anything but ideal. A scalpel. She had to make sure she grabbed a couple of scalpels to help in the extraction process. That should do it. She tore out the page, folded it, and shoved it in the pocket of her jeans.

Sandi dropped a twenty on the table and left. As she headed out the door, she heard the old lady say, "Hey! You gotta pay for that." Sandi kept walking, knowing the waitress would figure out she'd not only paid for her meal but left a ridiculous tip for the service given.

When she returned to the hotel, she stopped by the front desk to add an additional day. She needed more time before facing off with her father. As she approached the front desk, the night manager said, "Are you Sandi?"

"Yes. Is there something wrong?"

"No. You have a message."

"What kind of message?"

She passed the small pink paper across the counter. The spaces were filled in with, "From: Alan, To: Sandi Powell, Re: Stop being a spoiled brat and get home." The time stamp on it was 9:42 p.m.; it was signed with the name that was on the night manager's badge.

"Thanks," Sandi said in monotone as she turned away to go back to her room. If nothing else, she knew her father to be resourceful. She considered skipping school the next day but figured that *would* bring on a manhunt. She needed to keep things as normal as possible to have the opportunity to carry out her plans.

When Sandi's alarm sounded the next morning, she started to get up from the bed, but instead of her normal body response, she felt achy. All her joints hurt. She lay there thinking over the events of the day before. Nothing unusual or physically taxing. She hoped she wasn't coming down with something. She didn't have time to be sick. Come to think of it, she couldn't remember the last time she had been ill. She pushed herself up from the bed. A hot shower would do wonders.

Sandi had a birthmark on the top right of her left breast in the shape of a swirl. As she ran the washcloth over it, she felt a twinge of pain. She looked down. It appeared as it always had. No discoloration or abnormality in shape. That was odd. She finished up but didn't feel the relief in her muscles from the hot water that she always did.

She didn't have time to sit and eat something for breakfast. She had a longer drive than usual to get to school on time. She grabbed a Danish and an apple at the Continental breakfast setup as she passed through the lobby. She put the fruit in her book bag and dropped her room key on the counter. Since her father had found her, she wouldn't be staying an additional night after all.

Throughout the day at school, Sandi kept feeling like she was being watched. She often felt that way, but more so today. She was just being paranoid. *Get over it,* she reprimanded herself. *You're not that important.*

Sandi left school before Study Hall. She could use the extra time to get things done. Also, she was anxious to check on Max. She hoped he was fine and she hadn't lost ground while being gone.

As the garage door opened, she felt a physical release of tension at not seeing her father's car parked inside. She knew he would never miss work, especially for her.

Although she didn't intend to be there long, she lowered the door. She didn't want to draw any attention. Since it was so early, she didn't know if some of the nosy neighbors would take it upon themselves to get in touch with her father, if they noticed her home already.

She set her purse and backpack on the kitchen table and ran upstairs to change out the clothes in her overnight bag. She then went to the basement to check on Max. She was stunned to see his growth. She would have to think of an alternative soon. He wouldn't be much longer for that space. She did her measurements and tests and recorded her findings. With her gloved hands, she gently touched the mass. It was a bit less firm than skin but bounced back as flesh did. It was almost translucent.

After returning him to his shelf and repositioning the heat lamp to allow more room, Sandi gathered the supplies on her list from around the room. Sticking the notepaper back in her pocket, she started up the stairs. She remembered she would need to put the bone marrow in the freezer when she returned, so went back down to the deep freezer to be sure there was room. She wanted to be certain she could not only house it there but keep it hidden from her father's view, should he open the freezer. All set. She climbed the stairs, unable to take them two at a time as she always did. She needed to shake whatever this was off. It was infringing on her productivity.

Sandi knew the layout of Memorial Hospital best, so she checked into a hotel close to there. She was all on her own because there was no one she knew who would help her break the law and do anything this underhanded. She reasoned that acting under the cover of night was going to be her best bet since there would be less activity and less chance of getting caught.

Sandi took her things to her room and settled in. She ordered a pizza and watched some television. There wasn't anything interesting on the standard hotel channel lineups, so she put on a mindless drama just for distraction and company.

As it got later, she felt her anxiety growing. She had to keep her wits about her. She couldn't afford to make mistakes. Sandi pulled the ice packs from the small freezer in her room refrigerator. Just the two had filled the little space, but it had kept them frozen. She dressed in a set of scrubs and her tennis shoes. She had left everything else in her car.

Once she got to the hospital, she put on her white lab coat, slid the ice packs into the cooler with all her supplies, and headed in through the front doors. She knew that at that hour, all the remaining doors would be locked. There was no one in the lobby. Good, one less lie to tell. She knew she would be captured on the cameras placed throughout the halls. She kept her head down and turned from view. She went to the lowest level where the morgue was located. She would be safe from prying eyes once inside. She knew there were cameras, but they were only turned on when performing an autopsy. Otherwise, they were deemed unnecessary. As she was about to open the door, she heard loud Latin music and saw light from under the door.

Great! Just great, she thought. Who was in there at this hour? She really hoped it wasn't some doctor working to catch up on overdue work. She wanted to get in, get the job done, and get out quickly. She had no intention of hanging out half the night. She slipped into the adjacent office and took a seat to wait it out.

It wasn't long before she heard the music retreating down the hallway. She peeked outside the door to see a cleaning cart being pushed into the next bank of rooms, where Sandi knew radiology was located. She quickly left the office and entered the morgue. She thought about leaving the lights off and being guided by her phone flashlight but knew it would be more of a hindrance than help. She'd be quick.

Sandi set her things on the steel examination table. She looked for the doors with the "occupied" display tag showing. There were twenty available spaces, but only four contained any bodies. She hoped there was at least one male who hadn't died of some disease. She pulled door six. It was a seventy-two-year-old male who had been autopsied, discovered to have expired due to cancer. He had been dead three days already. That was pushing her time limit as it was, but the diseased cells would not be a viable option.

Door ten housed a young woman who had passed that morning from blunt-force trauma to the head. That would be ideal, had she been a man. She closed that door and opened door twelve. A thirty-four-year-old male involved in a motorcycle accident this afternoon. Bingo! This was the one. His note stated no autopsy was to be performed on him. Even better.

She swiftly gathered her necessary supplies, then rolled the corpse on his side in order to access his back. She apologized to him as she made a small incision in the center of a bruised area on his right buttocks. She inserted the long, hollow needle into the center of his large pelvis bone. The fluid easily drained from the target. She repeated the procedure at his clavicle, skull, and rib cage. After filling almost two bags, she repositioned him as she had found him and slid him back into place. "Thanks for your donation to science," she said and dropped them in the cooler.

She checked the last occupied door to find it was just the cadaver table filled with supplies. *Great, now what?* she wondered. She was concerned she wouldn't have enough marrow to accomplish what was needed. She had no intention of going through all this again. She needed to make this happen in one shot. That just left the woman behind door ten. She slid her out and started at her head since that would be the least noticeable area of incision.

Sandi easily obtained the marrow from her skull at that point and moved to her torso. She needed to work from the rear on this woman too. Sandi rolled the woman on her right side and began her next cut into the spinal area. As she was withdrawing the marrow from her sternum, she heard the familiar Latin music coming closer. She didn't have time to clean up her things and turn off the light without being caught. Sandi scanned the sterile room for a place to hide. Nowhere.

In a panic, she pushed in her lady, quietly closed the door, pulled open door nine, quickly climbed on the table, and pulled the door closed as best she could from her position. She lay motionless, breathing softly so as not to be discovered. Her heart was pounding so hard she was afraid it was echoing throughout the room. She heard the door to the morgue open and saw the light go out from the crack left in the freezer door. Phew, that had been too close!

As she was breathing a sigh of relief, the light went back on. Why?

She heard movement in the room. She was starting to get really cold. This cleaning lady needed to get out before Sandi's body temperature dropped too low. She heard her things on the table being shifted. Oh great! Hopefully, the woman wouldn't call someone to find out why Sandi's things were out when they hadn't been a short while ago.

"Hello?" a female voice called out. "Anyone here?"

There was the sound of one of the distant drawers being opened, some things being shifted, and the door closed. She wondered if the woman had put her things in the drawer being used for storage. That was fine with her as long as she was out of this locker soon. Not only was she cold, but she was also beginning to feel a bit claustrophobic. At least this wasn't one of the few spaces fully enclosed, reserved for those with communicable diseases. Although it was dark and creepy knowing she was closed in beside a dead body, she at least had a sense of additional space.

As she lay there waiting for the intruder to leave, she thought about Houston. She was making her own boyfriend, but she wished Max was simply an experiment and Houston her real boyfriend. She was so cold, she wished she had him here to keep her warm. Even his hoodie would be some relief about now. Then her mind wandered to thinking about stealing some DNA from Houston to make Max resemble him. If she couldn't have the original, maybe a knockoff would do. But how was she going to do that? What she was doing now was crazy enough.

Her door snapped shut. Adrenaline flooded her body, her mind began to race, and her breath came in short, sharp gasps. Sandi began to shake all over from the fear. As cold as it was in here, she felt feverish. If she banged on the door or cried out for help, she'd never be able to explain. That wouldn't bode well for her cause. She was now in panic mode and her brain seemed to have shut down. *Come on, Sandi, think!* she pleaded with her mind. *You've got to get out of here.* All she could smell was death; Sandi was now acutely aware that she was surrounded by it. She hadn't noticed it before, when they were in here and she was out there. Right now, she needed to think, she needed to get out of this ice casket of death. *Just breathe, girl. Slow and steady. Panicking isn't going to help this situation.*

Sandi heard the door to the morgue shut and began scrambling for her cell phone. She turned on the flashlight and started assessing her situation. The more solution-oriented she was, the clearer her thoughts became. It wasn't like there was a backup exit from within. The people inside didn't need a way out. She looked the door over and felt along the seams. On the backside of the handle, she found some screws. She used her scalpel to turn the screws, which loosened the handle. Sandi gave the door a shove, but it didn't budge. She returned to the screws and this time removed them completely. Her fingers had become numb with cold, making it more difficult to work. She took off the plate of the handle. There was a hole she could fit her finger in. She shoved at it, but it didn't drop out as she anticipated it would. She used her larger middle finger to wedge into the space and turned it counterclockwise. It dislodged from the casing. She shook it off her finger and let it clang to the floor. She pulled the latch from the side of the hole where the handle had just been, releasing it from its clasped position. This time when she pushed, the door easily opened. She was free!

She pushed the drawer out and jumped to the floor. Sandi was so cold, the impact hurt her knees. She briefly rubbed them, then got back to work. She originally was going to put the drawer door back together but instead set all the hardware on the table inside and closed the door.

She pulled open the storage door where she suspected the cleaning lady had put her things. Sure enough, there they were. She took them back out. This time though, she would work by her flashlight. She was almost done anyway.

After returning the woman to her original position and closing her back up, Sandi labeled her two and a half bags full of marrow with the word "female", placing them in the cooler and positioning the last ice pack on top, she noticed the woman's bone marrow was redder than the yellow tinge of the man's. She must have had less fat content in her marrow. Too bad hers would be the backup since Sandi wanted male stem cells.

She cracked the door to the hallway and peered down both ways. There was no sound and no one in sight. Sandi slipped from the room, secured the door behind her, and rode the elevator to the first floor. She tried to maintain an air of assurance as she crossed the lobby. This time there was a guard sitting at the reception area with his feet propped on the desk, playing on his cell phone. He quickly removed his limbs from the desk top and stammered, "Ah, sorry, doc. I didn't know anyone was here."

Sandi waved a hand in the air and said, "Carry on, I'll never tell."

"Thanks," he called after her.

Once inside her car, she shook from the adrenalin dump. She drove across the street to a convenience store where she purchased a bag of ice. Since she would need to keep the extracted fluid iced to preserve it but the small freezer in her room barely held the two ice packs, she would need to keep it in the cooler overnight. She would miss school tomorrow, wait until she knew her father had gone to work, and go home to take care of this. She was filled with excitement at the next step.

Sandi left the cooler in her trunk with her lab coat draped over it and went up to her room. She was exhausted and wanted a hot shower to warm up completely. She cleared the door, flipped on the light, and screamed.

Six

"Daddy! How'd you get in here?" Sandi shrieked.

"It's amazing what one will do with enough motivation. What are *you* doing here, is the more appropriate question."

She paused for a long moment before saying, "I wasn't ready to deal with you yet."

"Is that right? Well, you can call this an end to your preparedness. You're coming home tonight. Speaking of tonight, it's actually morning now. Where have you been? I arrived hours ago."

"I don't think that's any of your business."

"You're my daughter and still underage. Everything about you is my business."

Sandi began gathering her things then stopped. "I'm going to sleep here tonight. I'll be home tomorrow after school."

"You're done telling me what you will and won't do. You're coming home now. End of discussion."

"But I've already paid for the room."

"That's not my problem. Home. Now. Or I'll call the police and let you spend the night in jail."

"On what charge?"

"Oh, sweetie, do you really want to go there?"

As she resigned herself and finished packing her few belongings, her father rose from the chair and crossed the room to her. He stood to the side of her with his left shoulder to her right for a moment. She froze in place. She wasn't afraid of him, but she was apprehensive of what he would say. He said nothing.

"I'll be home shortly," Sandi said.

He said, "Not more than ten minutes after me." He left the room, allowing the door to slam behind him.

Ooh, he made her so mad. What did he care? They were little more than roommates occupying the same house as it was. He wouldn't have missed her just one more night. He was so controlling. She would never control her children the way he insisted on domineering her every move.

Sandi entered a dimly lit house. She locked the door behind her and turned out the lights as she ascended the stairs. She was glad her father had already gone to his room, so it didn't create an awkward situation. She dropped her things on the bed, then snuck out of her room and down to the basement to put the bone marrow in the deep freeze. She checked on Max. No obvious change. She was tempted to just go forward with introducing the bone marrow now but thought she was treading on thin ice as it was. Better to deal with that later.

When Sandi returned to the second story, she saw her father's bedroom light was now off. Good, she needed sleep. She ached as she crawled beneath the covers. That ice chamber had done her in. She hadn't felt her spry self as it was, but after being cooped up in that freezer, she was seriously feeling the negative effects throughout her body.

Sandi awoke to her morning alarm. As she got in the shower, she noticed again the ill effects on her body from the day before. She added the pulsating showerhead to her hot shower. She made the water as hot as she could stand, allowing it to beat on her sore muscles, back, and neck. Maybe she should tell her father she was just going to stay home from school. She would tell him she wasn't feeling well and needed a day in bed. As she considered it, she thought better and knew she'd go to school in order to avoid any further confrontation with her hard-headed parent.

In the morning, she went to the kitchen to find her father holding out her glass of disgusting juice. "Seriously," she said with disdain, "can't you just give it a rest? I haven't drunk that stuff in several days and it's been wonderful. I'm wonderful. The world is wonderful. It hasn't fallen off its axis or anything."

"Drink," was all he replied.

She yanked the vessel holding the bane of her existence from him, tossed it back, and said, "Happy?"

"Now, eat."

He had eggs and toast on a plate at her place at the table. She knew it was futile to fight him when he got like this. She just didn't want their typical nonsensical morning discussion. He sat beside her with his cup of coffee. She could feel his eyes boring into her. She refused to look up, focusing on getting this over with.

Sandi pushed from the table, rinsed her dishes, put them in the dishwasher, and went back upstairs to brush her teeth one more time. She always brushed her teeth while she ran the water for her shower. Today, she particularly wanted that taste of juice out of her mouth and not having had her morning java, she felt it necessary. She wanted nothing to do with her father, not even to sit next to him long enough to drink a cup of coffee.

When she returned to the kitchen, he was leaning against the counter. She gathered her purse and backpack to head out the door.

"No kiss goodbye?" her father asked.

She stopped in her tracks, considered it, then walked out the door.

Sandi drove away with no intention of actually going to school. She just needed to appear as if she was. She went instead to a park at the nearby lake. She got out and wandered the water's edge, waiting out the time until her father went to work. Although he was so set in his routine, she would allow extra time today in case he decided to be late going in.

Mid-morning, Sandi returned home and went to the lab. She sterilized the area she would be working in. She pulled the container holding her experiment from the shelf. She carefully set him on the lab table and uncovered him. He was no more than a big translucent mound of dough-looking substance. *Not for long,* she thought. He was about to become her greatest creation.

Sandi ran to her room in obedience to a wild hope and desire. She pulled Houston's hoodie from beneath her covers. She smelled it again. Houston's scent was fading and hers was taking over. She hugged it close. As she thought about Houston being her boyfriend, she was inspired. She would make Max her own Houston. She turned the hood inside out looking for hair. She found several strands and ran to the basement to preserve them.

Sandi pulled out a petri dish and some tweezers. She laid the hoodie on the lab table. Carefully, she picked off each strand she found that had a hair follicle attached. She was glad she'd never pulled the hood over her own hair, thus preserving his precious few. She had to have at least three pieces of hair at least one centimeter in length. She found two and was afraid she couldn't gather all she needed. Just one more. *Please, God, give me just one more.* There it was at the tie! She held it with the tweezers to the light. She had it! She quickly processed the offering.

She was excited about what she'd accomplished here. She would actually create her very own boyfriend. Someone who would love only her, be devoted to only her, stand up for her, protect her. She would teach him and increase his intelligence. She would guide him in kindness and love. He would be perfection.

She went to the freezer and pulled out just one bag of male bone marrow for the time being. It was the most desirable, given her current plan. She supposed she should be more focused on just creating a human than specifically on a man. But her motivation had always been to create a mate to love her, so the man's stem cells first. The woman's if necessary.

Sandi ran the apparatus to transfuse the marrow and Houston's DNA into her Max blob and prayed for the desired effects. The thought of going to this next level and creating something she might have to destroy was unthinkable to her. If she had struggled with her father's insistence on getting rid of Max when he was nothing more than a couple of ingredients, not unlike cake batter, what would she do when he had body parts? She refused to entertain the thought anymore. She injected the whole amount from the PVC bag into Max and waited. Was it too much too fast? She couldn't afford to make mistakes. From her research, she believed she was doing what was necessary correctly.

After there was no change, she considered giving it some time. She returned the slightly heavier container to its shelf, cleaned everything up, returned all her paraphernalia to their rightful spaces, and went to her room for a nap. She really wasn't feeling well. She knew rest would heal her body. She'd just sleep whatever this was off. She had hours before she would have to prepare for the dinner drama she anticipated. She liked it a lot better when she wasn't answering to her obsessed father. She knew she was in for one of his lectures.

Sandi awoke to the sound of the garage door opening. She threw back the covers and placed her feet on the floor. She was feeling a bit better. It must have been the drama she had been through over the past week that had worn her out. She stretched, went to the bathroom, freshened up, and read while she waited for the familiar call to the dinner table by her father.

Instead, there was a knock on her locked door. She heard the door handle jiggle. She was glad she had thought twice and locked it. She said nothing.

From the other side of the door, her father said, "Sandi, I need you downstairs. We need to talk."

She remained silent.

"We are not doing this again, young lady. You want to act all grown up, you will deal with me as a responsible adult. Five minutes. Downstairs. Or I'll take this door down."

She heard him leave. *Crap!* she thought, *this was not how she had envisioned this going.* She gathered her wits and went downstairs. He was sitting in his chair in the living room. Oh, this was going to be worse than she anticipated. He never "had a talk" with her in this room unless it was bad.

Sandi sat down on the sofa at the end farthest from her father. He had his fingers steepled, holding up his chin. They sat in silence. She had no intention of starting this conversation. She wasn't about to say something in a direction he didn't plan to go and bring up more issues than necessary.

Eventually, he laid his hands in his lap. "I understand you're mad at me," he began. "However, the way you have been behaving is unacceptable."

Oh brother, she thought, *here we go with the "unacceptable" speech he always fell back on.* She didn't look at him, only at the rug on the floor. By now, she knew every row and knot of the commissioned throw rug her father took great pride in. She had been in this spot before. She doubted this would be the last time. At least she knew what was to come.

He droned on and on about respect, responsibility, and boundaries. Just once she hoped he would find a new platform to preach from. Something different would be nice. She'd heard this same sermon too many times before. He needed new material.

She waited for him to bring up her experiment, but he never did. That was a good thing. Avoidance worked for her. She wasn't going to remind him how all of this began. She was surprised he never brought up her visit to his father. There was less love lost between her father and grandfather than between her father and herself. She had no idea what had gone wrong in that relationship, but she had her suspicions. Both men were rigid and immovable once they took a stance. Her grandfather often came across as caring, but only as long as there was the possibility of the public looking in. She could only imagine how her father had lived in her grandfather's shadow.

A common thread in her family was the lack of female influence. She had never known any grandmothers. Her mother had died in childbirth, but her father had never made her feel as though she was the cause of his wife's demise. She had never been introduced to her maternal grandparents. Her grandfather had no family she was aware of. Her father had no siblings. If her mother's side had family, they were never discussed.

Whenever she had asked questions growing up, her father would change the subject. Sandi occasionally longed for a sense of family. She didn't feel she could turn to her father. Their only real conversations always revolved around science. It would be nice, just once, to talk about something nonsensical or meaningless, but that wasn't who he was. Everything in his world had a purpose or was disposed of.

Sandi recalled having a small, square music box when she was young. She loved listening to the tinkle of the music as she watched the little, pink, plastic ballerina spin whenever she raised the lid. One day while she was sitting, mesmerized by the movement, her father had reached over her and closed the lid to end the dance and music. She protested that she had been playing with it. He informed her that it had no purpose and therefore was nothing more than a waste of time. He smashed it with a hammer and dumped the pieces in the trash.

She was pulled from her thoughts when she recognized the familiar "Do I make myself clear, young lady?"

She hadn't heard a word he'd said, but she could guess. She simply said, "Yes, sir."

"Then I don't expect to go through this with you again. Understood?"

"Yes, sir."

"Good. Now, let's eat dinner."

She got up and numbly walked to the kitchen. The table was already set. She sat down while her father pulled a baking dish from the oven. She recognized the pan as the one he always used when he made one of Sandi's favorite dishes.

Sandi ate in silence while her father droned on and on about his latest project at work. She didn't even try to seem interested. She was never concerned with what he did at work. Since he stopped doing experiments in the basement alongside her years ago, she found nothing he did of significance. He didn't seem to notice.

When she had finished eating, she sat momentarily with her hands in her lap and her eyes averted. As her father's tone changed, indicating he had almost concluded his rambling, she got up and began her chore of cleaning the kitchen. Her father put his dishes in the sink and attempted to hug her. She stood stiffly. He went upstairs. Since she figured he would probably not be back out for this evening, she slipped down to the basement to check on Max.

When she stepped into the aisle where his shelf was, there was a protrusion in the row with the curtain draped over it. She raised the gray fabric to find the container had tipped on its side and Max lay on the floor. "Oh no!" she exclaimed as she dropped to her knees to put him back in the plastic bin. He was much bigger now and wouldn't fit. She had figured this was coming, she just hadn't thought it would be this quickly. She lifted the mass and carried it to the lab table. When she set it down, there were several odd-looking bulges from various places around its circumference. She carefully examined them. She had no idea what they were, but this was the first sign of any shape other than round. She knew it had to be due to the introduction of bone marrow and DNA.

Sandi wondered what a full twenty-four-hour period would do. She knew she had to return to school the next day. She was sorry she couldn't slack off one more day, but she had just gotten over being in trouble, so she had better lay low and keep to her normal routine for now. After so much growth in just an afternoon, she was anxious to see how big Max would be when she returned from school. But right now, she needed to make a better arrangement than a bin on the shelf.

She went upstairs to the spare linen closet for blankets and pillows to make a pallet on the floor between the shelving unit and the outer wall. Sandi laid out several blankets the length and width of the aisle, placed pillows at both ends, and turned the heat lamp to beam down in the space where she would place Max. She picked him up from the table and walked back to his new bed. She noticed he was warm. She hadn't noticed when she brought him out because she had just taken him from the heat lamp. He wasn't feverish, just warm as a body might be. Her heart leaped in her chest. She just might be able to do this. Another day would be very telling.

Sandi gently laid him on the makeshift bedding, covered him with a down comforter, and said, "Sleep well, little Max. I'll check on you tomorrow." She climbed the stairs with more of a lift in her step. When she was famous, she wouldn't have to put up with her stringent father. She would have the last laugh. She would move out of this house and never return. He would no longer be in control or calling the shots. Her grandfather would regret not assisting her, too. She would share none of her findings with either of them.

As she crawled into bed, she was feeling noticeably better. One full night of rest, she thought, should have her back to her old self.

As she trudged through her day, Sandi recognized she was dealing with the same stuff she always did, the same foul people, the same unfair situations, the same frustrations, but today it felt different. Today, she let more simply roll off her back. She didn't feed into the attempts to hurt and anger her. She paid no attention to the usual suspects and thorns in her side. Her full focus was on getting through this day to get back to Max.

She had made sure to accomplish everything necessary by the end of her last class, so she could leave her book bag in her trunk. There would be no need for it tonight.

Sandi went quickly to the basement to see what developments had occurred overnight. She was thrilled to see Max's form was larger. When she removed the comforter, she was startled to see fuzz on what appeared to be forming into a head. It was a start. There were parts of him that resembled the shape of a growing fetus. She wondered if she should have done all this in a fluid sac to replicate the womb. It was too late now. If she had to start this process over, she would consider that variable then. Once this first one succeeded, she would make adjustments to future creations.

As she lifted Max, she felt the weight difference. To her naked eye, he appeared the same size in general, though with various additional formations he didn't have the day before, but there was no question he was a little heavier. Sandi knew muscle weighed more than fat. She wondered if he was developing muscle mass, so not showing larger but weighing more. Additionally, she wondered about his organs. She set him on the scale and recorded her findings. She drew a bit of fluid and ran tests. Now, there was evidence of red blood cells. Nothing more was registering. She used her stethoscope, there were sounds internally but they were by no means normal. Maybe it was still too soon, but she was hopeful. His formation continued to concern her. His coloring was less opaque with a tinge of blue. What was the purpose if he was not much more than an amoeba? She wanted a boyfriend. Someone whom other girls would beg for, but who was only loyal to her. Someone who was all about her. She knew it was a lot to ask. She also knew once he was fully formed and she had a chance to teach and train him the way she wanted, he would be just right for her.

She went to the freezer and pulled out the second bag of the male bone marrow to thaw. Sandi set the bag on a folded towel, so it would avoid contact with the stainless steel of the lab table while she gathered the necessities to do an additional transfusion.

Once the contents of the last of the male marrow had been pumped into Max, she carried him back to his bedding, covered him, cleaned up her mess, and went to the living room until dinner.

While sharing their nighttime meal, her father asked what project Sandi was currently working on. When she said nothing, he launched into another lecture. This one had to do with overcoming disappointments and moving forward. *If he only knew,* she thought.

Back in her room, Sandi was restless. She wanted to check on Max but not having any experiments to work on put her at a disadvantage. She needed to make up something believable. This might take some thought. She wanted to maintain this feeling of being the creator. She better understood how God must be so proud of His world.

Sandi was never sure of the origins of her atheist father's rantings that there was no God. But she was beginning to see why he would be so adamant about the subject. If humans were capable of creating life, what was the need for a belief in a God of creation?

It was going to take her some time to come up with an additional believable experiment. She wouldn't force it or rush it. Maybe she could think of a past experiment she hadn't fully worked out so her father would let her spend all her time in the lab but not be interested enough to check on her activities. That was what she needed to play with. Now, to think of what that would be. She always discussed her experiments with her dad. Was there anything she hadn't covered with him that she could believably reinvent quickly?

Sandi woke in the middle of the night with an idea she had done briefly while working on a bigger, better project. Since she was awake and she was curious how Max was doing, she chose to slip downstairs to check. Sandi quietly made her way to the lowest level. When she entered the storage area and looked to the left there was the deformed appearance of something sticking out from under the comforter into the main thoroughfare. It looked like it would eventually become a foot. It was a beginning shape without the development of bones. When she threw back the comforter, she was both thrilled and revolted by what lay in front of her. His form was really taking shape. She could tell where limbs were beginning to develop. She really hoped this would end up more encouraging than just random parts protruding from various spaces.

There was a bulbous extension at the top that should eventually become a head. It housed three protrusions and three holes. It looked like the eyes and nose were beginning to form. A hole in the front would most likely become his mouth, but there were no holes in what should become the nose. She hoped she didn't need to cut them into his face. There was a hole on either side of his head, they must be the formation of what would be ears. This was so exciting.

He began to visibly shake. He must be cold. Sandi drew the comforter back over him and the shaking stopped. She ran for her stethoscope. Her excitement grew at the faint sound of air going in and out. He must now be developing lungs. Her guess was that he was bringing air in through the holes in his head, passing it through his developing lungs, and expelling it back out through the same holes. How thrilling! What was louder and stronger was the beating of a heart. This development was crucial to his continued formation. Neither sound was normal, but they were measurable.

What was disconcerting to Sandi was his formation, or lack thereof, of actual limbs. There were, in fact, four extremities, but each was of different lengths and shapes. His right what-should-be arm had three long fingers at the end. It stuck straight out at a ninety-degree angle to his torso. His left arm had no evidence of a hand being formed. It lay beside him, extending down his side. She carefully lifted it to see it was attached to his quasi-torso all the way down, as she feared. However, when she picked it up, he became agitated and began to squirm. That suggested the development of muscles and nerves.

Max's legs were expanding as his arms were. The longer one had no foot at the end of it, it was just an extension out the bottom of the torso on his right side. The left had a malformed foot on the end of the protrusion. She was disenchanted by having created a freak instead of a boyfriend. She covered him back up and tucked his legs in. She had to get back to bed.

Sandi tossed and turned the rest of the night over what she should do about this. He may not have formed the way she desired, but he was a living, breathing being now. There was no way she would be able to destroy him. She also could not take him out in public. She was already the butt of too many jokes, this would be her undoing. She wished she could spend her days working on this instead of wasting her time in this foolish education system. Eventually, her morning alarm sounded, and she dragged herself from the bed. She was tired but the thrill of coming home to Max would motivate her to just get through the day.

Looking at her reflection in the mirror after her shower made her pay closer attention to all her parts. What a miraculous thing, she thought, that all ears, mouths, noses, and eyes were unique but maintained the same basic structure. Would Max's? She had to hope. There *must* be a God to create miraculously, as He did.

Downstairs, she went through the same routine with her father as she had almost every day of her life, then out the door to fight her way through a nasty society.

She now walked with more arrogance, in the belief that it wouldn't be much longer before all these mean people would eat their words. She would no longer be irrelevant, a loser, with no one to love her. She would never lower herself to fall in with the "populars," but she would also no longer be chastised and made a laughingstock. She just couldn't say anything yet. If her experiment went terribly wrong, she would be an even bigger joke.

Seven

S andi couldn't wait to get home. It was the same crazy day at school that she'd been through hundreds of times before. The difference was that she really felt like she had something to go home to. The first thing she would do was check on Max's progress. Every day was showing more development. He had come so far!

She dropped her bag at the back door and ran downstairs through the basement to the back room, to the area she'd managed to keep hidden from her father.

Sandi pulled back the blanket to find two fleshy pink arms and two similar-looking legs. All were *still* at various stages of growth. It wasn't as if any of these appendages could be of use. She was disappointed. What if her father was correct? What if she'd created a monster? No, it wasn't a fully functioning human, not even close, but it was still living. She could never destroy it. *Think, Sandi, think.*

She had to get him on the examination table to fully assess the situation. She tried to pull the tray she had him on, but he was too heavy now. She tried to lift him in her arms like a baby, but he was too long and gangly. She knelt, pulled him from his bed, carefully lifted his torso to her, and gently shifted him over her shoulder. His head had gotten so big, it was throwing off her balance. She had to be careful not to knock him into something. Once she felt his weight was properly distributed, she slowly rose to her full height. She had this.

She laid him on the examination table, grabbed her notebook, and began her observations. She was pleased with his coloring. It suggested blood flow. His weight had increased by 170% overnight. What if she was in way over her head? How would she get him to stop growing? She clearly hadn't thought this all the way through.

She measured his head. It was quite large in proportion to his body. There was a nose with two holes, opaque eye lids, and the beginning formation of lips. At this stage, there wasn't really a shape to his face other than a long oval. His right arm was 10.2" long, his left was 12.7". He had what looked like it might become a hand protruding from his right limb, but no such feature was on his left still. His right leg was 15.5", but his left leg was only 12.3" long. Both legs now had the beginnings of feet. They were both severely deformed at this stage.

Sandi pulled out her stethoscope. She turned him on his side and listened to his back. There were, in fact, strong, regular breath sounds. She jumped up and down in circles squealing. There was nothing her father could do about Max now. There was no way he could kill a living, breathing being.

She did take note he appeared to be a eunuch. Since his development was not like that of a fetus, she wasn't sure what to expect to form and at what stage genitalia developed. What was obvious was that she had to find a better solution to hiding him while allowing him to continue to develop.

Sandi wasn't sure how his digestive system was forming. She had to nourish his body but wasn't sure what he could handle. She used her stethoscope to listen for blood running through veins. It was faint, but clearly there. She pulled an IV bag from the back room. Her father was always afraid that something would happen, and she would need it. She suggested if that was the case, he should take her to the hospital. He always brushed her off. Right now, she was glad they had such an extensive supply.

Sandi located the strongest vein, set up the IV, and stuck the needle in. She was shocked when Max's body flinched. He could feel! This was a wonderful discovery. While she let the drip run its course, she cleaned out the last bottom shelf on the far end of the supply room. He needed room to grow. Sandi wanted to be certain he was kept warm and comfortable. She took out the shelf above the bottom one, set it on the floor beside the lowest shelf, and laid a board over both shelves to make the base of a bed. She fetched an old twin mattress in the attic. She made it up with a spare set of her favorite Jersey-knit sheets, so he would stay warm. It was the only set of twin sheets they owned. Her father had gotten them once when they thought she would be going on a camping trip, but it never happened. She laid out the old comforter she had been covering him with. It now looked like a nice bed for an actual person.

She pulled the heat lamp into the aisle and set it up in the corner at what would now be the top of his head. She checked the outer wall for drafts. She felt confident he would not be compromised here. She tacked the gray sheet to the top of the shelf and let it hang down to hide all the shelves of the last unit. It blended in well, and with all the stuff stacked on the other shelves, it wasn't really noticeable, even though she was looking for it.

Sandi ran back to check on the IV bag. It hadn't run dry yet. She tried to sit and wait out the final drips but couldn't stay still. She was so excited about this progress. Her adrenaline was pumping like crazy. She kept sitting down and jumping right back up. She paced the large room and checked often on Max. He looked more like an alien experiment than a person. She didn't know what she would do if he never formed properly, but she knew she could never destroy him. As the bag emptied, she withdrew the needle and added pressure and a bandage to ensure clotting.

Sandi cleaned up behind herself and returned to assess the needle entry. The bleeding had stopped. Another win in her books. She laid her torso across Max's, hoisted his top half over her right shoulder, and carefully lifted him. She felt she had better control this time around. She carried him to his new home, knelt, put her hand behind his head, and laid him out on his new bed. Sandi straightened him out across it and tucked all of him in for warmth. She slid a pillow under his head. His facial features were forming but were still a bit translucent. She could feel the slight breath on her hand from his nostrils. She smiled. She sat

61

back and just watched him. The sense of pride she felt right now was more than she imagined possible. She had created this person.

Sandi had to get everything put away and be upstairs before her father got home. Now, more than ever, she had to be sure she gave him no reason to visit the basement. She leaned over, pressed her cheek against what she hoped would one day be Max's cheek, turned the heater on, and ran back to the lab. There wasn't much to tidy. She made quick work of it. When she reached the top of the stairs, she heard the garage door open. She shot upstairs to her bedroom before her father came in. She had to calm herself before the inquisition began.

Sandi sat on the edge of her bed doing deep breathing to slow her heartbeat and change her physiology. She moved into a meditative state, which shifted everything for her. Yes, she was the one in control now, not her body. She felt she could face her father without drawing suspicion. She went to her bathroom to splash cold water on her face when she heard the familiar rap on her door and her father's announcement that dinner was on the table.

"Coming," she called out.

When she rounded the corner into the kitchen, her father had just put the last dish on the table. He turned to hug her and place his customary kiss on her forehead.

Sandi slid into her seat at the dining table.

"So, how was your day, princess?" her father asked.

"Same as every other day in my life. I hate school and wish you would let me test out."

"Sorry, kiddo, not happening."

"Then we might as well talk about your day instead." As long as her father had the last say, it would never happen.

She didn't understand how he could be paid the ridiculous salary he was to do mundane, nonsensical research that, in her opinion, would lead to nothing. She was more surprised that, with the resources he had at his disposal from his father, he would continue to work at a dead-end job for so many years. He said he would retire from his current place of employment. He was nowhere near retirement age. It would be a long, slow life for him. She felt sorry for him. He was fond of the quote, "We all make choices, then our choices make us." She supposed he was right.

His choice to remain at this job had slowly stripped away any enthusiasm for life he might once have had. Now his life was a boring routine with no excitement. Spending his evenings seeing how many *Jeopardy!* questions he could get right was not a life.

Sandi knew his lack of desire for more was not her concern. She just hated watching her father go through the motions of an insignificant life. It wouldn't be long before she was out of the house, and he would be all alone. What a sad existence that would be.

"Sandi!" her father said sternly.

"What?"

"Have you heard one word I said?"

She could lie, but the truth was she had no clue. If she tried to act like she had been listening, she would be busted for sure with the first quiz question. And there was always a pointed question asked. "I'm sorry. What did you say? I was going over a test I have coming up in Physics tomorrow."

"Oh, that's okay. That's much more important than what I was talking about. Anything I can help you study for?"

"No, not really. If you're done, I'm going to clean up and head upstairs to cram."

"Sure. I'm full. I'll help, so you can get at it. Don't be up half the night reviewing. You know it's in there, you just need to retrieve it."

"I know, Daddy."

She did have a test in a few days, but she was fully prepared for it. She would like the extra time to do more research on the human body and development. She kissed her father on the cheek and bade him goodnight.

"I love you, princess."

"I love you too. Goodnight."

Eight

Sandi had checked on Max twice a day for a week now: early in the morning before her father got up and right after school before her dad got home. He was gaining better form and weight and growing more than just peach fuzz on the top of his head. His limbs were beginning to even out. He had developed his genitals and was excreting more daily. There was now no question Max was a male. She believed she was going to have to start coming home for lunch to change his diaper at this rate. It was all coming together as it should be. She was hopeful for the completion when she would finally share him with her father. She knew he would change his mind about all of this then. He would be so proud of her and her accomplishments. Maybe then he would finally agree to let her test out of this hellhole they called high school. *One thing at a time*, she thought.

When Sandi came through the back door, she heard crying. She froze. There was no way that was coming from Max! If it was, how would she keep her father from knowing what was going on in the basement? She raced down the stairs. This had never occurred to her. What should she do? Her mind raced. Where would she hide him?

As she got closer to where she had stashed him, the crying got louder. He was uncovered, sprawled across the bed, and shivering.

"Oh, Max! I'm so sorry. I'm right here. Don't be afraid. I've got you. Here, let me help you."

Sandi repositioned him and covered him back up. His crying slowed, but he continued to shake. She laid down beside him and wrapped her arms around him to share her body heat. His crying ceased. His breathing became deeper. She figured he had fallen back to sleep. He felt good lying in her arms as he was. It wasn't long before he was softly cooing in his sleep.

Usually, Sandi only looked at Max in quick scans, trying to gather as much data as she could before her father got home at night. But lying this close to him, she was able to observe far more. She could see the tiny eyelashes that had formed. They were dark, as the tiny, fresh hair on his head was. She saw his eyeballs moving, as he was apparently in REM sleep. His eyelids were now thicker. They were no longer just thin, translucent coverings. She wondered how long it would take until they opened—if they ever opened and functioned as real eyes should. His lips were fully formed and parted. There was no question his lungs were in great shape. She had only two IV bags left. Tomorrow, Sandi would have to find more. She wasn't about to let him starve.

That was not her worry today. Today, she still had one to give him once she could bear to leave his side. She wasn't sure how long she'd lain there with him. She better get a move on. She couldn't be caught before Max was fully formed and ready to be presented. As she slowly backed away from him, he began to stir. She halted. She went slower. When she finally was able to extricate herself from him without waking him, she made quick work of prepping him for his feeding. She had left his IV in, changing it only once a week to avoid infection. She hooked him up and went about her measurements. She was only weighing him every few days. He was getting so heavy. She felt he was fine not being weighed daily.

Sandi was so excited. His arms were finally the same length, with fully formed hands and fingers. At the end of his legs were feet with toes. The left foot was not at the angle it should be but was pointing straight down. That might take some conditioning once he was able to walk. Her bigger concern was that his legs were not closing the gap in their length, as his arms had. She was worried he would be left with a severe limp.

As the IV dripped along, she began to rub both legs to increase circulation and hopefully stimulate growth. She noticed there was no real muscle mass beneath the skin, over the bones. She would have to figure out how to rectify that. He would never be able to walk without muscle to move him forward. Or even stand, for that matter.

Instinctually, Sandi put her hands on the bottoms of his feet and began moving them in the motion of riding a bike. Max remained sleeping. She figured he must not mind. As long as he was nourished, warm, and allowed to peacefully sleep, he didn't care what Sandi did to him. She moved his legs in many different formations and repetitions. She knew it might take a long while before she began to notice muscle beneath this frail skin. For now, she would be patient. She had a lot to figure out before he reached maturity.

Sandi quickly changed his diaper, which was becoming a challenge with his current size. As she was tidying everything up and putting things away, she heard the garage door going up. She began to panic. There was no way for her to make it past the top of the basement stairs before her father discovered her. She didn't want to answer any questions. She knew he would have them if she was emerging from the cellar. She waited in the lab trying to formulate a plan. She returned to Max to make sure he was all tucked in before she had to leave him and prayed, he wouldn't make any noise. All set. It was then she came up with a story to tell her dad.

She ran to the top of the stairs, turned out the light, and closed the door behind herself.

"Oh! Dad, I didn't realize you were home."

"What were you so engrossed in that you didn't hear me come in?"

"I was researching."

"Researching what?"

"Muscles and how they grow."

"And what did you discover?" her father asked sincerely.

"Nothing much, yet."

"Are you interested in becoming a physical therapist?"

"No. I don't think that is my life's path. I'm interested in more than just being a therapist, of any kind. The whiny people would make me give up too easily."

He chuckled. "Well, whatever you decide, I'll support you."

"Whatever..." Sandi allowed the word to dangle and see how her father responded.

"Yes, of course. You'll always be my baby. I'll always want the best for you. I'll always encourage you in your endeavors."

"That's all I needed to hear. Thank you, Daddy." She kissed his cheek and ran upstairs to her room. She would see if he meant what he said soon enough.

Her father called out to her from below, "Make quick work of whatever you're doing. Dinner will be ready in about fifteen minutes."

Nine

T he next night, Sandi heard her father upstairs. She didn't care if he came down. There was nothing he would find. She had quickly taken care of Max: he was changed, fed, tucked in, and peacefully sleeping. If he wanted to share research tips, she was all ears. Instead of coming down, her father called down to her that he'd brought a pizza home for dinner and to come eat before it got cold.

"Be right up," she called after him. She might as well; she was useless tonight.

Sandi bound up the stairs humming and washed her hands at the sink while asking her dad how his day was. He hesitated long enough that she looked over her shoulder at him. He was staring at her.

"What?" she asked.

"You seem in an exceptionally good mood tonight. What has you so upbeat?"

"Oh, please. I'm usually in a good mood."

"Not since you were about twelve."

"Stop it."

He proceeded to drone on and on about his boring day. It was the result she was looking for. She had no interest in talking about hers. And this gave her an opportunity to daydream while he talked.

After the pizza was gone, Sandi put the plates in the dishwasher, took the empty box to the trash can in the garage, kissed her father goodnight, and headed upstairs. She had no interest in doing anything with her dad tonight. She chuckled to herself as she climbed the stairs two at a time. She had yet to return Houston's hoodie to him. She just wanted to feel like he was with her under her roof.

She didn't really have anything to do, she just couldn't focus on anything substantial. She jumped in the shower, primped a bit, climbed into her bed, and turned on the TV. Sandi didn't usually waste her time watching TV but was going to give it a try, if for no other reason than to distract herself. She lay there in the bed feeling restless, channel surfing. She got up and went to her closet to retrieve the hoodie.

Once she was back in the bed, she laid it across her chest. It seemed to soothe her, and she was able to find something to watch to occupy her time and mind. Intelligent programming was a luxury. She had to settle for the mundane. For a brief moment, she forgot Houston's garment was an inanimate object and not the person himself. It didn't matter. It was more than she'd ever had before.

She woke with a start and looked at her clock. It was 2:30 in the morning. She'd fallen asleep watching mindless banter on a sitcom. Sandi turned off the TV and the lights and curled up with the sweatshirt. She didn't wake up again until her alarm went off.

Sandi got up and ran downstairs to change Max and keep him settled for the day. She ran to her room, washed her face, brushed her teeth, and got dressed—all the while wondering what she should do about the hoodie. She wasn't ready to part with it, so she made the sweatshirt up in her bed to wait until the night. She would consider what to do throughout her day.

It felt like forever until third-block Physics, the only class Sandi shared with Houston. She slipped into her seat. Houston's, beside her, was empty. She hoped he wasn't out. She was starting to feel like one of those mindless, gushy teenage girls—the ones who revolved their lives around their boyfriends, never had an independent thought, and didn't make a move unless told to do so. Her problem was, Houston wasn't her boyfriend. As the time ticked closer to the final bell and he still wasn't here, her heart began to sink.

Megan Malhomme walked in and said loud enough she could have been heard in all the surrounding rooms, "Hey, Klutzie, have you managed to stay on your feet today?"

The room erupted in laughter and jeers.

"I was pushed, moron! Did you push me? You seem to know so much."

"You're such a loser," Megan responded. "No, I didn't push you. I was simply lucky enough to be there to witness your latest disaster."

While bantering with Megan, Sandi had missed Houston's entrance just as the bell rang. When she looked to her right, he was sliding into his seat.

"I haven't seen you much. Are you okay since your fall?" he asked.

Sandi nodded and said, "Yes, I was a bit sore, and my ego took a bad hit, but I'll be fine. Thanks again for helping me."

The guy sitting behind her put on a falsetto and said, "Ooh, Houston, thanks again for helping me. I'm Sandi the simpleton with no social skills."

Houston rolled his eyes, lowered his voice, and said, "Just ignore them."

Sandi nodded. The teacher took roll. Sandi naturally slipped into her academic mode. Physics was one of her favorite classes. Too soon the class was over, and it would be another 48 hours until she saw Houston again. When the bell rang, Houston sprang from his seat and was out the door before she could even say, "Bye." Obviously, he didn't feel the same way about her as she did for him. It would feel like a lifetime before she saw him again. She figured he wouldn't have even a passing thought about her. No matter. She knew soon enough she would have a Houston of her own. He would think of her all the time. She would teach him to be her perfect mate. Attentive, intellectual, capable of more than a half dozen words to her.

Fourth block dragged. She just wanted to go home. Much like her other classes, she didn't feel they had anything new to teach her. It was the main reason her days dragged by. They weren't challenging.

Somehow, she had to make her father see reason. In university, she would be around more people like herself, and learn with no ceiling, at her advanced ability.

She was hungry. She was now skipping lunch to run home to take care of Max. It would be too long until dinner. She swung through the drive-thru of the local fast-food restaurant, called The Burger Joint. "What can I get you?" came through the intercom.

"Just a cheeseburger," Sandi said.

"$4.78 at the window."

Sandi drove around and was shocked to find Houston at the window. "I didn't know you worked here."

"I didn't know you ate here," he replied.

"I usually don't. I was just hungry."

"So, you chose here?" He quirked an eyebrow and gave her one of his brilliant smiles.

"Yeah, well, it's fast."

"And what you don't know, won't hurt you."

She laughed. "How long have you worked here?" Sandi handed him a five-dollar bill.

"Just a week. It's not a career choice, just a way to make some extra money."

She laughed again.

He handed her the change and a bag. "See ya at school."

"Sure thing." She drove away wishing their encounters weren't always so brief.

Ten

S andi found herself looking forward to one class only: Physics. It became the highlight of her week. If it was the week with three Physics classes, she was even happier. She was always elated just to see Houston, even if they didn't get an opportunity to talk. She was always thinking of things to discuss with him if he got to class early enough. He was apparently making more of an effort since they were having a few moments before class started. On the days she didn't have class with him, Sandi was making a habit of going by the Burger Joint just for the chance to see Houston. He wasn't always on. She wished she could get his schedule. Too many of their burgers and she'd start to get fat. She knew they were loaded with preservatives and things not good for her body, but they sure did taste good. She wondered if there were addictive additives in them. She was beginning to crave them. Or did she just crave seeing Houston?

Max was coming along nicely. He now had hair all over his head, his limbs had evened out, his vitals were strong, and his heart and lung sounds were steady and solid. Sandi talked to him all the time. It had been quite some time since she found him crying. He rarely even opened his mouth. She had explored the inside. He didn't have teeth yet, but the structure was there. He had a fully developed tongue. She was disappointed he had not opened his eyes yet. She was running him through physical movements to help develop his muscles. They were growing. Sandi regularly sat him up. She always strapped him into a chair, but he was doing much better sitting on his own now.

When she had run out of their stored IV bags, she made him baby bottles with high-protein formula. His instincts had him naturally sucking down the offerings. She hoped he was getting enough nourishment. Although his body was that of a full-sized person, she believed his insides would still be developing, as a baby's would.

Sandi decided today would be the day to try to get him on his feet. She hoped it wasn't a disaster, since he was now longer than she was. If he fell on top of her, there was no telling what would happen.

Sandi dropped her bag by the back door and ran for the cellar. Max was wailing. It was a good thing she had gotten there before her father. She rounded the corner to his bed. He was sitting up with his eyes open, yelling. She tried to calm him, let him know she was right there, and quiet him. When he heard her voice, he settled down. She knelt in front of him and rubbed his arms. He was looking right at her. She was slightly disappointed that his eyes were dark and not blue. She knew babies were usually born with dark eyes and it sometimes took a year before their color came in. She just figured since his formation was not that of a baby, his eye color might have already been established. Her disappointment was overshadowed by the fact that his eyes were now open, and he appeared to be able to see her.

Sandi pulled him gently to her and wrapped her arms around him. Max laid his head on her shoulder with little after-sobs from crying too long.

"Shh, it's okay. I'm here now. You're okay. Are you hungry? Let me go get you a bottle." Sandi started to rise, but Max held on tight. "Okay, let's see if we can get you on your feet and you can come with me."

She kept her arms around him, while gently lifting him with her. He followed. With Max at his full height, she came to just above his chin. She put one arm around his waist and took a step. He didn't move. "Follow me, Max. Move your foot to take a step."

He did nothing.

She bent down and pulled his right foot forward, then moved his left. She looked up and he was just staring down at her. It was kind of creepy. She went back to his right foot, then his left, back to his right. It was going to take them much longer than she knew they had before her dad was home.

"Come on, Max, please? You have to come with me. You're too big for me to carry anymore. We just need to get to the next room."

Nothing. He just looked at her. She wrapped his right arm around the brace of the shelving unit. "Stay here. I'll be right back."

Sandi ran to the lab to grab one of the chairs on wheels. As soon as she was out of his sight, he started crying out again. She ran back with the chair to find him slumped on the floor. She again lifted him up into the chair and wheeled him to the lab with her.

He watched while she prepared his bottle. She noticed a slight change in the look on his face. She believed he was showing joy. He didn't have a smile, but he did look happy.

"Are you hungry? Is this what you want?"

He drank down the contents in record time and started crying again.

"Okay, I'll make you another."

After four bottles, he seemed satisfied. She had to find something more for this growing boy. Also, taking in this much was going to increase the output. She was not going to have enough time in her day.

SANDI SAT EXPECTANTLY IN PHYSICS, as she always did. She knew Houston all too often arrived just as the final bell was ringing. She felt robbed on those days because it didn't give them the time to talk that she so craved. Houston was open and talkative if she kept the subject to intellectual topics, but always cryptic when it came to his personal life. Sandi tried, but she was so curious to know him better that every so often, she would try to slip in something personal. As she pensively sat waiting, it occurred to her that she never talked to anyone about herself. Sandi didn't think it was for the same reason as Houston. Any time she had told anyone anything personal, they used it against her. But everyone liked Houston. What would he have to be afraid of?

The final bell rang: no Houston. He had never missed a class. He might slide in by the skin of his teeth at the end of the last bell, but he was always there. Now she was worried. Where could he be? Was he sick? Had something bad happened? Was he detained in his last class? Where was he?

As always, class started right on time. Today, Sandi couldn't focus. It was a good thing she *knew* Physics. She was barely paying attention. She wanted to be done with this class and find Houston.

Class ended, but where would she even begin to look for him? She had no idea of his schedule. She only knew he always shot out of this class and went to the right. Her last class was to the left. Once she cleared the door, Sandi stood in the hall debating which direction she should go. There were a lot of options to the right. She had to get to her next class.

People started yelling at her to move and pushing her out of the way. She really hated it here. Reluctantly, she turned to the left. She would have felt a lot better if she could even glimpse him to know he was here and all right. He could be anywhere in this vast school. And then again, he might not be here at all. She ran for her last class. She would go by the Burger Joint after school to check on him.

Sandi's last class was just as torturous as Physics since she didn't have a clue if Houston was alive or dead. But when the last bell of the day rang, she made a beeline to her car and prayed she'd see Houston at his job.

Instead of taking a chance at the drive-thru, Sandi went inside. If he was cooking or cleaning in the front, she'd be able to see him. She scanned the front and back and didn't see him. She went to the counter and asked the pretty little thing taking orders if Houston was supposed to work today. Sandi found herself jealous. She was petite and beautiful, with long blonde hair pulled back in a ponytail, big, brown doe eyes, and a perfect peaches-and-cream complexion that needed minimal makeup. Maybe Houston was dating her. Or at the very least, more interested in her than he ever could be in Sandi. Maybe that's why he never engaged in talk about his personal life. He was a kind person. He probably didn't want to be mean and insensitive to her plain-Jane self.

"Who?" she said.

"Houston MacAvoy. Is he scheduled to work?"

She batted those brown eyes at her and said, "I don't know who that is. Can I get you something?"

"No. Not today. I'm looking for Houston."

"I don't know him."

"Could you look at the schedule and see for me?"

"I can't leave my station."

"Can you ask someone?"

She turned, looking lost, and said, "Matt, do you know a Houston somebody? This girl wants to know if he's working."

Matt shouted back, "He's off today."

The girl turned back to Sandi and said, "He's off today."

"Yeah, my hearing is fine."

"So, can I get you something?"

Sandi just walked out. She highly doubted Houston would be interested in Blondie. Jealousy averted. She might be pretty, but without enough gray matter to appeal to Houston.

Sandi drove home still worried, but she had Max to focus on.

She stopped by the store to get baby food. He was growing and his body needed a lot more nourishment. She had no idea what to get him. Although he physically didn't look it, his internal organs needed a slow introduction to food, just like a baby did. She stood in front of an entire row of shelves from the floor to about two feet above her filled with various foods and stages. She didn't know how these "stages" went, so she pulled one that had a one and another that had a two on the jars. She read both and determined that they went up in numbers as the baby grew. Her baby was full-grown, though. What stage should she use? Sandi felt it better to err on the side of caution. She bought a few of everything labeled with a one. There was a lot. Although Max was much bigger than a baby, she wouldn't allow him to starve.

As she checked out, she was grateful she came from so much money. How did ordinary moms and dads make ends meet? This stuff added up to a hefty bill.

When she opened her car door in the garage, she heard Max yelling as he had the day before. Sandi grabbed a bag and ran. She would get back here to get the rest later, hopefully before her father got home. She knew Max had to be hungry.

Sandi rounded the corner into the storage area to find a huge mess. Max was lying on the floor, yelling and crying. "Shh, it's okay, I'm here now," she said.

He stopped his wailing and looked up at her.

"What happened here?"

Max turned over and started pulling himself toward her.

"No, wait right there. I'll get your chair." She ran down the aisle to where she'd left the chair on wheels the night before, grabbed it, and ran back. Max had continued dragging himself toward her. He had to have rug burns from all this hauling. He was getting better with muscle strength but wasn't quite there yet. She tried to help him up into the chair. He had gotten so big, she wasn't strong enough to just pick him up and set him in the chair. She lowered her left shoulder to his midsection to try to drape him over her to hoist him up on the chair. He just sat there. "Come on, buddy. Work with me here."

Sandi put both his arms over her shoulder and tried again. It was like trying to lift a dead weight. When she attempted to push to get him up on her shoulder, she only succeeded in pushing him backward on the floor. She sat down hard in front of him. He just looked at her. "Do you understand I'm trying to get you into this chair?" She patted his behind then patted the seat of the chair. "Let's try this again."

She got on her knees, put his arms over her shoulder once again, slid her hands under his legs, and tried to push him over her shoulder. Success! She attempted to stand, but his weight landed her on her backside with him on top of her. "Oh, for the love of all that's holy! Come on, Max. We haven't got all night." She sat up and was going to try to push him toward the chair. Maybe she could land enough of him in the seat to work this out. When she tried, the chair shot backward down the aisle, and he landed on his behind with Sandi across his lap.

She stood up, retrieved the chair, and backed it up to the end of the shelving. "Okay, I need to be smarter than the problem." She took the belt she intended to strap him in with, sent it through the shelving, and secured it to the chair. Sandi bent down, tried again to send Max over her shoulder, and started to stand. She couldn't quite make it, but all she needed was to get him up high enough to hit the seat of the chair. She let out one good grunt, lifted his torso, and almost made it. "Again," she said. The next attempt was successful. He was half on, half off, but she could work with this. She scooted him over more securely in the seat.

As soon as Sandi got him situated on the chair, he hugged her hard. She tried to explain that she needed a bit of room to strap him in, but he wouldn't let go. She couldn't see the belt, so she had to feel her way to unfasten it from the chair and pull it from around the shelves. She scooted Max along with the chair toward her to reach behind to wrap it around the seat and Max. He wouldn't let go. Her face was into his side, under his arm, reaching around for all she was worth. "Max, you're going to suffocate me here." Sandi was fastening the belt between her and Max's death grip on her. When she'd accomplished her goal, she was exhausted and dropped on Max's legs. She tried to work her way around the chair to the back to push, but he wasn't letting up on her, so she pulled him into the lab while walking backward.

She had dropped the bag of food on the floor when she saw the mess. Sandi was trying to tell Max she needed the bag but couldn't reach it if he didn't let go. Nope. Not happening. She scooted the chair closer to the bag and put her foot around the back of the sack to pull it close. With Max's arms still wrapped around her neck, she lifted the bag into his lap. Sandi said, "Food, Max, food. I know you must be hungry. Let's eat."

It must have sounded like gibberish to Max. He just wouldn't let go. She had a lot to accomplish before her father got home. He probably wouldn't come down and see the mess, but Sandi wasn't taking chances. She couldn't accomplish it with an albatross around her neck.

She let Max hold on while she opened a jar. She worked it up between them to his nose. Once he got a whiff, he let go and grabbed the jar from her hands. He brought it to his mouth. While he was puzzling out how to get to the contents, Sandi shot to a drawer to get a utensil that would work as a spoon. Max was getting vocal at not being able to reach the food. Sandi tried to take the jar, but he refused to allow her. She got the spoon into the food, scooped an overflowing amount, and stuck it into Max's mouth. Success! Max shoved the jar toward Sandi but wouldn't let go. She scooped another and another until it was empty. Max was having none of that. She showed him she had a bag full of them. He gave her the space she needed to wheel him to the table, unpack the bag, and lay out the jars. She opened another. He devoured that one as fast as he had the last. And another. It wasn't until jar six that he began to slow down.

Sandi felt bad she had left him to be so hungry. She should have been feeding him before she went to school, but how, with her father always here? She had to work something out. This couldn't happen again.

Once Max seemed sated, Sandi put the TV on to keep him occupied while she got the rest of the groceries from the car. She had little time since she had wasted so much looking for Houston and shopping. She pulled a baby toy she'd bought from one of the bags. It was colorful, with many shapes to place in their respective holes. They needed to work on his cognitive learning and dexterity. The colors caught Max's eye, and he was immediately done with TV. Sandi gave him the toy. She went to the storage room to start cleaning the mess up. She worked from the most visible to the back. She wasn't nearly done when she heard the familiar sound of the garage door opening. She panicked. She was nowhere near finished. Max was mumbling to himself over his toy.

The door to the basement opened, and her father called down, "I'm home, princess. Dinner will be in about 30 minutes. I hope you're hungry."

"I am. I'll be up in a little while." Sandi was trying to get Max to be quiet, but he was having none of it. The more she tried the louder he seemed to get.

"Are you okay? Do you have someone down there with you?" her father asked.

"I have the TV on, Dad."

"Oh, I thought I heard someone. Okay, I'll let you know when dinner is ready."

Sandi collapsed in the chair next to Max. What was she thinking? How would she ever keep this secret?

"Max, you have got to be quiet," she whispered. "You're going to get me in trouble."

Max reached for another jar of food.

"Really? You're hungry again? How am I ever going to keep up with your appetite?" She opened another jar. Max reached for the spoon. There was a thought: Teach him to feed himself.

Sandi put the spoon in Max's right hand since that was the hand that reached for the jar. Sandi was left-handed. As she was showing him how to grip the spoon and dip it into the jar, she remembered Houston was right-handed. How fascinating this all was to her. Of course, she had no idea which hand was dominant on the stem cell donor. Odds were, he was right-handed as well since most people were right-hand dominant. After a few failed attempts, Max got it and beamed when he got the contents into his mouth. Sandi opened a couple more jars, left them in front of Max, and ran to the back to see if she could possibly get this mess all cleaned up before dinner was ready.

She cleared some shelves to store all the baby food, out of obvious sight. She wasn't as concerned with the food as she was with the person. How was she going to be able to hide Max much longer?

Sand returned to Max to find baby food everywhere: all over him, the table, the chair, and the floor. This parenting thing was crazy. Why did people choose to have children? They were exhausting! She knew she didn't have the time to clean everything up before her father called her. She wiped Max up as best she could. She would have to get him more clothes, but for now, she would settle for removing the bulk and doing a better job later. Her father called down that dinner was ready.

"Be right there." She grabbed Max's toy and wheeled him to the back in his little space. "Stay here and please be quiet." She set the toy in his lap and ran upstairs.

"Did you forget to turn the television off?" her father inquired.

"I did, I was in such a hurry. You said come hungry. It's okay though, I have more to do. I'll go back down after dinner, finish up, and turn it off then."

"You don't watch much TV, something special on?"

"Not really. I just had something mindless on to keep me company while I worked."

"What are you working on?"

"A Biology project I have to have done next week." *Oh, please don't decide to come down and see*, she thought to herself.

"Anything I can help with?"

81

"No, I've got this." She had to change the subject. "How was your day?"

That was it, her father started his ramblings about his latest project, allowing her to think through all the issues she had to find solutions to.

After a quick cleanup from the meal, Sandi announced she was going to the cellar but would be back up to watch something with her father in a little while.

"Okay, princess. Are you sure you don't need my help with anything?"

"No. I'm fine. I just want to finish this one part up and I'll be back."

She raced down the stairs and around the corner to Max. He was sitting peacefully playing with his toy. Sandi knelt before him, took his hand, and showed him how to put the piece in the proper hole. She pointed out the shape of the block, the shape it would go in, then how to line it up to drop it in. Once all the shapes had been inserted into the box, she showed him how to open the container to get all the blocks out, close the box, and begin again. Max was delighted. Sandi left him to it and went to clean up his mess from earlier.

As she was heading back into the lab, she spotted some old TV trays at the opposite end of the room. Perfect. She got one, took it back to Max, set it up in front of him, had him lay the box on it, spread out all the blocks, and left him to it. She found it much easier to get things accomplished without him underfoot. She went upstairs to get him some clean clothes.

When she hit the first floor, her father asked, "All done?"

"No. I just need something from my room. I won't be too much longer."

Sandi went up the next flight of stairs and pulled out a pair of her sweatpants and a T-shirt. Back in the basement, she ran soapy water in a plastic bin, threw a washcloth in it, and took everything to Max. It was too risky, letting him be near the bottom of the stairs while her father was home. He wasn't happy that she wanted to take his puzzle away, so she worked around it. She removed his shirt, washed everything on the top, put the clean T-shirt on him, then was faced with how to deal with the bottom half.

"I'm sorry, but we need to get you cleaned up, then you can go back to your toy." Sandi pulled the TV tray away from him and he started to scream. "No!" she said sternly. Max hushed. His eyes welled with tears. He was just going to have to cry. She had to get this done.

Sandi unbuckled him from the chair and wrapped her arms around him. He instinctively hugged her neck as she lifted him to a standing position. She really needed to work on teaching him how to walk. He had gotten so tall! He refused to let go of the block in his hand. She was fine with that. If it kept him quiet, he could keep it.

She needed to get him changed, get everything cleaned up, and make a plan for overnight.

She washed him down, put him in a fresh diaper, slipped the fresh pants on him, and while she still had him standing, wiped down his chair. Sandi sat him back down and buckled him in. She set the TV tray with his toys back in front of him, which made him happy.

Sandi went back to the lab, wiped everything down thoroughly, put everything up, and returned to Max. She didn't know what was best to do with him. If she put him to bed without his toy, she was afraid he would throw a fit. She couldn't leave him sitting in the chair all night. He was content at the moment. She would leave him as he was and come back down once her father went to bed.

She kissed him on the forehead. He looked up at her adoringly with those dark eyes. "You stay put, stay quiet, and stay out of trouble for me, okay? I'll be back in a little while."

Sandi turned off the television and prayed Max would remain quiet.

She watched several episodes of a sitcom with her father. It was one of his favorites, but she never enjoyed it. It seemed ridiculous to her, but it made her dad laugh. That was good enough for her. Just stopping to spend time with him kept him happy and out of her business. So, she would allow him this much time.

After they went upstairs, she acted like she was going to bed. She heard her dad's door close. She started to open hers when his opened again. She quickly, quietly closed hers. He must be getting something from downstairs. He was down there a long time. She began to panic. What if he had gone to the basement? She stood listening by her door and heard nothing. She couldn't stand the torture. She ran to her bathroom, took off her clothes, and put on her robe. She went downstairs to see what her father was doing. He wasn't in the kitchen or living room. Not in the dining room. The door to the cellar was still closed and she didn't see any light from under the door. She headed down the hall, she passed his office, and the light was off. He wasn't in their home gym. She found him in the library, sitting and reading a book. She startled him when she entered.

"What's wrong, princess?"

"Oh, nothing. I was coming to get a book. I've read everything I have upstairs."

"Great minds think alike." He smiled kindly.

"I'm just going to grab something and take it to bed with me. I'll be out of your hair in no time."

"You can stay here and read."

"It's okay. I like to read until I fall asleep."

She went to the fiction section and just pulled the first book she laid her hands on. She had no intention of actually reading it; this was all to discover what her father was doing. "Good night," she said and left the room.

Sandi was so glad he hadn't ventured downstairs. She considered just slipping down the stairs to check on Max. The problem with that was she wouldn't be able to hear when her father went to bed. It would be her luck to run into him while returning to her room. He would ask way too many questions. She would just hang out in her room until she heard him turn in for the night.

She lay on her bed. She could feel herself fading and was afraid of falling asleep. She usually slept straight through to her alarm. Instead, she grabbed a pillow and blanket along with her cell phone, cracked her door open, and looked down the hall—nothing. She took a deep breath, then slipped out of her room and down the stairs. She prayed she wouldn't run into her father. Once she was on the other side of the basement door, she let out the breath she now realized she had been holding. She went down the stairs using the flashlight on her phone to light her way. She rounded the corner of the storage to find Max as she'd left him. He was getting good at putting the proper blocks in the correct holes the first time. She noticed his dexterity was much better as well.

Sandi slid between the shelving and Max to lay her pillow and blanket beside his. That got his attention. He hadn't looked up until that point. Now, he stopped and was watching her to see what she would do next. She smiled at him and said, "How about having a sleepover tonight?"

He just stared.

She fed him a few more jars of food to hold him over until morning. While he worked on his puzzle, he allowed her to feed him. He was not nearly as famished as earlier. He ate two jars and was satisfied.

"Okay, time for bed. You're not going to be able to sleep in. I have to have you up and fed before my father gets up. Time for lights out, my big boy."

Max didn't like it when she started pulling his TV tray away again.

"No. It's bedtime. I'm going to be with you, though. Come on." Sandi wheeled him to the lab to change his Depends for bed. This would need to be done more often now since he would be taking in even more substance and getting rid of more excrement. She just had no idea how. That was a problem for another day.

When she laid him down in his bed and climbed in beside him, he gave her a strange look. She covered him up, pulled her blanket over herself, reset the alarm on her phone for earlier than usual, and cuddled into him. He cooed and went right to sleep, still holding a block in each hand. She imagined someday lying with him this way in a more romantic setting. Knowing she would have someone who loved and accepted her for who she was, who didn't make fun of her, who made her feel desired, would make all the effort worth it. Someone to spend time with, have intellectual conversations with, research, and discover with. Someone made just for her.

Eleven

S andi's alarm went off way too early. She'd have to catch up on sleep another time. She rolled over—Max was still sleeping. She slipped from the bed, stretched, and went to get everything set up for him. She pulled out several jars of food, a bowl, a spoon, and an apron. He was certainly too big for baby bibs. She had no interest in cleaning up messes like last night's after every meal. She ran back to Max to wake him.

He didn't want to get up any more than she did, but he had to. She didn't have much time before she had to be upstairs in her own bed, ready for her father to tell her it was time to get up.

Max was doing better with his muscle control. He assisted her in getting him into his chair. Sandi knew it wasn't ideal, but it had arms and wheels. It worked. After buckling him in, she pushed him while running. It evoked a giggle from him. It was the sweetest sound she had ever heard. She wanted to hear more of those.

After changing his Depends, she put the apron on him. He was puzzled. She tied the neck strings up tighter to pull it up closer to his chin. He was excited when he saw all the food laid out. He devoured her offerings and looked for more, so she grabbed a few more jars. If she weren't wealthy, she might go broke trying to keep him fed. How did parents on a tight budget stay afloat with growing children?

Sandi cleaned his face. "Ready for another run?" She started running with him again and got the same response. This was wonderful. Such a simple thing brought so much joy to not only Max, but her as well.

She sat him by the TV tray and toy. He immediately went to work on fitting the pieces into their appropriate spaces. She kissed his forehead. "I have to run, but I'll be back at lunch."

Sandi slipped back to her room and was brushing her teeth when her father gave the familiar rap on her door. "Time to get up, princess. Meet you downstairs."

She jumped in the shower and dressed. Her mind was racing. As well as Max was doing with his puzzle, it wouldn't continue to interest him for long. She had no idea how she would keep him contained much longer.

Her father gave her a warm embrace as she said, "Morning, Dad."

"Pancakes or waffles?"

"Pancakes are fine."

She drank her juice and wondered if this would be good for Max.

Her father said, "No snarky comment about the juice today?"

"Actually, it makes me feel so good, I was wondering if I would be able to have one in the afternoons after school too."

"Are you serious?"

"I am. Could I?"

"Yeah, I'll just make double batches for you. You're really going to choke two of these down a day?"

"Yes. You don't feel like it would help you to drink two of them a day?"

"I really hadn't thought about it. One is good for me. I never considered two. I'm no longer a growing teen though."

"Did you invent this?"

"No. Grandpa must have. He taught me the recipe. He drinks one every day too. I really don't know where it came from. It's just always been a thing in our family. You did feel the difference it made in your energy when you hadn't had it. So why would we not just take a brief moment in our day to swig it down?"

"Right. So, can you teach me? I can make it. And can you make it in any other flavor? I really don't like orange."

He laughed. "Sorry, sweetheart. Orange tastes the best."

"That's pitiful. Brilliant scientific minds, and we can't make it taste better?"

"I'll teach you how to make it on the next batch. In the meantime, yes, you may have two a day. Like vitamins, what your body doesn't use will be flushed out."

As Sandi ate her pancakes, she couldn't get Max's boredom off her mind. She told her father she was full and forgot something downstairs she had to get. He kissed her and told her to have a good day, that he was heading out shortly, and would see her at dinner. She was grateful it didn't come with all his normal questions.

"Make it quick," her father said. "You don't want to be late for school."

"I won't be. Promise."

In the basement, Sandi was sure there was another TV somewhere in the storage room. Max seemed surprised to see her. "I'm just finding you something to keep you occupied throughout the day."

She found the old, small flatscreen from her room that she had replaced with a much bigger one. She pulled another TV tray, set it up, put it on a kid's learning channel, and took off. "See you later. Please don't get into anything while I'm gone."

SANDI HAD A BETTER than normal school day. She was so focused on Max, his needs, and what she had to do after school that she didn't pay any attention to the people around her. She scanned every hallway for Houston but couldn't find him. She would just have to wait until the next day. She really hoped he was there. It would be Friday, and she didn't think she would make it all the way to Tuesday without seeing him.

After school, she went to the store. She wanted to be sure she didn't run out of food, and she wanted to pick Max up more learning toys. He needed more clothes too.

Sandi was pleasantly surprised when she got home and saw Max contentedly watching TV. He wasn't playing with his toy. The joy that spread over his face when he saw her made her want to burst. Of course, she knew her father loved her, but no one had ever been filled with so much joy over her presence. She hugged him. He wrapped his arms around her, with his head on her belly, and squeezed.

"Wow! We need to teach you your own strength! That's enough. Thank you. Are you hungry? Want to eat?"

He had learned that word fast. He got all excited and didn't have an issue with Sandi moving his tray away. She ran him down the aisle and this time she took the corner almost on two wheels. Max squealed with delight. Oh yes, she would not tire of that sound.

After cleaning him up from his meal, she took all his vitals and measurements. He was growing so fast! Sandi filled two buckets, one with warm soapy water, the other with plain warm water. She removed his clothes and started sponging him clean. As she washed his face, she saw the makings of a dimple and a cleft in his chin. Just like Houston. She was excited.

When Sandi lifted his arm to wash under it, he laughed. "Does that tickle?" She did it again and got the same response. She loved his laugh. "I won't try to tickle you. I don't like it done to me. I love your laugh though." Even just his sweet smile brought her joy she hadn't experienced in...well, come to think of it, ever. She didn't ever remember being this full of love and joy. Of course, she loved her dad, but he was always a bit distant. She wondered if he really loved her or just went through motions he thought were required, like his to-do list. She would make sure Max always knew how much she loved him, and that he was wanted. He would never question as she had so many times in her life.

She pulled the new toys from the bags, laid them in front of him on the table, and ran upstairs to fill one of his bottles with her father's nasty juice.

He took to it much better than she expected. He didn't seem to have the same aversion to the taste she did. Her father never did either. Maybe she was just the strange one.

Sandi was working with him on the learning toys when a most foul smell hit her. "You smell dirty. Let me check you. I bet this is the result of introducing actual food into your diet. Or else, something seriously died inside you!"

Max allowed her to lay him on the floor for the changing, as long as he could keep the new letter-learning toy she got him. She cleaned him up and wondered where she would hide a nasty diaper. She couldn't just throw it in the trash. It would elicit questions from her father. She would have to carry them with her in the mornings and throw them out in a dumpster on the edge of the school parking lot. This was all getting so complicated.

Sandi set Max up back in his corner. She had kept the television low so it wouldn't be heard from upstairs. She had some homework to get done, so she went back to the lab.

After dinner, she cleaned the kitchen and excused herself to the cellar. Her father went to the living room to watch TV. When she was done for the night, she changed Max for bed. She had gotten him some pajamas to wear now that he was getting bigger. When she got him into his bed and turned the TV off, he started to throw a fit. That wasn't going to work. There was no way she would be able to walk away without her father hearing him. She flipped it back on but didn't like the idea of it running all night. Yes, it was a learning channel, but his brain needed to rest. "In all things balance," her father always said. She turned the channel to 12-hour sleep music with soothing images and moved the TV around closer to Max, so he could see it. That satisfied him. She knelt beside him, kissed his forehead, and told him goodnight.

Upstairs, she found her father back in the library. "What are you reading?"

"Oh! Hi, princess. I'm just reading the newest mystery. Did you get your homework done?"

"I did and now I'm off to bed. I'm tired."

"Okay, sleep well. I'll see you in the morning."

Sandi kissed her father and went to her room. She would need to be up way before her father again to prepare Max for the day. As she lay in her bed, she began to fear what the future would hold. How long could she keep this secret from her father while they were all under the same roof? As Max got older, he would bring new challenges. She was going to have to start teaching him to walk and talk. He would be bringing in teeth soon. She had heard that was a terrible time of pain for babies. How would she keep him quiet through teething without her father knowing?

She drifted off to sleep with all these questions running through her head.

∾

SANDI HEADED to the basement with her nightie on. She wasn't wasting time getting ready for the day now. She would do that, as she always did, once her father told her to get up.

She found Max still asleep with the music still playing. When she turned the TV off, he awoke.

"Good morning, my little man. Ready for some breakfast?"

She was shocked when he crawled from his bed by himself.

"Good job! I'm so proud of you."

Sandi fed him, got him ready for the day, and set him back up with the TV in front of him and several toys laid out for him.

"I'm off to school. I'll see you later. Be good."

Physics class seemed to take a lifetime to come. Sandi was thrilled when Houston walked into the room early. She was glad they would have a moment to speak, even if it was brief.

"Houston! You're here. Are you alright? I was worried about you," she said.

"Oh, that's sweet. I'm fine. I just had some family things to take care of."

"I went by your work. There was a little blonde there who had no idea who you were. I asked if she could check the schedule to see when you would be on, but that seemed too much for her."

He laughed. "That would be Becca. She's new, but I don't think it would matter how long she worked there. She's clueless. It's a wonder she can remember her own name, let alone enter orders."

"She's very pretty." Sandi wondered if Houston had any interest in her.

"Really? You think so?"

"You don't?"

"Not really. She's as dumb as a box of rocks. I don't particularly notice girls who don't have two brain cells to rub together."

"Same for me. Well, not girls, but you know what I mean. That's really the reason I can't find interest in any of the boys in this school."

"Same here. Well, not the boys."

They laughed.

Jackson walked in and shoved Sandi and her desk. "What's so funny, brainiac? I didn't think you knew how to laugh."

"Go sit down. You have no business trying to think," Sandi said. "You might hurt yourself."

This time Houston laughed.

"What's so funny, MacAvoy?"

"That was clever, you have to admit."

Jackson went to the back and took his seat.

"I rest my case," Sandi said, in a lowered voice.

"Point taken," Houston responded in kind.

"I couldn't deal with anyone who couldn't mentally keep up with me."

"I'm looking for someone with intelligence too. I figured I'd be waiting until college. Then I met you."

Sandi was so shocked she couldn't speak for a moment. She felt a flush rise up her neck and was sure it showed on her face. "Same here. I could talk to you for hours. And I doubt I'd ever have to explain my sarcasm to you."

Houston smiled warmly. Then the bell rang, but instead of rushing out, Houston leaned over and asked Sandi if he could get her number. Fighting to still her trembling fingers, she took his phone and entered it under his contacts.

"Have a great weekend," he said as he left the room.

She sat in stunned silence for a moment. What had just happened there?

Sandi felt like she was floating through the end of her day. She hit the ground of reality when it dawned on her that she hadn't gotten his number. What if he was just trying to be nice? Would he ever contact her? She would never get his number. No, she couldn't think that way. He did make the comment about knowing her. She would just trust in that. And it was he who asked for *her* number, not her forcing it on him.

AT HOME, Sandi made Max's bottle of juice before letting him know she was home. When she approached him, he was delighted to see her. Well, two of the three most important men in her life made her feel wanted today. This was better than a month ago when she only had her father. She had no hope that her grandfather would ever make the list.

"Are you ready to eat? Here's your juice."

Max grabbed it greedily.

As Sandi fed him, he shocked her when he started saying the alphabet. He got mixed up at "M" and "N" and it threw him off.

"Good boy! That was great. I love your voice."

It had the sound of a young boy.

"I can tell you've been working on your letter-learning toy."

"TV," Max said.

"You learned that on TV? The whole alphabet? I thought they just did a letter a day or something."

"TV," Max repeated.

"Okay, you learned it on TV."

"TV," Max said once more.

"Oh, you want me to turn on the TV?"

Max pointed at the television.

Sandi turned it on and looked for the learning channel. Max let out a whine.

"What? I'm getting your station on."

He whined and pointed. There was a preview of a movie showing.

"You want to watch a movie?"

He grunted while pointing.

"Okay, but I have to find something age-appropriate." What was age-appropriate for him? They would start with a G-rated movie for now. Everything G-rated seemed to be in cartoon form. He seemed to want to see actual people. Sandi bumped the rating to PG and found *Lyle, Lyle, Crocodile*. He seemed happy with that.

Sandi watched him while he watched the movie. He was glued to the television but all the while working with his toys. He was a multitasker like her. They would get along just fine.

When Sandi heard the garage door, she quickly wheeled Max to the back. He started to become vocal.

"Shh, I'll put it on back here. You have to be quiet. My dad can't know about you yet."

Max quieted down. Did he really understand her? Whatever made him hush was fine with her.

She put the movie back on but had to start it from the beginning again. Max didn't seem to care.

"Okay, I'll be back later before bed. Be good. Please," Sandi begged.

She ran upstairs and met her father when she opened the door.

He hugged her while kissing the side of her head.

"Hey, princess. Still working on your project? When is it due?"

"Wednesday." She would have to think of something else to be occupied with in the basement after Wednesday.

AFTER SCHOOL, Sandi went to the tech store to get Max a tablet. She asked the clerk about learning games and apps. He said, "You look too young to have a kid."

Sandi laughed. "No. This is for my younger brother."

He loaded it up with several games for kids while he obviously and openly flirted with her. Now that she was no longer—so she hoped—in the market for a boyfriend, she was getting this attention. Where was this guy previously? Who knew, she might be back if things didn't work out with Houston.

"Max, I'm home," Sandi sang out as she went down the basement stairs.

"Home!" Max said clearly.

She held out the bag for Max to take. His face looked puzzled.

"It's a present for you. Take a look."

Max looked in the bag, pulled out the tablet and looked up at Sandi. "Mine?"

"Yes. It has loads of things you can watch and learn. Let me show you."

"Eat," Max said.

"Oh, of course. Hang on. I bought you some more food. We're up to level 4. You're going to be eating big-boy food soon. I'm going to have to start cooking for you."

"Eat," Max said again.

"Come on, let's eat."

Sandi set him up in the lab and ran upstairs to fill a sippy cup she'd bought him. When she returned, he was done and looking for more. She opened a few more jars and set the cup in front of him. He picked it up, turned it upside down, then jerked back and dropped it when the contents poured into his lap. Sandi laughed. "It's okay. This is different. Let me show you." She raised the cup to her lips to show Max how to drink from it. Handed it to him and he put his lips on the protrusion on the lid. He was a quick study. How could he not be brilliant? Look whose DNA he possessed.

While Max ate, Sandi showed him how to turn the tablet on and navigate around to the various apps loaded for him. She showed him how to get to the few movies she put on it, where to find learning games and those for hand-eye coordination. She had even added a couple of programs to learn Spanish, French, and German. She had heard kids were more adaptable to learning language at a young age. When she heard the garage door go up, she noticed Max looked up as she did. He said, "No go."

"I'm sorry, buddy, I have to. I really need you to be a good boy and be quiet for me. Want to go *whee*?"

He nodded his head with a big smile on his face.

"Here, hold this tight." She gave him the tablet.

He squealed with delight as she ran him back to his corner.

"Play for a while, and I'll be back later to get you ready for bed, okay?"

"K," he said.

She kissed his cheek and ran off.

Twelve

decorative flourish

Sandi entered the kitchen to the smell of bacon. Her father didn't often include bacon or sausage in their breakfasts except on the weekends.

"Good morning, princess. I figured the smell of bacon would bring you to life."

"Morning, Daddy. It sure did."

"What do you have up for today?"

"I haven't made any clear plans yet. You usually make up the juice for the week on Saturday. Are you going to show me how?"

"Oh, I'm sorry. Since we ran out yesterday, I already made it up and accounted for the additional amounts and days. Next time."

Sandi was disappointed but glad she would have enough to continue giving Max some too.

Her cell phone dinged. It was a text from a number she didn't recognize. Her heart skipped a beat. Maybe it was Houston.

> Whachu doin 2day?

the text read. Followed by,

This is Houston, BTW

She suddenly felt giddy. She responded with,

Nothin. U?

Wanna go 2 the Museum of Tech w/me?

Would <3 2. Want me 2 drive?

No. I'll pick u up. What's your addy?

Sandi sent it back and asked what time.

11?

I'll b ready.

"Who are you texting with at this hour?" her father asked.

"A boy from school. We're going to the Museum of Technology today."

"A boy, huh? I want to meet this boy, you do know that, right?"

"Yes. Please don't embarrass me. We're not dating or anything. I'm just really interested in him. He's the only intelligent one in my school, I swear."

"What's his name?"

"Houston MacAvoy. He's really nice, Daddy. I think you'll like him. Just don't scare him off."

He laughed.

She didn't understand why. This was no laughing matter. What if he embarrassed her?

"I won't. I promise. I just want to know what sort of boy my little girl is riding off with. What time?"

"He's picking me up at 11."

"That's respectable. He better not sit in the driveway and honk, or you won't be going anywhere with him."

"He's not that type. I'm sure he'll come to the door."

After Sandi had cleaned the kitchen, she raced through her Saturday chores so she could get Max taken care of and get changed. On a normal Saturday when she had no plans, she would take her time, stopping and starting throughout the day. Her father didn't care as long as she was done by the end of the day. He always hurried through his own chores, then tinkered in the garage or yard.

With her father distracted, she was able to fill Max's bottle with juice and slip down the stairs.

Max was awake when she got to him. He was mesmerized by the images on the screen that went with the sleep music.

"Good morning! I hope you slept well. We have to put a hustle in it today. I have a date."

Max just watched the screen.

Sandi had picked up a Diaper Genie to keep the odor at bay while not having to run by the dumpster daily. Max's messes were really nasty now. She did notice that his body was filling out better.

She got him ready for the day: she added rice cereal to two 8-ounce bottles and set them in a small cooler beside his chair, then turned on his learning channel, which thankfully, he didn't fuss over. She kissed his forehead, and he suddenly hugged her without her hugging him first.

"Bye," Max said.

"Oh!" Sandi was startled. "Bye, sweet boy. I love you."

She riffled through all her clothes trying to figure out what to wear. In the end, she decided on her normal go-to of jeans and a T-shirt. Houston had only seen her in these. She didn't want to scare him off by treating this like a real date. The hot shower helped to calm her nerves. She debated makeup and settled for just lipstick as usual. She wasn't one to fool with her clothes, hair, nor makeup once she was ready for the day, so she used a stay-on lipstick. A hint of her fresh-smelling perfume and she would wait out the clock.

Five minutes before 11:00 a.m., she saw Houston pull in the driveway. She hadn't known what car he drove but recognized it now. She ran down the stairs, but her father beat her to the door just before the doorbell rang.

"I told you he'd come to the door."

He smiled at her while opening the door. Extending his hand, he said, "Come in. You must be Houston."

"Yes, sir."

"Did you hear that, honey? He called me sir. I do believe I like him already."

"You promised," Sandi said under her breath.

Her father grinned. "Come in, Houston, you're not under a time restraint, are you?"

"No, sir. We're just going to go check out the new exhibit at the Technology Museum. No particular time."

Sandi just wanted to go. She had waited so long to be able to speak freely with Houston, and her father was cutting into her time.

Her father led them to the living room. "Have a seat. So, what are your intentions with my daughter, young man?"

"Daddy!"

"I'm just kidding."

Houston let out a huge laugh.

"You are so frustrating!" Sandi said.

"It was pretty funny," Houston said.

She shot them both a glare.

"Seriously, though what are your plans for college?" her father asked and winked at her. She didn't find him as funny as he believed he was.

"I'm currently looking at Cornell in New York."

"That's a great choice. Sandi has considered that one too. Did you know that's where he was thinking of going?" He addressed his question to Sandi.

"I had no idea, but I'm not surprised. It's a great university. I wouldn't consider it if it weren't."

"What are you planning to study?" her father asked.

"I'm very interested in creating better prosthetics for those who have lost limbs."

"Do you have someone close to you that could benefit from that technology?"

"Yes, sir. My mother lost her left arm and leg seven years ago. They are so expensive just for ones that look fake, are difficult to attach, and leave terrible sores because they rub. There has to be a better way."

Sandi was shocked. She'd just learned more in five minutes with her father's inquisitions than she had a clue to on her own. Houston had never mentioned any of this to her before. She better understood why he was evasive when it came to personal matters.

She just sat back and listened to the two men discuss many subjects —none of which she had ever had the opportunity to ask. The more she heard from this boy, the more she admired him. She had so many more things she wanted to learn about him. Having time alone without all the distractions of school would allow her that luxury. She just had to get these two to shut up so they could get out of there.

Sandi finally spoke up, "Should I leave the two of you alone, or are you ready to go?"

Houston said, "Oops. I'm so sorry. Yeah, we can go. It was nice to talk with you, Mr. Powell."

"Likewise. Feel free to stop by any time. You have a good head on your shoulders. I have a hard time with most kids your age because they can't carry on an intelligent conversation. Sandi does too. She's always begging me to let her test out of high school. I just think it's important to get the whole experience of each age to appreciate the journey when you are older. I'm glad she has someone her intellectual equal to talk with. Maybe now she won't be so anxious to move on."

"I understand," Houston said. "I lose all patience with most of my peers. They don't even try to learn or be more. It's been hard to find a girl who isn't acting dumb, if not being dumb, to fit in with the crowd. They have to be all about the latest trend and not comfortable in their own skin. Can't carry on a conversation unless it has to do with them and their friends, and refuse to eat anything more than a salad. You do eat, don't you, Sandi?"

Her father talked over her. "Oh, she eats."

She blushed. *Great*, she thought, *now he's going to think I'm not concerned about my weight, and I eat like a cow.*

"Let's just go," she said while shaking her head.

Houston got up, shook her father's hand, and started walking with Sandi to the door. He called back over his shoulder, "It was nice to meet you. I'll be back to continue our conversation another day."

"Any time," her father said. "Don't be out too late."

"I have to work at six, so I'll have her back long before then."

"Love you, princess."

"Love you too. Oh, wait here. I'll be right back." Sandi ran back in the house and came back with Houston's hoodie. "I washed it for you."

"My hoodie! Where'd you find it?"

"You dropped it the day you helped me up from the floor. I tried to catch you, but you were too fast, and I couldn't find you. I brought it home, washed it, and was going to return it, but then you were out, I'd forgotten about it. I knew I'd get it back to you one of these days."

"Thanks. I've been missing this. My dad gave me this; that's why I wore it so often. He's been gone awhile now. You didn't have to go to all that trouble."

If he only knew, she thought. She had no choice but to wash it because she had slept with it and worn it so much, it smelled like her.

Houston opened her car door for her. What a gentleman! Was there anything that wasn't perfection with this guy?

At the museum, their conversation came easily. As they browsed the exhibits, Sandi said, "Why don't you ever talk to me like this at school?"

"I'm sorry. I usually try to ignore everyone in school. Keep my focus on my goal and go home."

"What changed your mind and made you talk to me?"

"Little things. I always thought you were just a pointlessly angry girl. After you were pushed in the hall and I noticed the mean things kids were saying and doing to you, I made a point to talk to you more and liked what I learned. I don't know, when you showed so much concern for me, I was touched. I saw beneath your mask."

"Oh wow! I figured it was because you had a girlfriend outside of school, so just got through to be able to see her after school."

He laughed. "A girlfriend? That's funny. I've never had time for girls. Since the accident, all my spare time has been taking care of my mother or studying to make my dreams come true."

"I had no idea about your mom. I'm really sorry."

"Don't be. I mean, I appreciate your kindness, but I'm not one for regrets. I believe everything happens for a reason. Her accident gave me my purpose. I have a clear vision of what I want to do. I want to be the one to impact the world of quadra- and paraplegics. I know I can come up with a more cost-effective option. I just have to find out more about the human body, so I can invent something better that the everyday person can afford. I know I can do it. That's part of the reason I love science. I'm always looking for the answers to questions not yet discovered."

"That is so cool. I admire you even more now."

It was Houston's turn to blush. "I can't believe I'm telling you all this. The only one I've ever talked to about all this is my mom. Well, then your dad today. He's very easy to talk to. Now, you. It's a new day for me, I guess." He chuckled.

"I'm glad you feel that way. We're not pretentious people."

"I know your family has a lot of money, but you've never come across that way."

"Not exactly. I just like simplicity. I can spend whatever I want. I just don't want for much."

"It must be nice."

"Not really. The only time anyone has ever been nice to me was for what I could buy them. I stopped making friends when I saw the true nature of people."

"I never thought of it that way. You know I'm not like that, right?"

"I'm sure hoping that's true."

"It's true. You'll see."

"You're the only person, teachers included, that I've ever felt was intelligent enough to spend any time talking with."

"Thanks."

They walked into the new exhibit. Houston looked like a kid in a candy store. She was fascinated by the change in him. Then she saw the subject of the exhibit: *Prosthetics in the New Era*. Oh, from what he'd said, it was no wonder he wanted to visit today.

Sandi found herself fascinated by what they learned. She saw a passion in Houston she hadn't experienced in anyone outside of herself. She felt he would be able to understand her excitement creating Max. Her thoughts leaped forward: Would she somehow be able to help him with his goal by what she was doing with Max? What if they could put their heads together, research together, and come up with a solution to this problem? She would address all this another day. For now, she was just trying to absorb as much as she could about a subject she knew nothing about before today. When she had researched quadra- and paraplegics, she was looking for answers to building muscle mass for Max. She never really thought about what it was like to live that way.

As they walked to the car, Houston said, "Thanks for coming with me today. I appreciate your enthusiasm for my benefit."

She explained it wasn't just for his benefit. Since it wasn't anything that had popped up on her radar previously, she hadn't realized there was a flaw in the technology. She was glad to learn this and hoped she could help him find a solution.

"Do you want to stop for a bite to eat?" Houston asked when they got in the car.

"I'd love to. Just not burgers, okay?"

He laughed. "I'll be serving them all night. I'd prefer something else. How about Greek?"

"I love gyros!"

Sandi had to keep remembering to eat. She was so engrossed in all she was learning from Houston about the plight of those with prosthetics, especially those with limited means. Their conversation was easy, not forced, at no time awkward. She was having the best time and didn't want it to end.

"I'd better get you home," Houston said. "I almost lost track of time. I have to get to work."

"I can call my dad, he'll come get me, so you can go."

"No, I'll be fine. I just got lost in our conversation."

"What a nice thing to say. I could sit and talk with you for days."

As soon as Sandi closed the front door of her house, she laid her back against it, lost in thought. Her father called from the kitchen, "I'll have dinner ready in about 30 minutes."

"I'm not hungry. We stopped and ate." She really wanted to just go down to check on Max. She had been worried he would alert her father while she was away. She paused to gauge his reaction to this news. He didn't say anything, so she turned the corner into the kitchen. "I'm sorry. I should have called to let you know. I guess I was too wrapped up in Houston."

He looked hurt. But said nothing and shook his head.

"Give me just a few minutes. I'll come sit with you while you eat. I'll tell you all about the museum."

That did it. He perked up. "Sure. It will be about a half hour, so you have time."

She ran down to the basement. Max became very animated when he saw her. "Shh...I need you to be quiet. I'm so sorry I was gone so long. Let's get you fed."

She wheeled him to the table in the lab. He got very excited as she slipped the apron over his head. He knew his food was coming. She needed to wash the apron but wouldn't have the opportunity until Monday after school. She really needed to pick up several to change them out. It was a good thing she had taken on the chore of laundry for them several years ago. She would never be able to explain what was now in the hamper without giving away her secret.

He ate so much she believed she should move him up a level. She had to look to see what levels she had left to go up in. Thankfully, he ate fast. She wouldn't have much time. He was getting much better at controlling how much made it to his mouth. She was stunned at his dexterity and coordination. As she opened the various containers, she carefully enunciated what each item was. Occasionally, he would try to repeat what she said. He was like a sponge, absorbing so much so fast. She had known he would have to be smart. She believed intelligence was a combination of nurture and nature. As long as she continued to nurture his learning and taught him everything she could, she would see he was sharp. Then her father called down to her that his dinner was ready.

"Be right there."

She wiped Max's mouth, left the apron on him, rolled him back to his corner in the back, set him up with his toys and TV, and promised she'd be back soon. "Please play, be good, and for heaven's sake, be quiet."

Max nodded his understanding and approval.

Sandi ran up the stairs and slipped into her seat as her dad took a bite of fish. "Are you sure you don't want anything?"

"No. I'm good. I'm full from lunch. We had gyros from the Greek restaurant downtown."

"So, tell me about the museum."

"I had no idea about prosthetics and how advanced they are and what a deficit they had been."

"Yes, your granddad has a whole division that has been working on them for decades."

"Why haven't you ever done anything with them?"

"I did at one time. Just briefly. My interests took me in a different direction. If you think it's something you would be interested in, I'm sure he would make room for you in one of his facilities."

"I'm not sure. I'd need to think about working for him."

"I understand."

"Is that why you don't work for him?"

"It's complicated, princess. If you want me to talk to him about it, I will."

"No. If I want to, I'll have that conversation with him myself."

"You could always communicate better with him than I ever did."

"That's scary. That man doesn't really communicate. I thought it was just me."

Sandi covered some of what she'd learned over the afternoon while her father ate.

She cleaned the kitchen as usual. Just because she didn't eat, she didn't think it fair not to help, since she hadn't given him a heads-up beforehand.

"I'm going to be in the library the rest of the night if you want to join me in there," he said as he excused himself, giving her a side hug.

She didn't respond. She probably wouldn't go to the library. She really needed to spend some time with Max and prepare him for the night. She needed to figure out how she was going to manage going forward. Things were moving so fast, and she felt like she could barely keep up. There was no telling what even another day would do at this rate.

She filled one of Max's bottles and went back downstairs. When she rounded the corner, he was desperately pulling at the straps around his neck, saying, "Off."

"No, no, darling, let's leave that on for the time being. I brought you a bottle." That was all it took. He let it go and reached for the bottle.

Sandi dropped to the floor beside his feet. She needed to get off this hamster wheel.

When he was done, he pulled at the front of the apron and asked, "Off?"

"Are you still hungry? Do you want more to eat?"

"Eat," he said.

"That's what I thought. Let me get you more." This time she brought the food to him.

He ate three jars. When she lifted a fourth, he shook his head and said, "Off," as he pulled at the apron.

"Okay, I guess you're done." Sandi removed it, wiped his mouth, and brought a chair from the next room to sit with him awhile. "What have you learned today, my sweet boy?"

He said, "Earn."

She enunciated, "Learn."

He parroted her.

"That's right, learn. Good, boy. I'm so proud of you."

"You," he said.

"Good." She pointed to herself and said, "Sandi."

He looked puzzled.

She pointed to him and said, "Max." Back to herself, she repeated her name. Pointed back to him and said his name again. He still didn't seem to understand.

"I am Sandi. You are Max."

"Andy. Ax."

"Good. You're close." She made more effort to show him how to formulate the words. She had to hand it to him, he was trying. She tried counting and holding up her fingers as she went. She stuck to one through ten. Then she held his fingers up one at a time while counting them. By the third go-round, he was catching on and trying to mimic her. She praised him profusely. He beamed.

"Okay, that's enough for today. You play. I'll be back down later to put you to bed." She put her finger over her lips and said, "Shhh."

He nodded.

She just might pull this off. She just didn't know how long.

Thirteen

~

Sandi checked on Max in the night. He was much more agreeable. She had read that children liked clear boundaries, set schedules, and knowing what to expect. She fed him, changed him, and put him back to bed. He seemed to understand it wasn't time to be up for the day, just to take care of his needs and go back to sleep. She tucked him in, kissed his forehead, and told him she would see him in the morning. She loved the sweet smile he had on his face as he closed his eyes and cuddled into the stuffed bear she'd bought him to sleep with.

She opened her eyes to a new day, and as she stretched, a slow, big smile crossed her face. She lay there a moment recalling the events of the previous day. It still felt surreal, but she had gone on an actual date with Houston MacAvoy. She was dying to text him but didn't want to seem too forward and push him away.

Sandi got in her shower to be ready for whatever the day brought. She was excited and hopeful to hear from Houston. She had a pep in her step and a song in her voice. "Morning, Daddy! How'd you sleep?"

"Good, princess. I take it you did too?"

"Oh, yes."

"What are your plans for the day?"

"I'm not sure. I'm hoping I'll hear from Houston at some point today. Other than that, just hanging out in the lab. You?"

"It's great to see you so happy. I don't have any major plans. I'm going to do yard work and read a bit. What would you like for breakfast today? Eggs and toast acceptable?"

"Sure. It really never matters to me. I only eat because you make me." She crossed the kitchen to pour a cup of coffee. He wrapped his arms around her.

"Sit down. I'll have it ready momentarily."

Sandi pulled the newspaper from her father's place while he cooked and browsed the headlines. Same stuff, different day, but the world seemed brighter to her. She had a strong feeling it had everything to do with the day before.

After cleaning the kitchen, Sandi raced through the chores she hadn't done thoroughly the day before. She wanted to be ready for anything. If Houston called her to do something, housework wouldn't keep her from that.

She went to check on Max. Her father was busy outside. She was actively teaching Max new things, and he was learning fast. His diction was coming along, and his intellect was growing exponentially. She felt too young to be a parent, but she had brought all this on herself. She had just wanted someone who would love her, whom she could show off. She had only considered the end result; she hadn't thought through what the interim looked like and how it would naturally put her in a parental role.

As the day went on and she hadn't heard anything from Houston, Sandi began to worry she'd gotten the wrong impression. Maybe it was over before it had even begun. She felt her mood shifting. She was no longer floating on the clouds. She went to the kitchen to get Max his juice bottle. She had just opened the refrigerator door when her father said, "Oh, hey, princess! Can you pass me a beer?"

Sandi was so startled, she jumped. "Daddy!" She shoved the bottle in the fridge, laying it down on the bottom shelf, and pulled out a beer bottle. She closed the door behind her back as she turned and held the cold glass out to her dad.

"Thank you. I'm sorry. I didn't mean to surprise you. I thought you heard me come in. Were you hungry? You want me to make you something for lunch?"

"No, no. I'm fine."

"What were you doing?"

"Oh, uh, yeah. I was just getting my afternoon juice."

"Good. Do you feel like it's helping you, having it twice a day?"

"Um. Sure." She now realized her father was standing there bare-chested before her. Not that she hadn't seen him without a shirt before, but this time she noticed the swirl on the left of his chest about the same location as the marking on her left breast. Wow! How had she missed this in the past? She started to walk away. Her father stopped her.

"Forget something?"

"What?" She pulled herself from her thoughts.

"Juice."

"Oh! Yes. Juice." She turned back to the fridge and opened the door. She couldn't fill the bottle with her father here.

"Glass," he said.

"Yes. Of course." She pulled a plastic cup from the cupboard. She added the juice but had no idea where to stash the baby bottle for the time being. She quickly slid it down into the vegetable crisper. Once her father had gone, she would retrieve it. She tipped the cup to her lips, but she had no intention of drinking the stuff.

"Something has you distracted. I'll call you for dinner. I'm going to go take a shower."

When he left, she quickly pulled the bottle from the fridge. Her phone rang and she jumped. She pulled it from her pocket and lit up as Houston's name was displayed across the screen. "Hi!"

"How are you?"

"Great, now I'm talking with you." Oh, how corny. She really needed to get over being such an infatuated girl.

He laughed. "What are you doing?"

"Just working in the lab today."

"In the lab? What lab?"

"We have a full lab in our basement."

"You never said anything about that."

"It never came up."

"What are you working on?"

"Anything I can dream up at the moment." She laughed. She couldn't tell him.

"You'll have to tell me about it. It would be so cool to have a lab. I don't know where I'd put it, though. My house isn't nearly as big as yours."

"You're welcome to use ours anytime."

"That's really nice. I just might take you up on that. So, are you busy or can you be interrupted?"

"I will always welcome an interruption by you." She needed to just shut up. She felt like she was opening her mouth and stupidity was falling out.

He chuckled. "Would you want to catch a movie and a pizza? I'm off work now."

"Absolutely. Let me just check with my dad. Can I call you back?"

"Of course. Let me know. I'll pick you up. The movie's in an hour."

"I'll call you back." She hung up, quickly poured the juice into the bottle, rinsed the cup, put it in the dishwasher, and raced downstairs to Max.

With Max all set and content, she went back upstairs to find her father.

"Daddy, would it be okay if I went to a movie and out for a pizza with Houston?"

"Tonight?"

"Well, now. He's going to pick me up. The movie starts in less than an hour."

"This is pretty short notice."

"You haven't started dinner. Don't you remember being young and spontaneous?"

"I was once young, but I have never been spontaneous. I always plan ahead."

"Please?"

"Okay, fine. Are all your chores done?"

"Yes. I finished them all this morning."

"Alright. Have fun."

"Thank you, Daddy! I will."

She called Houston on her way to her room to freshen up. As she hung up, she was so giddy, she jumped up and down while pumping her fists in the air. "Yes!"

Sandi had just gotten to the front door when she saw Houston's car turn into the driveway. She took a moment to compose herself. She didn't want to look like a fool in front of him, acting like a schoolgirl with a crush—although she felt just that way right now.

As she was walking down the sidewalk, she heard her father behind her, "Did you forget something?"

She turned to look at him. He was tapping on his cheek. Dang it! Didn't he know this was embarrassing? Couldn't she just leave the house one time without him making a big show of it? She ran back to him, gave him a quick peck on the cheek, and ran for the car.

He called after her, "Don't be too late. It's a school night."

She didn't even give him a response, she just nodded. Houston was waving at him like they were long-lost buddies. Seriously?

"Hi! Let's go before he invites you in for coffee and we lose the whole evening."

"You're funny. It's sweet your father cares."

"Sure. Sweet. What movie are we going to see?"

"The new one that just came out Friday. Someone at work was talking about it this morning. He said it was action-packed. Oh! I didn't even ask you if you like action movies."

"I like all kinds of movies. Great! I wanted to see this one."

They discussed the movie over pizza: what they would have done differently to make it better, what they thought was done well, and a prediction on box office draw.

"I love going to the movies," Houston said. "I used to go all the time with my mom. It's too painful for her anymore, so she doesn't go out unless she has to. I usually end up going by myself."

"I am happy to go with you anytime. I'm trying to teach my father he needs to be more spontaneous, so I should usually be able to go."

Sandi was pleasantly surprised when Houston liked his pizza with so many of the same toppings she did. The only thing she didn't like were anchovies, which he didn't even suggest.

"Tell me about your lab."

Sandi went down through the list of all the supplies and paraphernalia they kept stocked. Houston's face lit up. He asked loads of questions. Sandi didn't see why she couldn't help him right now, at least where his mother was concerned. What was the use of having all this money and knowledge if she couldn't make a difference in people's lives? She was excited to have a new venture to research and work on. It was a big bonus that it would involve working closely with him.

She was lost in Houston's excitement about what he'd like to accomplish when she was struck with the thought of Max. She had not thought this through. This was not going to work. She would never be able to explain Max to Houston. She also was afraid her father would be drawn in with Houston there. There would be no hiding Max from either of them. She might have a better chance explaining it all to Houston, but she knew her father would hit the roof.

"Do you agree?" Houston asked.

Crap! She was so lost in thought, she had missed what he was saying. She didn't want him to think she was ignoring him, but there was no hiding her lapse. "I'm so sorry. Say that again."

"I'm the one who's sorry. I'm sure you're not interested in all this. Never mind. That was sweet of you to offer."

"No. Really, I'm very interested. I was lost in thought, considering the problem in my mind, and I just missed that last part."

"Are you sure?"

"Yes. I promise. I think we start with your mother and scale up from there for the public at large, don't you think? Would she be willing to be a guinea pig for all this?"

"So, you did hear me. I'm sure she would, but I have to make this disclaimer: We don't have any money."

"You don't have to worry about that. We've got this."

"I'm not looking at you for your money, you know?"

"I know that. Well, I believe that. It's on you if you're not being truthful with me. I want to make a difference in society, so I'm all in. I can see how detrimental ill-fitting prosthetics can be after going through that exhibit yesterday. That it's your mother who is being affected really drives it home. Let's work together to make her life better. Who knows what we'll discover along the way?"

"Wow! Thanks. It means a lot to me."

Sandi lowered her head, then looked up into those piercing blue eyes. "Stop."

"No. Really. No one ever does something this significant for nothing."

"We haven't done anything yet."

"I know, but I believe together we can."

Sandi liked that...together. Yes, she agreed they should be able to come up with something. And for something of this scope, she imagined her father just might get involved, if she asked for his help. She just had to figure out what to do about Max. Since she didn't have to figure it out right this minute, she would have time to work that out another day.

When Houston pulled into her driveway, he put the car in park and hesitated. Was he going to kiss her? Then he said, "Can you show me the lab?"

"Um...it's a mess. I'd want to clean it up first."

"Oh! Sure. I understand. I wasn't trying to put you out. I'm just excited."

Sandi paused for a long moment, looking at him, searching his eyes, deciding if he could be trusted. "Since this is really going to happen, I need to be able to trust you with a secret."

"A secret?"

"Yeah. A big one."

"From?"

"Well, mostly my father, but I wouldn't want this getting out to the people at school either."

"Okay."

Sandi paused long enough that Houston said, "Is it bad?"

"I don't think it is, but my father would have a cow if he learned I went against his wishes."

"Okay. I won't tell. What is it?"

"I created a human."

"You what?" The shock and look on Houston's face left Sandi wondering what he was thinking. Did he think she was unbalanced? Did he think she was insane? Was he concerned she had created a monster?

There was such a heavy silence between them, and she couldn't read his reaction. "Say something."

"I...I can't."

"Do you hate me?"

"Hate's a strong word."

"Forget I said anything. Never mind." Sandi reached for the door handle. Houston reached over her and pulled her hand away.

"No. Just give me a minute to wrap my brain around what you just said. Never in a million years would I have thought those words would have come from anyone's mouth, let alone yours. That's a big...um...a big..."

They sat there. The silence was deafening. She felt he needed to speak first. When he said nothing, she opened her door and stepped out of the car. She was almost to the house when Houston ran up behind her and grabbed her arm to turn her toward him. "Wait! You need to give me a minute to process this. You can't just drop something like this on me and not give me time to process it. I'm not sure if I should be shocked or ask the million questions that just ran through my brain all at the same time. How does your father not know? Where is this human?"

"In the basement. When I first started down this road, I was asking questions thinking my dad would help me. He did something similar years ago. When I approached him about it, he flat-out said no, and I was forbidden to take it any further. That's when I made him believe I destroyed my research and kept Max hidden."

"Max? You named it?"

"Well, yes, he's a boy."

"And he's here?"

"Yes."

"And your father really doesn't know?"

"He said he would destroy him if I didn't, so I have to keep him a secret. I just don't know how much longer I can. He's gotten so big, he's learning so fast, he's developing exponentially."

"I want to see him."

"Another time, when my dad is at work. Do you want to come with me tomorrow at lunch? I come home to feed and change him every day during my lunch."

"Yeah, I'll come with you. This is unbelievable."

"It's just science."

"Just science? Sandi, this isn't done in science or anywhere else. What if you just accomplished in a home lab what corporations have tried for decades to do? Do you know what this could mean? Do you understand the ramifications of what you've done?"

Sandi stood there wondering what Houston was so stirred up about. Of course, she understood this was a big discovery. What she didn't know was whether Houston was truly behind her or horrified. Would he spill her secret?

They stood just looking at each other. Sandi had imagined one day Houston would walk her to her door and kiss her goodnight. Right now, she figured, that was the furthest thing from his mind. Would this end what they had barely gotten started? The suspense was killing her. "Would you say something?"

"I don't know what to say. I don't know what to think."

"Just please don't betray my confidence."

"That I won't do. Just let me sleep on this."

"Sure. Good night." Sandi turned and walked into the house, leaving Houston standing on the sidewalk. Sandi was mad at herself now. Why had she gone and dumped all this on Houston before she even knew she could trust him with her secret?

Sandi dropped her purse by the back door and walked through the kitchen into the living room to find her father sitting in his wingback chair and Max sitting on the sofa. She stopped dead in her tracks, the air gone from her lungs. She felt lightheaded. She looked from one to the other.

Her father said sternly, "I think we need to talk."

Fourteen

Sandi sat down next to Max on the couch and took his hand.

She could tell by the look on her father's face that this was a lot worse than the time she was caught rewiring their house. She had believed she could save her father a lot of money on a solar-powered device she had created that just plugged into an outlet. Instead of going through the breaker box, the house needed to be connected to the solar panel she had made and attached to their roof. She was almost done when her father came home from work, saw what she was doing, and almost had an out-of-body experience. Instead of being proud of her ingenious design, he made her put everything back the way it had been and throw her panel in the trash. That was what she called ignorance.

He had a similar response when she was caught with the homemade bomb. In her fourth-grade mind, she simply wanted to connect their house with the park a block away, so she could come and go whenever she wanted. She would just make it deep enough to go under all the neighbor's yards. It would have involved a lot of digging, so she was going to expedite the process by blowing a hole in their yard, then dig from there. Maybe use a few additional explosives if she encountered any rocks. It was just chemistry, after all. Her father wouldn't listen. In her opinion, at the time, he had jumped to all kinds of crazy conclusions that were just not true. She tried repeatedly to explain, but he kept cutting her off with his standard question, "Do you have any idea what you have done?"

"I didn't do anything yet," Sandi had come back at him. "If you'd just give me a minute, I could have shown you."

He had droned on about her irresponsibility and having more brains than sense. He didn't even want to hear her ingenious way of creating it. She had used her knowledge of chemistry and was pretty proud of her accomplishments. Her father? Not so much. He was furious!

He had grounded her for a month for it. She hadn't felt any different. It wasn't like she went anywhere or had any friends or events she was missing out on. He made the statement that she needed to take this time to think about what she had done. It was lost on her what he thought was such an offense. It wasn't like she would disrupt anyone's pristine lawns or put some blemish on the holier-than-thou Home Owners Association. It would all be underground. She figured if anyone was interested, they could always connect from their yard down to her tunnel and reap the benefit of her ingenuity. But nooo...her father came unglued instead.

Sandi was pulled from her remembrance and back to the present when her father asked, "What have you done?"

"Let me explain."

"No. You let me explain! I told you not to do this. What would make you go against my wishes?"

"You were being unreasonable. I had already created him. I asked for your help. You refused."

"I had good reason to deny your request. Did it ever occur to you I'm older and wiser? Did you ever stop to think of the ramifications of something like this? You wonder why I won't let you test out to go to college early? You can't follow simple directives. How can I trust you to be on your own? I can't!" He was now bellowing.

Sandi sat in silence, and Max began to shake.

"It's okay. I'm here. You're okay," Sandi said softly. She put an arm around his shoulders, and he laid his head on hers. He was so much taller than she was.

Sandi looked back at her father. She couldn't read him. She usually could guess what he was going to say next. Not this time. He sat stone-faced, saying nothing.

Sandi stood and started to pull Max up with her. "I'm going to take him back—"

Her father cut her off. "You'll sit back down this instant."

Sandi sat. Max looked unsure.

"I told you what would happen if you continued."

"You're not going to kill him. He's a fully developed male. You were talking about if it all went wrong. It didn't. He's growing, he's learning, he's smart. You can't *murder* him and I'm certainly not going to. You're just sore I figured it out without you."

"Careful," her father said levelly. "I have a lot of questions right now."

"I bet you do. It would have been nice if you had actually worked with me on this. Then, you wouldn't have all the questions. You would know how I did it."

"Those aren't the questions I have. Did you ever think I might already have all those answers? I had good reasons for forbidding you to do all this."

"What good reason could you have for limiting my learning?"

"Humans have no business playing God."

"Oh! Is that right? The God you don't believe in?"

"Don't start! I'm serious."

"God gave me the brains to figure this out. Why wouldn't I?"

"You are too young to be messing around with things you don't fully understand. You don't have the years of wisdom I have established. Your brain isn't even fully developed. It won't be until around age 25. There is so much about life you don't know yet. You keep trying to push it. Why can't you just be happy being a teenager? Why do you insist on growing up too fast?"

"There's the bottom line. You're just afraid for me to grow up and be gone. You're the one driving me away. Did Grandfather do the same to you? Is that why you don't have anything to do with him? I'm not you. And I'm not him. You can't keep me down. I will make a name for myself, with or without you. Let's go, Max."

Sandi stood and took him by the hand, and he followed. She knew her words stung, but she also knew she was probably right. They never talked about her grandfather. They so rarely saw him. They never spent the holidays together as loving families did. There were only the three of them that she was aware of. She would have thought they could at least try to be a family, but her questions on the matter when she was younger had always faced a brick wall from her male elders. She was going to be different with Max. She would raise him to know he was loved. After tonight, she knew he was her only family now.

At least she no longer had to keep him quiet or hidden. She was working with him in the lab on his tablet when her father called down, "Sandi, come up here."

He had to be kidding.

After a long pause, he said, "And bring Max."

Sandi's head snapped toward the direction of the stairs. Did she just hear that right? She said, "Well, come on, Max. Let's see what he wants."

Her father was sitting at the kitchen table. She brought the tablet with them and laid it on the table at the seat beside hers. She wanted to be positioned between her father and Max, with Max on her left so she could help him with the tablet. Her father sat in silence.

"He's right-handed," her father said.

"Yes." Both of them and her grandfather were all southpaws.

Max began to work on his tablet. There was silence. Sandi was well aware her father was studying Max. He never said a word. She helped Max and praised him when he did well.

Her father finally broke his silence. "So, how'd you do it?"

Sandi didn't even look at him. "What do you care? You already long since surpassed me, remember? You don't need my menial knowledge."

"I guess I deserved that, but I'm still your father and will not tolerate your insubordination."

"My insubordination? I'm not one of your employees. I'm the daughter you never treat as such."

"I'm sorry you feel that way. Let's call a truce. As one scientist to another, I'm asking you what your process was. I know what mine was. I'm curious."

Sandi sat and stared at him for a long while. She was brought back to reality when she heard the slap of Max's hand on the table.

"Max eat," he said.

"Hang on, I'm sure you are hungry." She stood and hesitated. "Please keep an eye on him while I get him some food, will you?" she said to her dad.

"Yeah, I'll watch him."

Sandi ran downstairs and came back with her arms full. Since her father was aware of him, she would be able to keep more of his things upstairs. She let him pick what he wanted to eat and sat back down.

"So, tell me how you did it," her father said once again.

Sandi began from the beginning.

"I want to see your research and how you did all this."

"Well, come downstairs with us and I'll show you."

He asked Max pointed questions. Max responded with single-word answers.

She noticed some of his words were in other languages.

"Wait! What'd you just say?" Sandi asked.

"He said yes in French," her father said. "Have you been teaching him other languages?"

"Not yet. Not really. I just loaded some other language apps on his tablet, but he's only had those for 24 hours."

"As you said, he's smart. He reminds me of you."

Sandi faced Max and said in French, "*Comprenez-vous ce que je dis, Max?*"

Max responded, "*Oui.*"

She said in Spanish, "*¿Y ahora, me entiendes ahora,* Max?"

Max said, "*Sí.*"

"Oh my, wow, Dad! Do you hear this?" She faced back to Max. "*Kannst du mich jetzt auch verstehen?*"

"*Ja,*" Max said.

"This is incredible. I'm so proud of you, Max. You're my smart boy! Dad, can you believe this?"

When he didn't say anything, she turned to look at him. He just nodded.

"This is remarkable. That was just one day. What will he do with a week, a year, a lifetime?" Sandi wondered aloud.

"Just be careful."

"Why would you be such a wet blanket? Why can't you just be happy for me? We need to tell the world about this."

"No!" her father bellowed. Max let out a whimper and started shaking.

"Don't scare him like this! It's okay, sweetheart. He's more bark than bite. Stop being a bully," she addressed her father again.

"I'm not a bully. I'm looking out for you."

"By not supporting me? That's not looking out for me."

"There's more to this than you know."

"You're not killing him!"

"No. I'm not going to kill him. We just need some time to think this all the way through."

"I've had plenty of time."

"I haven't. I've just learned about this."

"How did you discover Max?"

"I heard a noise downstairs and thought you'd forgotten to turn the TV off. Imagine my surprise! I didn't know what to do with him."

"What *did* you do with him?"

"Just did a lot of observing. He is remarkable."

Sandi was shocked. It was the closest she guessed she'd get to a compliment from this man. He didn't hand them out often. "Thank you. I wish you would have worked with me on him."

"I guess now, I wish I had too. I don't like that you broke into the morgue and took something that wasn't yours."

"He wasn't going to use it anymore. It would have just gone to waste. But think of the things we can do in science with what we now know."

"The world isn't ready for all this."

"How do you know? Maybe not when you were creating your being, but today is a different time. I think we can make great strides with our understanding of the replication process. I've been thinking about situations like Houston's mom and prosthetics. What if we were able to regrow limbs? If we can create a full human, what's an arm or a leg?"

"Whoa. Slow down. I'm telling you from experience, the world is not ready. You need to trust me on this. I know you're a teenager and teens believe their parents have no sense and know nothing, but I'm telling you right now, society isn't ready. What do you think your grandfather has spent decades working on? You are not the first to cross this threshold."

"He said he didn't do anything like this when I went to see him."

"He lied. Look, I don't want you to get hurt."

"What do you care? It's my reputation, not yours. Or are you concerned it will throw a bad light on you as a parent?"

"We need to get over this barrier you have constructed between us. When did this all happen, when you were told *no*?"

"I didn't build the wall, you did. Unless it's forcing me to eat something or drink that gross crap you make me ingest every morning, you hardly even interact with me. You retreat to your corner and have nothing to do with me. You haven't worked with me in the lab in a very long time. You don't really talk about my days or how hard it is for me in school. As long as you're allowed to go on and on about whatever project you're working on, or general niceties, you have nothing to say to me."

He sat so still she wasn't sure he hadn't petrified in place.

"Never mind. I get it. It's my problem." She turned her back on him to face Max.

He stood behind her and placed his hands on her shoulders. "That's not what I'm saying. I just figured I was giving you the space you desired. I figured you'd outgrow the childish antics of the other kids at school if I just stood my ground."

"It's not just the kids, Dad. The teachers are just as bad if not worse. I think they're threatened by my intelligence and take it out on me. That's why I've wanted to advance. I figured if I went on to college, the IQ would be higher, and I would no longer be a threat. I would be able to learn at a higher level and maybe even be able to collaborate with others with my same interests."

He turned her around to face him, knelt in front of her, took her face in his hands, and looked into her eyes. "We'll discuss it, I promise. Now, show me what you've been doing."

Sandi pulled her journals with all her notes, measurements, and findings. He sat down at the table to read through them. Sandi took Max to the back to set him up with his toys and tablet. When she returned, her father looked up, now with what appeared to be a look of pride on his face. "You did all this." It wasn't a question; it was a factual statement.

"Yes. I did. I told you I would."

"You took Houston's DNA."

"Well, he doesn't know that. I'd be mortified if he ever found out."

"It was pretty brilliant."

"Tell me about my mother. Do I look like her? Do I act like her? I want to know more."

"That's for another day. Right now, we need to get your young man into his own bedroom. You can't leave him locked in the basement in a corner. He won't thrive that way."

"You're not going to off him?"

He laughed. "No. What kind of a monster do you think I am? I'm not going to kill him. I told you that. I'm going to help you raise him."

Sandi wrapped her arms around her father's neck and thanked him.

"I know I'm not good at showing it, but I really do love you, princess."

He led the way to where Max sat contentedly watching his tablet.

"Max, you're moving upstairs to your very own room," Sandi announced. "Come on, big boy."

There were five bedrooms on the top floor. Three were spare rooms —not that anyone ever stayed the night. She guessed it was just in case. They dusted and vacuumed them on a regular basis. Other than that, they were never even entered.

They chose the room at the top of the stairs to the right, across the hall from Sandi's room. There were two bedrooms down the hall, on either side. One was next to Sandi's, with a shared bathroom between those two rooms and the other across the hall shared a restroom with what would now be Max's room. Her father's suite was at the other end of the hall, behind the stairway.

Sandi led Max into his new room. "This is all yours now. This is your bed. I'll put your clothes in here." She pointed to the dresser on the wall. She went to the closet and opened the doors. "This is your closet. We'll put your hang-up clothes in here. This is where we'll store your toys and shoes too."

"Toys," Max said.

"That's right. Come in here." She led him by the hand into the bathroom.

"Does he use the facilities?" her father asked.

"Not yet, but I'm about to start teaching him."

"Why don't we leave that to me?"

"Great!" Sandi said with relief. "Look, Max. You can learn to wash yourself in the bathtub."

"I'll be teaching him that too. He's very bright. I should be able to get him to take showers quickly."

"Fine by me," Sandi said gratefully. She felt like such a weight had been lifted from her shoulders, having help with Max's care. And even more because she didn't have to keep this secret any longer.

Max sat on his bed. A look of delight crossed his face. He started to bounce, then squealed with joy. Sandi couldn't help but laugh. Her father quickly followed suit.

"You go get the rest of his things. I'll get started on his bath."

By the time Sandi got back with the few pieces of clothing and a handful of toys, she heard splashing in the tub. She could only imagine the water she'd be mopping up later. For now, she relished the laughter she heard coming from her Max and her father's corrections of the child in him. She would talk sense into her father another day.

Fifteen

Sandi woke to Max screaming. It sounded like he was in pain. She jumped out of bed and almost ran into her father getting to him. She threw the door open. Max was thrashing around on the bed, crying, in apparent pain. She ran to his side. "Max? What is it? What happened? Did you hurt yourself?"

"Ow!" was all he could say. He was rolling back and forth with his hands on his face.

"He's teething," her father said.

"What? Are you sure?"

"I recognize this."

"Really? I did this as a baby?"

"Uh...yeah. You did." He looked away from her.

"What do we do?"

"Hang on. I think I still have a gum-numbing cream we can put on him. Be right back."

"It'll be okay, Max. Dad's going to get you something for the pain." She climbed into the bed beside him, gathered him in her arms, and rocked to soothe him. "I'm so sorry you're hurting. We'll make it better. I wish I could take it for you."

Her father returned, but Max wouldn't open his mouth.

"You have to let him put the medicine in your mouth to stop it hurting. Please trust us, Max."

"Noooooooooo," he cried. "Ow!"

"I know it's *ow*, but this will make it feel better."

"You hold him down and I'll get it in there," her dad said. "Once he sees it helps, he will be more open to it in the future."

"I hate to force him."

"Just this first time. Trust me."

Sandi pinned his arms down and wrapped her legs around him to hold him in place while her father pried his mouth open, rubbing the medicine he had on his finger on Max's gums.

"Oh, yeah, there it is," her dad said. "I actually think I felt two coming in."

"Really? I thought they came in one at a time."

"You brought through several at a time. This is going to be a long week, sweetheart."

"Week? It takes a week for a tooth to come in?"

"Um..." he stammered. "At his rate of development, I don't think it will take as long as normal."

Sandi realized that while they were talking, Max had settled and was just breathing jerkily while lying in her arms looking up at her. Her heart burst with love and broke for his pain. "Shh, it's okay. You're okay. I'm right here."

"I'll leave this with you. Reapply it as directed. Try not to hit his tongue or it will be numb too. Stay just ahead of the pain by making sure you add it about 10 minutes before whatever time it says to reapply. You'll want to set alarms. Goodnight."

Sandi lay there a moment absorbing everything her father just said. Did he really just leave her to do this alone?

~

SANDI DRAGGED herself down the stairs aiming for the coffee pot. Her father hugged her and handed her a fresh cup of coffee. "Rough night?"

"Thanks, Dad. *Long* night."

"Where's Max?"

"Sleeping. I'll get him something to eat when he wakes up—or his next dose, whichever comes first."

"Not so fun now, huh?"

"Really? Funny. What am I supposed to do? I can't go to school and leave him like this."

"You need to get him a sitter. Take today off to take care of Max and find someone to take care of him, work with him, tutor, and raise him. He probably shouldn't have been left on his own as much as he was."

Her father set her juice and breakfast in front of her at the table.

"I guess the good thing to all this is he'll be able to eat everything we eat soon enough," Sandi stated.

"Good point."

Sandi heard Max calling for her from above. "Be right back."

"I'll get him some scrambled eggs."

She returned with Max, who was looking a bit bedraggled. Her father smiled.

"What?" Sandi asked.

"Nothing. I just remember these days. They weren't that long ago."

"Here Max, eat, you'll feel better," Mr. Powell said.

Sandi had never seen Max so forlorn. It broke her heart. "He will feel better soon, won't he?"

"This too shall pass. I've got to get to work. See what you can line up as quickly as you can. You don't need to miss much school." He hugged her while placing a kiss on the top of her head and started to walk away.

Max said, "Me."

Her dad stopped, looked at Max, smiled and went to his side. "Yes, Max, you too." He kissed the top of his head. "Have a good day. I hope you feel better."

MAX SAT NEXT to Sandi on the sofa, watching a documentary on elephants, while Sandi called care centers and services. She was hoping to find someone soon. She was going to line up the interviews for the evenings. She wanted her father there since he had more experience at this sort of thing than she did.

Sandi searched her phone for sitters. After changing Max yet again, she realized she probably should focus on finding a special-needs sitter. The first service she called didn't deal with special needs of any kind. After contacting six different businesses, she managed to line up four interviews for the next evening.

Sandi didn't remember having a sitter, only her father. She struggled to recall her childhood, but she could only come up with vague impressions. Her memories were strong and thorough beginning around the start of high school. Didn't kids remember at least some things from their childhood? She had heard some of her peers talk about things that happened in their youth. She wondered why she had no earlier memories. She would make sure Max could remember these days. Although maybe not the pain of this moment. She hated that he was in such pain.

Sandi's dad came in while she was reading resumes. "Hey! What are the two of you doing?" he asked.

"Gorilla," Max said.

Sandi chuckled. "Good boy, yes, he's watching a documentary on gorillas. I believe we've gone through the whole animal kingdom at this point. I've set up some interviews for tomorrow night. Does that work for you, or should I reschedule?"

"No. That's fine for me."

"I really wanted a selection to choose from. It looks like we have four. The agencies emailed me their resumes and references. I forwarded them on to you."

"Great. Hopefully, one of them will work and be trustworthy. It's hard letting strangers into your home. Are there any day care options?"

"One, but I didn't know how that would make Max feel, being with a bunch of babies."

Over dinner, Sandi read the resume for her favored woman from her phone to her dad. "Doesn't she sound like just the person for Max?"

"She sounds great. I like that she has so much experience, not only with little ones but the elderly. That should be a good mix for our situation."

"Agreed. I scheduled her last. This way we can compare her to everyone else. What if we don't like any of them?"

"We go back to the drawing board."

"I was thinking today about my childhood. I can't remember it."

"Young minds don't always recall clearly."

"I don't remember anyone but you. Did I have a sitter?"

"No. I raised you on my own."

"How'd you do that and work?"

"I didn't start with this company until a couple years ago."

She had no idea he hadn't worked there longer. "So, after I started high school?"

"Yes. How'd Max fare today?"

Nice change of subject, Sandi thought. "How'd Max fare, or how did I fare?"

"Well, both of you." He chuckled.

"You were right—his teeth are coming in fast. It was hard, but we're making it. Do we wait until they all come in before having this sitter start? Otherwise, how do we explain that he's bringing in a mouthful of teeth all at once?"

"Yeah, we can ask if they can start next week."

"Next week?"

"Um...yes. My guess is he'll get them all in this week."

She searched her father's face. What could he know to make a prediction like that?

"So, I have to miss the whole week of school?"

"It was your decision to go against my wishes, so you need to deal with the consequences. Email your teachers, so you keep up on all your schoolwork."

"Okay, I'll go do that now."

AT 5:55 P.M., the doorbell rang. Sandi's dad started for the door. "Do you mind if I get it?" Sandi asked. "Technically, I'm the one looking for the sitter."

"Oh! Sure. Be my guest." He stepped to the side.

Sandi opened the door to a girl who looked to be in her early twenties. She didn't want to discount her based on her appearance, but she didn't know how much assurance she could have that Max would be properly cared for. Would she ignore him to be on her phone or entertain a boyfriend? Would she take her responsibilities seriously? "Hi! You must be Marie," Sandi said while extending her hand. "Come in. This is my dad, Mr. Powell. This is Max. Max, can you say 'Hi' to Marie?"

"Hi, Mree," Max responded.

Marie simply smiled.

"Come have a seat, Marie," Sandi's dad said. He led her to the kitchen table. He pulled out a chair for Marie, directed Max to sit in his seat at the head of the table, and sat beside Sandi on the same side of the table.

Sandi was surprised by more than their positioning. She would have taken her to the living room.

Marie answered all their questions and when asked if she had any, she said, "What are Max's special needs?"

Sandi and her dad exchanged looks. Her father said, "Max is behind in development in some areas. He's now learning quickly, but, as you can see, he's a big boy. He needs guidance, teaching, and companionship while playing catch-up cognitively."

Sandi liked that answer. After saying their goodbyes, Sandi said to her dad, "What'd you think?"

"She's got a solid background. Good schooling and her references look good."

"Don't you think she's too young?"

"She's older than you."

"True. Can I ask why we're doing this in the kitchen?"

"You were thinking the living room?"

"Yes."

"I felt that setting would be too relaxed, less formal."

The doorbell rang.

By the time applicant number four was to arrive, they both had agreed on the strengths of each. Sandi was ready to be done with this process but wasn't entirely happy with any of them.

"Promise you won't just settle, Daddy. I want the best for Max, no matter how long this takes."

"I promise. I'm hopeful, but I promise. Now, go answer the door."

"Have a seat, Ms. Fields," her father said while pulling out her chair. He smiled and gave Sandi a look she couldn't understand.

Ms. Fields was an older woman. She appeared to Sandi to be about her father's age. She looked well put together, refined, but laid-back and relaxed. She gave Sandi a good feeling.

"Please," the woman said smiling, "call me Gretchen."

"Okay, Gretchen, how are you this evening?" he asked.

"I'm fine, thank you." She looked at Max and said, "And you must be Max."

Sandi loved this woman already. She was the first one to address Max past the formalities at the door.

"Max, can you say, 'Yes, ma'am, I am'?" Sandi said.

"I am Max," he said.

Gretchen smiled and said, "How old are you?"

Oh, no! They hadn't considered that before now. Sandi looked at her father, who didn't look like he was caught off guard.

"Max is a very special boy," Sandi's father said. "His age is a bit deceptive."

Good answer, Sandi thought, glad she didn't have to come up with something.

"I'm sure we'll do just fine together," Gretchen said in a sweet voice, leaning a bit toward Max. When she sat back, she looked at Sandi's dad and said, "What is it you'll need from me, Mr. Powell?"

"Well, actually, most of your instruction will be coming from Sandi."

"Oh! Is that right?" She looked a bit confused. "Is this your...son?"

"Not exactly," Sandi said, a bit self-conscious now.

"I'm sorry, dear. I didn't mean to be assumptive. You're just so young, and he looks to be almost your age. So, tell me what you would like me to do for your Max, here."

"As my father said, he's a special boy. He's learning and growing very fast, but he's still got a long way to go. He's pretty good at entertaining himself, but I'd like someone to tutor him, teach him, and bring him up to speed in all subjects. He likes to watch documentaries. He does feed himself and gets more in his mouth than his aprons now. He uses sippy cups, but he's getting better with regular ones. He's not yet potty-trained, so he'll need help in that department. He wears Depends at this time."

"That's just fine, we can work on that. I've had many elderly with dementia who needed help to use the toilet. I can teach Max."

"Great. Although he's still learning, he is learning fast. He speaks bits of seven different languages. He listens to various shows in all those languages. I don't always know what they're saying, but he seems to. As good as I am, he's surpassed me in linguistics. We will need you to work with him on his English. He isn't saying more than a word or two at a time in all languages."

"What I don't know, we shall learn together," Gretchen said.

Sandi was pleasantly surprised. Gretchen was the first one not to be put off by his ability to speak so many languages. The second woman had actually said she wouldn't be able to help him with anything but English.

Gretchen was very open when asked about the many months it had been since her last assignment. She had been with a kind, elderly man as more of a companion than caregiver who had unexpectedly taken ill and passed quickly. She had needed time to mourn his loss.

"I'm glad he's so healthy. I do understand and will look forward to preparing him for school. Do you have any other questions for me?"

"Yes," Mr. Powell said, "would you be able to start next Monday?"

"Dad!" Sandi exclaimed.

"I'm sorry. This is your call."

Sandi looked at Gretchen. "Would you be able to start next Monday?"

They all laughed.

"Yes, I'm happy to."

"Great!" Sandi said. "Let's show you around and where everything is."

When Gretchen left, Sandi's dad said, "I think she's going to be great with and for Max. Good call."

"It was more your call."

"No. I really wanted it to be up to you. I just had such a good feeling about her. I liked how attentive she was to Max and how he interacted with her. She certainly has the experience we need. I also liked that she didn't push on his age versus his experience. She asked just the right number of questions without being intrusive."

"Yes. I really do like her and think she'll be a perfect fit for Max. I'm still going to run home at lunch just to check on them. At least for a little while."

"I'm sure it will give you peace of mind. I'm going to be in the library if you need me."

Sixteen

Gretchen was at the kitchen table drinking coffee by the time Sandi and Max came downstairs Monday morning.

"Good morning, Max," Gretchen said, sounding genuine.

"Morning," Max said.

Gretchen said, "We're going to have some fun today, sweet boy."

"Fun," Max repeated.

"Good morning, Sandi," she said. "How'd your sleep, dear?"

It was too early for all this sweetness in Sandi's mind. "Fine. Thank you."

Sandi turned for the coffee maker, but her father placed her favorite mug in her hands with a big smile on his face. Sandi just rolled her eyes, hugged her dad, took the mug, and sat in her seat.

There was toast and the dreaded juice at her place. Max had already started on his grits and juice.

Gretchen said, "I thought we would walk to the park today. Would that be all right?"

Sandi just sipped her coffee, looking over the rim of her cup at Gretchen, who was across the table from her. She wasn't sure if he would be all right in public yet. He hadn't even left their yard yet. She then shifted her eyes to the right to take in her father while she continued to sip and think.

Her father laughed. "I don't think Sandi's fully awake yet. She's not really a morning person. Let's let her drink her coffee and mull it over."

Gretchen chuckled. "Of course. I'm sorry, I've been up for a couple hours. I forget not everyone wakes up happy. Drink your coffee and just let me know before you leave."

"I think that's a great idea," Sandi's dad said.

"Would you like to play at the park today, Max?" Gretchen asked.

"Park," Max said.

"He doesn't know what that means," Sandi added.

"Oh, he will soon enough. Is there anything in particular you would like me to work on with his lessons?" Gretchen asked Sandi's dad.

"I think work on full sentences. He seems to be absorbing things like a sponge, but he's not fully communicating in more than a couple words. Anything else you'd like to work on, we're fine with," he responded.

"I'll get a feel over the next few days to gauge where he's at. If I feel like we need class materials, would I be within my rights to purchase some?" Gretchen asked.

"Absolutely," Sandi said. "I can leave you money or we can order online and have it sent here."

"Look who's awake," Sandi's father said.

They all laughed.

"Don't give me a hard time just because I'm dependent on caffeine," Sandi shot back.

"It's fine, dear," said Ms. Fields, "I am too. I've just had a head start on you. I'll learn to give you some time to have your coffee in the mornings before I jump in and start asking questions.

"I'll be running home on my lunch break at 11:45 am," Sandi said.

"You have my number. If you would prefer, you can just give me a call. I hate for you to waste your lunch coming home for no good reason," Gretchen said.

"How about I come home today, and if all goes well, we can talk on the phone going forward," said Sandi.

"That's fine, whatever you think best," Ms. Fields said.

Sandi finished her toast and juice, picked up the table, and ran upstairs to brush her teeth. She felt a bit lost on what to do next. She was so used to making sure Max was all set up for the day. Now, with Gretchen in place, that wasn't necessary, and it was throwing her off. She went back downstairs to find Max with Gretchen in the living room.

"Well, if no one needs anything more from me, I'm off," Sandi announced.

"Have a great day, dear," Gretchen said.

Sandi went to her father and kissed him on the cheek. She went to Max, bent down to him on the floor, placed a kiss on his forehead, and said, "You be a good boy for Gretchen today. I'll see you at lunch."

"Good," Max said.

Sandi walked to her car, wishing her father had known about Max sooner. Gretchen was going to be invaluable to her and free up so much time.

It had been a long, hard week. Although Sandi had enjoyed being able to do her homework at her own pace, without all the high school drama, Max had managed to bring in a mouthful of teeth in a short period of time.

She had left Gretchen with instructions on the oral medication. Bless her, she didn't ask any questions. She told Max not to bite Gretchen and to remember that the goo helped him feel better, even if he didn't like the taste. She began smiling at the one and only time Max bit her. She was sure she would leave half a finger in his mouth. When she yelled, she scared him, and that was the last time he chomped down while her fingers were in his mouth.

"What's so funny, Smelly?" Kristy asked.

"You caught me, I was thinking about you. That's hysterical!" Sandi shot back.

"You're so weird."

"Back atcha."

"Girls," the teacher said. "I'd like to teach if you'd care to learn."

There wasn't anything this or any other teacher in this school could teach Sandi. She just had to pretend for the time being. She focused her attention on the front of the class. She heard her instructor's voice like

the teacher in the Charlie Brown cartoons—"Whawhawha...whawha"
—and smiled again.

Sandi hated it here. She'd rather be with Max at home. Anyway, she
could complete her assignments in a fraction of the time it took these
morons to explain so simply that the whole class would understand.

As she went through her day, she felt extra flak from the other
students. She felt like they had saved up all their insults for her return.
She wanted out!

She ran home during lunch to check on Max and be sure Gretchen
was okay. When she cleared the door, Max was at the table with his
apron on, eating his lunch.

"Oh!" Sandi said with surprise. "I guess all is well?"

"We're doing just great," Gretchen responded.

"Great," Max said.

"Well, wonderful."

"Can I make you something to eat?" Gretchen asked.

"No. I haven't been eating lunch. I really don't have time to get
here, take care of Max, eat, and get back to my next class."

"That's the beauty of having me here. Tell me what you do and
don't eat, and I'll have your lunch ready for you by the time you get
here, dear."

"Wow! That's really sweet. If it's in this house, I eat it."

"I'll be ready tomorrow then, unless you just want to use the phone
instead of wasting your time coming home."

If she only knew Sandi preferred having an excuse to leave that
dreaded place. "Thanks so much for that. I'll be here at this time every
day. So, what have you been up to today, Max?"

"*Je suis en train d'apprendre la langue Allemande,*" Max said.

"German? Is that right? You've been learning German, but you tell
me in French?"

"Yes, along with some Math and letters," Gretchen said.

"But he knows his letters."

"Oh, yes, I saw that, but I had him writing them."

"Great!"

"*Ich schreibe Briefe,*" Max announced that he was learning to write
his letters, this time in German.

"That's better," Sandi said. "Don't cross language. When you're speaking about German, say it in German, and French in French."

"*Warum?*" Max asked.

"Why? Because it can be confusing to the rest of us." Sandi laughed. "You're so smart I'm sure you keep it all straight in your head. All of us get mixed up."

Gretchen said, "He really is very smart. I don't know how long you'll need me at his rate of learning."

Sandi smiled. If she only knew. "Is there anything you need from me before I go?"

"We're good. You have a great rest of your day, and we'll see you this afternoon."

Sandi hugged Max, he wrapped his arms around her, and she kissed his forehead. "Be good for Gretchen. I'll see you later."

Seventeen

⌒〜⌒

Sandi awoke to the feeling of someone watching her. She opened her eyes and sucked air. Max was standing over her.

"What is it? Are you alright? What time is it?" She looked at her cell phone; it was 7 a.m. on Saturday. "Oh, wow! We slept the whole night through. You must be hungry. Come on. Let's get you dressed and me a cup of coffee."

She led him back to his room, pulled a jogging suit, a fresh Depend, and his wet wipes from his dresser.

"No," Max said.

"No, what?"

"No diaper. Potty."

"You want to use the potty? Hang on, let me go get my dad."

"I do."

"Really? Are you sure you don't need help?"

"No help."

"Wow! When did this happen? Gretchen didn't say anything. Okay, have at it. I'll be right here when you're done."

He went into his bathroom and closed the door. Sandi wasn't entirely confident, so she ran downstairs to get her father.

"Hey, Dad."

"Morning, princess."

"Can you come with me? Max says he's using the potty by himself. I just don't know if that's feasible. Can you check on him?"

"I can, but he's learned. He did it on his own last night."

"No one told me."

"I'm sorry, sweetie. I figured you knew. I can go check."

"No. That's alright. We'll be back in a few."

She ran back up to find Max standing in a pair of underwear while pulling a T-shirt over his head.

"Well, look at you. Using the restroom on your own, now getting dressed by yourself. Gretchen's taught you a lot this week."

He held his hand out and said, "Pants."

Sandi looked at her hands. She was still holding the jogging suit. "Here you go." She handed him both pieces.

He put the jacket back, said, "Hot," and proceeded to pull on the bottoms.

"I have to grab a quick shower. I'll meet you downstairs."

Downstairs, her father had already completed a stack of pancakes and was finishing up the bacon in the pan.

"Hungry?" he asked.

"I think Max is probably starving. We didn't wake up in the night like we usually do. We slept straight through."

As Sandi made her way to the coffee maker, Max took his same seat.

"How does pancakes and bacon sound, Max? Having teeth is making things easier," her father said.

"Not to mention no longer costing me a fortune in baby food. I'm sure he eats a lot more than babies do."

Sandi filled Max's sippy cup with the nasty juice and her regular glass for herself.

"Ah," her father said, "now I understand the need to double the recipe."

"Yeah, well, I was trying to help him grow and be healthy. The good thing is, unlike me, he likes it."

"It's good for you."

"And tastes terrible."

A cell phone chimed. "Not mine," Sandi's dad said. "Must be yours."

"There's no one I want or need to talk to. It's probably just spam."

"What about Houston?"

"I think Houston is done with me. I wasn't in school for a whole week, he never returned any of my texts or calls. He's avoided me all this past week." Sandi set down two platters with the pancakes and bacon from the warmer. She placed a white carafe of warm maple syrup on the table. Max's nose went up, and he said, "Umm..."

"You think so?" Sandi said. "Do you think it would hurt him?" she asked her dad.

"This early in the day, I doubt it. We'll see how he reacts to natural sugar."

Sandi poured just a bit in a ramekin and set it next to his plate. "Like this." She took Max's hand holding the fork, stabbed a piece of pancake, dabbed it in the syrup, and guided it to his mouth.

"Umm...more," Max said enthusiastically. "More."

They laughed. "I guess he likes it," Sandi said.

"Now, let's hope it doesn't make him hyper," her father responded.

Sandi had to tell Max to slow down so he wouldn't make himself sick. She sat watching him while drinking her coffee.

"Make sure you eat some too," her dad said.

"I know. I will. I'm just enjoying my coffee at the moment. You told me everyone is not ready for this," she said while nodding her head toward Max. "What do you know about everyone not being ready?"

"Where's Houston now? You said you told him. And what was his response?"

Sandi realized the truth in what her father was saying. This was not what she expected from him. She had trusted him, and he had avoided her. "Okay, point made."

"I'm not in this to win. I understand all too well. I had a gal I was seeing back in the day."

"Yeah, I know, my mother."

"No. Her name was Elizabeth. I called her Beth."

"What happened to her?"

"She left me as soon as she learned what I had done. She accused me of having a god complex. Maybe I did. Maybe I do. I don't know anymore. She walked away, and I've been alone ever since. I haven't dared let anyone else in."

Sandi felt bad about all her thoughts on why her father was alone. She could now relate to why he would choose to be alone. If she didn't have Max, she would probably have ended up the same way. "What about my mother? When did she come into the picture? She didn't leave you on purpose. She couldn't help it that she died giving birth to me. And what happened to your creation? Did Beth make you kill it?"

"I really don't want to dredge all this back up."

The phone dinged again.

"Ding," Max said absently while he continued to devour his breakfast.

She ignored it. A few minutes later, it sounded again.

"Ding," said Max.

A little while later, it went off again.

"Ding," Max said again.

"If you don't respond to it, I will," her father said.

"It can't be mine. It must be yours."

He held his up in his hand. "Not mine."

"Oh, alright. What?" She said in irritation. She got up, crossed to the counter, picked it up, but didn't look at it until she'd sat back down.

"Who is it and what do they want so early on a Saturday?" her dad asked.

She opened her phone to see several missed texts from Houston. "They're all from Houston." Without reading them, she laid her phone face down on the table.

"Ding," Max said as he continued to eat.

Sandi glanced at Max, shook her head, and picked up her phone. She really wasn't in a mood to deal with whatever Houston had to say. She was still too hurt over his treatment after she had been so vulnerable and trusting with him. She had talked herself into believing she didn't need him. Soon enough, Max would be grown, and she would have with Max what Houston would never be to her. This pain from rejection was hard to deal with. Her finger hesitated over the button to switch it off.

"Just answer the boy," her dad said. "Prolonging the inevitable is going to solve nothing."

Sandi opened it to read his litany of messages.

> "We need 2 talk"
>
> "R u up?"
>
> "Can u chat?"
>
> "I'm off @ 4. Chat then?"
>
> "Plz. I'm sorry. Just talk 2 me"
>
> "Just answer me"
>
> "Don't hate me. That was a lot u laid on me"

Sandi set her phone back down on the table.

"What'd he say?" her father asked.

"He wants to talk."

"Well, you owe him that."

"I don't owe him anything. He's the one who stonewalled me after I opened up to him."

"I'm sure he was overwhelmed. This is no little thing, Sandi."

"And it took me a lot to share."

"You're not going to get anywhere being stubborn. I know all too well."

"Fine." She picked up her phone and shot him a simple response,

> "Fine"

Houston came back with,

> "Fine as in I can call u when out?"

Sandi sent back,

> "IDC"

"U'll answer?"

She sent a thumbs up emoji. She set her phone back down on the table. "Happy?" she asked her father.

He just smirked.

In such a short period of time, her morning joy had been turned into irritation—and to think, just the thought of Houston had once made her giddy. If this was what relationships were made of, she wondered if she should do without.

After breakfast, Sandi set Max up on the living room floor, turned on the TV, gave him his tablet, and set a few toys on the carpet around him. "Sit here and play. I have some work to get done." This was so much easier than trying to hide and sneak around.

She made quick work of her chores. She wanted some time to work with Max on his learning. She didn't have to sneak around to get their laundry done, she just threw it in while doing everything else as she once had. She was mopping the kitchen floor when she heard the TV channels changing. She rounded the corner to find Max with the remote.

"What are you looking for?" she asked him.

"*No esta,*" he said.

"Not this?"

"*No esta.*"

"Alright. Let me find you something else." She couldn't remember what she had put on for him, but she would clear it with him from now on. "What about this?" she asked when she stopped at a PBS station.

"*No esta.*"

"Really, everything in Spanish?" She changed the station to a cartoon.

"*Pas ça.*" And he wrinkled his nose.

"Funny. What do you want to watch?"

"*Tigre.*"

"Tiger? You want a documentary? Haven't learned about every animal on the planet already?" Sandi switched to the National Geographic channel, and Max started bobbing his head and bouncing up and down.

"Well, alrighty then. A documentary it is." Sandi heard what sounded like Chinese coming from his tablet. She leaned over to see he had added a Chinese program to his others. "How'd you do that?" She took the tablet, and he threw a fit.

"Mine!"

"I know it's yours. I'm not taking it. I just wanted to know how you got this program on it. Let me look. I'll give it back."

Sandi scrolled his apps; he had added several. There were many varied language apps including Latin, Portuguese, Cantonese, and Russian.

"You like languages?"

He nodded.

He had added some math and science apps as well. At this rate, she wasn't sure he wouldn't surpass her intellect soon. She was pleasantly surprised at the speed he was learning. She wanted to hurry to get her work done. She wanted to discover how much he had really learned in such a short period of time. She did want to move him past single word sentences, regardless of the language.

Sandi was involved with Max and teaching when her phone began to ring. She had lost all track of time. Two weeks ago, her heart had jumped for joy at just the thought of Houston calling her. Now, it sank with dread. She debated answering it. Her ego was telling her all the reasons she should ignore it and continue on with Max instead. It stopped. *There*, she thought, *decision made*.

He sent her a text,

"On my way 2 u now. Hope this is ok"

Crap! Sandi didn't want that. She couldn't think straight in his presence. She called him back.

"Hey," Houston said on the first ring.

"Hey. You wanna talk? Talk."

"Please don't be like this. I thought we were friends."

"So did I until I opened up to you and you left me feeling like a freak."

"I didn't mean to. I just didn't know what to do with the bombshell you dropped on me."

"Why do you want to talk now? What is it you want?"

"Can I come over?"

"What difference will it make? I don't know if I'm ready to see you. You really hurt me."

"That's part of why I want to do this in person. I feel really bad about how I left everything."

"How you left me."

"Yes. How I left you. Please, can I come over?"

Sandi paused a long while thinking about if she would be able to stay strong with him right in front of her. She didn't think so.

Houston begged, "Please."

"Fine."

"I'll be there in a couple minutes. I'm around the corner."

Sandi wasn't even going to try to hide Max. This would be the moment of truth. The doorbell rang. Her dad called out, "I'll get it."

She let him. She remained on the floor with Max.

Her father sounded thrilled to have Houston here again. "Come in, come in, so glad you came back. Give Sandi a chance to explain herself. I did. Max is pretty remarkable. I can't believe she did all this on her own. Come, they're in the living room."

Sandi never moved. When he stood above her, her heart betrayed her as she knew it would. It did flip-flops in her chest. She meant to be firm, unmovable, but seeing him here, in her house, she caved and stood up. "Hi."

"Hi. Sandi, I—"

She cut him off, "This is Max. Max, can you stand up and greet Houston?" She reached her hand out to him. He took it and rose.

"*Bonjour*," Max said.

"*Comment vas-tu?*" Houston replied.

"You speak French?" Sandi asked.

"A little. Not as much as I'd like. Max speaks French?"

"He apparently understands many languages but is always surprising me with new ones. He's working on it."

"Did you teach him?"

"No." Sandi looked at the floor. "I got him a tablet with language programs loaded on it. He took it upon himself to download more."

When Houston said nothing, she looked up at him. "What?"

He was staring at Max. "Nothing. This is incredible. You made him? By yourself? I knew you were smart. I just had no idea."

Sandi blushed. "Yeah, well, it's not like you gave me a chance."

"About that—"

"Forget it. What did you want to talk to me about?"

Her father excused himself and retreated to the library.

"Please forgive me for being a jerk," Houston said.

"The jury is still out. Tell me what you want first. I'm not giving you the opportunity to hurt me all over again. Speak your piece."

"I hate that I made you feel that way. I'm really sorry. I want to be able to move past this and get back to where we were."

"You mean before I allowed myself to trust you? Before I let myself be vulnerable to you? Before you abandoned me?"

It was Houston who now looked at the floor. "Yes," he said in a low voice. "Then."

"I don't know if I can ever get back there. How can I trust you not to betray me again?"

"You can give me a chance to prove it, I guess. To earn your trust back. Please?" The pleading look he had in his eyes made her want to believe him.

"We'll see."

In two strides of those long legs, he was scooping her up in a bear hug. "I won't let you down again. I promise. Thank you."

He most certainly was strong like she knew he would be. "You're welcome." She knew he had just come from work. He smelled like a deep fryer and sweat. Being in his embrace let her forgive him for not taking a shower before coming over. Also, it made her believe he meant what he was saying.

He set her back on her feet. Max came to her, wrapped his arms around her and picked her up off the floor. She and Houston laughed. "You can put me back down, my big boy." He set her down. "Good boy," she praised him.

"Really? You made him? I'm fascinated. How?"

"There were a lot of components, a lot of patience, a lot of terror at keeping him a secret. I studied my father's notes, but he left a lot out. From what I knew and researched, I filled in the blanks, and here he is."

"Amazing," was all Houston could say.

"Zing," Max said.

They laughed. Sandi stood in front of him and enunciated her words, "A-maz-ing."

Max tried to parrot her.

"Good job," Houston said. "How old is he?"

"That's hard to say. Technically, a few months old. He's growing at a much faster rate than a baby. It's a bit difficult to know what to introduce at what points because he's not like dealing with the growth rate of a baby, toddler, nor child. He is now fully formed, but still growing."

"What do you mean?"

"Well, as he grew, he wasn't exactly growing proportionately. I was really worried I'd created a monster. I keep his vitals and measurements, and he's still progressing, but now everything has evened out. I just hope it remains this way. Until recently, he had a limp because one leg was slightly longer than the other."

"How tall is he?"

"6'2"," Sandi said proudly.

"That's my height."

"Hi," Max said.

"That's right, high," Houston said. "And all his vitals are good?"

"Yes. Once all his organs developed, we had about a week of instability, but now they're consistent and strong. As he is."

"That really is remarkable."

"He got all his teeth in the week before last."

"Is that why you were out?"

"Yeah."

"And all of them in one week? That's fast, isn't it?"

"Yes. It can take up to a year and a half to two years. He accomplished it in one week. It was a rough week, but we're through it."

"Wow! You have to adjust the timeline up a lot, huh?"

"Yes. We started him on pancakes and bacon this morning. I gave him soup with crackers this afternoon for lunch. So far, so good."

"What's for dinner?"

"Steak, vegetables, and potatoes."

"Well, Max, what do you think of the world?" Houston asked.

"Word," Max said.

"Close," Houston encouraged. "When and how did your father find out? Did you tell him?"

"No! When we were out, he heard the TV from downstairs that I'd left on for Max and discovered my secret."

"Like the night we went to the movies?"

"Yeah."

"Was he mad?"

"He was more shocked than mad. He's going to help me finish raising him, which I'm so grateful for. He's getting too big for me to handle on my own."

"Tell me how you did it."

Sandi went through most of the process. She left out the part about it being his DNA.

"Impressive. How'd you come up with all this? You said your father gave you his journals after you had already conceived of the plan. So, what made you want to even try?"

"I was lonely. I wanted a companion."

"Usually, people make friends, they don't literally make a person."

"I was raised with scientists. My grandfather has a huge facility where they research all day every day. I guess it's in my blood."

"I never would have had the guts to even try to do anything like this on my own. I admire you."

"You do? Then why'd you ignore my calls and texts, then deliberately avoid me all week?"

"I don't really know. I'm not sure, I had to have time to really wrap my head around all this. I was intimidated, I wasn't sure I could keep a secret this big, and didn't know how I would react to meeting Max. Until I was sure I could handle it all, I thought it best to keep myself from being backed into a corner and have to lie."

"Sure, but you didn't think you could just talk to me? You felt it necessary to abandon me?"

"That's the second time you've put it that way. I didn't abandon you. I was just keeping my distance until I was sure I was ready."

"It felt like abandonment to me. Even if you just said you needed some time to process it. Or asked me more questions. Instead, you just left me high and dry..."

"Hi!" Max said.

"Yes, Max, high," Sandi said. "You gave me no hope you wouldn't tell someone or ever talk to me again."

"I'm sorry. I didn't handle it right. I just didn't know what to say, what to do. It took me a lot longer to process than I thought. But I did keep your secret. It was hard not to talk to my mom about it, but I didn't. I didn't talk to anyone really over the past two weeks. I said what was necessary. My mother keeps asking me what's wrong. The rest of the time, I was pretty much lost in thought. I didn't sleep much. I guess I'm a bit slow." Houston chuckled.

Sandi just smiled.

"Can I see your lab?"

"Max lab," Max said.

"Yes," Houston said, "Max came from the lab."

Sandi was crossing the living room. "Come on, boys, to the lab."

Max took Houston's hand and said, "Lab."

Houston looked down at their hands, seeming a bit uncomfortable, and said, "Uh, yeah, sure, buddy."

Sandi flipped on the lights to bring the space to life. Max went to the back, past the drapes, and said, "Max room."

Sandi corrected him. "Was Max's room. No longer."

"Longer," Max said.

Sandi turned to find Houston standing at the bottom of the stairs, staring at the huge lab.

"What?" Sandi asked.

"It's just..."

"Yeah, I know. I get it. It's a lot."

"He was living back there?" Houston inquired as he peeked around the curtains.

"Yes. I had to keep him out of my father's sight. My dad has since given him his own room upstairs, though. We all slept well. Not living in a secret is freeing." Sandi went to the back to retrieve Max, and Houston followed.

"Wow," he said. "Look at all this stuff. Now I understand how you could keep something like this from your father. This is a big space. I was thinking the lab in the other room was big, but this is better than double what's out there. It all looks pretty organized and orderly."

"It needs to be in order to pull what is needed when necessary. As you would need to do in any laboratory environment."

"Are those refrigerators?"

"Yes, and freezers."

"That looks like a full kitchen back there."

"It is."

"You've got two kitchens in this house?"

"Well, yeah, but other than minor things I cooked there, we only really use the one upstairs."

"But two full kitchens?"

"Back in the day, my father did most of his work and experimentation down here. I guess he needed two kitchens. Since it's always been here, I never questioned or second-guessed it."

"I could tell this was a big house when I was here last time. I had no idea, though. It's deceptive from the outside."

"Come on, let me show you around the lab." Sandi led him back to the other side of the curtains. Max followed.

Sandi showed Houston where everything was, how it was laid out, and some of the things she had used to make Max. There were rows of microscopes, beakers, glass vials, centrifuges, microwaves, and several rows of counters with cupboards above and below.

"I think this lab is bigger than ours at school. It's certainly better outfitted," Houston said in awe.

"I know I prefer to work in my lab instead of the crappy school one. I just thought it had more to do with the company than the equipment. Now that you say that, I think you're right, and that's probably why I prefer it here. Max, do you want to show Houston your new room?"

"Womb," Max said.

"R-r-oo-m," Sandi said.

"Womb," Max said slower.

Houston laughed. "Let's go see your room, buddy." He held his hand out for Max. Sandi loved how good he was with Max. Max was not really a kid, but mentally he was nowhere near an adult yet.

Sandi led the way to the second story, to Max's room. She opened the door and stepped back. She was going to give Max all the bragging rights.

Max led Houston into his room with pride. He took him to his bed and sat down on the side. When Houston didn't sit down right away, Max pulled at him. Houston sat down beside him. "Nice bed, dude. It's big." Houston looked at Sandi. "This looks like a king-sized bed."

"Yes. All our beds are king."

"I'm moving in. Do you mind sharing, Max? It's big enough for both of us."

"So, you'd rather sleep with Max than me?" Sandi said.

Houston blushed, then started to stammer. "We...well, that's not what I meant. I was just playing."

"Oh, relax. So was I. Besides, if you stayed the night, you'd be in one of the guest rooms down the hall."

"So, it has a king bed too?"

"Yup."

Max started bouncing up and down on the bed. Houston stood up. Max looked crestfallen.

"It's okay, you bounce without me," Houston said.

Max got up, took Houston's hand, and led him to the bathroom. Sandi heard him say, "Max tub."

"I see that. Sandi, do you share the bathroom with Max?"

"No. I'm across the hall."

Max pulled at Houston and said, "Sandi room."

Sandi followed them.

Max went straight to her bed, sat on the side, and bounced up and down.

"Whee!" he said.

Again, Houston and Sandi laughed.

"Nice room," Houston said. "Dang! That's a big screen," he said, looking at her TV on the wall.

"I guess."

"You guess? It's twice the size of the one in our living room. Two kitchens, all these bedrooms and bathrooms. Yeah, I guess!"

"Oh." Sandi wasn't sure what to say. She didn't want to make him feel bad about things she didn't ever really think about. She wasn't materialistic, but she'd never wanted for anything. It never occurred to her that everyone didn't live as she did. She just assumed, in her sheltered life, that everyone else had it better than she did. She just didn't know how. Never having friends, she hadn't been exposed to how other people lived. She'd never been to anyone else's house—ever— except her grandfather's, and he lived much more opulently than they did.

They stood in deafening silence until Max passed gas. They both looked at him. He looked innocently at each of them. Then Houston and she laughed.

"I guess solid food is making its presence known," Sandi said.

"I'd say. He doesn't even know what just happened, does he?"

"No. Why would he?"

"His size is really throwing me off. I forget he's still so new."

Sandi's dad called up the stairs, "Are you kids going to be here for dinner?"

Sandi looked at Houston. "Want to stay for dinner?"

"Let me check with my mom, but probably."

"Houston's checking with his mom. We'll let you know in a minute, Dad."

At dinner, Houston sat across from Sandi on her father's right side. Houston was impressed at Max's dexterity and how well he fed himself. Her father agreed with him, boasting about Max's quick development. Sandi felt proud that these two men, who meant so much to her, acknowledged her accomplishments. She reveled in their easy conversation and enjoyed sitting back, listening, and not having to participate in her father's endless drivel about his work. She was glad Houston seemed to enjoy his stories. He was saving her from truly having to pay attention.

When Max was done, he wanted to get up. "Wait just a minute, let me get you cleaned up," Sandi said. She went to the sink, wet some paper towels, and returned to wipe Max's face and hands, but there was nothing to wipe up. "Good boy, you've gotten really good at feeding yourself. I'm proud of you. Actually, you don't need this apron anymore."

"Hey, Max, why don't you come with me?" her father said. "We'll get your bath done and get in PJs. Want to help, Houston?"

"Um...sure. Be right back, Sandi."

While the men were gone, she cleared the table and cleaned the kitchen. Sandi took a seat in the living room to wait for them to return. Max was being very good, but she was hoping for some time with Houston alone. She wasn't sure if that was in the cards tonight, though. While she waited, she flipped through channels on the TV. She was looking for a movie they could all watch. Something not too childish, but nothing so advanced as to lose Max and his attention. She searched for a family movie. That was a strange thought. She found a movie about a boy and his dog that seemed suitable. She queued up the movie and waited. When they all returned, Houston said, "I'd better get going. Thank you for dinner, Mr. Powell. It was nice meeting you, Max. Can I call you tomorrow, Sandi?"

"Um. Okay. Sure." She was disappointed he was not going to stay to watch a movie with them, but his asking to call her the next day was encouraging. "See you later."

Her father was the one to walk him to the door. This was too much friendship and not enough romance. She would have to do something about changing his attitude toward her.

Eighteen

Sunday morning, while Sandi was enjoying her cup of coffee, Houston texted her.

"Morning!"

She responded,

"Mornin"

"Whachu doin?"

"Breakfast"

"I'm off. Can I come over?"

"Sure"

Sandi said, "Houston's on his way over. Is that okay?"

"Of course," her father responded. "I like him. I'm glad you two worked everything out."

"We'll see."

"What do you mean by that? He's a nice boy, he's highly intelligent, and he seems kind. You're not going to find better than him out there."

"He abandoned me when I trusted him."

"So, he hurt your feelings for a bit. Don't be so stubborn. Get past all that. Dr. Phil asks, 'Do you want to be right, or do you want to be happy?' So, do you want to be happy?"

"Of course, I do."

"Then get past it and move on. What you laid on that boy is huge. It's a wonder he came around as fast as he did."

"That just makes me wonder what he wants."

"Oh, honey, not everyone has an ulterior motive. Sometimes you have to open up and let people in."

"Like you? You haven't let anyone in since Mom. You barely let me in."

"That's not fair. I do the best I know how with you. It's not easy being a single parent."

"That's been your choice. You could have remarried."

"I haven't found the right one."

"You haven't even looked, Dad."

"It's hard."

"You would have to open up. You'd need to make yourself available. You might just have to get out of your rut and try to engage with women. It's not going to be long before I'm gone, and you'll be all alone. I want you to have someone to share your life with."

"I'm happy as I am."

Sandi just sipped her coffee, refusing to look at him, while Max worked on his French toast pieces. He sure did like maple syrup. Her father wasn't going to listen to her. He never did. One day soon, she would be able to walk away, and she would never look back.

"All I was trying to say," her father continued, "was don't be so stubborn and give the boy a break."

"How about you don't talk to me about *stubborn*? I apparently learned it from you."

Silence.

Sandi got up and refreshed her coffee. She had to distance herself from him for a moment. She was without a mother because of his stubbornness. Who was he to insist she get over Houston's pain so quickly?

The doorbell rang. "I'll get it," she said. She was the one currently standing.

"Hi!" Houston said enthusiastically. "Are you done with breakfast?"

"No. Come in. Want some French Toast?"

"Naw. I ate. It smells great, though. Hi, Max! Hi, Mr. Powell."

"Hi, Stun!" Max said.

Sandi laughed. "It's Hou-ston, Max. Can you try again? Houston?"

Max tried and got closer.

Mr. Powell pulled at the chair on his right. "Have a seat. Sandi, get the boy a plate. Surely, you can eat a few pieces of French toast and some sausage."

"Do you want a cup of coffee?" Sandi asked.

"That I'd love. Just cream, please."

Sandi set a cup of java in front of him.

"A plate," her father said.

She got him a plate and fork and sat back down.

"You still need to eat too," her father said, addressing her.

"For the love of all that's holy, I will! I just want to enjoy my coffee."

Her father shook his head. "So, Houston, what's on your agenda today?" her dad asked.

"I'm not sure yet. I was going to see what Sandi was doing and what she wanted to do. I do want to discuss prosthetics with her and possibly using your lab."

"And there it is," Sandi said as she set her mug on the table.

Both men looked at her.

"Of course, you can use our lab, son," her father said.

Houston asked Sandi, "There what is?"

"I wondered what you wanted me for. You think you need me for the lab. Well, I'll tell you what, it's technically my dad's lab, so I'll leave you two to it. I'm going to my room. I've lost my appetite." She set her mug on the table and got up to walk away.

Houston shot to his feet to get in front of her before she could leave the room. "Now, wait one stinkin' minute. The lab is *not* why I'm here.

I'm here for you. I made a mistake. I'm trying to make it right. You have to give me a chance."

"I don't have to give you anything more. I was just trying to figure out what it was you wanted, and now I know."

"Apparently, you don't. You don't know me, and you're not even going to give me a chance?

"Why should I? I can't trust you. You only want me for what's in it for you, like everyone else.

"Sandi!" her father said. "I'm sorry, Houston. She's been saying things like this since before you got here."

"Please, Sandi, don't be like this. You haven't even given me a chance to prove I just want to be your friend."

Ooh, there it was again. He made her so mad. He just wanted to be friends. Couldn't he see her for more?

He continued, "You can't even give me a chance? I didn't tell your secret. I won't betray your trust again. Let me prove it."

Sandi stood in silence, looking up at him.

"Well, say something," Houston begged. "Anything."

"Okay." It looked like it was friends or nothing.

"Okay?"

"Okay."

Houston gathered her up in his arms in a warm embrace. "Thank you. I won't let you down, I promise."

"Don't make promises you can't keep."

"I'm not. You'll see."

"Now, can we eat the rest of this meal without drama?" her dad asked.

"Ama," Max said.

They all laughed. Sandi's dad dropped a couple of pieces of French Toast and some sausage on the plates on either side of him. "Now, eat."

Halfway into the meal, her father started asking questions about Houston's thinking on making prosthetics better and more affordable. They were instantly lost in conversation over it. Sandi had ideas of her own but would let them hash out their theories.

Sandi cleaned up the kitchen while her men sat at the table and chatted.

"Do you want to play downstairs with us, Max?" Sandi asked.

"Play," Max announced.

"Come on. Let's get you set up. Meet us down there whenever you're done." She led Max by the hand. "You're my good boy."

Max said proudly, "Gooboy."

"That's right. Good boy. I trust you will never betray me. Let's work on your sentences, shall we?"

Sandi had worked with Max for over an hour and had given up on Houston joining her today. Her father was going to monopolize all his time. She was a little disappointed he seemed to only want to be friends. She had secretly hoped for more.

Houston did have fresh thoughts and ideas. She wanted to be the one to think these things through with him. She knew her father well enough to know he wasn't going to give him up without a fight. When Houston came down the stairs with her father on his heels, she wasn't surprised. So much for just the two of them discovering a solution. What happened to her father not being interested in working with her in the lab anymore?

"We've been talking about the regeneration of limbs based on your work with Max," Sandi's dad said.

She just nodded.

"Yeah," Houston added, "what do you think about trying to use stem cells to grow out the partial limbs paraplegics have to work with already?"

"Funny you should ask. That's what I wanted to talk to you about," Sandi said.

"I think we can do it," her father interjected.

"You didn't want anything to do with working with me on this when I came to you. Why are you so interested in this, Dad?"

"I was concerned, and rightly so, that you would end up creating a creature and have to dispose of it when it went wrong. I didn't want you to get hurt. Thankfully, it worked out. We always used to do experiments together."

"That was a long time ago, and I've begged you," Sandi said sadly.

"There's no time like the present," her father said. "Let's do this. We first need to see if and how the stem cells will attach to existing tissue.

We need to take tissue scrapings and work from there. Nothing like creating a human being, but the concept should be similar. We just aren't breathing life into it. Just motivating the cells to reproduce."

Sandi had to admit, this was exciting. This way would be the most natural and cost-effective. No longer would people have to lose everything they had worked for due to the loss of a body part. Especially, in her mind, a limb. There was no reason they couldn't extend limbs. But why hadn't someone figured this out before the three of them in a home lab? Why hadn't her grandfather, with his enormous team of research scientists?

"Who's going to give up some of their tissue for this experiment?" Sandi asked.

"I will," her father offered.

"Actually," Houston said, "what if we use my mother's? She's numb on the ends of her stumps. I'm sure she would let us use hers. Especially when she learns what we intend to do. I told her about Max last night. She was shocked and fascinated. She shouldn't be too surprised by our thoughts of taking your research a step further. Can I call her?"

"That's not a bad idea," Sandi's dad said. "Yeah, call and see if she'll be a willing participant."

Houston called his mother. As he was explaining, she was obviously asking many questions. He climbed the stairs to leave them.

"I would imagine she would have questions," her dad said.

"Yeah, but this could be huge for her. What if we can restore her limbs and give her back her life?"

"It's still a big *if.*"

Houston returned. "She'd like to meet all of you and ask some questions. She's skeptical, to say the least. Not that I blame her, but I've tried to make her understand. Do you mind going to my house? I offered to go get her and bring her here, and she refused."

"Not at all," Sandi's father said. "Let's go. Do you just want me to go with you, Houston?"

"If you don't mind, will all of you come? She'd like to meet Max and ask Sandi some questions as well."

Sandi looked shocked. "She wants to talk to me, not my dad?"

"Oh no, she wants to talk to him too. She just has a lot to discuss. I figured since we were just talking about a small amount of tissue, she'd be okay with the donation, but she had too many questions. Since I wasn't involved in the Max experiment, I can't answer them. I'd feel better if all of you would talk to her."

"Sure, son, we'll go with you. Right, Sandi?"

"Yes, of course. Come on, Max, let's go get cleaned up. You're about to go on your first car ride."

"Oh!" Houston said. "I'm really sorry. Our house is pretty small. It's just us now. I try to keep it up, but I'm no housekeeper."

"No apologies necessary," Mr. Powell said. "We don't consider things like that. Let's just see if we can answer all your mother's questions and get to work on making her whole again."

SANDI HAD QUITE a time showing Max that he would be all right with the seatbelt across his body and it would keep him safe. Max had no intention of being strapped down in one place that wasn't his wheely chair, and he'd never had a belt across his chest. Her father wasn't out of the house yet, so she finally asked Houston if she could show Max what she would be doing using him. Since Houston was riding shotgun, and Max would be behind her dad, she knew Max would be able to see. As she was leaning over Houston to make the connection, she paused and looked up at him. He grinned down at her. Sandi blushed, her heart skipped a beat, and they both looked away.

After Max saw Sandi buckle Houston in, he agreed to let her plug his seatbelt in too. Then she sat in the seat beside Max and showed him she was going to buckle up as well. Her dad got into the driver's seat and hooked his seatbelt.

Sandi said, "See, Max, we all have to be safe."

Houston's house and yard were pretty. There were flowers in the garden beds, and the house was a pretty yellow with white trim. He was right; it was much smaller than the house she'd grown up in, but she liked it. It looked cozy, not cold, as she always thought their own house felt. Inside was a simple ranch-style on a single level with minimal furniture. She guessed it was necessary for the wheelchair. It was a home, not just a house. There were family photos around the room and on the walls in the hall. This was what she imagined a home felt like.

Houston's mother had made a tray with tea, cream, sugar, cups, spoons, and butter cookies.

"You didn't have to go to any trouble," Mr. Powell said.

"No trouble," she said. She was a pretty woman. Sandi guessed the accident had taken a toll on her. She must have been stunning before. Now, she had dark circles under her beautiful blue eyes. Sandi knew where Houston's came from. "Houston, will you carry the tray to the living room for me?"

He did as he was told.

"Please, everyone have a seat," his mother invited. "Make yourselves at home. From what I hear, it's nowhere near as grand as your house. It's the best we could do."

"This is a lovely home," Sandi said.

"You're sweet, dear. I see why my son has taken a shine to you."

"Mom," Houston piped up.

"Mrs. MacAvoy, this is some boy you have here. You must be so proud," Sandi's dad said.

"I am, and please, call me Grace," she responded.

"Grace. What a beautiful name," her father said.

Sandi and Houston passed a look between them.

"So, this is the infamous Max," Grace stated.

"He is," Houston said. "Max, can you say hello to my mom?"

"Hi, Mom," Max said.

They all laughed.

"Her name is Mrs. MacAvoy," Sandi corrected. "Can you say 'Hi, Mrs. MacAvoy?'"

"Hi, Ms. Mavoy," Max said.

"Good job," Grace said. "He's very smart for as young as Houston said he is. His size is quite deceptive."

"This is all Sandi," Mr. Powell said. "I had no idea what she was creating in the lab."

"Yes, which leads me to the questions Houston said he couldn't answer. What made you do this? Create Max. Was there a purpose? A reason? A necessity?"

"No," Sandi said, lowering her head to hide her shame. She had no intention of telling her true reason. "I just conceived of it. My dad had done research in this area years ago. He gave me his research journals, and I took it from there."

"Now, do I have this right—you're *the* Powells?"

"Well, I believe my father is who you're thinking of," Sandi's dad said.

"Still, it makes sense that you're from that family. And Sandi's mother died in childbirth, is that right?"

Sandi's dad looked away.

Sandi said, "Yes."

"You never remarried?" Grace asked.

"No. I was busy raising Sandi and just got lost in my work. I opted for a career over a relationship."

"I'm sorry to be so intrusive."

"No. You're fine," he said. "What is it you do?"

Grace looked down in seeming embarrassment. "I'm no longer able to work. I'm on disability now," she said with an undertone of hostility.

"What did you do previously?" Sandi's father persisted.

"I was in sales. I sold real estate. I wasn't the highest producer, but I made a good living. We lived well."

"I'm sure you did," Mr. Powell said. "I'm hoping that, between the four of us, we can get you back there."

"That's a bit farfetched, don't you think?" she retorted.

"No. I don't believe so. If we can apply similar principles from Sandi's discovery, I don't see why we can't restore your limbs. They may not be exactly as they were previously, but from what I understand, what you've been left to deal with is more painful than helpful," her father explained.

"That is very true," Grace said a bit more softly.

"Mom, we were talking at breakfast this morning, and I think we're on to something. I would love to try if you're willing."

"At breakfast?" she asked. "I thought you ate breakfast here."

They all laughed.

"Don't blame him," Mr. Powell said. "He's a growing boy. I insisted he eat with us too."

"I see. So, what would I need to do?" Grace asked.

Sandi spoke up, "We would start with harvesting some of your stem cells. We would then do a light scraping at the ends of your limbs, then introduce your stem cells into the sampling. Once we see if they will grow, as we believe they will, we would like to graft them back onto you and encourage the regrowth of your limbs."

"What makes you think you can do something like this when no one else has done it? No offense," Grace said.

"None taken," her father interjected. "The fact is, others have been doing this work for some time now. My father, for one."

"Then why isn't it out there?" she asked.

"Some brilliant ideas get lost in red tape."

"Why me?"

"Why not you?" he responded. "You are in a unique situation. You have a brilliant, passionate son, who has a brilliant, passionate friend."

His mother grinned. "So, brilliant, passionate minds."

"And I'm going to help them," Sandi's father said.

"What do you anticipate happening?" Grace asked.

"We believe we can regrow your arm and leg," Mr. Powell said.

"I don't believe that will happen, but I'll go along for the lark and in the name of your research," Grace said. "How are we going to do this?"

"It can't hurt to try," Houston said. "What have you got to lose?"

"If you don't mind," Sandi began, "I'd like to secure a scraping from both limbs. I'd like to see if one does better than the other and how that will work."

"Now? Here?" Grace asked with surprise in her voice.

"No. Ideally, I'd like to do this in our lab. We will need to extract your stem cells as well. We have all the equipment to do that back at the house."

"I can carry her," Houston said. "You know, into the house and up and down the stairs."

"We can both do that," Mr. Powell said.

"She's not heavy. I don't mind," Houston said.

Sandi now understood where his muscle development had come from.

"Can I sleep on this?" Grace asked.

"Of course you can," Sandi's dad said. "Take all the time you need. We're not going anywhere."

"Good. This is a lot to take in. I don't want to be given false hope. I would love to have my life back. I just don't want to be disappointed. I've lost too much already."

"If I didn't believe we could do this, we wouldn't be here having this conversation," Mr. Powell said. "We would be working with any tissue in the lab instead of giving it practical application on the first shot."

"Speaking of the 'first shot,' how many times do you anticipate it will take to get it right?" Grace asked.

"I'm hoping no more than three," Sandi said. "Thankfully, Max was my first try. I had researched a lot before adding the oxygen, which started the whole ball rolling. With this, we're trying to be very specific on what we're growing and how it is to grow and develop. I say no more than three."

"I would agree with her on that," Sandi's father said. "Given what we now know, I won't be surprised if we get it right on the first try, but certainly no more than the third. Are you game?"

"This isn't a 'game' to me! This is my life, my future you're suggesting you play with," Grace said.

"I wasn't suggesting in any manner this is something to toy with. It was a simple figure of speech. Please accept my apologies if I came off as insensitive."

"Sure. I'll give you my answer tomorrow."

It was getting late. Sandi had let Max eat too many cookies to hold him over. "We need to get home and get Max some dinner."

"You are welcome to eat with us," Grace offered. "Just give me a moment to dig something up."

Mr. Powell spoke up. "If you don't mind, I can order some pizzas. We don't want to put you out."

"It's no bother, but we love pizza. I'm sure it sounds good to Houston, He could eat pizza for dinner every night."

"Mom!" Houston said.

"That sounds great," Sandi spoke up. "I could certainly do pizza."

"Then it's settled. What toppings does everyone like?" Sandi's dad was back in control, where he was most comfortable.

Nineteen

When Sandi got to school, Houston was standing on the sidewalk in front of her parking space. Her heart leapt, then plummeted. *Was something wrong?* she wondered.

She got out of her car pulling her backpack with her. "Did something happen with your mother? What's wrong? What's happened?"

He laughed. "Wrong? Why would there be anything wrong?"

"Well...you're here... you've never—"

He cut her off. "I was early, so just thought I'd meet you before school started."

"Is your mother okay? Has she made a decision?"

She heard someone say, "Eeugh, Houston, get away from Messy, you might catch something!"

Someone else responded, "Looks like it's too late."

"You should go, I don't want to ruin your reputation," Sandi said in almost a whisper.

"No. You're my friend. They can get over it. Just ignore them," Houston demanded.

"Where have you been all my life?"

He laughed. "Right here, oblivious to who you are. We should start every day like this."

"I agree completely. Where do you park? I'll be happy to meet you there some mornings."

"No, I can meet you here. It's easier. I'm in general parking. There's never any telling where I'll be."

"I'm sorry. My father insisted I have an assigned space."

"Don't apologize. If I could, I would."

"I just don't want it to be a thing between us. My money, I mean."

"Oh, it's not. I'm not too proud to let you pick up the tab when necessary."

They laughed.

"I've got to get to class. I'll see you later in Physics?" Houston queried.

"Yup. Bye," Sandi said to his retreating back.

"Bye," Kristy said in a nasty parroting tone.

Seriously? Kristy had to destroy her moment. Sandi wanted to slice her with words, but she remembered what Houston had said about ignoring them and held her tongue. It was so hard. She hit her key fob to lock her car, ignored Kristy, and walked into the building. Kristy followed, taunting her the whole way. Sandi stood her ground. She was really pretty proud of herself. This was the first time she didn't even attempt to retaliate.

"I'm talking to you, little maggot. Answer me," Kristy said, now indignant.

Sandi walked into her homeroom and took her seat. She was going to make herself a countdown sheet to be out of this hell hole. This made sense. Maybe if she continued to simply ignore the haters, they would eventually give up and go away. It took at least two to fight. If she didn't give them fuel, sooner or later, the fire would have to go out. She sat through roll call feeling pleased with herself.

In her first block class, as sure as the sun was coming up every morning, Jackson began his torments as soon as her butt hit the seat. She said nothing. He kept it up. She held her tongue. He yanked her ponytail, "I'm talking to you, smelly."

"Jackson!" the teacher said, "Keep your hands to yourself. Sandi, are you alright?"

Sandi was shocked. Her teacher had never stood up for her before. She had only ever given Sandi a hard time. Why this change? All year, at some point in every class, Jackson would pull her ponytail, usually several times. This teacher had never said anything before. "Yes, ma'am," she said in response.

Jackson said in a whiny voice in Sandi's ear, "Sandi, are you alright?" She ignored him.

At lunch, Sandi was thrilled when she returned home to find Max happy and content. Max greeted her at the back door with a big hug. "Sandi home."

Ms. Fields was true to her word. At her seat was a plated sandwich and iced tea.

"Sandi eat with Max," Max said.

"Wow! Good job!" Sandi was impressed at his ability to form a full sentence so quickly under Gretchen's tutelage. "That is wonderful progress, Gretchen. Thank you."

"Oh, it's nothing. Max is very smart. We have had a great morning, haven't we, Max?" she said.

"Went to park," Max said proudly.

"You did? Did you have fun?" Sandi asked.

"Fun on swing," Max announced. "Whee!"

Sandi chucked. "I'm so glad. What's on the agenda for this afternoon?" Sandi addressed Gretchen.

"I don't know any other languages, but Max has thrown some words at me this morning. I was thinking maybe I could learn some of them along with him. I do want to continue to work with him on basic math as well."

"That's ambitious. Good for you. He seemed to do well yesterday with the German. I hate to eat and run, but I can't be late for class. I'll be back. Have a great afternoon."

"Bye, Sandi," Max said.

Sandi hugged him and left with a heart full of pride.

Sandi's afternoon went much like her morning had. The typical harassment by peers and staff. She felt she was getting better at not responding. She wasn't sure how long she could keep this up. Every time she thought about lashing out, she thought of Houston and kept silent.

Houston was at Physics class before her. He gave a big smile when he saw her. Butterflies were going crazy in her stomach. She felt like she was glowing. She liked seeing Houston like this but hated that he would become the butt of everyone's jokes. She slipped into her seat.

He leaned across the aisle and said, "Hey, how's your day?"

There erupted a huge commotion, and all the tongues started wagging.

"What are you doing?" Sandi asked.

"What? Talking to my friend. Is it supposed to be a secret? I didn't know," Houston said.

"I was going to keep it a secret for your sake. You just put a huge target on your back."

"Oh, please. Like I care! Let 'em talk. It's the truth, isn't it? Aren't we friends?

"Well, yeah. But you could have saved yourself a lot of harassment if you kept it between us."

"I don't care."

"You know they all hate me here. Now they'll transfer that to you."

"Seriously, what are they going to do to me? Act like high school?" Houston had a very matter-of-fact look on his face.

The teacher walked in. The commotion didn't subside as usual. "This is still my class, right? Settle down!"

Silence.

When class was over, Houston leaned over to whisper in Sandi's ear, "Stay put."

She did as he instructed. Once the class had fully dismissed, he stood and nodded at her. Sandi picked up her backpack.

"Zip it up," he said.

Grinning, she did as he said.

"Now, pay attention on your way to your next class. Be alert. I have to work tonight, so I'll call you after, okay?"

"Ah, sure. Why did we wait?"

"Because this puts us in control walking out of class, so no one can blindside us. Stay aware. Why this has started something makes no sense to me, but the less we make of it—while staying vigilant for now—the quicker it will die down. They'll all move on to their next pettiness. Trust me."

"I do trust you."

"Have a great rest of your day. Call ya later."

They turned in opposite directions toward their respective classes.

Sandi felt like she was floating, which made it hard to keep her head and pay attention to everyone around her, as Houston had warned her to. Snide comments followed her all the way to her last class, but she ignored them all.

Kristy followed her to her car. "What are you holding over sweet Houston's head to make him talk to you?"

Sandi kept walking, trying to ignore her.

"I'm talking to you, scab."

Sandi did as Houston said and didn't answer.

Kristy shoved her. "Don't ignore me. I'm talking to you."

Like magic, Houston appeared by her side. "Problem, Kristy?"

"Yeah, as a matter of fact. You are too good for the likes of this maggot."

"Careful. That's my friend you're talking about."

"Why?"

"Why what?"

"Why her?" Kristy drew out the word "her."

"Why not her? She's got a brilliant mind, she's kind, and she's good company."

"Ugh. Gross. She's pond scum is what she is."

It was taking all Sandi had not to fight this battle herself, but she kept her mouth shut.

"What's she ever done to you that you didn't bring on yourself?" Houston asked.

"She's breathing the same air."

"That's not an answer. Has she ever done anything to you that you haven't provoked?"

Kristy opened her mouth, then closed it.

"That's what I thought," Houston said. "Now, go away and stop harassing her. You're better than being a bully, Kristy. You lead and the rest will follow."

She turned on her heels, flipped her blond head of hair over her shoulders, and stomped off.

"I can't believe you're here," Sandi said. "I thought you had to work."

"I do. I saw her going after you and thought I'd rather be late than allow her to torment you. What is her deal with you?"

"Your guess is as good as mine. We've never really been friends; she was always nasty to me, but every year, it just gets worse. I don't get it. She's got a mom and a dad, an older sister, all these friends, and I think she gets decent grades."

"She could be jealous of you."

"For what? I don't have anything."

"You are a Powell. I'm sure, like everyone else in this place, she knows you come from money."

"You said that's not what you want me for."

"I don't. You're fun to be around, you have a quick wit, but mostly, I want you for that big brain of yours."

"It's not like I'm pretty, like the other girls here are."

"Are you kidding? You can't be serious! Their beauty comes from products, yours comes from within. Yours is natural."

"No one has ever suggested I'm beautiful in any way. I'm just a plain Jane."

"There's nothing plain about you, and your name isn't Jane." He winked at her. "I've gotta run. I'm gonna be late if I don't go." He ran off in the other direction.

Wow! She had never seen herself as any kind of beauty. What did Houston see that she missed? It was no matter now; he had come to her rescue yet again. She was grateful. This is what she'd always imagined it would be like to have someone who was on her side. Someone who appreciated her for who she was. Not her family's money, not the school punching bag, but intelligent Sandi who could hold her own in a debate or speak with authority on any subject. She wanted to see herself as Houston saw her. She would have to work on it.

AT 9:30 P.M., Sandi's phone rang. Her heart skipped a beat when Houston's picture appeared on the screen.

"Hi," Sandi said.

"Hi yourself! I hope it's not too late to call you. My mom always had the rule: no phone calls after 9 p.m. But I told you I'd call after work, and I just got out."

"No, you're fine to call me any time."

"Hey! I wanted to talk to you about this afternoon. Did something happen between you and Kristy that I'm not aware of? I know you said she's always been this way to you, but what exactly happened to make it start?"

"She's never been nice to me. I do know that years ago, she asked me for help with her homework. It turned out, what she really wanted was for me to *do* her homework. When I refused, she became unbearable. She's not that bright. I usually talk circles around her, and I think it makes her even more angry with me. I can't seem to help myself. She's such an easy target. I never take the first shot, but I won't just stand by while she humiliates me."

"Nor should you. I just wondered if there was something I was missing. A couple years ago, she came on to me pretty heavy. When I wasn't interested, she got nasty with me. I know most people don't tell Kristy *no* for anything. I think because you aren't afraid of her, there's nothing you need from her, nor anything she can do for you, she targets you more than others. Good for you the way you stand your ground. It can't be easy. Especially since so many in this school follow her lead. I just think if we stand firm together, we show we're not backing down, and stay aware of our surroundings, like this afternoon when Kristy was blatantly coming after you—"

"I had no idea she was there. I didn't know to look for her."

"Right. That's what I'm talking about. For now, until they get tired of us and move on to the next thing, just pay more attention to who's around you, where you're going, who could be targeting you, so you aren't blindsided by Kristy, her Barbie girls, or Betty the Beast and her goons."

"Okay."

"It shouldn't take long before they get tired of falling on their faces. You tend to stay lost in all your thoughts. I get it, there's a lot going on in there." He chuckled.

"Sure."

"After this week, does it look like you'll eat lunch with me?"

There was a long pause.

"Sandi?"

"Yeah, I guess. Are you sure about all of this? High school is tough enough, you don't need to make it harder trying to make it look like we're friends."

"I thought we *were* friends."

"No, we are. I just don't want you to take the harassment because of your association with me. I'm accustomed to it. You've never had to deal with it."

"I really do like spending time with you. I want to talk with someone who can keep up. I want you to talk projects with me. I've never met a girl who can carry on a conversation about more than makeup and gossip. I should have given you a chance sooner."

"Why didn't you?"

"You're so strong and self-assured, I just knew you wouldn't want to be bothered with me. So I kept myself busy with everything else I have going on and tried not to think about you much."

"You thought about me?"

"Of course! You really don't get it, do you?"

"Get what?"

"Never mind."

Sandi laughed.

"You're a threat to most. You give me a run for my money, and I'm smarter than the average bear. You come across as untouchable, so no one tries. I took a risk, and it paid off."

"It almost didn't."

"Yeah. I know. I was scared. I really thought you were way out of my league, and I needed to walk away. Thanks for giving me another chance."

"I thought you were going to blow the whistle on me, and the authorities were going to raid the house."

"Really? That thought never crossed my mind. I told you I wouldn't tell on you."

"Thanks. I'm glad I can trust you."

"No matter what happens between us, I will never betray your trust. Even if we never fixed our misunderstanding, I would never try to hurt you."

"Wow! Only my dad has ever been on my side for anything, as I'm sure you've witnessed at school. This is something new for me. It's always been this way. If you hadn't noticed, the teachers are just as mean to me as the other students."

"That's because they're afraid."

"Afraid of what?" Sandi said indignantly.

"Your brains. I'm sure they're all threatened because you probably know more about every subject they teach than they do. How would it look if you corrected something they didn't have right, or filled in with more than they know? If they keep you down, they can remain above you in the sight of everyone else."

"I never thought of it that way. You're probably right. It's dumb but accurate. Do I come off as a know-it-all?"

"No. You come off as highly intelligent. That's a threat to most."

"Not to you?"

"No. I've gotten to know you. I'm encouraged and only want to learn everything I can from you. I think we can make a great team, and I'm excited to see what we come up with."

"Me too. That makes me very happy."

"You know what I was most surprised by, as I've gotten to know you better?"

"What?"

"You're open to others' ideas and thoughts. Just because you're smarter than me, you don't dismiss my ideas."

"That's how we learn. And I don't think I'm smarter than you."

"Well, you are. You don't treat me that way, but you are. I'm okay with that."

"I've always just wanted a friend. Thanks for being that for me."
"You're welcome. It's getting late. I have to go."
"Okay. Good night."
"Night."

Twenty

She emerged from her shower to find Max sitting on the floor, watching her. "Max! What are you doing in here?" She quickly wrapped a towel around her nakedness.

"Sandi takes a stand-up bath?" he asked innocently.

"Yes. I take a bath standing up. You shouldn't be in here."

"Why?"

"Well, because..." How was she going to explain this one? He didn't take his baths alone. "I'm a girl, and you're a boy. Girls and boys shouldn't be in the bathroom together."

"Why?"

Oh boy! "It's not proper. You're getting big enough that you won't need someone in the bathroom to help you much longer. I'm old enough, I don't need assistance anymore. It's not polite."

"What's polite?"

"Polite means to be respectful and considerate of other people."

"Max is not polite?"

"You are learning."

He rose and left the room. Phew, that was awkward. She couldn't imagine the questions that she would have to field in the future.

When Sandi got to the kitchen, Max was already eating.

"Max is not polite, and Sandi takes stand-up baths," Mas announced.

Sandi blushed.

"What?" her father asked.

"Well, we had to learn that men and women use the bathroom alone."

He quirked an eyebrow at her. She waved her hands dismissively.

"I think Max is ready to learn to take showers now."

"Okaaay," her father said. "I'll just trust you on this. So, what do you have up today?"

"Houston has to work until this afternoon, but I think he's coming over after, and we're going to work in the lab."

"Has his mother made a decision yet?"

"I don't think so."

"Max work in the lab with Houston and Sandi," Max stated.

"Sure. You can work with us."

"I was thinking we should give Max some of his own Saturday chores," her father said. "What do you think?"

"Yeah, I like it. What would you like to start doing, Max?"

"Max do chores."

"Yes. I'll teach you to dust and vacuum. How does that sound? I can let him do the spare rooms and his room."

"Sounds reasonable. When he's a bit older, he can help me in the yard too."

After breakfast, Sandi started cleaning up. Max joined her. "Sandi teaches Max?" he asked.

"You want to learn to clean up the kitchen with me?"

"Yes."

"Well, okay. We rinse off the dishes and put them in the dishwasher like this. Cups, glasses, and bowls go on top, everything else goes on the bottom, the silverware and utensils go in here. At the end of the night, we run it. I'll let you do it with me a few times, then we can take turns."

"My turn?"

"I'll let you do the lunch dishes. Just watch me this time."

"Okay, I will watch."

"You're getting really good at your sentences. I can tell how much you and Gretchen have accomplished."

When they were done, she took him upstairs to show him how to tidy his room, strip his bed, vacuum, and dust. For now, she would clean both bathrooms. Once they were done with his room, she took the vacuum and duster to the room adjacent to his.

"Now, you vacuum and dust this room and the one across the hall while I clean the bathrooms. We don't change the bedding in these two unless we have guests. Understand?"

"Understand."

"If you have any problems, come get me."

"Max can't go in the bathroom with Sandi."

"If the door is open, you can stand in the doorway and talk to me. You just can't open the door and come in if it's closed."

Max tagged along with Sandi throughout all her chores. She taught him how to clean the glass, wipe down the kitchen, sweep and mop floors, make the beds, and do the laundry. When they all came together for lunch, her father asked how it was going.

"I think by next weekend, we'll each have our own set of chores. Max caught on fast, as usual. He's going to do the lunch dishes, and I'm going to supervise."

"Nice. Many hands make light work."

"What means 'many hands make light work?'" Max asked.

Sandi's father explained.

"Ooh. My hands are many?"

"Your hands plus my hands make many," Sandi said.

Max picked Sandi's hand up to look at it. She noticed how the simplest things they took for granted were new and different in Max's eyes. His gentle, attentive touch warmed her heart.

After the dishes were done, Max asked what was next. Since together they had kicked out everything she was responsible for, she told him it was free time, and he could do whatever he wanted.

He went to the living room to watch TV on his tablet.

"I'm going to be in the library if you need me," Sandi told him.

"Bye."

Sandi smiled her way down the hallway.

About an hour later, she went to check on Max.

"What are you watching?" she asked. It looked familiar.

"*When a Man Loves a Woman,*" he answered.

"Really? You're watching romance movies?" Sandi walked away shaking her head and chuckling to herself.

At 5 p.m., Houston showed up. Sandi's dad, who was making dinner, informed him he was eating with them.

"I don't want to intrude. I had just gotten off work, ran home to shower, and came here since we won't have a lot of time."

"No intrusion. When Sandi said you'd be here late this afternoon, I planned for you. You should have brought your mom. What's she having for dinner?"

"She always finds something. She's not ready to visit yet. Sorry."

"No need for apologies. I can only imagine what it must be like. We're going to do everything in our power to change that for her. Has she made a decision?"

"No. Not yet. She's nervous about all of it."

"Nervous about what?" Sandi asked.

"Well, she's concerned about the growth starting, not forming properly, and her ending up with limbs that can't be properly fit to prosthetics, then having to have them surgically removed."

"Oh dear," Sandi said, horrified. "No, we won't let that happen. Besides, I really don't believe that would happen. Look at Max. It was slow going for a bit, but everything formed as it should. I know it will happen for her too."

"I can understand her apprehension," her father said.

"Me too," Houston concurred. "Let's just give her time to think it all the way through. I feel certain she'll end up giving it a try."

After dinner, Mr. Powell told the three of them to head down to the lab, and he'd clean up the kitchen.

"I will help. Many hands make light work," Max announced.

"Sure," Sandi's dad said.

"This way, you can show him how to start the dishwasher, Dad."

"Happy to. Come on, Max, help me clear the table."

Houston followed Sandi to the basement. They started pulling beakers and Bunsen burners.

"What are we going to experiment with?" Houston asked.

"I'm not really sure. I'd like to work with cells to see their interaction when just looking at them without the whole being. You game?"

"Why? Are we using mine?"

She laughed. "Nope. Anonymous donor I've got in the freezer."

"Are you serious?"

"I am. My dad doesn't know, so don't tell."

"You know keeping secrets isn't a good idea."

"Yeah, well, it's left over from making Max. What he doesn't know won't hurt him, and I hope to learn enough to properly help your mom."

While they were working and talking, Sandi was telling Houston about Max watching romance movies.

"Do you think it's a case of hormones?"

"I hadn't thought of it. Could be. He just finished teething."

"He's not on a normal growth development path, you know?"

"Very true. I hope it's not up to me to tell him about the birds and the bees."

Houston laughed. "I don't want to be the one to tell him either. You need to leave that up to your dad."

Sandi suddenly realized that she couldn't remember him ever having that talk with her.

"You look like I just lost you. Where'd you go?"

"I was thinking about the fact my father has never talked to me about sex."

Houston thought for a moment and said, "My mom has never really talked to me about it either. Once, when I was about to leave on a date, she told me to make sure I never have unprotected sex, and that was it. I didn't quite know what to do with that. It wasn't like I was planning on going too far with her anyway."

"Have you gone too far before?"

He hesitated for so long, she figured that answered her question.

"How many times?" she asked.

"Just once."

"Do I know her? It was a *her*, right?"

"Yes, of course. We were too young, and we let our hormones get carried away."

"Did you love her?"

"Lust for her, yes. Love her, no."

"You never answered if I know her."

"I'm sure. It was a long time ago. We don't have any classes together. Whenever we're in the same vicinity, we avoid one another."

"Who is it?"

"What does it matter?"

"It might not, but it might. Is it someone who hates on me? Who wouldn't want us to be friends?"

"I doubt it. She's not like that."

"So, tell me who it is."

"Jana Proctor."

"Seriously? She's in my homeroom. She's one of the mean girls. You and Jana?" Sandi turned and began to walk away. Now, she understood the increased nastiness from Kristy, Jana's bestie. Just great!

Houston grabbed her arm. "Wait! Where are you going? We're long over. That was in middle school. We only dated for a few months. She means nothing to me. She didn't really mean anything to me then: she was pretty, and I was newly hormonal. It happened, it passed. I'm over it, as I'm sure she is too."

"Is that what you think? Boys are so clueless! Were you her first?"

"Yes. What does that have to do with anything?"

"Men really are from Mars! She and her pal Kristy have upped the ante since the school found out we're now openly friends."

"Kristy maybe, but not Jana."

"Oh, give me a break. Yes, Jana! A girl never forgets her first. How many people have you dated since her, and how has she treated them?"

"No one. Since my mom's accident, I haven't really had time for girls. More like, I haven't wanted to make time for girls."

"So, you haven't dated anyone else?"

"I've been on a couple casual dates, but nothing past an evening or event."

"Who broke it off?" Sandi asked.

"With Jana? It was mutual."

"Who started the conversation to end it?"

"I don't even remember. It was too long ago. We both weren't happy and decided to go our separate ways."

"Who first?"

"I'd really have to think back on it. I don't remember. It might have been me, but we both agreed."

"No. She may have agreed, but if she wasn't really ready to end it, she may still be holding onto something she wasn't ready to relinquish."

"What are you talking about? It's over. It's been over. We agreed. We moved on."

"*You* moved on," Sandi said. "You have no idea how she's now feeling. Jana has dated a lot of guys, but no one for any length of time. How do you know she's moved on? What you took from her, she can never get back. You'll always be her first. Girls hold onto those things for life. We don't forget anything. We're wired differently."

"You're being serious right now."

"Yes. This is very important. You can't take her feelings for granted. You moved on. What if she didn't? What if she just said what she thought you wanted to hear?"

He stood in silence a moment. "She would have told me."

"No, she wouldn't. She would need to save face, and as long as you believe it was mutual, the rest of the school believes it was mutual, and she isn't embarrassed."

Houston had a strange look on his face.

"What?" Sandi asked.

"I like having a girl for a friend. I had no idea."

Yeah, just a friend, not a girlfriend, Sandi thought. She had longed for Houston to be her boyfriend, but obviously, he lusted after the Janas of the world, not the Sandis.

Max bounded down the stairs. "Dishes done." He broke the awkward silence that had momentarily hung between them. She wished she could know what Houston was thinking.

Max inserted himself between them and hugged Sandi. "My Sandi."

She smiled, hugging him back. "And my Max."

Houston wrapped his big arms around them both and said, "My friends."

He really was clueless.

Twenty-One

A few weeks later, Sandi had gotten to the top of the stairs on the second floor. Max was waiting there for her. "Hey, Max. What's up?"

"Do you love me?"

"What?"

"Do you love me?"

"Of course I love you. Where's this coming from?"

"You don't kiss me."

"I kiss you all the time."

"No, you don't. You kiss me like you kiss Dad."

"Oooh...I see. Too many romance movies? Well...that would be because what you're talking about is a romantic love. We have a more familial love, so I kiss you like your family."

"I don't want to be your family. I want to be your romantic love."

"Oh, boy. We need to think about this. This is a little different. Come in here, let's talk about it."

Sandi led him into her room. She had him take a seat in her easy chair, and she sat on her bed.

"I'm not really sure where to start."

"At the beginning," Max said plainly.

"Good place. So, I created you, you understand that?"

"Yes."

"Well, the reason, at its core, was because I was lonely. I had no friends, and everyone at school was mean to me. I thought if I made myself a boyfriend, I would have at least one friend."

"A boyfriend?" Max stated simply.

Sandi looked at her hands in her lap. "Yes, a boyfriend. I thought it would validate me in the school if I had a good-looking boyfriend that other girls would want."

"Me?"

"Yes."

"I'm your boyfriend?"

"Well, no."

"Why?"

"There's nothing romantic between us. We're more like family. I hadn't thought it all the way through."

"Why can I not be your boyfriend? You don't love me?"

"No! I do love you, Max."

"You don't want me?"

"No. That's not it."

"What is it?"

"I don't know. I can't exactly see myself making out with you now."

"What is making out?"

"Kissing you passionately."

"Oh. I'm not kissable?"

"I didn't say that."

"Why can't we try?"

"I have to think about it. I don't know if that's really what I want anymore." Her mind went to Houston. "I do love you. Very much. I just don't know if I can love you romantically."

"When will you know?"

"Is this because you just want to kiss a girl?"

"I don't want to kiss a girl. I want to kiss you."

Sandi had to look away from his piercing blue eyes that reminded her too much of Houston's.

"Do you want to kiss me?" he asked.

"Oh, Max. I'm not sure. Can you let me think about it?"

"Yes." With that, he got up and left the room. He was always so matter-of-fact.

Sandi immediately felt as if most of the oxygen had been sucked from the room. She couldn't help but notice how physically attractive Max had become. She'd have to be blind to miss it. This was what she wanted, wasn't it? She wanted a boyfriend. She wanted someone the other girls would want but not be able to have.

When he was near her, she felt her body come alive; when she was away from him, she somehow no longer felt whole. She had always been attracted to Houston, but this was something more, something deeper, something almost visceral. She knew that if Houston someday walked away, she would mourn his loss but eventually get over it and move on. Not Max. If she ever lost Max, she wasn't sure she would ever get over it, if she would ever be able to move on to find someone else. She would no longer want to live in this world. Her life would never again be complete.

But she had created him. Now that he was reality, not just in her imagination, could she see herself romantically involved with Max? Sandi dropped herself backward on the bed and lay there looking at the ceiling a long while. What was she supposed to do with all this?

She absolutely loved Max, but could she be *in* love with him? She certainly noticed how sexy he'd become. Could she see him as desirable like that, wanting to kiss him more than just the occasional peck on the forehead or cheek? Or would she only ever see him as a family member, making her think any real relationship to be incestuous? This was too much right now. She would have to sleep on it. She was grateful Max hadn't pushed the issue. She wasn't sure how she would have responded with her back against the wall.

She began thinking over everything so far. If she hadn't created him, she would seriously want him as her boyfriend. He was smart, caring, good-looking, tall, dark, and handsome, with eyes she could get lost in and a smile to light the darkest room. He had an infectious personality that made her want to spend every minute of her day with him.

Sandi's father called up to her for dinner. She dragged herself up to get to the kitchen. She sure hoped this talk didn't make things weird with Max. There was only one way to find out.

When she got to the table, Max was standing beside her chair. She glanced quickly at her father and back to Max. Max smiled kindly at her and pulled out her chair for her. As she sat down, she said, "You don't need to pull my chair out for me, Max."

"I want to."

Her father's head snapped up like he had missed something. Sandi discreetly shook her head. He quickly looked down at his plate.

The meal felt strained and awkward for a bit until Max asked her father about his day in fully formed sentences in Spanish.

They both looked at Max as he raised his fork full of food to his mouth, paused looking at them over his potato-filled fork, then said, "What? Why are you looking at me like that?"

They both began to laugh. The scene struck Sandi as funny, and Mr. Powell said, "I just wondered if I'm supposed to answer you in Spanish or English."

"Either one. I fully understand them both."

"Oh, we are well aware," Sandi told him.

SEVERAL DAYS LATER, as Sandi was leaving her room, heading toward the stairs, Max was doing the same. His long legs took a couple of extra steps to put his hands on Sandi's waist. Backing her against the wall, lowering his lips to hers, he kissed her full on. Once the shock wore off, she put her hands around the back of his neck and kissed him back. She had never felt such a fire as was instantaneously ignited in her body. He intensified the passion, and she became lost in his taste, his feel, his love. Her knees grew weak, and she was glad he was holding her in place. When he pulled away, she felt like the room had gone cold. He gazed into her eyes for a long moment.

"How about now?" he said.

"How about now, what?" Sandi replied with a shaky voice.

"How do you like me now?"

"Um...uh...I..."

"Can you see me as your boyfriend now? I want you to be my girlfriend, Sandi."

She couldn't think straight. What could she say? If she ever had a doubt, it had just gone straight out the window. "Yes," was all she could manage to say.

"Yes, you'll be my girlfriend?" He lowered his head to be level with her eyes.

"Yes. I will be your girlfriend."

"I'm so happy."

He took her hand to head for the stairs. She quickly pulled out of his grasp. "Wait."

"What?"

"Not yet?"

"Why not?"

"I need to prepare my father. I don't think this is going to be easy for him."

"We can tell him together."

"I would prefer to tell him by myself."

"Okay, when?"

"This weekend."

"We can't be together until this weekend?"

"We are together."

"No, we aren't. I want to kiss you whenever I want. I want to make love to you—"

She cut him off. "Whoa there. We're not crossing that line."

"You don't want to make love with me?"

"I didn't say that. I'm saying not yet, not this weekend, maybe not ever."

"Why not?"

"That's a whole other level that I don't believe either of us is ready for. Let's just take this one step at a time. The first step is for me to tell my father. The next will be to date. Then to kiss like you just kissed me. Then, and only if we're both ready, will we take that last step."

"That will be a long time."

"You'd be surprised. Please, we need to take this slow. For my sake."

"For you? Okay. I will take it slow."

"Thank you. Now go see if dinner is ready, and I'll be right there."

～

SANDI SENT Houston a text asking him to call her on his way home from work. Moments later, her phone rang.

"Hey," she answered.

"What's up?"

"Are you out of work and on your way home?"

"No. I'm at home. I got out early. Is something wrong?"

"No, nothing's wrong. I needed my friend to talk to."

"Really? What happened?"

"A funny thing happened in the hallway tonight."

"In the hallway? What hallway? What happened?"

She led with the conversation several days ago and ended with Max telling her he wanted to make love to her.

"Whoa...wow!"

"Yeah, I know."

"What are you going to do?"

"Exactly what I said I was going to do. Talk to my father about it and get his blessing first."

"Do you think he'll give it?"

"I don't know, but I won't sneak around behind his back in his home. I was wondering if you would mind talking with Max for me?"

"Me? About what?"

"About sex. About safety. About the ramifications and what a big step this is. I've never been a teenage boy. I don't know what's going through his mind. I'm not willing to be a warm body just because he has raging hormones."

Houston laughed. "I get ya. I thought we were going to put that on your dad."

"That was before we were talking about his daughter."

"Yeah, I'll talk to him. It will have to be this weekend. I work every night this week and have a project due next week."

"That's fine. I told Max I'm not going to talk to my dad until this weekend anyway. Thanks, Houston."

"Don't thank me yet. I haven't talked to him yet. He may not go for this."

It was Sandi's turn to chuckle. "I trust you wholeheartedly."

THE WEEKEND CAME TOO QUICKLY for Sandi's liking. She knew she was about to have a difficult conversation she'd really rather not have with her father.

When Sandi got to the kitchen, Max was already at the table. It had been a strained few days with him. She was so glad to have had Gretchen for a buffer. She did keep him busy and hadn't asked questions regarding his obvious growth and development. Her father had already taught him how to shave. His voice changed overnight, and he sounded so much like Houston, it was unnerving at times. She noticed he was looking more like Houston every day, which made it that much more difficult to try to control herself.

Max's face lit up as it always did when she entered the room. She, on the other hand, tried hard to shut down her emotions whenever she was near him now. She quickly looked away and headed for the coffee pot.

"Good morning, Sandi," he said.

"Morning, Max, Daddy."

"Morning, princess," her father said and hugged her. "Plans today?"

"Not entirely fleshed out yet. Houston is coming over before he goes to work."

"Should I make extra for breakfast?"

"No, he's fine. He eats with his mom."

"No news on that front?"

"Not yet. I get where she's coming from, I just wish she'd let us try."

"It's a big deal. Scary. Give her time."

"I am."

Her father turned to Max. "What are your plans for the day, Max?"

"Whatever Sandi's are."

Sandi froze mid-sip while leaning against the counter. She looked up to see both of them looking at her expectantly. Her brain seemed to shut down. "I need at least one cup of coffee before I can answer that."

"Come sit down and eat," her father said.

She took her seat, and her father made her plate. She really wished he wouldn't always push food on her.

"Daddy, please. Can't I, for once, just have coffee?"

"Not on my watch." He laughed.

She shook her head.

"Have you decided yet?" Max asked.

"Decided what?" Mr. Powell inquired.

Sandi shot Max a look. "Not yet."

"Decided what?" her father asked again.

"After breakfast, we need to talk."

"You and I need to talk?" he queried.

"Yeah. If you don't mind."

"Nah, I don't mind. You don't want to talk about it now? Is it something Max can't hear?"

Why couldn't he just leave it alone? She just wanted to drink her coffee and fully wake up before having to address this with her dad.

"It has to do with me, so why can't I be here?" Max asked.

"Oh, for the love of all that's holy!"

"What?" her dad asked.

Sandi heaved a huge breath and said, "Fine. Now it is."

Her father set his fork down and looked between Sandi and Max.

"Okay." Sandi began. "You know the reason I made Max."

"Yes."

"And you know Max is now fully grown."

"Obviously."

"Well, Max has asked me to be his girlfriend."

"Is that right?"

"Yes."

"And what did you say?"

"I told him I needed time to think about it and to talk to you."

"I see. And what conclusion have you come to?"

Sandi felt her palms grow sweaty. Her brain felt like it wanted to shut down. She looked at her hands in her lap, then wiped them on her jeans.

Max reached over, taking both her little hands in one of his big ones. "I love her. I was made for her. I want her to be my girlfriend."

Sandi couldn't look up. The warmth of his hand on hers ran like an electrical current through her whole being.

"I see," was all her father said.

"You do?" Sandi asked.

"I guess the two of you are making yourselves pretty clear right now."

"Can Sandi be my girlfriend?" Max asked.

"That's not my decision to make," Mr. Powell said. "What do you want, Sandi?"

"I'm not sure. I do have feelings for him. This is a big step. I know it's what I wanted. Back then, it was just conceptual. Now that we're actually here, I'm not sure what to do. What do you think?"

They sat in awkward silence for a long time. He was taking the time to choose his words carefully.

"Well, there are going to have to be some boundaries put in place if this is what you both want. I don't think you should cross inappropriate lines. What does being Sandi's boyfriend look like to you, Max?"

"It looks like treating her like a princess, taking her on dates, pulling out her chair for her, putting my arm around her, making her feel safe and protected, talking to her about everything, listening when she has something to say, hugging her, and kissing her on the lips."

Wow, Sandi thought. He had really given this some thought, and she couldn't have asked for more from any boyfriend.

"It sounds like you have it all figured out," her father said. "Sandi, what are your thoughts?"

"Wow! Actually, I was thinking I couldn't have asked for more from a boyfriend. And yes, I would like to be your girlfriend, Max."

He leaned over and hugged her.

Her father cleared his throat. "Are the two of you willing to abide by my rules?"

Sandi wasn't really clear on what that was but nodded her head.

Max said, "Yes, nothing inappropriate. What is inappropriate?"

Sandi so wanted to laugh, but her father was being so serious, she knew that wouldn't go over well.

"It means you will not be having sex with my daughter. There will be no hot and heavy makeout sessions. It means if you can't control yourself around her, you will be taking cold showers."

At that, Sandi did laugh. She couldn't help herself.

"Why do I take a cold shower?" Max asked.

Sandi looked at her dad, who seemed at a loss for words. "To cool your jets, son."

"I don't have jets," Max said.

"Trust me on this. It will help you control your hormones," her father replied.

Sandi really wanted this meal to be over. She got up to refresh her coffee.

"You're not done until you eat something," her father said.

"I know. I'll eat. I just need more coffee."

"Yeah, for this conversation, I'll let you refill mine too."

SANDI WAS JUST FINISHING CLEANING up the kitchen when Houston arrived. Max was in his room. Sandi opened the door before Houston could ring the doorbell. She put her finger to her lips to indicate he should be quiet, pulled him into the house, and led him to the basement.

"What's the big secret?" Houston whispered.

"Oh boy! Before I could talk to my father, Max told him he wanted to be my boyfriend."

"Oh boy is right! What'd your dad say?"

"He said we just couldn't do anything inappropriate."

"Really?"

"Yeah, and he told Max, if necessary, he needed to take cold showers."

They both laughed.

"Shhh," Sandi said. "I wanted to talk to you alone before Max figures out you're here."

"So, what'd you decide? You going to date him? Is that weird for you?"

"I don't know. I thought it would be, but he's been so kind, so attentive, so tender, and loving. He has grown into what I made him for, a boyfriend."

Houston didn't say anything and just searched Sandi's eyes.

"What?" she finally said.

"I don't know. Are you sure this is what you want to do?"

"It's not like the boys are beating down my door." She wanted to state the obvious: that even he wasn't interested in her that way.

"But you shouldn't just settle."

"I don't feel like I'm settling." She looked at the floor.

"What?"

She shook her head.

"What? Tell me what you're thinking."

"It's embarrassing."

"Your father telling Max to take cold showers in front of you is embarrassing. Just tell me."

"The truth is, I had always hoped it would be you."

"Oh." Houston turned around. "I'm...I'm sorry, Sandi. I...I didn't know. You told me from the get-go you made Max for that. I think a couple should have a spark. You know what I mean?"

"Actually, I do because I did feel it when Max kissed me."

He turned back to face her. "You did?"

"Yeah, I sure did."

"Well, I guess there's your answer." The look on Houston's face was impossible for her to read. She wondered what was going on in his head.

"I guess it is."

"Do you want me to go?"

"No. Why would I?"

"I don't know. I don't want to get in your way."

"You've made it perfectly clear you just want to be friends. I have been maintaining that. I thought we were going to try to solve this problem for paraplegics together?"

"Me too."

"Well then, let's do this."

"So, it sounds like you don't need me to talk to Max anymore, right?"

"Actually, if you don't mind. I really would like you to still have that conversation with him. He should hear from someone who has been there what a big step having sex is and how you can't take that back."

"Well, I'm not sure I'm the right one for that talk. Remember, I was a bit clueless until you explained it to me."

"I don't feel like it should be me who tells him. I've never been a boy."

He chuckled. "You've got a point there. Okay, where is he?"

"In his room."

Houston took a deep breath and said, "You owe me one. And it's going to be a big one."

"You got it." She smiled.

Twenty-Two

For the first few days after the proclamation of Sandi and Max's relationship, things felt a bit strained. This was navigating new territory for both of them. Sandi had never had a romantic involvement before. Obviously, neither had Max. She needed to figure out how to move this into a place of normalcy.

"Hey, Max, what do you say we catch a movie and get a bite to eat after?"

"Outside the house?"

"Yeah, I was thinking like a date."

"Yeah, I want to go on a date with you."

"Great. You pick the movie, and I'll pick the restaurant. I'll let Dad know not to plan on us for dinner."

Max had never been to a movie theater. Sandi was excited to be with him to experience it for the first time. He was in awe. When the movie started and the sound was loud all around them, he looked at her with big eyes. She smiled and nodded her head.

He leaned over and whispered in her ear, "This isn't like home."

She shook her head.

He put his arm around her. She laid her head on his shoulder. She felt something she'd never experienced. She felt safe, secure and loved.

After the movie they went to her favorite pizza place. Over a large pepperoni, Max said, "Teach me how to drive a car."

"You want to learn to drive?"

"Yes. Then I can drive you on our dates."

Sandi chuckled and put her hand over her full mouth. She nodded. "After dinner, I'll take you to an empty parking lot and teach you like my dad did me."

"What have we here?" Kristy's voice cut through Sandi like a knife. This was going to be hard to not engage her like she'd like and instead heed Houston's advice.

"Kristy," Sandi said coldly.

"Who are you? You look familiar. Have we met?" Kristy said.

Max stood up while wiping his hands on his napkin, extended his right hand to her and said, "No. Hi, I'm Max."

"Shut the front door!" Kristy said. "You're Max?"

"I am."

It was taking everything Sandi had to keep her mouth shut.

"I thought you were just a figment of Crazy's imagination."

Max looked confused.

Kristy looked at Sandi. "So, where'd you find him?" Then looked at Max and said, "And what on Earth is someone as fine as you doing with the likes of her?" She hitched her thumb at Sandi.

"Sandi is my girlfriend."

"But why?"

"Because I love her."

"Well, then it's obvious you're not that bright."

"I possess an IQ of 152."

Kristy was momentarily rendered speechless. "Honey, you can do a lot better than her. If you're that smart, you should run."

Sandi couldn't stand it anymore and finally said, "Kristy. Mind your own business and get lost."

"I don't know what you're holding over Houston's head and now Max's, but it must be really big. No man would really want to be seen with you."

"I do," Max said defiantly.

"Then you need your head examined." She walked away.

"Who was that?" Max asked.

Sandi took a cleansing breath and looked at the table. "She's actually the reason I made you."

"She told you to make me?"

"No. She and her friends treat me like that all the time, so I decided to make you, so I would no longer be alone."

"Now you aren't. And you have Houston. What did she mean about holding it over Houston's head?"

"She thinks the only reason Houston is my friend is because I'm forcing him to be."

"But you're not. Are you?"

"No. We got to know each other and became friends. She's just jealous because he said she came onto him once and he shut her down."

"What does that mean?"

"She tried to get him to go out with her once and he wouldn't. He thinks that's why she is so mean to me, but she's always been mean to me."

"I'm sorry. She doesn't know you, does she?"

"No. She doesn't, and I have no interest in knowing her any more than I do. Are you ready to go?"

"Yes. Let's learn to drive."

SOMEHOW, Sandi's dad got Max the paperwork to validate him as a 16-year-old male born in another state. She didn't ask any questions. With that, Max was able to obtain his driver's license. Mr. Powell bought Max his own car. They had a four-car garage, so they might as well use it. Max couldn't wait to take Sandi on a date, giving him the opportunity to drive them.

Sandi suggested they visit the botanical gardens since Max had never been there. It was a beautiful, sunny day, and everything in the world just felt right to Sandi. They wandered the gardens holding hands. Max was so attentive, kind, and gentle with her. He opened her car door and always let her go ahead of him. She wondered where he had learned all this from, but he was so industrious, there was no telling. She was just glad for it. He really made her feel special. The way she'd always wanted to feel.

When they left, Max asked, "Where to?"

Sandi directed him to a place she'd only ever heard of, never been to. When she told him to stop, his response was, "Wow!"

She agreed. It was breathtaking. It overlooked the entire city. She could only imagine what it would look like at night. They got out of the car, walked to the edge of the cliff, and sat down, dangling their feet over the side. Max took her hand.

"You have made me so happy, Sandi."

"Me too."

He leaned over and kissed her. When he pulled back, she knew she wanted more. She let go of his hand and slipped it behind his neck, pulling him back to her lips. He intensified the kiss, and she felt her body catch fire. She pushed her tongue inside his mouth and felt his breath hitch. He laid her back, partially covering her with his body. He was so muscular, so desirable. She wanted him, body and soul.

Max abruptly sat up, catching his breath.

"What's wrong?" Sandi asked.

"I need a cold shower."

She laughed. "I do too. I really love you, Max."

"I really love you too. I want to make love to you, but we aren't allowed."

Sandi thought about it for a moment and said, "One day we will."

"Really?"

She just nodded, getting lost in those pools of blue.

Twenty-Three

At the end of the school day, on her way to her car, Sandi was doing as Houston had always warned and going slow, watching out for all those around her. That was why she was able to stay on her feet when Betty came barreling at her from her left. Sandi caught the motion out of the corner of her eye, took a step back when Betty threw herself at Sandi, and the Beast went down on the ground hard. Her momentum had sent her almost completely past Sandi. Sandi gingerly stepped over Betty's feet and picked up her pace to get to her car before Betty could recover and come after her. She locked her doors before starting the car. Betty ran after her and pounded on the window as Sandi backed out of her parking space. Betty was mad and yelling after her as she drove away. She knew she would be in for it the following day, but today, she was feeling very satisfied. In the past, she would have been tackled to the ground and left as the brunt of jokes for several days to come. Instead, maybe it would be Betty as the recipient. She didn't think so. She only hoped so.

Her phone rang. It was Houston. "Well, Mr. McAvoy, to what do I owe this pleasure?" Sandi said with a smile.

"What'd you do?" he asked.

"When?"

"Just now. I was going to my car, and people were talking about what you did to Betty."

She laughed. "I didn't do anything to Betty. Betty was her own undoing. I did as you said and was paying close attention to my surroundings on my way to my car. Betty came charging at me to mow me down like she often does. I saw her coming at me, took a step backward, and she hit the ground instead of me."

Houston belly-laughed. "That's brilliant! Well done."

"Yeah, well, she's pretty mad. I can't imagine what I'm in for tomorrow. She was pounding on my windows, telling me she was going to get me."

"You're right. You're gonna have to watch your back for a while, I'd imagine. Eventually, it'll die down."

"I've been dealing with this my whole life. I don't know if I have a sign on me somewhere, but I've taken it off, and I'm not putting up with this anymore. I just never thought to not fight back. Thanks for that."

"Sure. Just do me a favor."

"What?"

"Try not to be alone anywhere at school."

"There is nowhere to be alone at school."

"You know, don't go to the restroom without a friend."

"Maybe you haven't noticed, but you're my only friend in that school. I can't wait for you to escort me to the potty. I'll be fine."

"Just try."

"I will."

"I just pulled into work. I'll talk to you later."

"Sure." Sandi hung up the phone with a big grin on her face. It was nice not to feel like she was all alone anymore.

Sandi faced an empty first floor when she got home. Where were Max and Gretchen? She raced up the stairs to Max's room. They weren't there. She went to the basement: still no one. She began to panic when she heard them in the kitchen. She went back upstairs to an animated, happy Max. Her relief was replaced with anger. "Where were you? I was worried."

Gretchen looked stricken. "I'm so sorry. We went to the mall and lost track of time."

"*¿Cómo te fue en la escuela, Sandi?*" Max asked.

Sandi's anger was replaced with an adrenaline dump, and she started to cry.

He rushed to her side and wrapped his arms around her. "Shh. What's wrong? Did something happen? You're okay. I'm here."

"I'm sorry. I was just worried when I got home and no one was here. I couldn't imagine what had happened to you."

Sandi bear-hugged Max.

"Too tight," Max said.

"I'm sorry," Sandi responded. "I didn't know where you were. Too many bad thoughts ran through my head at once."

"We'll make sure we're here when you get home from now on," Gretchen stated.

"No. It will be fine. I will be fine. I'll know in the future. It didn't occur to me that you would be at the mall. I couldn't imagine what had happened. Let me get a drink and calm my nerves."

Sandi grabbed a glass from the cupboard and filled it from the water dispenser on the fridge. She now understood her father's reactions to her being missing in the past. She felt like she'd been on a rollercoaster ride of emotions in less time than an actual ride would entail. She noticed that as she pressed the glass for the water, her hand was shaking. When she turned from the kitchen, Max had a big smile on his face.

"Sandi, come sit with me," he said gently.

She nodded her head. He guided her to the living room.

"I'm okay. We just lost track of time."

"Let me make you two a snack," Gretchen offered.

"That's fine," Sandi said as she began to get up. "I can do it. You can go home."

"Are you sure? I don't mind."

"No. We're good. Enjoy your evening; we'll see you in the morning. I really appreciate everything you do for Max, for me, for us." Sandi said.

"I'm really sorry. I didn't mean to scare you."

"No. It was all me. I had a scary end to my day. I should have known you'd never let anything happen to him. Please forgive my overreaction."

"Nothing to forgive, dear. Have a good night."

Gretchen gathered her things and headed out the door.

"I sure missed you today," Sandi said.

Max wrapped his big arms around her as they sat on the couch. "No more crying. Nothing happened to me. We're okay."

"I know. It's just silly. I had a run-in with a mean girl at school."

"Was it Kristy?"

"No. This girl's name is Betty. She's really big and often plows into me, crashing me to the floor. They call her Betty the Beast."

"What? She knocks you down? Are you okay?"

"Yeah, I am."

"This has happened before?"

"Yeah." Sandi huffed a breath. "Too often."

"Why hasn't anyone ever done anything about it?"

"I've never had anyone on my side."

"What about Houston?"

"Actually, it's because of what Houston told me that I was able to avoid being bowled over by her today."

"What'd he tell you?"

"To be alert."

"I'm glad you're okay. I'm sorry for all the times she's hurt you. I'm sorry I wasn't there."

Sandi felt so safe wrapped in Max's arms. She loved him so much. "Now, tell me what you learned today."

He led her to the library. He stopped in the hallway, leaned down, and kissed her. I missed you too."

"I wish I'd known to make you sooner."

"We're together now."

"So, show me what you're studying."

He explained how Gretchen felt she could no longer keep up with him, so he had taken to being the teacher and she a willing student, which in turn helped him learn the material. He was currently learning the differences between alpha, beta, delta, gamma, and theta waves and showed Sandi his findings.

They turned in unison as they heard the garage door opening.

"Dad is home," Max said.

Sandi couldn't help but smile. "Let's not both call him 'Dad'—it makes what we have a bit icky."

"What should I call him?"

He had a point; what should he call him? "Well, for both of us to call him dad makes our relationship feel a bit incestuous."

"Incestuous? What does that mean?"

"That's when family members get together in more than a familial way."

"What's wrong with that? They used to do it in most of the monarchies to keep the royal lines pure."

"That is true, but it also led to genetic mutations and severe birth defects."

"There's no part of you in me, right?"

"Right. I almost used my stem cells, but decided against it since I did want you for more than just an experiment."

"I'm glad you did." He stole another kiss.

"Come on. Let's go greet...Dad."

During dinner, Sandi and Max caught him up on their day.

"Max, you are too smart to be schooled by whatever you were finding on TV or the internet, and if Gretchen can no longer keep up," her dad said, "I believe you might be ready to go to school."

"No. He can't go to public school," Sandi demanded.

Her father's head snapped up to look at her.

"I'm sorry," Sandi said. "Max is special. I know firsthand how horrible the kids are at school. I won't do that to him."

"He needs the interaction of others his age."

"There are no others his age, Dad."

"You know what I mean."

"I do, and I won't allow it."

"Let's see how he does. If he continues to learn at this rate, he may be able to skip many grades and won't be looked at as an oddity. Start out on solid footing."

"We'll see." Sandi had no intention of subjecting Max to the taunts and ridicule she had put up with. She just needed her father off the subject. "So, we have a question. What should Max call you? It seems a bit weird for both of us to call you Dad when we're dating."

"Hmm..." He thought. "I hadn't considered that. I'm really not your father. I guess we need to think of a story if he's going into school."

"I don't want him in school."

"No matter. We still must have something plausible."

"He has the Powell last name when you got him his license. We just can't be related and dating."

"True. "I could have a brother who adopted him."

"That would work, but where's the brother?"

"He died."

They laughed. This was complicated.

"Should I call you Mr. Powell, like Houston does?"

"No. Uncle Al will work. You're my deceased brother's adopted son that I took in."

"Okay, Uncle Al," Max said.

It sounded so odd to Sandi.

Sandi and Max cleaned up the kitchen. When they were done, Sandi said, "I've got some homework that shouldn't take me long, if you don't mind."

"We've got this," her father said. "Come on, Max, let's go find something good on TV. Join us when you're done, princess."

Twenty-Four

S andi kept herself on high alert at school. She didn't know when or where, but she could rest assured Betty the Beast would retaliate. Nothing happened. At lunch with Houston, she told him about the dinner conversation the night before.

"Yeah, I didn't think about that, but I can see where that would get strange. Eeugh."

"Eeugh is right," Megan Malhomme said as she passed by them. "How can you eat lunch with her and actually keep it down?"

"And here I thought you were so much better than that pettiness, Megan," Houston said.

Megan huffed out an indignant breath and stormed off.

"It doesn't look like the harassment has died down," Sandi said. "I'm really sorry. You know you don't have to be seen with me. I will fully understand if you want the target taken off your back."

"Oh, stop. It would take a lot more than a few mean girls to make me stop hanging with you. Or are you trying to tell me something, and I'm just not taking the hint?"

"No. I just hate how this is still going on for you. I'm used to it. You're not."

"I'm not going anywhere. Come on, we've got class. I'll see you in Physics."

She waited for Houston in Physics. He slid into his seat just as the bell sounded and the teacher stood up.

Sandi whispered across the aisle, "Is everything alright?"

Houston nodded.

The teacher said, "Ms. Powell, are you through? May I proceed?"

Sandi nodded. "Sorry."

After class, as they were talking in the hall, Houston said. "I don't have to work tonight. Would it be okay if I came over right after school?"

"Of course. Stay for dinner."

"No. I have to make dinner for my mom."

"Sure. That's fine. Whatever. You know if you're there during dinner, my dad is going to make you eat."

He laughed. "Gotta run. See you—"

They were slammed to the floor. Sandi's head hit the tile over concrete, and she saw stars. Houston was on top of her, and she couldn't breathe. Everything went black.

When Sandi came back around, she started to get up, but pain shot through her head, causing nausea. "Ooh," she said.

"Don't move," Houston said. "Your head is bleeding."

"What happened?" Sandi asked

The hall was thick with kids staring at them. Some started to make jokes but were quickly silenced when the whispers about Sandi's head spread. The nurse pushed through the crowd to kneel beside Sandi.

"What happened here?" she asked.

"That's what I want to know," said Sandi.

The nurse asked again, "Who saw what happened?"

No one said anything.

She looked at Houston. "Did you do this?"

"No! I was knocked to the ground with her."

"Who did this?" she demanded while wiping blood from Sandi's head. "Someone call 911. How many fingers am I holding up?" she asked Sandi.

Sandi tried to focus, but for the life of her, she couldn't say with confidence. "My head hurts," she said instead.

The principal came up with his phone in hand. "I've called, and an ambulance is on the way."

The nurse said, "This is going to need stitches, and I believe she's concussed. I want to know what happened."

"Done. Everyone in this hall to the gym. Now!" bellowed the principal. "Someone knows something, and I want answers. If no one wants to talk, we'll be here all night. You can explain to your parents."

"I want to go with her," Houston said.

"You'll go to the gym with everyone else," said the principal.

"No, he'll need to go with her," the nurse said. "He needs to be checked out. He was knocked to the floor too."

"Did you see what happened?" the principal demanded.

"No, sir. All of a sudden, we were on the floor. Whoever did it came from behind me."

"How do you feel?" the nurse asked.

"I have a wicked headache. I don't think I hit my head, though."

"Mr. Smith! Where do you think you're going? That is not the way to the gym. Everyone in the gymnasium, now!" Mr. Llewellyn, the principal, was a nice guy until you crossed him. Sandi worked hard never to cross him.

Before she knew what was happening, Sandi was being strapped to a board and loaded on a gurney. Her saving grace was that Houston was next to her. They were loaded in the ambulance and taken to the hospital.

Sandi was taken to a space where a curtain was drawn around her. A nurse was recording her vitals as the paramedic rattled them off and removed her from the board. A young doctor walked in, asking questions. The nurse handed him Sandi's chart. He shone a bright light in Sandi's eyes, and she winced.

"What's your name?" the doctor said.

"Sandi."

"Sandi what?"

"Powell."

"Who's the president?"

"Um…" Sandi knew she knew this. "Give me a minute."

"How many fingers am I holding up?"

"What's with the fingers?" Sandi said.

"Just answer, please."

"They're a bit blurry."

"Get her down to imaging for a CT scan. I'm sure you have a concussion. I just don't know about any internal bleeding. I'll stitch you up when you get back. I'd like to leave this compress on in the meantime. You don't know how you hit your head?"

"All I know is I was talking with my friend in the hall between classes when we were plowed into and hit the floor."

"Is that him in the hall? The big guy?" the doctor asked the nurse.

Sandi started to speak when the nurse patted her hand. "He's asking me. You just rest. Yes, his name is Houston MacAvoy. He has a headache but doesn't think he hit his head. He doesn't know what happened either. Unlike her, his vision is clear with no cognitive deficits."

Sandi wanted to ask questions, but the pain was muddying her thoughts.

"Does he appear to have any trauma?" Sandi heard him ask as they wheeled her away in the opposite direction of Houston. She wished he could stay with her. She'd never been a patient in a hospital before. Every bump the gurney rolled over felt like it shot straight to her head in an explosion. She gripped the sides of her head in pain.

"Sorry, honey, I'm trying to be careful," the orderly wheeling her said.

Sandi just held on for dear life. She couldn't escape the pain.

When she returned from the scan, her father was in the hall with Houston. "That's my daughter," he called out.

"The doctor will be right with you," said the orderly.

"Sandi, are you alright?" he pleaded.

"I will be, Daddy."

Shortly after returning from imaging, the doctor came in and talked with her dad. They had hooked her to an IV and put something in it to ease the pain. All she could feel was relief. She had thought if she didn't get out of the pain soon, she'd lose her mind. Now, she didn't care what they did as long as they kept the agony at bay.

Sandi drifted off to sleep. When she woke up, she was in a different room with a curtain drawn around her bed, and a different nurse was with her. "Good," the nurse said, "you're awake. Look here for me." She shone a light in Sandi's eyes. "Good. How many fingers am I holding up?"

"Three," Sandi said.

"Great. How do you feel?"

"Like I've been hit by a Mack truck."

"That's to be expected. Get some rest."

Sandi realized she had been fighting to stay awake to answer the nurse's questions. She closed her eyes.

When she awoke again, she was in an actual hospital room with her father beside her. She looked around. "Where's Houston? Is he okay? Daddy, what happened?"

"It's okay, he's okay, you'll be okay. You had some bleeding on your brain. The doctor did surgery. You're going to be alright."

"What about Houston?"

"He has a concussion and some bruising. He was released and is back home with his mother."

"What happened? Does anyone know what happened?"

"Not yet, sweetheart. Mr. Llewellyn is going to call me as soon as he gets to the bottom of this."

"What time is it?"

"It's almost 9:30 p.m."

"Oh no!" Sandi started to jump up, but the pain in her head stopped her. "Max!"

"Max is fine. He's pretty worried. Gretchen is with him. I promised I'd let them know when you're in the clear. She's a good woman. She's going to be looking for a raise!" He laughed.

She couldn't laugh. She knew the pain that would accompany it.

"Don't worry about anything right now. You just concentrate on getting better. You gave me a real scare."

A nurse came in. "You're awake. How are you feeling?"

"Like I was hit by a freight train."

"That's to be expected. Everything is looking good now, though. A few days' rest and you'll be able to ease back into it. We're going to keep you here overnight for observation. If all goes well, you should be able to go home tomorrow. Mr. Powell, I'm going to have to ask you to leave now. We'll take good care of her. I'm about to give her a sedative for the night."

"I just woke up," Sandi protested.

"And the more rest you get, the sooner your body will heal," the nurse said.

Her dad came to her side and kissed her forehead.

"Wait!" Sandi said.

"What, princess?"

"Please give Max a big hug for me. Don't let him be afraid."

"You know I won't, and yes, I'll hug him from you, not like you, just from you." He smiled. "Anything else?"

"Yes. Where's my phone? My purse? Does Houston know what's going on?"

"Yes. I've kept him up to date throughout the night. He's been worried too. He'll like to know you're awake. I'll call him from the car."

"No. I want to talk to him."

"I don't think that's a good idea," the nurse said. "You need your rest."

"If you want me to rest, you'll let me talk to him."

"Fine. But when I get back, you need to be off the phone, and your father needs to be gone."

"Deal," Sandi said.

Her father dialed the number on his phone and hit the speaker button.

"Where's my phone?" Sandi asked while it was ringing.

"In the bedside stand."

"Mr. Powell?" Houston asked with panic in his voice. "Is Sandi all right?"

"I'm fine," she responded.

"Oh, thank God!" He said while blowing out a huge breath. "I was so worried. I'm glad you're awake. You've been out for hours."

"I'm gathering that. Do you know what happened?"

"No, not yet. My mom called the principal, but he said he'd let her know as soon as he could get a clear picture of what went down. I can't go back to school or work until Monday. Can I come see you tomorrow?"

"I would hope you would."

"We'll get your car to you tomorrow, Houston," Mr. Powell said.

"Oh, thanks, I'd appreciate that. I don't like being without wheels if there's an emergency. I'm not supposed to drive, but that doesn't mean I wouldn't."

"If you need anything, young man, don't hesitate to call me. I'd come get you and take you to your car tonight, but you shouldn't be behind a wheel right now."

"Yeah, that's what the doctor said, but I really need to see Sandi for myself."

"Just rest tonight. I'll pick you up in the morning and bring you up here."

"What about work?" Sandi asked her dad.

"What about it?" her father asked. "You're more important than any project at work. We're going to let you go, Houston. Sandi needs her rest, as do you, and if I'm not out of here before Nurse Rutcherschmut gets back, I'm in big trouble."

Sandi couldn't help but laugh, even though it made her head hurt. Her father had given that nickname to her first teacher when she was unreasonably nasty to Sandi. She didn't remember the teacher but remembered the story.

"Who?" Houston asked.

"My nurse. I'll tell you about it tomorrow when I see you. Sleep well. I'm glad you're alright."

"You too. See you then. Goodnight. And thanks again for the lift home, Mr. Powell."

"Not a problem. Night."

He leaned over her and gave her a gentle squeeze. "Sleep tight, princess. I'll be back in the morning after Gretchen gets there."

"Night, Daddy. Thanks for taking care of everything."

"Of course." He opened the door just as the nurse was coming back in. He looked over his shoulder at Sandi, and they both chucked. He walked out the door.

Twenty-Five

S andi hoped she could go home. She had fallen fast asleep shortly after her father left the night before, but the hospital is no place to sleep. It was busy with people coming and going all night long. She still had a lot of pain in her head. She wanted her own bed and silence.

"Good morning," came a too-cheerful-for-7-a.m. voice. "I'm Tiffany, I'll be your nurse today. How are we feeling?"

"I can tell how you're feeling, but I need coffee to get to where you are."

Tiffany laughed. "I'll get you a cup as soon as I get your vitals. You might be able to go home today."

"No. I better be going home today. This is not the place to rest."

Tiffany chuckled. "It's not that bad." She giggled.

Sandi wanted to correct her but kept her mouth shut. Too much of this little Miss Perky and Sandi was going to run!

"I've seen Dr. Abernathy making rounds already, so he should be able to tell you your prognosis. You took quite a fall."

"Coffee?" Sandi asked.

"Yes, how do you take it?"

"Black and strong."

"I'll be right back."

Tiffany returned with her cup of coffee and a refill of ice water in her pitcher. "Enjoy your coffee but be sure to drink plenty of water too."

"Yes, ma'am."

Sandi held the Styrofoam cup like it was a golden chalice. She inhaled the beloved smell deeply before taking a sip. Oh, that was good for hospital coffee. She wondered if this was from the nurses' station and not for general consumption. She didn't really care at this moment. Just the fact she felt it slide down her throat and hit her brain was good enough for her.

Her door opened again, and Dr. Abernathy walked in. "Good morning. How did you sleep?"

"You can't be serious. Who sleeps here with a revolving door?"

He chuckled while reading her chart. "Someone is sharper than she was yesterday. Who's the current president?"

"No one I'd vote for. The country's a mess right now."

He laughed. "How many fingers am I holding up?"

Today, there was no hesitation. She could clearly see his three fingers on one hand and one on the other. "Nice try. Four."

"Great. Let me have a listen to your heart and lungs and take a look at your incision. Are you still experiencing pain?"

"Yes. A lot of pain in my head. My body aches today."

He placed his stethoscope to her chest and listened intently. "Great. Nice and strong." He sat her up and listened to her lungs. "Good. They're clear. Good sign. Let me see how your head is." He removed the bandage and poked a bit. Sandi was surprised at how gentle his touch was. She had been dreading that part. "It looks great, and the swelling is coming down."

"Can I go home?"

"I'd like to keep you here for one more day."

"I really want to go home. My dad will take good care of me. He's a scientist. He's more than capable. We don't live far from here. Please," she begged.

"We'll see. Let's watch you throughout the morning, and I'll reconsider this afternoon. Fair?"

"Fair," Sandi said with disappointment.

"In the meantime, I need you to keep pushing this button as soon as you feel any pain. I need you out of pain to heal faster."

"Out of pain sounds wonderful. What's the button trigger? They told me last night to push it if I had pain, but I was pretty out of it and didn't ask any questions."

"It's morphine. You can't overdose—it locks you out for a time after each dose. Okay, you rest, and I'll check back this afternoon."

He seemed pretty determined. Sandi relaxed into the pillows. It didn't look like she was getting out of here anytime soon. Nurse Sunshine came back with a syringe of something she placed into Sandi's IV. "This will help with the swelling."

It wasn't long before Sandi felt herself slipping away.

When she opened her eyes, Houston was in front of her. "Am I dreaming?"

He beamed that megawatt smile. "If you are, I'm in it with you." He leaned over the rail and hugged her gently. "How do you feel?"

"Better. I was in a lot of pain this morning, but they drugged me up, and I slept. I do feel better." She pushed her morphine button. "This helps."

"What is it?"

"Morphine. My friend."

They laughed.

Sandi looked around the room. "Where's my dad?"

"He dropped me off here, took my keys, and said he'd take care of getting my car home for me. He'll be back later."

"Why didn't he drop you at your car to get it yourself?"

"The doctor said he doesn't want me doing much of anything, including driving, until Monday."

"How are you feeling today?"

"I feel fine. I still have this headache, but other than that, I'm fine. I was really worried about you. You hit your head pretty hard, and all that blood..."

"Yeah, it happened so fast. Do they know what happened?"

"Oh, yeah. It was Betty the Beast. She was mad at you for making her look like a fool. She said she didn't mean for you to get hurt like this, but she wanted you to pay for what you did."

"Pay for stepping out of the way of being hit by that raging bull? What sense does that make?"

"None but Betty's. You humiliated her in front of the whole school, and apparently, kids were teasing her throughout the day. She was just planning on knocking us to the floor to turn the tables of ridicule. Of course, she didn't say ridicule, that's too big a word for her."

They laughed.

"Wow! How angry do you have to be to hit someone that hard?"

"Pretty angry. I'm a pretty big guy. I would hate to think what would have happened if she'd hit you directly. I figured they would suspend her, but the principal expelled her. There're rumors she has to go to an in-treatment facility for anger management."

"Good! She needs it. She's not a linebacker, and we certainly weren't on a football field. Did anyone else get hurt?"

"Some girl who was behind you had bruises, but she'll be fine."

Sandi sat in silence, thinking about all he'd just said. She couldn't imagine such a poor error in judgment altering someone's life in a split second. Not that she felt sorry for Betty, but she couldn't help but contemplate what all that anger had done to her.

Houston interrupted her thoughts. "My mom has decided to move forward with our plan. I was hoping to do the stem cell replacement this weekend, but we need to put that off until you're better."

"No. We can do it. I'll be fine."

"She said she's been this long, so what's a few more weeks? And she understands it may not even work."

"Oh, it will work. And there is no need to wait. I'll be fine by tomorrow. Besides, it's not like I'm the only one who can do it. My dad certainly can."

"Really?"

"Really. Where do you think I learned?"

"Yeah, but what about you? You need to rest and recuperate. I know you. You won't be able to help yourself, you'll be all up in the middle of it."

"I promise to sit and observe. Dad can do all the heavy lifting."

"Let's pass it by him when he gets here. I don't want him to feel obligated."

"You know, as a scientist, it isn't a sense of obligation; it's thrilling to make a difference. It excites him as much as it does me. I don't understand why he didn't follow through with his same experiment all those years ago. What I do know is, he was on the right track, and he's been very excited about Max. He was enthusiastic about working with your mother. Besides, I think he really likes her."

"Really? Like *likes* her?"

"Yeah. I'm not so sure it's not mutual. Did you notice how they were together?"

"I'm a guy, we're not as observant as you girls. I still want to check with him first. Now, let's see what trash we can find on TV."

They were engrossed in a True Crime drama when Sandi's dad walked in. "You're awake! How are you feeling, princess?"

"That seems to be the catchphrase of the day. I'm better, Daddy. Where's Max?" Sandi felt Houston stiffen beside her on the bed.

"I'm glad you're better. Max is home with Gretchen. He's really worried about you. Your car is back at your house, Houston. As is yours, Sandi."

"Thank you, Mr. Powell. I really appreciate it. I'll pay you back. I promise."

"Don't be silly. It was my pleasure. In a way, I owe you for cushioning the blow to my little girl."

"I'm not little anymore."

"You'll always be my little girl. If you had taken a direct hit from that brute, as she intended, there is no telling what she would have done to you. I hate you were hurt in the process, Houston, but so grateful your large frame protected Sandi, as it did."

"I just wish I could have completely protected her," Houston said, looking down at his hands in his lap.

Sandi wanted the subject changed. "Daddy, do you think we can still do the stem cell replacement with Mrs. MacAvoy this weekend?"

"Oh, is she ready?"

"Yes, sir," Houston said.

"I don't know, honey, you really need to rest."

"That's what I said," Houston chimed in.

"And I said I would be willing to be a silent observer if you'll do the actual work."

Houston laughed. "I'm sorry, but you're usually not silent."

"I can be," Sandi offered.

"Let's see how you do today. You know I'm happy to do it," her father said.

"That's what I said." Sandi shot a glance at Houston.

The nurse came in. "You're awake. How are you feeling?"

"When can I go home?"

"Dr. Abernathy will be in to discuss that with you shortly. I just need to check your vitals and change your bandage."

Sandi was getting stir-crazy stuck in this room. She wanted to see Max. "Max understands I'm doing alright and will get better?"

"He was upset when I told him what happened to you. He told me to tell you he hopes you get better and come home to him soon. It's a good thing I know several languages in order to follow what he was saying because he ran them all together."

"Oh, wow! That's my Max."

Houston got up from the bed.

"Where are you going?" Sandi asked.

"Just need to walk around a bit."

It looked more like pacing to Sandi.

"I can't wait to meet this Gretchen," Houston said.

"She's really sweet and so good with Max," Sandi added. "Now, I just want out of here and go home so I can introduce you."

"Patience, princess."

"You know I don't possess that. I'm not about to start now."

Houston sat back down beside Sandi on the bed and unmuted the TV to continue watching.

"Sit back with me," Sandi said, patting the bed beside her.

At 4 p.m., Dr. Abernathy came in. "How do you feel? Any better? Has the pain subsided?"

"I feel ready to go home."

"You've continued to be stable. I'll let you go with the understanding that you will stay down and rest."

"She will, I'll see to it," her father said.

"And I'll help him," Houston declared.

"You've got a good father and boyfriend here."

"Oh, no, he's not my boyfriend. Just a friend."

Houston quickly got up from the bed. A strange look passed over the doctor's face. "Alright. I'll send the nurse in to set you free from all these tubes."

He turned to her dad and said, "Continue to monitor her temperature and change the bandage daily. If you see any signs of infection, call right away. Make sure she gets lots of rest and plenty of fluids. I'm sending you home with a prescription-strength Tylenol she can take for pain. If you feel she needs something stronger, call my office, and I'll get it for you."

"Thanks, Doctor. We'll take good care of our girl," her dad stated.

"Okay, I'll go fill out the discharge papers, and we'll get you out of here. Take care."

Sandi hadn't realized she was holding her breath until he walked out of the room. "I was so afraid he was going to tell me I had to stay another night. This is not the place to sleep."

Twenty-Six

J ust the sight of the house made Sandi happy. She couldn't wait to see Max. She hadn't realized she would miss him so much. When she got in the house, he came running. Her father stepped in front of her.

"We have to be gentle with her, Max."

"I'll be very gentle," Max said and stepped around her dad.

She welcomed his tender embrace. "I missed you so much."

He started rambling in several different languages all at once. She was catching most of what he was saying, but this was taxing her brain.

"Whoa. One language at a time. My brain is still a bit foggy."

Instead, he went silent and just tenderly held her.

"How are you feeling?" Gretchen asked.

"Like that question should be stricken from the English language," Sandi responded.

"I understand, dear. I'm just glad you're going to be all right and are home now."

"Me too."

"Let's get you to your room," Houston said.

"Oh, would all of you stop smothering me. I know the way to my room. I can do it myself."

"No. Let Houston help you. This is a lot more than you've had to do, and we don't know how you'll handle the stairs. Don't be stubborn."

"But that's my middle name. You say it yourself," she said with thick sarcasm.

Max easily lifted Sandi in his arms.

"Put me down, I can walk."

"Not today."

He ascended the stairs and set her on her bed.

"I'm just going to use the restroom first. And you're not carrying me there."

He laughed. "No. You do that all on your own. If you need help, though, just call out."

"I won't, but thanks."

He leaned into her and kissed her. "I was so worried about you."

"Thanks. I'm going to be okay, you don't have to worry anymore."

When she returned, she had changed into a long nightshirt. Max was sitting on her bed with his back against the headboard on the far side. Houston was standing beside her side of the bed. Her bed had been turned down. She slipped between the sheets. Houston covered her up and sat on the side of her bed, facing her. "You have no idea how scared I was. What that hateful girl did is unforgivable. All over the same kind of teasing she does to you on a regular basis. She needed treatment a long time ago. I just wish it hadn't come at your expense." Max placed a protective arm around Sandi, and she curled into him. She felt Houston get up from the bed. She easily slid into sleep, feeling protected and loved.

IT WAS dark outside when Sandi awoke. She opened her eyes to see Max still sitting on the bed beside her, watching his tablet with headphones on.

"Hey," she said.

He looked up, and a big smile spread across his face. "You are awake."

"Yes, I am."

He set his tablet on the bedside stand, stretched out beside her, and cuddled into her. She put her arm around him and just let him hold her.

Her father walked in with Houston on his heels.

"Sandi is awake," Max announced.

"I see that," her dad said. "Are you hungry?"

"I'm starving," Sandi responded. "And thank you for not asking me how I feel."

"I knew better."

"How *do* you feel?" Houston asked.

They all laughed. Max looked confused.

"Everyone keeps asking me how I feel," Sandi explained. "I'm just tired of the question. I'm fine. Much better now that I'm home."

"Good. That's what we like to hear. Come on. Dinner is on the table and getting cold."

Halfway down the stairs, Sandi recognized the smell of Italian. "Is it lasagna?"

"It certainly is. Your favorite," her dad said.

"Yum. I was hungry but didn't realize how much until now."

Sandi was led to the dining room instead of the kitchen table. She was surprised to find Grace waiting for them. "Oh, I didn't know you were here," Sandi said.

"Your father insisted. How are you feeling?" Grace asked.

Everyone laughed, including Max this time. She looked bewildered.

"I'm much better, thank you," Sandi stated.

"Grace and Houston will be staying with us for a few days," her father declared.

"Staying here?" Sandi asked.

"Since you two kids need to lay low, Houston can't drive. I didn't want to leave them in a position to be stranded. We certainly have the room, Grace agreed to come here for the time being."

"You really have a lovely home," Grace said.

"Thank you. I know it's too big for just the two of us...three of us," he corrected himself, "but I bought it for the basement. I was able to build the lab of my dreams."

Sandi had never known why they had such a big house just for them.

Talk over dinner was light and easy. Grace was full of great stories from before her accident. She praised her son for the way he had taken care of her since that time. She didn't say much about anything else since the crash. Any time she did mention anything since then, she lost her joy and turned somber.

Mr. Powell kept steering the conversation to things that made everyone laugh. Sandi had never experienced her dad in social settings and had no idea he had it in him. He always came across to her as all business. He rarely attended work functions, and when he did, she wasn't included. She wondered why, after all these years, he remained alone. She imagined her mother would have wanted him to remarry. It wasn't right that he didn't have a companion.

After dinner, Sandi started to take her plate to the kitchen. Houston beat her to it. He took her dishes and directed her to the living room.

"I can clean up the kitchen," she announced.

"No, you can't," three voices said in unison.

"I'll clean up the kitchen," Houston declared.

"I will help," Max said.

"Good, that's settled," her dad said. "Let's go to the living room." He went behind Grace and pushed her wheelchair into the Living room. "Is this good?"

"Yes, this is perfect," Grace said.

Sandi took her seat on the end of the sofa where she usually sat. Her dad sat in his favorite wingback chair facing Grace. Sandi observed the easy dialogue and interaction of the two adults. Hmm...this was interesting. She kept quiet and listened. Houston and Max joined them. Max sat beside Sandi and took her hand, and Houston took a seat in the other wingback chair next to her father.

"Would you rather I take you back to your room?" Houston asked Sandi.

"No. I'm thrilled to be anywhere but bed at the moment."

"Would everyone like to watch a movie?" her dad asked.

"I'm good with conversation or a movie," Grace said.

"Conversation it is," he announced.

They talked way into the evening. Sandi felt herself fading. She rose to go to bed, and before she was fully upright, Max was on his feet, lifting her up.

"Put me down. I can walk." She immediately regretted her phraseology.

"I know you can. I also know I'll feel better carrying you," he said.

"I believe I'll be next," Grace said.

To Sandi's surprise, her father walked over and easily lifted Grace in his arms. "Let me show you to your room. I'll bring your wheelchair up as soon as I get you set up."

She giggled. "No one but Houston ever picks me up. I hope I'm not too heavy."

"Not at all," her dad responded.

This is interesting, Sandi thought. Grace was a slight woman, and Sandi knew her father regularly worked out in their home gym, but she'd never realized what strength he possessed.

Max set Sandi on her bed. Houston had followed them and said, "If you two are all good, I'll go help your dad with my mom."

"Something tells me they'll be just fine," Sandi said with a smirk.

Houston turned back to her. "Really?"

"Oh, yes."

The look of surprise on his face said it all. She knew he hadn't been paying attention in the living room.

"I'm not sure how I feel about that. I mean, I hate that she's been alone since my dad, and I really like your father. I just didn't see that coming."

"Neither did I."

"You wouldn't feel strange about us if they got together?"

"Why should I? It sounds like you might, though."

"I don't understand," Max said.

"She would be my sister if they married," Houston explained.

"Your stepsister," Sandi clarified. "And don't rush it. He just carried her to her room."

"You're right. Although, on second thought, maybe I should check on her."

"Leave them alone. They're fine. I'm just going to use the

restroom." Sandi jumped up from her bed as she always did, and an intense pain shot to the top of her scalp. She quickly sat back down, cradling her head in her hands. "Oh, owww."

She immediately had Max on one side and Houston on the other.

"Sandi!" Max said, panicked. "Are you okay?"

"I'm sure she just stood up too fast," Houston said, putting his arm around her shoulder. "You have to be careful. It's not going to hurt to baby yourself for a little while."

"I just had forgotten. I was reminded right quick though." This time, she began to stand slowly.

Max helped her to her feet. "Are you good?" he asked.

"Yeah, I've got this."

She headed for the bathroom.

"I'm getting your medicine. I'll be right back."

"I'll get it, buddy. You stay here with her," Houston said.

Sandi felt doubly blessed at this moment.

IN THE MORNING, Sandi woke with considerably less pain in her head. It was now a dull ache. She would take Tylenol at breakfast to hopefully subdue the throbbing. She carefully got up from her bed and padded to the bathroom to get ready for the day. She really wanted a shower. She could do with letting her hair go for another day, but she wanted the heat and pounding of the water on her body. Her muscles ached from the impact of the floor and Houston on top of her.

She dressed, brushed her teeth, and brushed through her hair as best she could. It was painful. One more day and she would attempt to wash it to get all the blood out. She went into Max's room. He was on his tablet on his bed.

Houston walked in through the bathroom. "Hey, guys! What's up?"

Her dad announced from the hallway that breakfast was ready. She turned to see him holding Grace in his arms. "In the dining room, princess."

"Be right there."

Max picked her up.

"I can walk," Sandi said indignantly.

"I know, but I like holding you. Let me take care of you." He leaned in and kissed her.

She smiled, wrapped her arms around his neck, and rested her head on his shoulder.

The bane of her existence was at her space and Max's. "Really, we can't catch a break from the orange nastiness?"

"You went a day without it. It will help you."

"If it helps so much, why aren't you sharing with Houston and Grace?"

"They're not accustomed to it. Their bodies have adapted without it. Don't argue with me, just drink it."

"What is it?" Houston asked.

"It's the foulest juice on the planet. Max seems to like it, but I think it's disgusting!"

"Can I taste it?"

"Be my guest. Drink it all."

"No," her father said.

"I just want a taste," Houston said, put it to his lips and licked his lips. "You drink this every day?"

"He insists," Sandi replied.

"It's not bad," Houston stated.

"You're just as sick as they are."

"I don't mind it either," Sandi's dad said.

"Let me try it," Grace said.

Houston passed the glass to her, looked back at Sandi, and said, "Do you mind?"

"No, not at all."

Grace tipped the liquid to her mouth, took a small sip, and passed the glass back to Houston with a disgusted look on her face. "You like that? It is foul. I'm with Sandi. That's horrible. You make her drink that every day?" she asked Sandi's dad.

"It's good for her, and it doesn't taste that bad."

"Oh, but it does. It must be a male thing if all of you don't mind it. I agree with Sandi on the taste. I think I'd shoot myself if I had to drink that every day."

"Thank you," Sandi said, glad someone finally agreed with her about the gross juice.

"Drink," her father said to her as he passed her the glass he'd taken from Grace.

Sandi downed it and followed it with a big swig of coffee.

Mr. Powell returned with a platter of pancakes and sausage.

"You did not need to go to all this trouble," Grace said.

"No trouble. We usually have pancakes on Saturday, isn't that right, Houston?"

"He's telling the truth. He cooks like this all the time."

"I could get used to this, but I'd end up being as big as a barn. I don't metabolize as well as I did in my younger years," Grace said.

"Don't worry, I took all the calories out of these," her father said.

"Really?" Grace asked.

They all laughed.

She looked embarrassed. "That was dumb. I thought with as brilliant as you two are, you had discovered something the rest of the world didn't know."

"That's not dumb," her father said. "As a matter of fact, you may be onto something. When we're done with stem cell replacement for growing limbs, I'm going to look into that. It had never occurred to me before. We could make a healthier option and reverse the damage of obesity. What do you say, Sandi?"

"I'm in," she announced.

"Now, eat before they get cold," Mr. Powell said.

"He has a thing with food getting cold," Sandi said.

"Because certain foods were intended to be eaten hot," he defended himself.

"These are delicious," Grace said. "You're really a good cook. Lasagna last night, pancakes this morning."

"Thank you. I enjoy cooking. To me, it's similar to science. The right formula, created in the right way, yields wonderful results."

"Always the scientist, Dad," Sandi said.

"You've never complained," he retorted.

"And I'm not about to start now. These are exceptional, especially after hospital food."

While Houston and Max cleaned the kitchen, Sandi followed her dad while he carried Grace to the lab.

"Wow!" Grace exclaimed. "This is huge. It's impressive. I understand why you like to work here."

He set her in one of the two dentist chairs he had installed. It was very comfortable. Sandi had taken many naps in it over the years. She never knew why. Now, watching her father set everything up around Grace, she better understood. It was the perfect setup for transfusing. He carefully explained everything to Grace as he set up the equipment. He was first going to extract her stem cells. He explained everything as he went along. He would use a mild sedative on the end of her arm and leg, excise some skin from each, place them in separate petri dishes, add in the stem cells, induce heat, and let them begin to grow.

Grace looked at Mr. Powell with admiration. "I trust you. I hope this works."

"If it doesn't, we will keep trying until we succeed," he replied.

"I'm ready," she said bravely.

Sandi was proud of herself for taking a back seat in the process and allowing her father to work. She did start to stand up a couple of times, but each time, she sat back down. She had offered to help when he began, but he said he had it well in hand, and indeed he did. She saw her father in a new light. It had been years since they had worked on anything in the lab together, and they had certainly done nothing of this magnitude. She watched with awe at the way he thoughtfully handled Grace.

Now, they would just have to wait and see. She really hoped they were successful with this first attempt. She realistically knew it probably wouldn't happen this go around. Sandi had already begun to think about what to do differently going forward.

Houston was so good with his mom. He held her hand throughout the whole course of action. Just then, he caught her staring at him. She smiled, and he beamed at her. He mouthed the word "What?"

She shook her head with a smirk. "I'll tell you later."

"I'll hold you to it," Houston responded.

An hour later, her father asked Grace if she felt she was stable enough to proceed. She was. He reopened the end of her arm and injected the tissue with stem cells. She took it well. He moved on to her leg.

"You don't think we should see how my arm does before moving onto my leg?" Grace asked.

Sandi spoke up. "We want to do them simultaneously to see if possibly one takes better than the other."

When the procedures were finished, he leaned over to pick her up, but Houston said he could get her. He stepped in front of Sandi's father, gently lifted his mother, and carried her upstairs to her room.

Sandi slowly, carefully climbed the stairs to the first floor. Max was right behind her. She had planned to make something for lunch, but instead had to sit down and let her head stop pounding. She had felt like it was crazy for Max to keep carrying her around. Now, she was grateful for his doting on her.

Her father walked in. "Are you all right? What's wrong?"

"Max hasn't let me walk anywhere. Just climbing the stairs caused a headache."

"I'll get you some Tylenol. Are you hungry? I can make some lunch."

"I was coming up here to do just that. I don't think I can now, though. I would rather go to bed, if you don't mind."

"Max, would you mind taking her to her room?"

"No. I promise I can walk. Just a bit slower."

"I've got this." Max lifted her.

"Here," her father said. "Take this first." He handed her two pills and a glass of water. "I'll get lunch ready, Max. Don't be long."

Houston walked in. "My mom is asleep already."

"Good," Sandi said. "Her body's been through a lot. I want to talk with the two of you about options if this doesn't work. I just need to rest for a bit."

"I believe this is going to work. Just trust," Houston said.

"I do trust. I just don't want you to be too disappointed if we don't succeed this first time."

Her father interjected, "All the science gives every indication it will work. We'll be able to adjust according to the results."

"My mom's patient. She's excited there's a possibility she may be able to have natural limbs instead of prosthetics. She's willing and determined. Whatever it takes, she's gonna do it. Between what the two of you know about cloning and stem cells and what I understand about prosthetics and loss of limbs, I know we can do this."

"Then together we'll make this happen," Mr. Powell said. "A big piece of this is that your mother is a willing participant. None of us have her perspective. This is a big risk for something untested."

Sandi turned to look at her father. The look on his face was one she'd never witnessed before. She felt certain he was falling for Grace. She had no point of reference since she had never seen him with her mother or any other woman. Wouldn't that be something if her dad had finally found someone? Sandi's gaze drifted to Houston, who tilted his head curiously at her. She slightly shook her head. He gave a small nod.

Max walked her upstairs. "I'm going to stay with you until you fall asleep."

"My father said he'd have your lunch ready. You know how he is about his food. He did say to hurry."

"He'll have to wait. You're more important to me than my next meal and if it's fresh."

He gently kissed her. She intensified it while he laid her down on her bed.

"We better stop before we both need a cold shower," Max said.

She laughed. "You're probably right."

He gently brushed her hair from her face, then gingerly ran his fingers over her bandage. "Do you wonder if that girl is sorry for what she did to you?"

"I don't know, but as long as I never see her again, I'll be all good."

"Sleep now, and I'll be back when I'm done with lunch."

"You don't have to. Go do whatever you want, something fun. I'll be fine. I just want to sleep and distance myself from the pain, even if it's just for a little while."

"I understand, but I want to be with you even if you don't know I'm here," he said, covering her with the throw from the foot of her bed and lying down next to her. He leaned over and kissed her. "Rest, my sweet Sandi."

Twenty-Seven

When Sandi awoke, the sun had set, and it was dark in her room. She saw the glow of Max's tablet and smiled. She sat up and quickly laid her head back on her pillow. This pain had to subside, and soon. She couldn't function this way.

"Hey, careful," Max said.

She sat back up, but slower this time. When her equilibrium had returned, she slowly rose to her feet. She stood still a moment.

Max jumped to his feet. "*Où vas-tu? Ich habe dich.*"

"I know you've got me. And that's two different languages. I thought you were going to speak in one at a time. I'm just going to the bathroom. I promise I can do this myself."

"It's not like you don't know what I'm saying."

When she returned, Max carried her downstairs. "So much for walking on my own two feet."

"You don't understand. I love the feel of you in my arms. If this is all I can get right now, it makes me happy to help keep you out of pain."

Everyone, including Grace, was in the living room watching a movie. "You can set me down now, Max."

He lowered her to the sofa and kissed her. "Can I get you anything?"

"Maybe in a bit. I just want to sit with everyone a minute."

Houston stood. "Let me get your dinner for you."

"I can get it," Sandi responded.

"Don't be silly. I can heat your dinner up for you if you're ready to eat," he said.

"Sandi, just sit with me while he warms it up," Grace implored.

She did as she was told. "You feel like you're tolerating the procedure alright, Mrs. MacAvoy?"

"Remember, you were going to call me Grace. I'm doing well. I've been up for a while and was able to eat dinner with everyone."

"Is there any pain at the surgical sites?"

"I really don't feel anything. Other than phantom pain occasionally, I never feel anything at the ends where my appendages were removed. I guess that's a good thing."

"Can I take a look?"

Grace held her arm out.

"It looks good. No apparent adverse reaction."

"Sandi, your dinner is done. Where do you want to eat?" Houston called out.

"I'll just eat in the kitchen. Be right there."

"I'll join you," Grace said and began pushing her wheelchair with her good arm. Sandi's dad came behind her and began pushing her.

Sandi sat carefully.

"Are you still in pain?" Houston asked.

"Yeah, I just can't get away from it."

"Let me get your medicine. Oh! While you were sleeping, you had a visitor," he said.

"I had a visitor?" Sandi asked.

"Yeah. And you'll never guess who. Betty."

"You're not serious."

"He is," said Grace.

"Her parents were with her and made her come to apologize," her father interjected. "I refused to wake you and said I'd relay the message."

"Do you think she meant it, or was she just appeasing her parents?" Sandi queried.

"She seemed genuine to me. Don't you think so, Mom?"

"She did seem remorseful. I think the magnitude of what she did to you hit her hard. Maybe she'll think before she does anything like that again," Grace responded.

"I would hope so," Sandi offered.

"Her parents seemed pretty nervous that you were going to sue them," Houston said.

"I should, but I won't. She's really not worth it to me."

"Your father said he was leaving that decision up to you," Grace said.

"Me?"

"Yes," he said. "It was you she wronged, and it's your decision to make. They asked to be notified as soon as possible. They asked Houston if I was going to sue them."

"Are you?" Sandi asked.

"No. They really look like they have less than my mom and I do. They shouldn't suffer for the actions of their angry daughter. I did say I wouldn't as long as Betty got help to learn how to manage her feelings. They assured me she was doing just that. Betty said very little and kept looking at the floor. I've never seen her so meek and mild. I do think it did something to her."

"Did her parents seem nice?"

"Her dad looked like a hard man. Her mother didn't say much of anything. She seemed beaten down. Watching the family dynamics, I can imagine where Betty's anger comes from," Houston said.

"I feel bad for her," Grace added.

"Bad for her?" Sandi said. "She's grown enough to know the consequences of her actions. I don't know. I'm going to wait to see if she actually follows through with help. If she doesn't get it and change her ways, I *will* sue just to maybe teach her a lesson."

Her father said. "She seemed sorry."

"Sorry she hurt us or sorry she got caught? There's a big difference," Sandi said. She stood up, but before she could take her dishes to the sink, Houston took them.

"Feel like doing any thinking work?" he asked her.

"It depends. How hard do I have to think?"

He picked her up and carried her to the lab.

"I really just wanted to hear your thoughts on what to do if this first process doesn't work for my mom."

"Oh, but you didn't need to carry me," she said smiling. She turned her head and gripped both sides in pain.

"I beg to differ. Are you all right? I've been really worried about you."

"I'll be all right. I just need to learn my limitations. Thanks for being here for me."

"Of course, it's what friends do. So, tell me what you're thinking if we have to do a round two."

"I was thinking about growing the tissue and stem cells out before attaching them."

"Oh, wow. That's brilliant! I bet that would work. I'm still optimistic on this first go-round, but that's a great option. I wonder if we should think about that in the future for other people. Maybe it would expedite the process."

"That's very possible. We should try."

"I can't believe we're really doing this. This is crazy."

"Why?"

"I've only ever imagined being able to make a change in the world, but we're actually going to do it."

"Of course we are. You know, I never would have thought of this if we hadn't started talking."

"Well, then I'm glad we did. Together, we make a great team."

Sandi wasn't sure what the look Houston was giving her was about, but it looked a bit like remorse. She wondered for what. Instead, she said, "Do you think your mom and my dad...?"

"I've been wondering. Their stolen glances haven't been lost on me."

"I've never seen my dad respond to any woman the way he does to your mother."

"I haven't ever seen her respond to anyone the way she does with your dad. Not even my own father. I think they had just settled into the routine of life and lost their spark—if they ever had one. I really don't know. I was too young. I know they had been together for a while before they got married."

"Then good for both of them."

"Hey! Where's Max? He hasn't left your side since you got home."

"I don't know. I really love him, but I was starting to feel claustrophobic."

They laughed.

As if right on cue, Max came down the stairs. "What's so funny?"

"Nothing. Come kiss me," Sandi said, reaching for him.

THEY WALKED into the living room to find Sandi's dad sitting on the sofa right next to Grace, who was out of her wheelchair, on the couch. Sandi exchanged a look with Houston. She knew she wasn't far from the mark. What Houston didn't know was that her father only ever sat in his own chair, even when they watched movies together.

She saw the blush that crossed Grace's face when they walked in on them.

Sandi said, "Hi, guys, we're going to be in the library if you need us, okay?"

"Sure, honey," her father said.

Sandi took Max's hand and led them down the hall.

"Now do you believe me?" Sandi asked Houston.

"How did you know?"

"Men are so oblivious."

"Hey! I wouldn't say I was oblivious. I just didn't think to look for it. Why's your father hitting on my mother?"

"My father? What about your mother?"

"I'm just not sure I'm ready to completely remove my father from the picture of the three of us. I know it's been a while. I just still miss him every day. Taking care of my mom after the accident allowed me to focus on something other than his passing. I had a lot of anger to deal with."

"I can understand. Unfortunately, you had no say over his passing. It was done without your permission. You know he's in a better place. Why not let your mom be happy again? Honestly, I'm shocked by my father. He's never showed the slightest interest in anyone since losing my mom."

"Why are you so surprised he's interested in my mother?"

"It has nothing to do with her. It has to do with all these years, all the women he's encountered. But your mom has him acting like a schoolboy."

"And that's a bad thing?"

"Stop twisting my words! I didn't say that. About now, it wouldn't matter who the woman was, I'm surprised he has an interest in anyone. I was worried about him. I would hate for him to be all alone, especially since I'm going to be gone soon. I think it would be great if it worked out between them. We'll make sure to give them space."

"Yeah, sure. I'm just not sure how I feel about all this."

"Don't you think she deserves to be happy?"

"Of course I do. I just didn't see it coming. It's going to take me a minute to process it."

"Well, I remember what happened the last time you needed time to process."

"What happened?" Max asked.

"I got myself in deep hot water, buddy. She had told me about you, and I didn't handle it well."

"Why not?"

"You really are a remarkable feat of science. I was overwhelmed, I guess. I needed more time than Sandi thought I should. That's behind us now."

"Thankfully," Sandi added.

"Anyone interested in a game of chess?" Max asked.

"Sure. I love chess." Houston said. "Unless you'd rather play, Sandi."

"No. I'd really rather watch tonight."

They went to the board her father always kept set up in the library. Houston said he hadn't played in a very long time. He used to have a buddy named Graham he would play with, but he hadn't been to their house in ages.

It was a long, close match. Sandi was surprised at Houston's skill. Max was exceptional, but Houston gave him a run for his money. When her father taught her, he had never gone too easy on her. She was glad because it made her a much better player. She taught Max the same way. He was even better than her dad.

"Good game," Houston said when Max won.

"Thanks. You're good at this," Max commented.

"My father taught me. It was something we enjoyed doing together. I don't have a lot of those memories."

It was getting late. "I really want to go to bed," Sandi said. "I need to get away from this pain for a bit. I'm sick of whining about the discomfort. I just want to be better."

"It's only been two days. You had brain surgery. Maybe tomorrow you should call the doctor about calling you in something stronger."

"Something stronger. You just reminded me of something." Sandi got up and went to the kitchen, with Houston right behind her. She opened the pantry door. "Here it is." She pulled out a mason jar filled with a purple liquid with strange bits floating in it. She took it to the counter, grabbed a fork, opened the jar, fished a piece out, and popped it in her mouth.

"What is that?" Houston asked.

"It's a tincture of ghost pipe. It's great for pain. I'd forgotten all about it since I'm rarely in pain."

"Ghost pipe. Is that dangerous?"

"Not if you don't do it too much or often. I would rather have holistic remedies. I'm surprised my father didn't think of this. I'll just run my diffuser with some lavender oil while I sleep. Both together will help. Tomorrow's a new day—hopefully, one with less pain. I'm going to bed if you two don't mind."

"I don't mind. You need your rest." Max picked her up.

"Hang on. I need to put this up."

"So, do it."

"Put me down."

"No. Deal with it."

She gave him a huge sigh. "You're infuriating."

"And I'm all yours." He laughed and kissed her.

As they passed the living room, they announced to their parents that they were going to bed. Max gingerly carried her up the stairs.

Sandi waved to Houston as he continued down the hall.

"See you in the morning," he said.

Max sat her on the bed, leaned down, and kissed her. "I'll see you in the morning. It's hard to sleep when you're right across the hall from me."

She chuckled. "Can't get me off your mind?"

"No. I'd love to crawl into this bed with you. One day, we won't be going to bed in different rooms."

"Goodnight, Max."

"Night. See you in the morning."

She was concerned the pain wasn't subsiding. She'd never experienced anything she couldn't easily and quickly bounce back from. But Houston was right—she had gone through surgery. She didn't know what the common recovery time was. She would have to look that up in the morning. She started her diffuser before going to the bathroom to get ready for bed. The tingle from the ghost pipe had already begun. She was beginning to feel relief from the hard edge of the pain. A good night's sleep and she was hopeful for the new day.

Twenty-Eight

S andi woke feeling much better than she had the day before. She
made her bed and headed for the bathroom. After her shower,
Sandi went to the kitchen. She needed some coffee. Her dad was
cooking breakfast, and Grace was at the table.

"Don't you two sleep?" Sandi asked.

They laughed.

"Good morning, princess," her father said. He hugged her, then
handed her the dreaded juice. "Have a seat, I'll get your coffee. Breakfast
is almost ready."

Max was at his seat at the table. He leaned in and kissed her.
Houston was nowhere in sight. "Is Houston up yet?" Sandi inquired.

"Not yet," his mom said. "I'm concerned he's not taking care of
himself worrying about everyone else."

"He needs to stop worrying about me," Sandi said.

"That's easier said than done. Houston is a worrier. Always has
been. Even as a little boy, he worried about things way beyond his years.
When his dad passed, he assumed an even bigger worrier role. I've tried
to get him to stop and just be a kid, but it's just the way he's wired. He
reminds me so much of his father. I love him no matter what."

"Speak of the devil," Sandi said as Houston walked in.

"What?" Houston said.

"We were just talking about how much like your father you are, my big boy," Grace said.

"Mom! Seriously, stop with the 'big boy' stuff. I'm grown; I'm not your baby anymore."

"I don't care how old you get, you'll always be my baby," Grace responded.

"I know that's right," Sandi's dad chimed in.

"Fine," Houston said. "You can at least not embarrass me in front of others."

"We're all family here," her father added. He was not helping Houston's cause.

"I understand how you feel," Sandi said in Houston's defense. "I hate when my dad treats me like I'm still two."

"It could be a lot worse," Grace said. "Too many kids are neglected by parents who keep themselves busy and miss these years that are so fleeting. I've known some like that. When their kids are grown and have nothing to do with them, they regret not giving them what they really wanted, which wasn't all the things they bought them, but their time and attention. I don't ever want to regret not giving you enough attention, Houston."

"You don't have to worry about that, Mom. I know you love me. I love you too."

"Now that we all know where we stand," Mr. Powell said, "let's eat." He set a platter of waffles and bacon in the center of the table.

Sandi sat nursing her coffee, watching the people who had become so important to her.

"Aren't you going to eat?" Houston queried.

Her father answered for her. "With Sandi, coffee comes first. Let her get her hit of caffeine and wake up, then she'll eat and talk and function."

Sandi simply smiled. Houston speared a waffle, placed it on Sandi's plate, and began to spread butter over it. She couldn't help herself from laughing.

"Now you see what I mean?" Grace addressed Sandi.

The two women laughed.

"I think that's really nice of him," her father said.

"I'm sure you do, Dad."

Max stopped eating briefly to say, "What's so funny?"

"I'm as clueless as you are, buddy," said Houston.

That made Sandi laugh even harder, which made her head pound. She went to the pantry to get more ghost pipe for the pain.

"Oh, yeah," her father said. "I should have thought to give you that a few days ago. I'm sorry."

"It's alright. That Tylenol isn't cutting it. I thought of this last night and slept better. I put on my lavender oil too."

"What is that?" Grace asked.

Her father explained. "Speaking of pain, are you experiencing any?" he asked Grace.

"No. None."

"Any changes?"

"I don't believe so." She held her limb out to him to inspect.

Sandi said, "I wonder if adding heat more consistently would help. That's how I got Max going."

"Hmm..." her father said. "It can't hurt. We can inject more stem cells and add the heat and see if that makes a difference."

GRACE WAS A TROOPER. She said nothing while they poked and prodded, injected and observed. Sandi thought she would do the same in the hope of regaining her mobility. She looked at Grace with admiration. She had dealt with losing a beloved husband, her arm, and her leg, all while raising a son on her own. She was someone to aspire to. Sandi knew from some family photos in the MacAvoy home that Grace did not give herself the care she once did, and her beauty had faded. It was hard to see that at this time. The woman was radiant. Especially when she looked at Sandi's dad. She hoped both parents would find love again and be happy.

Max sat at the table, contentedly watching his tablet. From the sounds of it, he was studying Italian. Sandi smiled and shook her head. She could never have imagined this scene around her a year ago. She was filled with love for all these people surrounding her today. Now that she had Max, she couldn't imagine her life without him. If she hadn't made Max, would they ever have thought to work with Grace as they were? Probably not. Then again, this was Houston's mission in life. They might have come at all of this from another angle, which might have taken them a lot longer to find a solution. She had to remind herself they had yet to discover the answer. She was so sure this would work, she had looked at it as a given.

After the injections and applied heat, Sandi's dad asked Grace, "How are you feeling? Would you like to rest? I can take you to your room if you would like to nap."

Grace said, "I'm good today. I want to stay up with everyone if it's okay."

"Of course, just give the word if you change your mind," her dad said.

Sandi noticed his hand remained on Grace's shoulder. Yeah, she knew she was right about them. She was happy.

Max suddenly blurted out, "*Vi amo tutti!*"

Sandi laughed. There must be something in the air. "We all love you too, Max."

Max beamed.

"What'd he say?" Grace asked.

"He said he loves all of us," Sandi said.

"How many languages do you speak?" Grace asked Sandi.

"I understand more than I can actually speak. Max has me beat. He also is more conversational with all his languages than I am."

"Do you speak multiple languages?" Mrs. MacAvoy asked Mr. Powell.

"I only speak four: English, Latin, Spanish, and French," he responded. "I never studied more. I took up Latin since it's the root of most Western languages, Spanish and French because I often go to France, Spain and Mexico. I was drawn to French for its lyrical sound, it's my favorite."

"Wow! I took French in high school, but can't remember any of it now," Grace said. "Houston took it for a couple years. I admire all of you knowing and speaking so many."

"I put a couple of language learning apps on Max's tablet," said Sandi. "He went and found all the others. He has a real affinity for them. He's good at them too."

"I can tell," Grace replied. "Now, if my cells can be as smart as Max, we may get somewhere."

"Be patient," Houston said. "I know this will work. Imagine once we figure all this out. I hate that you're a guinea pig. Just think of all the people we will be able to help."

"Then I'm happy to do it," Grace said.

SUNDAY MORNING, Sandi woke to the sound of a scream. It sounded like Grace. She had to get to her. Sandi jumped from her bed and quickly sat back down when the pain shot straight to her head. She had made so much progress the day before.

She got back up, slower this time, and headed for Grace's room by way of their shared bathroom. Just as she was clearing the door, she saw Houston come in with Max right behind him. Her father was already in the room with Grace, on the far side of the bed, holding her left arm.

"What happened? Are you alright?" Sandi asked in alarm.

"Look," Grace said.

Houston gasped.

"What?" Sandi asked, still lost.

Grace held up her limb with the end exposed to Sandi. There at the tip was obvious new growth. Sandi was thrilled.

"This is great!" she exclaimed. "I'm so happy for you. We did it, Dad!"

"It looks like it," he responded. "We're far from home, but this is a great start."

Houston turned and hugged Sandi.

Sandi laughed. "Need to breathe here, Grace's big boy."

He let her go. "Oh, sorry. I was excited."

"I can see that. Right up there with Max. I don't think you know your own strength," Sandi said, sitting down on the edge of the bed.

"I can't believe this is really working," Grace said with tears in her eyes. "I wished it would, but I couldn't imagine it was really going to work."

"Please don't get your hopes up yet," Mr. Powell said. "This is only the beginning. We not only need it to grow but to survive. We need it to continue to grow and then form properly."

"How will we make it create hands and fingers?" Grace asked.

"We don't, we can only speculate," her father said.

"God created our bodies, including your stem cells. We know science is doing a lot with stem cells. We have to trust God will properly form the rest," Sandi said.

"God doesn't have anything to do with this; we did all of this," Sandi's dad said.

"You are not still on that kick," Sandi shot back. "You're the one telling me I'm not God and to stop thinking I was. Well, you're not God."

"I'm not saying I am, but there is no God. This is all science." He looked very self-assured.

Grace pulled her arm from his hands and said, "You don't really believe that, do you?"

"Of course I do," he replied.

Grace had a look on her face Sandi couldn't read. Sandi looked at Houston. He left the room. Sandi followed him. "Hey! Where are you going?"

He turned to look at her. "Your father doesn't believe in God?"

"No. We've had this conversation several times over the years. There are so many miraculous things that happen, including Max, I came to believe, but have never been able to get through to him."

"My mother's faith is everything to her. We know only God got us through these hard years. My dad had a strong belief too, but it was after his passing that my mother's grew to what it is now. She's unwavering. If we thought they would ever get together, your father just destroyed that. She would never be with someone who didn't believe in God."

"I'm sorry. I wish he wasn't so hardheaded. I've tried to convince him for years of a God of the universe. I get nowhere with him. He's pretty set in his beliefs. Or nonbelief. I've got to get some coffee. Want some?"

"Yes."

"Houston," Grace called out.

He went back into her room. Sandi followed.

"I want to go home. Call me a cab and take me home. I can't stay in this house with this man," Grace said.

"Wait, Mrs. MacAvoy, I mean Grace, I know you don't agree with my father's beliefs, or lack thereof, but I really implore you to stay. I'll tend to you. You know I can. I would rather you were here where I can observe and care for you," Sandi begged.

"I don't know," Grace said.

"Dad, can you leave us, please?"

He left without a word.

"Please, Grace, stay. What is happening is wonderful. It's exciting. And everyone left in this room knows God is involved. My father has been set in his ways my whole life. He just needs some time, and I'll talk to him. I really want you to stay. I can't go back to school for a bit, he'll be going back to work. Tomorrow, it will just be the two of us working on this together, okay?"

"What about me?" Houston asked.

"I mean during the day, while you're at school, my dad is at work, and Max is with Gretchen. It will just be the two of us girls. I want to make this work. Can I take a look at your leg?"

Grace uncovered her left leg, and sure enough, there was growth there as well. Sandi hugged the woman. Houston wrapped his arms around them both.

"This is so wonderful. If you don't want my father involved, he won't be," Sandi said.

"Okay, but I don't even want to see him," Grace declared.

"You won't have to. Can I bring you up something to eat?" Sandi said.

"Yes, and some coffee, please. I was so excited, and now, I feel like someone has popped my balloon," Grace said mournfully.

Houston sat on the edge of the bed, wrapped one of those strong arms around her small frame, and comforted her.

"I'll be right back," Sandi said.

Sandi went back the way she'd come to use the restroom and brush her teeth. This was too much first thing in the morning, especially without coffee. What was her father thinking? She went down to the kitchen to find him cooking up breakfast as though nothing had happened.

"What is the matter with you?" Sandi asked him.

"What is the matter with me?" he replied. "Have none of you paid any attention? *We* harvested her stem cells, *we* excised her skin, *we* injected the cells, and *we* added the heat to help them adhere and grow. Now she wants to claim some god is responsible and not us, not science."

"You're the only one under this roof that doesn't believe God played a major role in this miracle. You're the minority here. Couldn't you just hold your tongue and let her believe what she wants to believe? Now, instead, she wants to leave and never see you again. I think I've talked her into staying and letting me work with her. You need to steer clear."

He passed her a cup of coffee. "Fine. So, when this works—and it is working—you plan on cutting me completely out of it?"

"You're not cut out of anything. You just need to keep your beliefs to yourself, and honor Grace's wishes by leaving her alone. She doesn't need the stress. Promise?"

"Sure. Drink your juice."

"You're incessant."

Max was eating at the table.

"Morning, Max. I didn't even get a chance to say anything to you in all the chaos." She leaned over to kiss him.

Sandi turned to her father. "Could I get a plate to take to Grace? She won't come down."

"If she wants to eat, she'll sit at this table," her father said.

"You're impossible. Never mind, I'll make it myself." She went to the coffee pot, poured a cup, and added cream the way Grace liked it. She took it upstairs.

Houston intercepted it. "I've got it."

"I'll go get her breakfast," Sandi said. "I'm really sorry about my father. He's impossible."

She went back downstairs. When she got to the kitchen, her father had set up the lap tray with two eggs, bacon, toast, milk, silverware, the salt and pepper shakers, and a napkin.

"Is this for Grace?" Sandi asked.

"Yes," was all he said.

She took it upstairs.

"I'm sorry to be so difficult," Grace said.

"You're not being difficult. My father is."

"How did I not know before now how he felt?" Grace asked.

"It hadn't come up," Houston said.

"You two need to go eat. I'll be alright here," said Mrs. MacAvoy.

"Are you sure?" Houston inquired. "I can sit with you until you're done."

"So can I," Sandi said.

"No, I'm sure. You kids go eat. I've got this."

"Call if you need anything; I've got my phone," Houston said as they left the room.

When they got into the hallway, Houston said, "I'm not sure who's more stubborn, her or your father."

"There's no question," Sandi said. "My father." But Houston said, "My mother," at the same moment.

Together they laughed while going downstairs.

Twenty-Nine

Monday morning, Sandi was drinking her coffee when Houston walked in. "Good morning. How'd everyone sleep?" he asked.

"Good," Max said.

Sandi smiled. "Is Grace up yet?"

"Not yet. I checked on her before I came down."

"We're having pancakes for breakfast," Mr. Powell said. "How many will you eat?"

"Four, please," Houston responded as he walked toward the coffeemaker.

He sat down across from Sandi and gave her a strange look. Sandi looked at him inquisitively. He gave her a brief shake of his head as her father set the plate down in front of Houston.

"Thanks, Mr. Powell. You don't have to cook for me. I can make my own meals."

"No trouble. I enjoy cooking. Sandi doesn't, so I always cook. She and Max do the cleanup."

"Then wouldn't you like to just sit and enjoy your morning coffee and let someone else serve you for once? I'd be happy to take tomorrow's shift for you."

"I've got this. You just enjoy. I'm simply happy to be able to cook for more than just two of us."

"Since I can't go to school yet, and your car is at your house, why don't you use mine for now? You can park in my space too," Sandi said.

"Really? Is that alright with you, Mr. Powell?" Houston asked.

Sandi's dad sat down with his plate of food. "Fine by me. So, what classes do you have today?"

"I have Social first block, English second, Physics third, and Communications fourth."

Sandi realized she hadn't known his schedule or classes until just now.

"What are your classes on B days?" Sandi asked.

"French, Biology, Calculus, and Choir."

"You sing?" Sandi and her dad said in unison.

"I do. I love to sing. I grew up singing in our church."

"I wasn't aware you went to church," Sandi said.

"I haven't been able to go lately because I usually end up working on Sundays. The next Sunday I have off, would you and Max want to go with me?"

"Yes." Sandi looked at Max, who nodded his head.

"I've never been to church, though," Sandi said. "I don't know what to do."

"You're going to buy into this religious stuff?" Sandi's dad said.

"Right now, you need to just keep your thoughts to yourself," Sandi responded.

"I just don't get why—" Mr. Powell began.

Sandi cut him off. "Your thoughts to yourself, Dad. I'm not kidding. You're the only one with this opinion, and your stubbornness isn't changing any of our minds."

Sandi got up from the table to start cleaning the kitchen. Houston took his dishes to her at the sink. He whispered in her ear, "Thanks for that."

Sandi smiled. "Hey, can you go see if your mom is up and ready to eat? I'll leave everything out and make hers when she's ready."

"Sure. Be right back."

"I'll make her some pancakes," Sandi's dad said.

"No. I think you've done enough. I can manage to make her some breakfast and coffee."

Max came to the sink with his dishes. "Why are you mad?"

Sandi took his dishes, dried her hands, and hugged him. "I'm sorry. It's complicated. I'll explain later. For now, I'll be better. I just saw Gretchen pull up. Can you go let her in and see if she needs any help?"

Houston came back in. "My mom is still sleeping. I wonder if she was up late. She never sleeps this late unless she went to bed late or isn't feeling well. Can you do me a favor and text me when she's up?"

"Sure. I'll let you know if she's not feeling well too," Sandi replied.

"I appreciate that. I'm gone. See you after I get out of work."

"Are you okay to work already?"

"If I don't want to lose my job, I have to be."

"You know you really don't have to work anymore?"

"I do. We have bills to pay, and I've been saving for college."

"Houston, we can help you."

"No. That's not going to happen." He paused, seeming to regret his curtness. "I'm sorry. I can't let you do that. I've got this. Thanks, though."

Sandi pulled her keys from her purse. Houston palmed them and headed out the door, throwing his backpack over one shoulder.

"Have a great day," Sandi said with a sense of loss. She'd gotten used to having him around.

Max and Gretchen came in the front door.

"Good morning, Sandi," Gretchen said. "I hope you're getting better. No school yet?"

"Not yet. Dad's still here. Houston's mom is still sleeping. I'm going to go sit with her and work on the schoolwork I've been sent until she gets up. I'll make her breakfast when she does, so I've left the pancake batter and pan out."

"What should I make for lunch?" Gretchen asked.

"Oh! I hadn't thought about it since I was going to be here. I'll think on it and let you know when I come down to get Grace's breakfast."

Gretchen turned to Max. "Ready to get started? I'll meet you in the library to begin lessons."

Max started off after Gretchen and Sandi grabbed his arm and pulled him back into the kitchen. He grinned mischievously and leaned in for a kiss.

"Wait!" she said. "I wanted to tell you something."

"Oh! What?"

"Since Gretchen probably wouldn't understand, we need to keep a fairly low profile around her."

"Sure. What's a low profile?"

Sandi laughed. "Sorry. We don't show any public displays of affection. At least no kissing on the lips, that sort of thing. It would be difficult to explain."

"I see. So, I'd better get a good kiss in now." And he sure did. Sandi thought her toes would curl.

Sandi went to the lab, gathered her laptop, and headed for Grace's room. When she got there, Grace was trying to maneuver to the edge of the bed.

"Oh! Grace, you're up. Let me help you with that." Sandi pulled her wheelchair to the side of the bed.

"I can manage from here. Thanks."

"I'll go get your breakfast and coffee. Are you okay with pancakes?"

"I'm really not hungry, but I'd love some coffee, if you don't mind."

"Be right back."

By the time Sandi had cleaned up the rest of the kitchen and returned with Grace's coffee, Grace was back in bed. Sandi handed her the hot coffee and sat in the easy chair across the room with her computer on her lap.

Grace sipped. Sandi sat in silence, waiting for Grace to speak first. Sandi didn't like to be bombarded when she first woke up, and she didn't know this woman well enough to know her habits yet.

"Is everyone gone?" Grace finally said.

"My father and Houston are. Max is with Gretchen in the library. It's just us. How are you feeling?"

"Physically, I'm good. I'm excited, there appears to be more growth." She held her arm up toward Sandi. "Emotionally, I'm spent."

Sandi went to the bed on the left side of Grace and examined the protrusion of new growth. "This is wonderful. And I'm sorry for my father's behavior. I've always lived with his unbelief. He usually says nothing to me when I disagree with him. We just agree to disagree."

"I can't do that on this subject. If not for God, I doubt I'd be here. He's been so good to me, to us."

"You and I agree. I just don't know if we can change his opinion. I'm sorry."

"Stop apologizing for something you have no control over. If it weren't for you, I'd be home right now. I do have to say I'm glad you are of one mind with my son and me on this matter. I think he would be devastated if you believed as your father does."

"Please, just give him some time. He may come around."

"He can take all the time he wants. I'm just glad I learned this now before it was too late."

"Too late for what?" Sandi inquired.

"Before I completely lost my heart to that man. For the first time since losing my husband, I began to imagine my life with someone else. That can't happen with your father. I could never be with a man who denies that God exists."

"I understand. That makes me sad. I thought the two of you were perfect for one another. I'm sorry he's as hardheaded as he is. I've never known him to believe differently. I can't imagine he'll start now." She wasn't about to tell her about her father's comments at the breakfast table.

"It's all right. If God has another man in mind for my life, he will be of the same beliefs as me. I just had a brief glimmer of hope that man might be your father. He seemed so accepting of my condition. I thought even if this didn't work, he might not reject me for not being a whole person."

"You *are* a whole person! Don't ever think like that. You're a beautiful, vibrant, intelligent woman. Any man would be lucky to have you. After seeing my dad with you, I'm certain he was seeing you the same way I do. This is his loss." She would have loved to see the two of them get together. She knew that would never happen now.

"I should just be grateful for the miracle God is doing with my limbs."

"Speaking of which, can I take a look at your leg?"

"Sure. But remember, you're supposed to be recovering."

"I'm feeling better than I did yesterday. Thank you."

"Gretchen wanted to know what she could make for lunch. Does anything sound good?"

"Honey, I'm good with anything. I'm not picky, and I'm not allergic to anything. Soup sounds good. Do you have soup?"

"We have all kinds of soups. Yes, we can do soup. Just tell me when you're hungry. Let me go tell Gretchen. I'll be right back."

Sandi went to the library, but they weren't there. She texted Houston to let him know his mother was fine. She suspected Grace had had a restless night over her father. When she returned to Grace, she was asleep. Sandi went to the chair to catch up on her schoolwork.

Several hours later, Sandi heard voices downstairs. She knew Gretchen and Max must be back. She left quietly to let Gretchen know what she and Grace had decided on for lunch. "So, where were you two?"

"The museum," Max replied.

"Oh! I'm so sorry. While you're here, would you prefer I clear it with you first?" Gretchen asked Sandi.

"No, it's no problem. I was just curious. Was it great?" Sandi asked Max.

"Wonderful! There's a lot to learn," Max said.

"He's just growing and developing so quickly. I felt I needed to seize the opportunity," Gretchen explained.

"You're right. Anything to challenge his mind."

Sandi returned to the chair in Grace's room. Shortly after getting back to work, she dozed off. She awakened to Max kissing her head.

"What is it?" Sandi asked.

"Lunch is ready," Max said.

Grace said, "Oh, good. I'm starving."

Sandi said, "You're awake. I'll go get your lunch."

Max walked over to Grace, picked her up, and turned to leave the room.

"Wait!" Sandi exclaimed. "Where are you going?"

"Lunch," Max replied.

"He's pretty strong," Grace said.

Sandi knew all too well. He'd been carrying her around for days. It was good that Grace could get out of the room for a time.

It was a fun afternoon. After lunch, Max brought Grace's wheelchair down for her to have more freedom. They taught Max to play a board game from Sandi's childhood. Sandi and Max left the two older women to watch a movie while they went for a walk. Grace protested at first, concerned it would be too much for Sandi. Max assured her he wouldn't let anything happen to her. Gretchen said she didn't get paid to watch movies. Sandi told her she did now. The pair walked out the door, chuckling.

Grace asked Max to return her to her room when they got back. She said she didn't want to be downstairs when Mr. Powell got home.

"I wish you'd talk to him and explain how you feel," Sandi expressed.

"I have nothing more to say to him," Grace replied. "He was so set in his stance that there is no God. I have no desire to frustrate myself with someone so closed-minded."

"I do understand. I also know if you appeal to his logic, he may come around."

"I'm sorry, sweetheart. I'm just not interested."

Grace seemed just as set in her way as her father was in his. She didn't think they would ever be able to bridge this gap.

After returning to Grace's room, Sandi said, "I brought the heat lamp that I used when I created Max. I kept it on him all the time. I thought we might try it for you to see if it helps expedite the process. Is that okay?"

"Yes, please. Look how well my arm is coming along."

Sandi asked Grace to get comfortable in the bed, then set the heat lamp so that it hit both her arm and her leg, pulled the covers around Grace, and gave her the remote to the TV.

"I think I'll just read for now."

"Sure. Can I get you anything?"

"I'm good. I've got my water right here and my book on my phone."

"Then if you don't mind, I'm going to go take a nap."

"Yes, please rest. You need to heal."

Sandi hugged the sweet woman.

WHEN SANDI OPENED HER EYES, it was dark outside. She hadn't intended to sleep so long. Her father must be home by now. It was odd he hadn't woken her up for dinner. She used the restroom, then went to check on Grace. She was sitting up and had adjusted the lamp to accommodate her current position. "How are you feeling?" Sandi asked.

"I feel great. How about you? Max brought me dinner a bit ago and said you were still sleeping. You must require it. I'm sorry I've been so needy and you haven't gotten to rest as you should. We'll do better tomorrow."

"No need to apologize. Today was all on me. So, you've eaten?"

"I'm good. Max has taken good care of me."

"Has my father been in to see you?"

"No. And that's fine by me."

"Can I take a look at your arm and leg?"

"Sure."

Sandi was pleased to see her theory regarding the heat lamp was right. There appeared to be a bit more growth to both, and the tissue was looking good.

"You should go eat some dinner," Grace suggested.

"It's so late, I'll just wait for Houston and eat with him."

"Are you sure? Sometimes, he eats at work, or he's so tired by the time he gets home, he doesn't eat."

"I'll be fine either way. Do you mind if I sit with you while I do my homework?"

"No. I would love the company."

She got so lost in getting as much done as she could before Houston's arrival that she didn't hear him come in until he entered the room.

"Welcome home, darling," Grace said.

"Hey, Mom. How are you feeling? What's with the heat lamp?"

"It's what I used with Max," Sandi said.

"Can I look?" he addressed Grace.

She proudly held up her limbs. "Looks good, don't they?"

He agreed.

"Are you hungry?" Sandi asked.

"Naw. I had a burger at the end of my shift."

"Why don't you go sit with Sandi while she gets something to eat? She was waiting for you." Grace said.

"You didn't eat?" Houston asked. "Why didn't you eat?"

"I took a nap and slept through dinner. I'm fine. I'm really not hungry."

"You should eat something. You need to keep your strength up to heal," Houston insisted.

"He's right," Grace said.

He grabbed her hand and led her out. "We'll be back," he called over his shoulder.

"Take your time," Grace said in response.

When they got to the hall, Max was standing there and looked down at their hands. Sandi dropped Houston's.

"Oh! Max! I missed you," Sandi said, kissing him.

Houston said. "Want to come sit with us while Sandi eats some dinner?"

"Meatloaf for dinner," Max said.

"Come on, Max, let's go eat," Sandi announced.

When she got to the kitchen, her dad was heating her plate. "Have a seat. Your dinner will be hot in just a few minutes," he said. "Houston, do you want some?"

"No, thank you. I ate at work."

"Max, are you hungry?" Sandi's dad asked.

"Always," Max replied.

They all laughed. Max pulled Sandi's chair out for her.

"Such an attentive boyfriend you are," Houston said.

Sandi leaned in for another kiss before taking her seat. She felt a glow all over.

"How was school?" Sandi asked Houston.

"It was no different besides missing you in Physics. A lot of people asked about you."

"They did? Why?" Sandi asked.

"Maybe they realized things went too far. I got a lot of ribbing for driving your car and parking in your space. Obviously, nothing I couldn't handle."

"What did you do today, princess?" her father asked.

"Some homework, took a long nap, went for a walk with Max. Grace's growth is going really well. I added the heat lamp."

"Really? Do you think she would let me take a look?" he asked.

"I don't think so. She's not happy with you. I would give her some space."

He said nothing.

"I'm sure she'll come around," Houston said after a long awkward silence.

"I don't think she is the one who needs to," Sandi spoke up.

Her father looked up at her. "They're simply my beliefs. Why is she allowed hers, but I'm not allowed mine, in my own home?"

"Because as strongly as she feels, you shut her right down and refused to even consider her side," Sandi said. "What if you actually listened to her? You should at least be open-minded about the subject. Find out why she feels as strongly as she does."

"What if she actually listened to my side, or doesn't that matter?"

"I never said it doesn't matter. You took her beliefs and essentially laughed in her face. That wasn't cool, Dad."

"I never laughed at her."

"You certainly shut her and all the rest of us down quickly."

"Okay, so what are her beliefs?"

"That's for you to find out from her."

"Houston, what is it your mother believes?" her father queried.

Houston started to open his mouth, but Sandi spoke up first. "That's not for him to say either. You should go talk with her. Don't shut her down by being a know-it-all. Listen to her. Try to understand from her perspective. What if you learn something?"

He sat for a moment longer, then went upstairs.

"You shouldn't be so hard on him," Houston said. "She can be just as stubborn as he is."

"I've seen that. But this isn't our fight. It's for them to work out between each other. If they can't, they should at least honor each other and try to understand what the other has to say."

"Agreed. I'm glad you and I are on the same page with this subject. How is it you have such a different belief from your father on this?"

"I don't know. I have always been open to new ideas. For me, it makes sense. All the research I've done leads back to God as creator, omniscient, miracle worker. My father's stance on the Big Bang—we came from nothing only to return to nothing—doesn't make sense to me. In reading, I've learned about too many things science can't explain. My dad has never given me enough evidence to change my mind, so it remains."

"Fair enough," Houston agreed.

After a long silence, Sandi said, "I was encouraged thinking our parents might develop a relationship. Now I just hope they can mend fences, so it's not awkward for all of us under the same roof."

"I had hoped the same. I'll be happy if they just come out of this on speaking terms. I would love to sit here with you all night, but I'm really tired. Will you be offended if I go to bed?"

"No. Not at all. You've had a long day. I took a long nap."

He stood, paused for just a moment, smiled, and left. She wondered what that was about. He had looked as though he was about to say something.

"Are you heading to bed?" Sandi asked Max.

"In a minute. I'm just going to finish up the kitchen first."

"I'll help you."

"No, you rest. I've got this."

She sat watching him. She knew he and Houston had been hitting their home gym pretty hard. She didn't realize just how hard until she saw the evidence straining his T-shirt with his movements. She'd never tire of looking at him. She went up behind him wrapping her arms around his narrow waist. "Do you have any idea how sexy you are?"

He leaned his head back into her with his hands in the dishwater. "Yeah, having soap suds all up my arms is really sexy."

"You have no idea." She gave him a squeeze. He turned in her arms wrapping her in his with his hands out to keep the dish water off her. He bent to meet her lips, sending bolts of lightning through her. She moaned and he intensified the kiss. She took a step back. "This isn't getting the dishes done."

"No, but it's a lot more fun." He turned back to the sink, and she swatted his behind as she walked away.

Thirty

The next morning, Sandi was pleased to find Grace at the table with everyone eating. They must have worked out their differences. She wondered how long it had taken. When she had gone to bed, her father had still been talking with Grace. She heard both their voices, so took that as a good sign. As she went to the coffee pot, her father headed for the stove.

"Waffles work for you, princess?" her dad asked.

"Sure, Daddy."

"Juice." He handed her the dreaded cup.

"Of course. Why aren't you pawning it off on Grace and Houston?"

"I'm sure they don't need it."

"Lucky them." She swallowed the liquid. "Yuck!"

"How can you force that horrible stuff on Sandi?" Grace said in Sandi's defense. "Just give her some orange or apple juice. Something that has the vitamins she needs but doesn't taste like dirty feet."

"Thank you, Grace!" Sandi said emphatically. "I've been saying this for years. He always thought I was just being difficult. I'm not. I was joking about it being a male thing, but what if that's not a joke? Maybe there's something in that Y chromosome."

"I never considered that," her father said. "Let me reconsider the ingredients. I thought you were just being belligerent."

"No, I was just being disgusted."

Houston got up from the table and kissed his mother on the top of her head. "I'm off. Thanks again for breakfast, Mr. Powell. Everyone, have a great day."

Sandi sat, drinking her coffee. Since she had all day, she might as well enjoy her morning in peace.

"What big plans do you have today?" her father asked her.

"Just finishing up my schoolwork. I'm going to stay down more today. Although I don't feel like I did a whole lot yesterday."

"I know you don't like it but maybe add an additional glass of juice this afternoon," her father suggested.

"No. I'd rather take a lifetime to heal than add another cup of that motor oil."

"It will help you heal faster."

"I don't care."

"Suit yourself."

"Make it palatable for me and we'll talk. Until then, no!"

"Gretchen is here, Max. Go let her in and see if she needs any help," her father said.

Max took his dishes to the sink, then went to the front door.

When Gretchen entered the kitchen, Mr. Powell asked if she'd like a cup of coffee as he began to rise.

"I can get it myself. Keep your seat," she replied.

"Then I guess I'll head to work," he said. "Are you going to be okay down here today, Grace?"

"Max can take me upstairs if not. For now, I'm fine. Thank you for considering me."

Well, that was a far cry from yesterday, Sandi thought. She wondered if they had worked through their difference in beliefs. They were at least being polite. She would ask Grace about it later. Her father bent to kiss the top of her head, and he was out the door. Gretchen took his seat at the table with her coffee.

"Would you like some breakfast?" Sandi asked. "It's waffles."

She smiled. "I'm fine, dear. I've eaten already." She turned to Grace.

"How are you feeling today? I noticed yesterday, the end of your limb is a bit inflamed. Would you like me to take a look at that?"

Grace covered it with her hand and stammered, "Oh, no, I'm fine. I'm having some treatments done on it at the moment. It's to be expected."

"Treatments? What sort of treatments? Are they monitoring you closely? I wouldn't want it to get infected."

"Actually, we're attempting to stimulate growth with the addition of stem cells," Sandi interjected.

"Really? That's fascinating. So, it's working?"

"It appears so," Grace said with a quick glance at Sandi.

"Grace, would you like to sit in the living room or have Max take you upstairs?" Sandi said.

"The living room would be nice."

Sandi got up, but Grace motioned for her to sit back down. She rolled out of the room.

"Come on, Max," Gretchen said. "Let's start your lessons. I'd like to take him to the aquarium today, if that's all right."

"Sure," Sandi responded. "I'm sure he'll love it."

"We're going to go learn a bit about water mammals, and then we'll head out. We'll be back by lunch."

"I can take care of lunch today."

"That would be great."

Sandi started cleaning the kitchen. When she was done, she went to the living room with Grace.

"Does Gretchen know about Max?" Grace asked.

"No. She knows he has grown and aged extraordinarily fast but hasn't asked for particulars."

"I thought I'd best err on the side of caution, so I said as little as possible."

"I appreciate that. I just don't know what she would say or how she would respond. For now, I'd rather she just focus on Max and his needs. Want to watch a movie?"

"That sounds like a plan."

"Let me take a look at you first."

Sandi examined her arm, then her leg. They had significant growth.

Previously, there was simply new tissue. Sandi saw there was now a measurable difference.

"Let me run up and get the heat lamp for you to sit under while we watch the movie. Be right back."

When Sandi returned, she had her notebook and a vernier caliper to get actual measurements and record her findings. "This is exciting, Grace. There is a full centimeter of growth on your leg and fifteen millimeters on your arm."

"Is that a lot?"

"It's significant. I'm very hopeful for you."

"I'll trust your instincts."

"Now, let's pick a movie."

At 11:30 a.m., Sandi started making sandwiches. She laid out lettuce, pickles, tomatoes, onions, and condiments for everyone to make theirs up individually. She set out drinks at everyone's place and went back to the living room to wait for Gretchen and Max to take a break.

SANDI STAYED HOME the rest of the week. She was getting stir-crazy but didn't miss school. She was glad to have a break from all those imbeciles. Her schoolwork certainly wasn't suffering. Maybe instead of pushing to graduate early and go on to college, she could talk to her father about homeschooling. She would miss Houston, but at this point, it would just mean missing him through a single class two to three times a week. The pros of not having to deal with the students and staff far outweighed the cons.

Grace and her father were getting along well. They seemed to be past their formalities with one another the day following their "talk" and were at ease again. It was nice to see them both so happy. Sandi wondered if her father's attitude about God had changed.

It was Friday night, and Houston had to work. Grace and her dad had retreated to the library after dinner, and Max was watching a show in the living room. Sandi didn't ever have time alone with her father anymore. If she had to talk about homeschooling, she might as well say it in front of Grace. It might work to her advantage.

Her father noticed her standing in the library doorway. "What is it, honey? Do you need something?"

"I wanted to talk with you about something."

"I can leave the two of you alone," Grace offered.

"No. You're fine. You feel like family," Sandi said. "I know I'm supposed to go back to school Monday, but I was thinking about it. I know you won't let me test out and go to college early."

"Right, and that hasn't changed," her father said.

"I know. So, I was thinking I could just homeschool. There are virtual programs I could do. Graduate when I'm supposed to but not have to deal with all the nastiness I've had to all my time in school. The only time I have felt as relaxed and at ease as I have this week is when school is out. I was through all my assignments for the week by Wednesday, and that was with taking a lot of breaks and doing extra research and work."

"Not happening. I've told you it's not only about entering college too young, but I want you to have the whole school experience."

"I am not having a normal school experience. I'm being bullied *all* the time. I hate living like this day after day. I do *not* want to go back."

"You're going back on Monday," her father said.

"How would you like to be in a place where you're tormented and bullied every day? How long would you remain there?"

"This isn't up for negotiation. You're going back to school."

"Why can't I do homeschool?"

"I said you're going back to school!"

"But what is the diff—"

Her father cut her off. "I said you're going back, and that's the end of this conversation."

"Alan," Grace began in her soft, kind voice, "don't you think you should listen to Sandi and try to understand where she's coming from?"

Sandi watched her father's demeanor change right in front of her. She had never seen this happen before. He seemed to relax and soften.

"What do you have to say for yourself?" he asked Sandi.

"That's not exactly what I meant," Grace said. "Sandi, why is it you don't feel you should try going back to school? You don't know that this accident hasn't changed people's perceptions of you and how you'll be treated. Do you think you should give it a try? If you do and things have not changed, we can always revisit this at that time. But what if things have changed? What if you're treated better? Wouldn't it be sad to have missed out on an opportunity to experience school and instead be isolated for the next year and a half?"

Wow! She was good, Sandi thought. She looked at her father. He sat stoically. Sandi looked back at Grace. "Okay, I'll try. If it hasn't changed, I need to know I can come back and have an actual conversation with you, Dad, not a staunch directive."

"I will try," he said. "We may have to have Grace in the conversation with us."

Sandi left the room, realizing she needed Grace in her life as much as her father did. She would love it if Grace just moved in permanently. She thought about going to the basement to cook up her next experiment but was too tired to think. She would lay in bed and watch something mindless on TV instead.

Sandi must have fallen asleep because she awoke to Houston's weight on the side of her bed. "You're home! I love your mother!"

"So do I. What'd she do?"

"She brings out the best in my dad. I told him I didn't want to go back to school and wanted to homeschool instead."

"Wait! What? Why?"

"He wouldn't even listen to me. She calmed him down and even made me change my mind about going back. How does she do that?"

Houston laughed. "I don't know. She's been like that my whole life. She was always able to calm my father down too. She would often make the two of us see the other's point of view. She has a way about her. I'm glad you're coming back. Even if just for little ol' me, please stay in school."

"The teachers and students don't bully you. I'm sick of it. I don't deserve it. I've been so relaxed this week and didn't realize what going to that place does to my mental well-being. I'm so sick of being everyone's punching bag."

"You have me now. You aren't and never will be my punching bag. You know I stand up for you."

"True. Before I got hit and everyone knew we were friends, they were still being cruel to me. Your mother seems to think things may have changed since the accident. I doubt it."

"A lot of people have asked me about you this week. She may be right."

"I'll try."

"I need you to tell me if people are still being mean. Maybe together we can combat this."

Sandi's father appeared in her room. "Houston, I didn't realize you were home. What are you doing in here?"

Houston jumped up.

"We were just talking," Sandi said.

"I'm heading to bed," her dad said with an odd look on his face.

"That was weird," Sandi said. "He's been so strange lately. What's his deal?"

"It's okay, it's his house."

"You're my friend," insisted Sandi. "We were just talking. It's not like we were doing anything wrong. I can't wait to leave here, and I'll never be back. He's the one driving me away. I hope he's happy."

"I don't think that's what he means to do. I know he loves you."

"I don't think more than he loves himself and his rigid beliefs."

"I disagree. I just don't think he's very good at communicating."

"Neither is his father. They generally have nothing to do with each other. He's developing our relationship to be the same as his with his father. I don't care for my grandfather either. I wouldn't lose a moment of sleep if I never encountered him again."

"That's sad. I have one grandmother left. I would give just about anything to have all my grandparents back. I loved all of them and couldn't spend enough time with them."

Sandi tried to imagine grandparents she wanted to spend time with, the loving grandparents so many had. It was nothing more than a fairy tale to her.

"I don't want you to break your relationship with your father."

"He's doing all this on his own. Why does he get so closed-minded on things and stop listening?"

"If you understand what his buttons are, steer clear of those subjects. If he gets heated about it, don't fuel that fire; just walk away."

"So, don't try to stand up for myself?"

"Is the way you're communicating now working for you?"

"No."

"There's my point. You know what's going to happen if you keep pushing him. He doesn't change his mind, he just digs in. So, what will happen if you just drop it and walk away?"

"Okay. I'll try. So, he gets his way, and I just get frustrated. Great!"

"I'm not saying he gets his way. You just need to take a step back and find a different approach to what you think and feel to help him see your point of view. What you're currently doing isn't working. Try something different."

Sandi thought about this a moment. He had a point.

"I'm going to go check to see if my mom is ready to go to bed."

"Go help her. I'm going to sleep. I'll see you tomorrow. Thanks for helping me feel better."

Houston's absence made Sandi long for Max more. He had gone to bed already. She crossed the hall and slipped into the bed beside him. He rolled over and cuddled her into him. She drifted off to sleep, feeling loved and secure. He was hers.

Thirty-One

Monday at school, Sandi found herself tense, just waiting for something mean to happen. It didn't. Houston walked her to her homeroom. She walked in, took her seat, and looked around. No one was saying anything. She was unnerved. This reaction was so different from all her school years that she wasn't sure how to react or what to do with it. The teacher took roll call, the bell rang, and she went to her next class. Many people said kind things to her. Maybe Grace was right. Maybe she could get through her remaining time.

Houston met her at lunchtime.

"I didn't think to bring a lunch," Sandi said.

"No big deal. We'll buy our lunch and eat outside."

"That's okay. I'll meet you at the picnic tables. I don't go in the cafeteria."

"Ever?"

"Ever. The last time I did, Betty threw me to the floor, and my lunch went everywhere, leaving everyone laughing at me. I've never been back."

"Well, isn't it good for you Betty is no longer here? Come on. I'm starving."

He led her through the line. No one did or said anything. She felt all the stares, though.

When they set their trays down on the table, Houston said, "See? That wasn't so bad, was it?"

"Did you see all those people staring at me?"

"So? Who cares?"

"Funny guy! Apparently, I care. I've been going home to check on Max for so long, I forgot what it was like not to race through lunch."

"I've been meaning to ask you if you think his aging will begin to slow down? I mean, does he just keep aging exponentially? Does that decrease his longevity?"

"I'm hoping it doesn't. I didn't think about the aging process."

"His intelligence seems to be matching his growth rate. He's really smart, Sandi."

"Yeah, I see that."

"What if he outsmarts you?"

"Be my guest. It doesn't take away from me, it just goes to show what I created," she whispered.

"Good point."

"Have you thought any more about enrolling him in this school?"

"I thought about it for just a moment, but I would never want to subject him to the same ridicule I have suffered."

"You can't protect him forever. He's a really nice guy. I think everyone would like him."

"You said you thought I was really nice."

"You are."

"Look how I'm treated."

"I know, but we're going to change that. By the way, I have to work tonight. I can run you home after school, if I can borrow your car. We'll need to get out right away so I'm not late."

"Sure. Fine by me."

"Okay. There's first bell; let's go."

As they walked to drop off their trays, Sandi said, "I have to say, today hasn't been bad. This is the first time I've ever said that about school."

"Come on, let's finish this out."

They went two different directions.

"You're pathetic," came Kristy's voice from behind her.

Without looking back, Sandi said, "Yeah, I missed you too, Kristy."

Sandi held her breath, waiting to see what came next. Nothing did. Kristy giving Sandi lip gave Sandi a sense of normalcy. She went to her next class with pep in her step. She just might be able to do this.

THE MONTHS PASSED. The McAvoys sold their house and moved in permanently with the Powells. It was senseless for Grace and Houston to try to maintain their home while everyone always stayed at the Powell house. Grace moved into Sandi's father's suite with him. They were so good for each other. Her father was the happiest Sandi had ever seen him. Sandi was glad to know he wouldn't be alone when she left.

Houston and Sandi spent their free time with experiments in the lab, ever perfecting the best way to grow limbs and give people an alternative to prosthetics. Max usually hung out with them but focused a lot of his time learning and using languages. He had been accumulating friends around the world to hone his skills.

Grace's limbs were developing better than expected—she had even grown fingers and toes. There was always the possibility that Grace's new limbs might not be as they originally were, but Grace was thrilled. She announced she would be going back to work. Mr. Powell had tried to talk her out of it, but she felt it gave her a sense of purpose and pride. In the end, they agreed she could work as she liked since providing an income was no longer the goal. She was finding greater success since she was no longer part of the cutthroat competitive aspect to beat out other agents. She was having a lot of fun now at what she loved to do. She still had a slight limp, but they were all hopeful that, with time and a bit more growth, that would go away.

Mr. Powell had begun talking with the local Veterans' agencies, explaining what they had accomplished and seeing if there were any others who would be willing to work with them to make a better way.

This year, the holidays were a lot of fun with a houseful. Max enjoyed experiencing all the festivities and excitement. Houston suggested they serve meals at the local shelter on Thanksgiving Day with his church. Sandi had never thought to do anything like it. She found it made the day more significant. She wanted to do this every year. They couldn't get her father to join them, so Grace stayed home with him to prepare the family feast together.

The shelter was packed with people in need, even full families. As she dished out stuffing, Sandi realized that she had never gone without anything she wanted, let alone needed. She had certainly never missed a meal. The woman she was serving with explained that for many, this would be the only meal they got for a few days. It broke Sandi's heart. She was now aware of so much need that she, in her sheltered life, had known nothing about. She refused to feel guilty, but that didn't mean she couldn't choose to do more in the future. She signed up, along with Max and Houston, to help at the soup kitchen once a month.

Christmas regained its magic seen through Max's eyes. It had been a long time since it held the level of excitement she felt watching Max experience all the wonder. He loved the decorations, lights, and gifts. He most enjoyed shopping for others. Houston's church sponsored a huge Christmas drive for inner-city children. Sandi, Max, and Houston had a great time shopping for the collection boxes. They bought food, clothes, shoes, toys, and games for the less fortunate. This year, Sandi felt more of the meaning of the season. For so many years, she had been ignoring this time of year, believing it was nothing more than a reason for consumerism. Sandi knew that, just like her, Max had everything he wanted or needed. When she asked him what he'd like for Christmas, he said, "Nothing but you."

Grace made the holiday extra special when she made a birthday cake for Jesus' birthday. Sandi was surprised her father didn't push back. He just went along with all of them. Sandi couldn't imagine what Grace had said to bring about this attitude adjustment in such a stalwart man. Max insisted on singing "Happy Birthday." Partway through the song, she noticed Grace was no longer singing, just looking at Max in a strange way. She prayed the woman wasn't thinking what Sandi thought she must be. Houston and Max looked like brothers and now possessed the same exceptional singing voice.

Occasionally, Sandi would see Grace looking between Houston and Max in quiet contemplation. She never said anything.

School had become bearable for Sandi, and the haters had stopped harassing Houston for being her friend, just as he said they would. Although some of the teachers were still threatened by her intelligence and talked down to Sandi, the overall response from everyone was much better than before the accident. Sandi and Max had been to church with Houston and Grace a few times. Her father refused to attend. Sandi was learning to walk away from fighting with her dad when she disagreed with him. Sometimes she would revisit the subject, but often, she just let it go. He was entitled to his opinion even if he didn't respect hers.

Mr. Powell suggested that Max test in and enroll in high school in the new year since Gretchen was having a hard time keeping up with him. Sandi was a nervous wreck. How would he be accepted? Especially when people found out they were a couple. Although Max scored off the charts, Mr. Powell convinced the school district to allow him to be a junior with Houston and Sandi. Sandi didn't understand why her father had to complicate things. She felt she and Max would be just fine homeschooling. No one would need to know anything. Her father still refused.

Sandi found herself more insecure than ever because every girl in the school was hitting on Max. He was always polite but made it clear he was with Sandi. She felt like no one in school liked her and everyone liked Max. She didn't understand why. They were both highly intelligent people. It was a clear distinction based strictly on gender bias. It wasn't fair.

When Max would kiss Sandi, other students would tell him that he should dump the trash. Girls even went so far as to put their hands all over him while she was standing right there with him. He seemed to really like the attention.

Max had been pushing Sandi to have sex. She assured him it would be soon. Although he lit her body up every time he even looked her way, she didn't know if she was ready to take that next big step yet.

One night, when she had him stop before they went too far, he asked, "Is it just that you don't want to make love with me?"

"No! I do. This is a big deal to me. I can never unring that bell."

"Why would you want to? Am I not enough?"

"Oh, yeah, you most certainly are," she said with a goofy grin on her face. "I just want to be certain I'm really ready."

"Are you sure it's not something else?"

"Something else? Like what?"

"What if Houston wanted to sleep with you, would you do it then?"

She was appalled. "Max!"

"That's not an answer."

"No! I wouldn't. I love you. I'm with you. I'm just asking you to be patient with me."

"I have been."

"I'm getting there. Seriously, what would make you think something like that? Houston is just a friend. We've never even ever kissed."

"Never?"

"No. He's not my boyfriend. You are."

"But do you wish it was him instead of me?"

"No! Why would you think that?"

"I see the way he looks at you."

She was shocked. She believed he must be imagining things. "Look, Houston had his chance but shut me down, saying he only wanted to be friends. It was fine with me because just after that, you kissed me and turned my world upside down."

"So, you only love me?"

"Yes."

"You only want to have sex with me?"

"Absolutely. That day is coming soon. Just please give me the time to mentally prepare that I need."

He smiled, raised an eyebrow, and began kissing her passionately again.

MAX, Sandi, and Houston were hanging out in the hallway between classes. Kristy walked up and stepped in front of Max, putting Sandi at her back. Kristy placed her hand on Max's chest and said, "Hi, Max. So good to see you. I'm having a party Saturday at my house, I'd love for you to come."

Max pushed Kristy's hand off him. "Sure. What time and what address?"

Kristy pressed a card into his hand. "Everything you need to know is on there."

"Great! We'll be there."

"Not Sandi, just you. You can come too, Houston."

Max handed the card back to Kristy. "Never mind. If Sandi's not welcome, I'm not interested."

"Fine. Bring her if you must." Kristy huffed and walked away.

"I've never been to a party," Sandi said.

"Never?" Houston asked.

"Nope. No one has ever invited me to anything."

"I didn't realize that. I'd have taken you to parties if I'd known. I just usually don't go. I'm not a drinker, and they're not that exciting to me."

"What do you mean, you're not a drinker?" Max asked. "I've seen you drink plenty of times."

"Alcohol, buddy. We're not supposed to drink alcohol at our age, but a lot of kids do. They usually can't handle it, so they make fools of themselves or make bad decisions—then have to face the consequences."

"Oh. We don't have to drink alcohol though, right?"

"Right. But make sure you don't accept drinks from other people and never leave your drink unattended."

"Why?" he asked.

"Because people can spike your drink."

"What does that mean, spike your drink?"

"They can slip something in it like drugs or alcohol."

"Got it."

Sandi was learning just as much as Max was in this exchange.

SATURDAY NIGHT, the trio showed up at the address they were given. There were a lot of cars parked on the streets. They followed the loud music and throngs of people. When they walked into the house, the guys were quickly pulled away from Sandi. She tried to keep up but lost them in the sea of bodies. She kept trying to find where they had gone but there were too many people. She found herself paranoid about ingesting anything after everything Houston had said, so she just wandered around, trying to find anywhere to fit in or find her boys. Neither happened. Eventually, she went to the front steps to wait until they got ready to go. People made snide comments as they passed her, but no one engaged with her.

Much later, Houston sat down next to her. "Hey! What are you doing out here?"

"Waiting for you two." She looked around. "Where's Max?"

"I was going to ask you the same thing."

"Both of you got separated from me when we walked through the door, and I couldn't find you."

"Yeah, Max and I got pulled in two different directions too. You good to go?"

"Absolutely."

"Let's go find Max."

"Are you sure you can't do it alone? I'm too short to see past the crowd, and I hunted for both of you all night. You're a lot bigger than me. I have no interest in losing you again."

"Oh, sure. I'll be right back."

Sandi sat waiting for what felt like forever. When they returned together, Max led the way and walked right past Sandi with Houston on his heels. It was Houston who grabbed Sandi's hand to pull her with him. She tried looking into Houston's eyes, but he refused with a strange look on his face. What had happened?

When they got to the car, Houston got behind the wheel to drive them home. Sandi climbed in the back seat behind Houston, and Max rode shotgun. There was a deafening silence. When she couldn't stand it one more minute, Sandi said, "What'd I miss?"

Neither of them said a word and just looked straight ahead.

"No one's going to tell me what's going on?"

Nothing. Now, she was worried. What could have been so bad that they weren't talking to her?

"Did you have a drink, Max? Is that what this is about?"

Still silence.

"You two are making me worry. What's wrong?"

"Now is not the time, Sandi," was all Houston said.

At least that was something.

When they got to the house, Max was out of the car before Houston had even turned off the engine. By the time Sandi had gotten out, Max was long gone. She grabbed Houston by the arm and turned him to face her. "Tell me what happened."

"You don't want to know."

"Clearly I do."

"Sandi, trust me on this."

She felt her insides go cold. She couldn't imagine what was going on, but the tone of Houston's voice and the look on his face told her whatever it was, she needed to leave it alone for now.

When they entered the living room, Sandi's dad asked how the party was and if they had a good time.

"It was my first and last," Sandi said.

"Max didn't even answer us. I think he went to his room. Is he alright?" Grace asked.

"It's been a night, Mom. The party was typical. Not my thing, and I don't care if I never attend another. I'm going to bed. I'll see you in the morning." He kissed Grace's cheek and went up the stairs without even glancing at Sandi.

The parents looked at Sandi like she had the answers. "Don't look at me. I'm clueless. I got separated from them as soon as we got there. Couldn't find them, so spent the night sitting on the front steps alone." She shrugged her shoulders.

"Were they drinking?" her father asked.

"I'm not sure. I don't think Houston was. He didn't smell like he had been, and you know I wouldn't have let him drive if he had. And Max just walked past me. I really don't know."

"Well, everything looks better in the light of day," Grace added.

Sandi sure hoped so because right now, she felt sick to her stomach.

Thirty-Two

When Sandi awoke, she was determined to find out about the night before. Max had never been that dismissive of her before. Houston was clearly mad but wouldn't say why. He hadn't been that way before he'd gone to get Max. Something must have happened in the house. Max didn't seem like he was drunk or not in control of his faculties. She couldn't imagine what else it could be. Had he been doing drugs? Whatever the case might be, she was going to know before sunset on this day. She'd had a horrible night's sleep, and that wasn't going to happen again.

Sandi showered and dressed before going to the kitchen. When she entered, Houston, Grace, and her dad were at the table, but there was total silence. No one was eating or drinking or speaking.

"Good morning?" Sandi said as a question.

Her father stood and hugged her to him but said nothing. He hugged her every morning, but this felt different. She looked at Houston, who wouldn't look at her. Even Grace, in all her sweetness, was saying nothing. This nightmare couldn't continue. She could tell she was going to need her coffee for whatever this one was.

After sitting down with her hot mug and a few sips, Sandi said,

"Alright, out with it. What happened? And why won't anyone talk to me? Where's Max?"

They all looked at each other and not at her.

"You're scaring me. Why won't anyone talk to me?"

"We don't want to hurt you," her father said finally.

"Hurt me? Not talking to me, not explaining to me what's going on, is what's hurting me."

Houston got up from his chair, sat down in Max's seat, and put his arm around her. What in the world was so bad that he felt the need to do this?

She pulled back to look him in the eye, and he looked away.

"I swear if you don't tell me what's going on right now, I'm going to go off on someone, and it won't be pretty!"

"I'm really sorry, Sandi," was all he said.

"For what? Who died?"

"I went to go find Max."

"No kidding. I was there."

"I found Max in a compromising position."

"Compromising how?" She looked at Grace. She had tears in her eyes. She turned to her father, who looked away.

"Very," was all Houston managed to say.

"Exactly how compromising?"

"He was in bed with Jana."

"Jana Proctor?"

"Yes."

Sandi felt all the blood drain from her face, and her hands began to shake. Houston covered them with his. She began to shake her head. "That can't be true. He was kissing Jana Proctor, of all people?"

Houston just shook his head.

Sandi sucked air. "No!"

Houston nodded.

"No! He was not having sex with Jana!"

"I'm really sorry."

Sandi began to tremble all over. Houston wrapped her in his arms. Over and over, Sandi shook her head, repeating, "No, no, no, no..." She crumpled into Houston's lap and sobbed.

Houston let her while rubbing her back. He kept whispering, "I'm really sorry."

Sandi had no idea how long she stayed in that position, but when she had no more tears to shed, she sat back up and just looked at each person at the table. She now understood their silence.

"How did this happen? Is it because I wouldn't have sex with him? Should I have let him make love to me like he wanted? Would he still be mine if I had?"

Sandi's dad and Grace started talking at the same time. Grace stopped and said, "You go, Al."

"Honey, you were not wrong. He's the one in the wrong here. Yes, you made him for you, but you can't control the decisions he makes on his own. He needed to respect your wishes and wait until you were ready. It's not like he wasn't told how to control his urges."

"But why Jana Proctor? I don't understand why her. She's a skank. Sorry, Houston."

"No apologies necessary. You're not saying anything I haven't thought."

"Really? That's how you feel, Houston?" Grace asked. "Isn't she the little girl you dated for some time?"

"Yes, which means I know what I'm talking about."

"Oh, dear."

"Where's Max now?" Sandi asked.

"He hasn't been down yet this morning," her father said.

Sandi got up from the table with determination.

"What are you going to do?" Houston asked.

"Confront him." She walked away.

At the top of the stairs, Sandi squared her shoulders, took a cleansing breath, and slammed open Max's door. "Get up!"

He jumped from the bed. "Sandi!"

"You want to act like a grown man, you'll face me like one. You had sex with Jana Proctor?" she demanded.

He hung his head.

"Answer me," she bellowed.

"Yes."

She waited. He said nothing more.

"Just yes?"

"Sorry?"

"Really? Sorry you got caught, you mean?"

"Yes.

"Oh, not sorry for cheating on me?"

"You didn't want to make love with me, she did."

"And you think that makes it okay?"

"I liked it. She liked it. She's pretty. She was very nice to me."

"Well, yeah, because she was going to make sure to hurt me by taking what she knew was mine."

"It wasn't about you. It was about me. She likes me. I like her. I liked having sex with her."

"If you think it wasn't about me, you're sadly mistaken, but I sure hope you have a great life with her. And you better hope you didn't catch something—she's slept with most of the guys in the school." Sandi turned to walk out of the room.

Max grabbed her around the waist to pull her to him. "Wait! I just had sex with her. That was all."

"Get your hands off me."

He dropped his hands to his sides.

"Don't you ever touch me again. I made you for me. To love me. To want only me. Not the likes of Jana. To live out life with me. Not to be the plaything of my haters to use against me to hurt me. I don't know how you could do that to me."

"I love *you*, Sandi."

"That's not love. That's betrayal. No one has ever hurt me like you just did. I'll never give you an opportunity to harm me again."

"I don't want her. I want you."

"Obviously, not enough. I'm no longer a possibility for you. Best of luck with the mean girls. You might as well run on back to Jana."

She went across the hall to her room, closed the door, threw herself face down on her bed, and cried.

Sandi wasn't sure how long she lay there. She didn't have a clue what time it was when Houston tapped on her door and let himself in. "Are you all right?"

"I don't think I'll ever be all right again."

He sat down beside her and rubbed her back. "I really am sorry."

"Thanks. I feel like such a fool."

"You shouldn't. You didn't do anything. This is on Max and Jana."

"I was so stupid to think I could fix how people saw me by making my own boyfriend, then showing him off like he was some prize. I thought that would make me valued, that I would have validation. The reality is, I wasn't fooling anyone but myself. No one likes me, and having a cute boyfriend only put a bigger target on my back. One more way to hurt me, to make me suffer and pay."

Houston gathered her up in his big, strong arms and pulled her to his chest. "Now, stop it. None of that is true. You are far from stupid. You are valued, and you don't need a boyfriend. It doesn't matter what the kids in this school think. It's really only what you think that matters. Once you finally recognize your value, you won't care what anyone else thinks of you."

"Yeah, sure, you can say that because you're so well-liked and heart-stoppingly good-looking." Sandi held her breath. She couldn't believe she just told him how she felt. She waited for him to drop her back to the bed and walk out.

Instead, he pulled his head back to look at her.

"Sorry. I'm a bit overwhelmed right now," she said in her defense.

"Is that really what you think?"

"It's what I know."

"You think I'm attractive?"

"Well, duh! You know you are."

Houston blinked a couple of times. "Really?"

"Really what?"

"I must be missing it."

"Wait a minute. Are you kidding me right now?"

He just looked at her with a lost look on his face.

"Houston MacAvoy! You are the most good-looking man on the planet. If you're fishing for compliments, I'm happy to oblige, but you must know it."

He just sat there staring at her, then he leaned in and kissed her. She knew she must be dreaming—she had wanted him for so long. She sighed against his mouth, and he intensified the kiss.

He sat back and said, "What took you so long to tell me?"

"You only wanted to be friends."

"No. I wanted more. You told me you made yourself a boyfriend, then when I met Max, there was no way I could compete with him, so I tried to focus on other things. I was just happy to get some time with you, to learn from you."

"No way. You're being serious?"

"Dead serious."

Sandi wrapped her arms around his neck and snuggled into him, inhaling his intoxicating scent. "Please don't ever leave me."

"I could say the same."

"Do you know how long I've wanted you?"

"I've wanted *you* since the first time I met you. I heard you talking, and I was done for."

She laughed. "You wanted me?"

"Oh, yeah!"

She was finding this too hard to believe.

"I'm no Jana Proctor."

"Thank God! Why do you think I don't have a girlfriend?"

"Wait! What? What do you mean?"

"In my eyes, no girl compares."

"But until just last year, you would never have anything to do with me."

"Not true. Sometimes, I felt like a stalker. How do you think I was always there when you needed me?"

"How did I not know any of this?"

"I told you that you tend to stay lost in your thoughts. You apparently just never noticed me."

"Oh, that's where you are so wrong. I noticed you all right!"

He kissed her again. "What do you say we start this day over? How about some breakfast?"

"What time is it?"

"True. How about some lunch?"

She laughed and got up.

He pulled her to him and said, "I'm so glad we cleared the air, and I'm not carrying around this secret anymore."

"How am I supposed to face Max?"

"It's not you who has to worry about facing Max, it's the other way around. That's on him."

"What's he going to think about us?"

"I don't care. Why would you?"

"He accused me of wanting to sleep with you as being the reason I wouldn't have sex with him."

"What? Why?"

"He said he saw the way you looked at me. I told him he was imagining it."

"Oops! It was hard to hide how I felt with you always so close. You loved Max. You were with him. I had no choice but to keep my feelings to myself."

"You said you only wanted to be friends."

"Because you told me it was Max you wanted."

"Houston!"

"What?"

"You really don't see it?"

"See what?"

She needed to tell him the truth, but she didn't know where to start. This would have been a lot easier if he had figured out that Max looked like him on his own. "I'm not sure how to tell you. I really can't live without you, and I'm so afraid you'll hate me forever."

"I could never hate you, let alone forever. Just say it."

"You never noticed how Max looks like you?"

"No, he doesn't."

She couldn't read the look on his face. She saw his wheels turning but couldn't make out where his thoughts were going.

"Way back when I conceived of Max..." She paused.

"Don't stop there."

"When I tried to think of the perfect boyfriend..."

She searched his eyes but knew he hadn't connected the dots.

"I've always wanted you, Houston."

"I don't get it. What's that got to do with you claiming Max looks like me?"

"Um, remember when you dropped your hoodie, and I picked it up?"

"Yeah."

"Um..."

"Um, what? Just tell me."

"You had some hair on it. I took it." She said it like ripping off a Band-Aid.

"You took hair off my—" he froze mid-sentence.

Sandi looked at the floor, wringing her hands together. She looked up at him.

He stared blankly at her a moment longer with his mouth open. "You didn't."

She nodded her head.

"Why?"

"I wanted you to be my boyfriend so badly. I didn't believe you could ever even notice me. I was so lonely. I believed if I couldn't have you, I could make the next best thing."

"Oh. My. God. Sandi!"

"I know. I shouldn't have. I just wanted him to have your intelligence, your personality, your good looks. It was wrong. I know that. I'm sorry."

He sat down hard on the bed, staring ahead.

"Please say something. Please say you understand, and it will be all right."

"I don't know if I do understand, and I don't know if it will be."

She went to him and knelt in front of him, taking his hands in hers. "Please, Houston. I can't lose you too. You mean the world to me."

"You're going to need to give me a minute here," he said, raising one hand in front of him at Sandi. "This is big."

"I know. I should have asked permission. At the time, it was just a theory. I never wanted to keep secrets from you. Once I'd done it, I was too embarrassed to tell you. I never dreamed he would look exactly like you. I used someone else's stem cells. I didn't know how to tell you. I never meant for it to go this far."

"It already has."

"I know. I'm sorry. Please forgive me and tell me we can get past this."

"Just give me a minute." He shook his head, looking at his feet.

She sat down on the floor and crossed her legs. She would give him all the time he needed. She prayed this wouldn't end badly. They sat in silence for the next two hours. It was killing her, but she would wait for him to make the next move.

"What are we supposed to tell people?" he finally said.

"I don't know. You're the one always telling me it doesn't matter what anyone else thinks."

"This is a lot bigger than 'You called me a mean name,' Sandi."

"I know it is, but I also believe together, we can get through anything."

"Oh, girl, you're too smart for any of us, especially your own good. What am I going to do with you?" He took her hands in his and pulled her up. She sat on his lap and wrapped her arms around his neck.

"Keep me?"

He shook his head. "We better come up with something good to tell the world."

"Should we just tell the truth?"

"What? That you made Max? That's not what I meant. No. If he really looks like me, we need to come up with a believable reason why."

Thirty-Three

Since Sandi had never been good at makeup, she set an appointment at her salon for someone to not only create a fancy updo but apply her makeup as well. When they were done, she liked her reflection, but she felt like she was looking at someone else. She had to get over her imposter syndrome before this evening. She wanted Houston to be proud of the woman on his arm. She still struggled with worthiness where he was concerned. She tried to keep in mind that her intellect was far superior to her peers, and that was what most appealed to her man.

She and Houston fielded a lot of flack from the kids at school. Max being with the "in crowd" didn't help. He started dating Jana openly and shunned Houston and Sandi in school. Sandi was sad he wanted nothing to do with her, but her betrayed heart allowed her to move past it.

Sandi slipped into the beautiful gown she had paid to have altered to perfectly fit her small frame. She put on her stilettos, which would help close the gap in their height. She added a flashy necklace and matching earrings. One last look in the full-length mirror, and she headed downstairs.

Partway down the staircase, Max said, "Wow!"

She froze and grinned. "You look pretty good yourself." He was in a tuxedo.

Everyone came to the bottom of the stairs. "You look beautiful," Grace said.

Her father's mouth momentarily hung open, then he closed it. Houston had a look she couldn't read. He just stared from the foot of the stairs, all decked out. He took her breath away. He was as handsome as Sandi had imagined he would be.

When she got to the bottom, Houston put an arm around her waist, pulled her close, and kissed her. "Oops! Sorry. Did I mess up your lipstick?" he asked.

She laughed. "No. It's a stay-on kind. You can't mess it up, but you can be my guest and try."

Her father found his words. "Grace is right. You do look beautiful, honey. You don't look like my little girl anymore. That makes me sad."

"Oh, Daddy." Sandi gave him a hug.

"Come on, the photographer is in the gardens waiting for all of you," her father said.

After countless pictures, Houston led her like a porcelain doll to the waiting limousine. The driver opened the door for them, and Houston motioned for Sandi to get in first. She could feel him gathering her dress into the vehicle behind her, and she smiled. He was so thoughtful. She wondered if having Grace as his mother was responsible for that. The driver explained that all the chilling bottles were sparkling cider of various sorts, so they were free to drink any of them. Mr. Powell cautioned Houston as they were leaving to take good care of his baby.

There was no way she was sharing a vehicle with Jana, so Max took his own car.

When they pulled to the curb at the prom, everyone stopped to see who was coming by limo. When they stepped out, the mystery was over, and everyone continued into the building. Sandi felt ten feet tall on Houston's arm. A few people complimented them, many just turned away. Some of Houston's friends fist-bumped him and made sexual innuendos. Houston seemed puffed up with pride, which made her feel even more special. The gymnasium had been transformed into a wonderland. If she hadn't known what it was by its location, she would never have guessed it to be the school gym. Music was playing, people were milling, and everything felt festive. No one was dancing.

"Wait here, I'll get us something to drink," Houston said and walked away.

"Look what the cat dragged in," Jana said from behind her.

Sandi felt a chill go up her spine and turned to see Jana in a fully sequined, floor-length gown, looking amazing as usual. Sandi's first instinct was to be nasty back, but she chose to be the bigger person.

"You look beautiful, Jana," she said instead.

"Of course, I do," Jana spat back. "Here alone? I'm not surprised."

Max looked down at the floor but said nothing.

"No. She's never alone," Houston said from behind Jana, handing Sandi a glass.

She spun to face him. She was obviously as struck by his appearance as Sandi had been.

"Oh! Houston, I hadn't seen you," Jana said sweetly.

"Play nice, Jana. You got what you wanted."

Kristy walked up. "I see the freak couple has arrived."

Sandi felt her blood boil. Houston squeezed her hand.

Kristy's date dropped her hand and man-hugged Houston. "Hey, dude! I didn't know you were going to be here. You clean up pretty good."

"You too," Houston said.

"You know each other?" Kristy said in surprise.

"Yeah, our parents used to hang out together all the time," her date said. "We were practically brothers."

Houston said, "Sandi, I want you to meet an old friend of mine. This is Graham. Graham, this is my girlfriend, Sandi."

"Eeugh! That is so gross," Kristy said. "Let's go." And she tried to pull Graham away.

"Is he your chess buddy?" Max asked.

Graham dropped Kristy's hand and extended it to Max.

"Yeah, this is him," Houston said. "Graham, this is Max."

"Nice to meet you, man," Graham said.

"I'm not spending my time with the maggot. Now come on, Graham." Kristy pulled at him once more.

"We'll catch up later," Graham called over his shoulder. "I want to know more about your date—she's hot!"

Sandi blushed. She knew that wasn't going to go over well with Kristy. Houston whispered in Sandi's ear, "Oh, yes, she is."

Sandi's blush spread more. A few couples stopped to talk to them before Houston took her cup, set it on the nearest table, and led her by the hand to the dance floor.

"What are you doing?" Sandi asked. "No one else is dancing yet."

"Then I think it's time to start," Houston responded. "I know I didn't just come to make small talk with people I see all the time. I came to dance with my unbelievable girlfriend and make the most of the night."

Sandi truly felt special. He pulled her close for a slow dance. The feeling of him pressed against her like this stirred feelings that were hard to control, but they felt so good. She could do this all night. She noticed more couples joining them on the floor as the music played on.

When the buffet opened, Houston led Sandi to a table, pulled out her chair, and told her he would make her plate. He certainly knew by now what she liked and didn't. She trusted him. "Save my seat," Houston said. "I'm sure every guy in here wants you for his date, but you're mine."

Sandi felt that familiar blush climb her neck to her cheeks. His declaration of possession stirred something deep inside her.

Houston returned and set their plates down. Right behind him came Graham. "Can we sit here?" he asked.

"Sure," said Houston.

"No!" I'm not sitting with the scab," Kristy announced.

"Come on!" Graham pushed back. "I haven't seen this guy in ages. I want to sit here."

"Go right ahead," Kristy said indignantly. "I'll be sitting elsewhere."

"It's okay," Houston said. "Go sit with her, we'll catch up later."

Graham obediently followed. Sandi saw them sit with Jana and Max. A few looks were tossed their way. Sandi didn't care. This was turning out to be the best night of her life.

After the prom, Houston gave the driver the address of their destination. They pulled up at the Ritz Carlton.

"I thought you didn't want to do the hotel thing," Sandi said.

Houston laughed. "No. It's not like that. This is the venue Preston's parents rented for the after-party."

Preston's parents were very wealthy. His father was a surgeon and his mother an anesthesiologist. Sandi liked Preston well enough, though they didn't run in the same circles. Houston and Preston had always been good friends. Houston led Sandi into the hotel. A staff member asked if they were with the Monroe party and directed them to the ballroom. There were a lot of people there. The ballroom opened to a tiered terrace, which led to an Olympic lap pool with tropical plants and soft, white lights surrounding it. It was magical.

"This is beautiful," Sandi said.

"See what money buys," Houston said, then quickly corrected himself. "I'm so sorry. I didn't mean it the way it sounded."

"It's all right," Sandi replied. "I understand. You're right. It does buy extravagance. I just haven't had the need for it."

"You and your father do live modestly for what you probably have. You don't flaunt your money in anyone's face. I would imagine you, alone, have more money than the Monroes combined, but no one would ever know."

Sandi considered that for a moment. He was probably right, but she tried not to think about it.

"Hey," Preston said as he approached them. "I'm glad you two could make it." He leaned in and kissed Sandi on the cheek. "You look stunning."

"Thanks, Preston," Sandi responded. "You look great yourself. Thanks for having us. This is beautiful."

"Yeah," Preston replied. "It's all my mom. She loves doing this sort of thing. My dad and I just go along with whatever she says." He laughed, and they laughed with him. "Get some food, some drink. The staff is circling with eats and stuff to wet your whistle. Make yourselves at home. Gotta mingle. See ya later."

"What a nice guy," Houston said when he was gone.

"Yeah, he's never been mean to me," Sandi said. "On the other hand, he's never had anything to do with me."

"I'm sorry. He's really one of the good guys and has always been a good friend to me. Actually, I'm not sure what I would have done after my father died if it weren't for Preston."

"I think everyone has always been a good friend to you."

"Not everyone."

"Really? Like whom?"

"Like him right there." He pointed at the school's golden boy, the star quarterback.

"You don't like Connor?"

"More like he doesn't like me."

"What'd you ever do to him?"

"I have no idea. He's not very smart, and he's all into sports, so we've never had much in common."

"I've heard you talk sports with people. What are you talking about?"

"It's different. He's obnoxious about it. He's a know-it-all and takes the fun out of discussing a game. He can't carry on a conversation about anything outside of sports, particularly football. He gets flustered and then defensive. He turns on anyone smarter than he is, which is everyone. I'm sure it's his insecurities."

"I didn't realize that."

"Yeah, I think it's why he and Kristy dated so long. Once she found someone to control, who didn't mind being controlled, they just worked."

"Do you know why they broke up?"

"I had heard it was because she wanted to see someone new. I'm going to have to fill Graham's ear another time."

Kristy walked up to them. "Who invited you?"

"Preston," Houston simply said.

"Well, you can go out the same way you came in. You're not welcome here."

"Back atcha, Kristy," Houston said.

Sandi's heart began to pound. She really didn't want a fight tonight.

"What'd you just say to her, scum?" Connor addressed Houston.

"Look, no one wants a fight. We were minding our own business. She started it," Houston said.

"And I'm gonna end it," Connor said, taking off his jacket.

"Whoa, big boy!" Preston came up from the side. "This is a party, not the football field. Now, go get a drink and cool off." Preston directed them to the nearest wait staff.

"You better watch yourself," Connor said to Houston, then stalked away.

"You okay?" Preston asked.

"Yeah, we're fine," Sandi said. "Thanks again."

"Sure, enjoy." And he walked away.

"Let's take a walk around the grounds," Houston suggested and took Sandi's hand.

They descended the terrace steps, walked around one end of the pool, and followed a path across the grounds. Sandi felt the tension leave Houston as they walked.

"He always knows how to push my buttons. He and Kristy were perfect for each other. I have no idea what Graham sees in her."

Sandi chuckled. "You make me laugh."

Houston stopped, turned to her, looked longingly in her eyes for a long while, lowered his mouth to hers, paused, then began kissing her. There went that flush through her body again. She loved his nearness, his touch, his taste on her lips. He drove her mad with desire. She just might make this their night.

"I better stop before I can't," Houston said.

"I didn't say you have to."

He stood just looking at her a long time. She saw his mind racing and wondered what conclusion he was coming to. She hoped he wanted her the same way she wanted him.

He said, "Come on, let's head back."

When they got to the pool, Graham was standing there alone. "Hey, guys!"

"Hi, Graham," Houston said. "Where's Kristy?"

"I don't know," he replied. "She said she saw one of her friends. I told her I was going to hang here."

"I'm glad," said Houston. "This gives us a chance to catch up. How's school?"

"It's good," Graham responded. "You know, it's school."

"Do you live somewhere outside our district? I've never seen you at school," Sandi said.

"I go to the private school," Graham explained. "My parents are education snobs."

"They should be. He's brilliant," Houston commented. "Any idea of where you'll go to college?"

"Naw. I'm actually thinking of taking a year off to find myself," Graham stated.

"Why?" Houston asked with a laugh. "Are you lost?"

"No, man," Graham said, laughing along with him. "I just have no idea what I want to do with the rest of my life."

"Do your parents know?"

"Not yet. I'm not saying anything until I know better what I'm going to do. You know they won't be happy. I've been accepted to every college and university I've applied to, and they keep badgering me to make a decision. They just don't know I have, and it's not what they're going to want to hear."

"What makes you happy?" Sandi asked.

Graham looked long and hard at her. "Happy? I'm not sure what you mean. I'm pretty good at Math, but I can't see myself working with numbers the rest of my life."

"No," Sandi interjected. "Not regarding academia. I mean, what do you like to do that gives you joy?"

"Oh! I have a couple hobbies I like," Graham said. "I love to sail. I like to hike, and I collect rocks and minerals."

"If you're going to take a year off anyway," Sandi began, "why don't you look into joining a sailing team. I know some people who are usually looking for crew. If you already know how to sail, I'm sure it would make you more attractive to them hiring you. I'd be happy to put in a good word for you."

"Really?" Graham asked. "You'd do that for me? That's a brilliant idea. I'd never thought about that."

Houston gave Sandi a side-hug and said, "That's my girl, brilliance!"

"Once you've gotten your fill of the sea, maybe consider studying geology since you are a collector," Sandi added.

"I never thought to turn my hobbies into a profession," Graham said. "That actually makes me excited to continue my studies. I do think I'd still like to take a year off."

"You'd probably go back into classes with renewed vigor," Sandi said.

"She's got a point," Houston chimed in.

"So, how did the two of you meet?" Graham asked.

"School," they said in unison, and they all laughed.

"Why haven't you told me about her sooner?" Graham queried.

"I must have been afraid you'd swoop in and take her from me," Houston replied.

They all chuckled. "Ah! That's because you know I would have won," Graham chided.

He wrapped Sandi up in his arms and pulled her away from Houston for a moment. They were all laughing when Graham let Sandi go.

The next thing she knew, she was pushed into the pool. Houston dove in after her. As she came up sputtering, she heard Graham say, "What is the matter with you?" Sandi saw a mad Kristy with her hands on her hips.

"We're out of here," Kristy announced. She grabbed Graham's hand to pull him with her.

He yanked his hand from hers. "I'm not going anywhere with you. You need to apologize to Sandi."

"It will be a cold day in hell when I apologize to that maggot," Kristy said.

"I beg your pardon?" Graham said, standing his ground.

A group was gathering as Sandi and Houston climbed from the pool. She was sure their clothes were ruined. She was horrified as everyone stared at them.

Kristy stomped her foot and proclaimed, "I said we're going!"

"No one tells me what to do. I'm not going anywhere with you. Not today, not ever. We're through. I have no interest in being with anyone who can be so hotheaded and mean. I'll find my own way home. Are you alright, Sandi?"

"Sandi?" Kristy screamed and started pounding on him with her fists.

"You're insane," Graham said. As he turned away, Kristy was thrown off balance, slipped, and went into the pool. No one jumped in after her.

She came up sputtering. "Someone get me out of here."

"Come on," Houston said as he took Sandi's hand. "Hey, Graham, we'll be happy to give you a ride."

They were walking away when Sandi felt Houston yanked from her grasp. He hit the ground with Connor on top of him. Graham grabbed Connor from behind and threw him off Houston. Just then, Jana jumped Sandi, and they went down. Jana was swinging and fighting like a girl. Houston grabbed Jana, pulled her off Sandi, and set her on her feet, while Max picked Sandi up and righted her. "Are you alright?"

"Yeah. I'm fine. Thanks."

Jana was still clawing at Sandi. Sandi kept pulling back to avoid connecting with the daggers Jana called nails. She wasn't going to dodge and weave like this all night, and Jana wouldn't stop, so Sandi leaned in and punched her square in the nose. Blood started pouring from Jana's face.

"Don't you *ever* touch me again," Sandi said, getting up in Jana's face. "I've had all I'll ever take from the likes of you. I hope I've made myself perfectly clear."

Sandi turned, took Houston's hand, and marched out of the party.

They passed Preston, and Houston said, "I'm really sorry, dude. We didn't start it."

"No, man. But you sure finished it," Preston said, laughing. "Are you all right, Sandi?"

"I am. I'm sorry. If there are any added expenses, let me know, and I'll pay them."

"Naw. You're good. From what I saw, you didn't do anything wrong. I'll pin it on Jana, Connor, and Kristy if there are. I wish you wouldn't leave."

"We're soaked and need to get into dry clothes," Houston said.

"I get it," Preston said. "Have a great rest of your weekend. Sorry you can't stay."

The trio left.

In the limo, Houston asked Graham if he would want to go back to Sandi's house and see his mom.

"I'd love to see your mother," Graham said. "Why is she at Sandi's house?"

"Oh!" Houston exclaimed. "We've moved in there. She's seeing Sandi's dad."

"Really?" Graham said in surprise.

"Yeah, it's a long story," Sandi added.

"Okay, sure," Graham agreed.

Sandi texted her dad to be sure he and Grace were still up.

When the pair saw the three of them climb from the car, Grace exclaimed, "What happened?"

"Sandi was pushed into the pool at the Ritz, and I went in after her," Houston said.

"Graham!" Grace shouted. "Come here! Were you at the prom or the after-party?"

Graham went to her, leaned in, and hugged her tightly. "Hi, Mrs. MacAvoy. Both. It's so good to see you. How are you doing? Wow! You look amazing. No wheelchair—nice!"

"I'm much better seeing you. What a nice surprise. Come in."

Grace said, "Alan, I'd like you to meet the son of some old friends of mine. This is Graham. Graham, this is Mr. Powell." They shook hands.

"Please, call me Al." Sandi's dad ushered everyone into the house.

"I'm going to go get changed," Sandi said.

Houston said, "Me too. Be right down."

"Have a seat," Sandi heard her dad say as he led them to the living room.

When Sandi and Houston rejoined the group in warm, dry clothes, they relived the evening for the adults.

"I'm so sorry," Grace said to Sandi. "This should have been a special night for all of you."

"It really was," Sandi said. "Until the end, it was the best night of my life. I had a lot of fun. Did you?" She looked between Houston and Graham.

"I did," Houston agreed.

"I would have had a better night with a stable date," Graham said.

311

Sandi and Houston laughed.

"It sounds like this girl has issues," Grace said.

"Yes," said Sandi, "with me."

"It's Jana's best friend, Kristy, Mom," Houston said.

"Jana, like your old girlfriend, the one Max is with now?" Grace asked.

"Yeah," Houston said.

"You used to date that wacko?" Graham asked.

"He did," Sandi confirmed.

"She didn't seem so unstable back then," Houston said. "She's had a real issue with me dating Sandi."

"And what's the story with the nutjob that took you down, Houston?" Graham asked.

"Took you down?" Grace asked in shock.

"Yeah, Connor. He's always been threatened by me for whatever reason," Houston said. "He used to date Kristy, who has never gotten along with Sandi. I think she's threatened by her intelligence. Connor is just threatened. He's a dumb jock who apparently works hard to stay stupid. Maybe he's been hit in the head too many times on the football field."

"Ah," Graham said. "He's a football player?"

"He's the school's star quarterback," Sandi said.

"Then Sandi punched some girl's lights out," Graham said.

"You what?" Sandi's dad demanded.

"It was totally self-defense," Houston said.

"What could have happened to make you punch someone?" her father asked.

"That girl Jana jumped Sandi from behind," Graham said. "Houston got her off Sandi, but that crazy kept scratching at her and trying to attack. Sandi landed one good punch to her face, and that was the end of that. She put up with her a lot longer than I ever would have."

Sandi's dad looked at her and said nothing.

"I always told Houston not to ever start fights, but if someone else threw the first punch, he was to throw the last," Grace said.

"Oh, she sure did, Mrs. MacAvoy," Graham said.

"It sounds like quite a night," Mr. Powell said. "You know I don't condone violence, but I'm glad you're all right. Now, where is Max?"

"No idea," Sandi said. "He did help me up and asked if I was okay."

"What does Max have to do with all this?" Graham asked.

Everyone in the room looked at each other and said nothing.

Grace finally said, "Max lives here too."

Sandi's father went to the street and let the driver go. He promised to take Graham home when he was ready. As the night went on and the old friends got caught up, it was getting late. Houston said, "Hey, dude, why don't you call your parents to see if you can just stay the night. Someone can take you home tomorrow."

When Graham called his parents, they were surprised to find out where their son had ended up. They said they would love to see Grace and would pick him up later.

Around 1 a.m., Sandi's dad ordered pizzas to be delivered. They all talked into the wee hours of the morning. As Sandi dropped into bed, she wondered where Max was. She could only imagine, and it frosted her.

Thirty-Four

S unday morning, Sandi awoke to the smell of bacon and coffee. She trudged to the shower to try to wake up. She was sore from the tussle with Jana, and the streaming hot water pounding on her flesh was a welcome relief.

When she entered the kitchen, only Grace and her dad were there. "Is Houston up yet?" she asked.

"Not yet," Grace said. "Both boys are still asleep. I don't imagine that will last long with your father cooking bacon."

"That's what brought me up from the dead," Sandi said.

Graham walked in wearing a pair of Houston's sweats. "Do I smell bacon?"

They laughed.

"You do," said Grace. "We figured that would help get you up."

"Would you like some coffee?" Sandi's father asked him.

"No, thank you," Graham said. "I don't drink the stuff. It'll put hair on your chest."

"How about a Coke or a Mountain Dew?" Sandi asked.

"Yeah, I do the Dew, if you have it," Graham said.

"We do," Grace said. "It's in the fridge; help yourself."

"Can I help with anything?" Graham asked on his way to the refrigerator.

"I've got it," Mr. Powell said. "Just have a seat at the table and enjoy your drink."

Houston arrived. "I smell bacon."

Everyone laughed. At that moment, Max walked in the back door in the clothes he had worn the night before. His tie hung loose around his neck, and the top buttons of his shirt were undone.

Graham said, "Uh, hi! Nice to see you again. Just getting in?"

"Uh, yeah."

Graham said, "So, that was your girlfriend that attacked Sandi last night?"

Sandi liked Graham. He was certainly straightforward.

Max lowered his head. "Yeah." He looked up at Sandi. "I'm really sorry. Are you all right?"

Sandi simply nodded her head. "Is Jana going to live?"

"Yeah. You broke her nose." He walked through the kitchen. "I'll see everyone later. I'm pretty tired."

"I bet," Sandi said sardonically.

Once Max was gone, the chatter returned to its previous level of joy.

AROUND 4 P.M., the front doorbell chimed. "I'll get it," Max announced.

"That should be my parents," Graham said.

Max led a man and woman into the living room as Grace stood to welcome them. The reunion was sweet. Grace invited them to have a seat. Sandi and Houston situated themselves on the fireplace hearth to make room for all.

"Oh, Grace, look at you!" Graham's mom said. "What have you done? I thought..." She trailed off.

"Yes, I know. I'd like you both to meet a very special man in my life and his brilliant daughter. This is Alan and Sandi Powell. Al, Sandi, these are the Crowleys.

Al shook their hands and offered them a seat.

Houston stood to shake hands with Graham's dad and hug his mom. "It's so nice to see you again."

"Look at you," Graham's mother said, standing back from Houston. "You're all grown up."

"That's what I said to Graham last night," Grace said. "They grow up so fast.

Sandi and Houston looked at each other and rolled their eyes. Parents!

It was a nice afternoon. Graham's parents were invited to stay for dinner, extending the afternoon into the evening. Sandi loved having so much activity in their home.

"Can I get your clothes back to you later?" Graham asked Houston.

"Keep them," Sandi said.

"Generous, isn't she?" Graham said.

"You have no idea," Houston said with a chuckle.

"Naw, I'll return them," Graham said. "It will give me an excuse to visit again."

"You never need an excuse," Sandi said. "You're welcome here anytime."

ON MONDAY MORNING, Jana showed up at school with a big bandage on her nose. When she saw Sandi, she got up in her face and said in a nasally voice, "You are going to pay for my broken nose and any cosmetic surgery to make it right."

"I'd suggest you get out of my face," Sandi said. "Or I'll give you more than a broken nose. You started this. It's on you!"

"This isn't the end of this," Jana called after her as Sandi walked past her.

Sandi stopped, turned around, and said, "Haven't you had enough? Go away, Jana. Everyone knows you're a mean girl. Now, they all know which of us is tougher. Let it go already." Sandi turned again and walked away.

"Never," Jana called after her.

"Your funeral," Sandi said over her shoulder.

"I heard that," Jana said.

"At least your hearing works," Sandi responded.

The kids in the hall started laughing. *Well, this was a nice change of events,* Sandi thought. She knew this was only fueling Jana's fire. Jana would never tolerate being laughed at.

~

A COUPLE WEEKS PASSED, and Jana approached Houston and Sandi at lunch. "Explain to me who Max is to you!" She looked Houston square in the face.

Houston spoke up first. "He's Sandi's adopted cousin."

"Sure he is," Jana said skeptically.

"He is," Sandi said. "My uncle adopted him."

"Why does he live with you?"

"His father died, and we took him in," Sandi answered.

"I don't think so," Jana said. "Something about him struck me when I first met him. I couldn't put my finger on it. The more I thought about it, I've finally figured out what it is."

"No one cares, Jana," Houston said.

"I'm sure that's what you want everyone to think," Jana shot back.

"What is it?" Houston asked with frustration.

"Funny thing is," Jana went on, "You want to say Max is *Sandi's* cousin, but he looks more like your side of the family."

Sandi's blood ran cold. *No, no, no, no, no,* she thought. *This could not be happening.*

"He's not," Houston said adamantly.

"Look at him and look in a mirror," Jana said. "He is too. How is that? What do you think attracted me to him? He is your spitting image."

Houston looked at Sandi and back at Jana. "Nice. Does Max know?"

"That he looks just like you? Yeah, I asked him. He said he didn't know."

"No, pea brain," Sandi said. "That you want him because you think he's Houston's doppelganger?"

"Don't turn this around on me!"

"You're the one who said it," Houston said.

"Just answer the question."

"He's adopted. I have no idea why he resembles me, and I don't really care."

"Some coincidence."

Sandi's blood ran cold. She couldn't believe this had gone on all this time, and now this cotton-brain was going to spill the beans.

"Go mind your own business, busybody, and stop trying to stir trouble. You're a sad excuse for a human," Houston demanded.

"Keep believing that lie," Jana said. "Sounds to me like there's something fishy going on with you two." And she walked away.

Sandi's body flooded with relief.

"That went well," Houston said when Jana was out of earshot.

"I knew we should have been better prepared."

"I know, but I had no idea how to come up with something feasible. Doppelganger. That was a good one."

Sandi said, "I feel a bit bad for Max, but he made his choice."

MAX HAD DISTANCED himself from the family, electing to spend way too much time with Jana. He was no longer working out with Houston. She and Houston were doing that together now. Max usually made himself scarce, which Sandi was happy for. She still struggled with his betrayal. It was hard for her to see him with Jana at school. He acted arrogant when he was around Jana, and she appeared to treat him like he was one of her couture handbags.

Sandi mourned the loss of the happy times she and Max used to have together. Now, he barely said two words to her in an entire day. She wondered if he was still learning more languages. She couldn't imagine what he and Jana found to talk about. His intellect was too high for her. Then again, she didn't imagine they did much talking when they were together.

Thirty-Five

Alan Powell had rented out his and Grace's favorite restaurant for an evening. Sandi was bent over, smelling some yellow roses, when she felt a presence behind her. She turned. "Grandfather, I'm glad you came."

"You look beautiful, my dear," he said and gave her his cold, cursory embrace.

"Thank you. Have you seen Dad?"

"Not yet. I just got here."

"Come. I'll introduce you to everyone."

She led him to the dining room where all their friends were mingling.

Sandi walked up between Max and Houston.

Her grandfather extended his hand toward Houston and asked, "And who is this?"

Houston shook his hand. "How are you, sir? I'm Houston MacAvoy. Sandi's boyfriend, Grace's son. Nice to meet you."

"Likewise." He turned to Max with an outstretched hand. "And you must be his brother?"

Max said, "No, sir. I am Max."

He looked between Houston and Max and raised an eyebrow at

Sandi. She knew he fully understood what she had done. "So, this is Max?" he said, not looking at Max but at Sandi.

"Yes, sir," Max said.

"I see," he said, and this time looked at Houston.

Before he could say another word, she said, "Let me introduce you to Grace."

He followed. She made the introductions.

Grace said, "I see where Alan gets his good looks. He looks just like you."

Sandi saw him visibly stiffen more than his usual stance. "I should think so," he said to Grace. "It's nice to meet the woman who will finally make an honest man of my son. I never believed he would marry."

"You mean marry again, don't you?" Sandi interjected. "Did you forget my mother?"

"No. I mean marry. He's never been married."

Sandi stood in stunned silence. She had always believed her father and mother were married. From behind her, she heard her father say, "Dad, glad you made it."

They turned to face him.

"I thought you had married my mother," Sandi said.

"Not now, Sandi," her father replied.

"But—" Sandi began and was cut off.

"It's not important," her granddad said. "Of course I made it. Thank you for inviting me to your engagement celebration."

Sandi felt the tension that always hung in the air when they were in the same space together. She never understood what had gone so wrong. She knew her grandfather wasn't a warm fuzzy, but she believed he loved his son and probably loved her. She always wondered if he had changed after his wife passed, becoming so cold and calloused. Now, she had to wonder if he had ever married her grandmother or if they had only had an arrangement, as her mother and father apparently had. She didn't know what to do with this information, but she would be asking questions later.

THE EVENING HAD GONE SMOOTHLY. Sandi was glad there had been no drama. There was no telling where her grandfather was concerned.

"There you are." Sandi heard her granddad's voice coming for her. "We need to talk."

Sandi's blood ran cold. The evening wasn't over, and her grandfather hadn't left. There was still time to cause a scene. She put a smile on her face and turned toward him. "Grandfather. Are you enjoying yourself?"

"I am. Your father seems happy. Grace is lovely. They were telling me what all of you were able to accomplish with her. I've known it was possible. We've never been able to perfect it, and not everyone would be willing to settle for anything less than they originally had."

"It allowed Grace to be free of her wheelchair. She's been very grateful."

"Well done, Sandi. Now, tell me about Max."

Sandi stood in silence, trying to decide how much to say.

"I take it he's the result of your visit to me last year?"

"He is. He is what made it possible for us to take it a step further to help Grace. Houston wanted to go to college to discover a way to help his mother. Since we've already done that, he's going to be working out a way to help the masses instead."

"I take it Houston donated something toward Max's creation. What was it?"

"I used his DNA."

"I figured. They look like twins. I'll have to talk with him later."

"Why would you do that? For what purpose? To what end?"

He now appeared to be gloating. "Why? He doesn't know? Did you do it without his permission? This is why I refused to help you when you came to me. You don't think. You just do what you want without paying any attention to the repercussions."

Houston seemed to appear out of nowhere. "As a matter of fact, she did have my blessing, sir."

"What has Grace had to say about this? And your father. Does he know?"

"Yes, Dad knows."

"I see. What happens when the world gets ahold of what you've done?"

"Why do you find it so hard to be supportive? You really are a hateful man. What made you this way? Who did what to you to cause you to be so mean?"

"I'm not mean. I'm practical. You should learn the difference. You need to learn responsibility."

"Oh, and that's what you think your role is? To make me responsible? You've done everything in your power to avoid us over these years. Now, you just want to ride in like you're the Right Police? You can waltz right back out the way you came in."

With that, Sandi walked away. That man boiled her blood. She was glad for her father's sake that his father was in attendance, but he always managed to stir up trouble when he was around. It infuriated her that her granddad didn't want to help her when she asked, understood what was involved in making Max, and was trying to call her out on it now. She was just grateful she had already come clean with Houston, and this wasn't a secret between them, or her grandfather would have had the fuel he was looking for to ignite an explosion.

Sandi went to the window, looking out over the grounds. Houston slipped his hands around her and pulled her back into him. "Don't let him get to you. What could he possibly do now? Just let it go."

"He's just a miserable man who works hard to make everyone else's life wretched."

"Just be glad there isn't anything he could hold over your head. What if you hadn't told me?"

"That's what he was banking on. He's a very powerful man. Last year, I went to him for bone marrow when I began my work on Max. Although he has an army of people and resources, he refused me. He was asking about Max. I really didn't want to get into it with him here. He kept pushing."

"There isn't anything he can do about it now." Houston kissed her neck. "God, you smell good."

She smiled.

"I would think he would be the first in line to want to know what you did. I'm sure it was just of interest to him. Do you think you misunderstood him?"

"There is no misunderstanding that man. He makes himself crystal clear. I just don't like his tactics and threats."

"I would think he would be proud of you."

"He's too narcissistic to be proud of anyone but himself. I'm sure he's mad that I was successful in my little home lab before him and his team of researchers in all his massive facilities. I really don't want to talk about him anymore. Let's dance."

"HEY," Houston said to Sandi one day at lunch. "You know our parents are going out of town this weekend."

"Yeah."

"They'll be gone, and Max is never at home anymore. We'll pretty much have the house to ourselves."

"Right."

"So, what do you want to do?"

"I'm not sure. What did you have in mind?"

He gave her a look and wiggled his eyebrows.

She swatted at him. They laughed and put their foreheads together. Sandi was struck by the familiarity of what she had imagined for herself so long ago.

Kristy and Jana came up beside them. Kristy said, "What did you ever see in him? They're both a couple of freaks."

Sandi looked up at Jana, who looked down at the ground like she was embarrassed.

"Go away, Kristy," Houston said. "This is a mean-girl-free zone."

"Come on, Kristy," Jana said while pulling at Kristy's arm. "Leave them alone. We got what we wanted."

"You got what you wanted," Kristy said.

Sandi held her breath.

Kristy continued, "But what did I get? The maggot is still here."

"Kristy, you need to leave now, before I say something you'll regret," Houston said.

"Like what, big man?"

"Should I share seventh grade with everyone?"

Kristy paled, grabbed Jana by the arm, and quickly retreated.

"What happened in seventh grade?" Sandi asked.

"Remember I told you she'd come onto me? Well, she did something she could be arrested for. I promised if she left me alone, I'd never tell."

"What was it?"

"I made a promise, and I'll keep it. But she'd better leave you alone."

She leaned over and kissed him.

FRIDAY EVENING, Max was out with Jana. Sandi figured he probably wouldn't be home most of the weekend. She was sad things were the way they were between them and hated that he had chosen Jana. Why did it have to be her, of all people? She guessed it was better than Kristy —but not by much.

"I love being with you like this," Sandi said, standing so close to Houston that she could lay her head on his broad chest. She inhaled deeply. He smelled so good.

"I do too. It was a good day. I love getting creative with you in the lab."

"Yeah, now what do you say we get creative in another room of this house?"

"Great minds think alike." While he kissed her passionately, he lifted her into his arms and carried her upstairs, never breaking contact with her lips. He laid her on his bed and pulled his t-shirt over his head.

She loved looking at him. He was so well-defined. Her heart skipped a beat, and she trapped her lower lip between her teeth while gazing longingly at him.

"Girl, you drive me wild when you do that."

"What?"

He gently bit her lower lip.

She giggled.

He kissed her while laying her back on the bed.

She felt an explosion through her body and moaned. He stopped. "What?" she asked.

He smiled, shook his head, and resumed kissing her while his hands roamed over her body. It was taking everything she had in her not to give in and go all the way with this man. She just didn't feel ready to take that next step yet. She loved Houston more for respecting her boundaries, but his skilled hands and mouth were making it difficult.

SANDI OPENED her eyes to light streaming through the window. It was morning. Wow! What a night. She turned her head to see him still sleeping. He was her dream come true. She didn't think she could be happier than she was right now. She was glad he was able to keep them under control. She loved waking up next to him. She could get used to this. She was going to talk him into the one more night they had.

He began to stir and opened his eyes. He rolled on his side and slid open the bedside stand drawer. Her heart started to thud. He pulled a box, flipped it open, and offered her an Altoids. He popped one in his mouth.

"Mmm, good morning, beautiful." He leaned in to kiss her. She grabbed a mint from the box. She understood now. "Morning, but I wouldn't go that far."

"What do you mean?"

"It's a good morning, but I'm not beautiful."

"You are the most beautiful woman in my eyes."

"Then I hope you never remove your rose-colored glasses."

"I don't get it. You don't have a problem knowing how brilliant you are, but you have no idea how beautiful you are?"

She looked away. She just didn't see herself the same way Houston seemed to. She got up. "Come on. I need a shower and some coffee."

"Shower with a friend and save water."

"I doubt that will save any water."

Thirty-Six

Sandi and Houston had enjoyed a wonderful weekend. Max had stayed away the whole time. She was sorry to have to return to reality Monday morning. Her whole body ached.

Her father met her in the kitchen with the usual juice offering.

"Oh, come on, Dad."

"Drink."

"No. I have been just fine all weekend without this foulness."

"That's what I was afraid of. And I bet you're feeling it. Now, drink."

"Feeling what? Repulsed. Yes, I am."

"Al, you really need to explain to her," Grace said.

"Explain what?" Sandi asked.

"Not now. Drink."

"Then tonight," Grace said.

"Tonight," her father agreed.

Max came down and went straight to the fridge. "Man, I need some juice this morning."

"I take it you went the weekend without it too?" her father said.

"Yeah. I'm sluggish today."

"Wait a minute," Sandi said. "No! Are you saying what I think you are?"

Her father just looked at her.

"No." She paused in thought. "No, it can't be true." She looked at Grace, then looked away.

Houston walked in jauntily and said, "Morning, everyone. How was your weekend?" He kissed his mother's cheek, leaned in to kiss Sandi, and stopped. "What's going on? What are all the looks for?"

"Yes, honey. There's a reason I've always forced you to drink your juice daily." He stopped and just looked at her.

"For some other reason than to torture me?" Sandi asked.

"Yes," he replied. "My experiment all those years ago didn't fail. You were my greatest success."

Sandi's head began to swim. "What are you saying?"

"I made you just like you made Max," he said.

She sank hard onto her chair. "No! That's not possible!"

"You know it's possible," her father said. "And there's more."

"More?" Sandi asked. "You've made others?"

"No," he replied. "But my father has. That is what his facilities are all about."

"I knew if I could make Max, he must be able to do more."

"Yes. He made me," her father admitted.

Sandi felt like all the air had been sucked from her lungs. "He what? You what? I don't understand."

"Like Max," he began, "I was created by my father in a petri dish. He was always cold and clinical with me. I was never anything more to him than a successful experiment. And his father made him. My father developed that juice you take to keep us alive. Do you remember when you rebelled against me when you were starting to develop Max, and you went a few days without that juice? Our bodies need it to continue to live. If we stop, our cells will break down and eventually, we will die."

"Why are you telling me this now?" Sandi asked.

"Because you need to know the importance of continuing to drink your juice every day. It's more than just a beverage with vitamins."

"Why didn't you tell me before now?" Sandi insisted.

"I never wanted you to feel you were just a science experiment. I really wanted you. That's how you got your name. Sandi stands for She And I. My name is an acronym for Artificial Life Accelerated Naturally. I had learned how to make humans from my father. I wanted to make you female. Much like you, I wanted a woman of my own. Funny thing happened, though. My feelings for you gravitated to parental instead of lover. I have loved you more than life itself. You became my everything. Until Grace, I didn't have an interest in becoming romantically involved with anyone. You and my work were all I wanted. I've been on dates, I've even had a few so-called girlfriends, but never anyone I would want to be serious about, until Grace."

"What am I supposed to do with this bombshell?" Sandi asked.

"Forgive me?" her father said. "I hoped I would never have to tell you. The problem was, you have to know, so you don't stop drinking the juice. I guess I had hoped you would never leave me."

"You knew I would leave to go to college one day."

"Actually, I intended to go with you. I was just going to buy a house wherever you went and have you continue living with me."

"You can't be serious. You had to have known one day I would leave you to make my own life."

"I'm very serious. This weekend, I told Grace everything. She convinced me to trust that you would understand and forgive me for keeping this from you."

"I don't even know what to do with that. Any of that."

"Forgive," Grace said. "I found it in my heart to forgive you for stealing my son's DNA. He was able to forgive you. You should be able to find it in your heart to forgive this man who gave you life and has loved you so deeply."

Sandi looked into her kind eyes. Oh! This woman was maddening. She was right, but Sandi didn't know if it was that easy. She sat thinking about what she'd done with Max. She had been raised in a loving home. Her father had not been that fortunate. She believed parents wanted better for their children. She thought about all the difficulties she had put her father through—yet he continued to love her.

He continued to look at her hopefully, expectantly. So much was running through her head. She wanted to run, but instead, she went to him, and he wrapped her in his arms.

"I love you, princess."

"I love you too, Daddy."

Thirty-Seven

S andi wrapped her arms around her man when she met him in the hall outside her bedroom. "Our parents seem really happy."

"Yeah, they do."

"You know, you could sneak into my room and sleep with me tonight."

"Won't happen."

"Why not?"

"I feel like I would be disrespecting your father in his own house. And now, my mother."

"You didn't have a problem sleeping with me over the weekend."

"Your father wasn't under the same roof at the time."

"We didn't do anything."

"I know, but I wouldn't feel right."

"You are so weird. You are not a normal teenage boy."

He laughed. "I'm your weird."

"You are, and I love you."

They both froze. She didn't know what to do. She wished she could take it back, but she didn't want to insult him if he was feeling the same way. Instead, she leaned back a bit to be able to look at his face to read his reaction.

Houston had a face full of conflicting emotions running across his face. She couldn't read him.

"I'm sorry," Sandi said. "It wasn't to scare you off. It just came out."

Houston remained silent, staring at her.

"Say something."

When he said nothing, she turned away and ran through her room into her bathroom and shut the door.

"No. Wait. Come back," she heard him saying on the other side of the door.

She leaned her back against the door, sank to the floor, plunged her face in her hands, and sobbed. How dumb of her.

An hour later, there was a soft tapping on the door from the guest room. She said nothing. The door cracked open, and Grace stepped in. "Sandi? Can I come in?"

Sandi quickly sat up. "Yes, of course."

Grace looked relaxed and beautiful in jeans and a T-shirt.

"Are you all right?" Grace asked.

"I will be."

She sat down beside Sandi. "Houston told me what happened."

"Yeah. I opened my stupid mouth when I should have kept it shut."

"That's not what I heard."

Sandi looked at her and thought she should just listen. Maybe he didn't tell his mother the whole thing.

"Houston said you told him you love him."

Yup. He had told her the whole thing. Sandi remained silent and hung her head.

Grace lifted her chin. "It's nothing to be ashamed of."

"I feel like such a fool. I had no idea he didn't feel the same way I do. I don't know what came over me. It just flew out of my mouth without thinking."

"Oh, honey, that's not true. You can't help how you feel. Men are a bit clueless and a bit slow sometimes. There's nothing to feel foolish about. Houston feels terrible he hurt you. He asked me to come find you and plead his case. It's not that he doesn't feel the same. He was just in shock that you felt this way. He said he froze and didn't snap out of it until it was too late, and you refused to hear him out. He said the last thing he ever wanted was to hurt you. He was just surprised. I think you should come out and talk to him. This isn't something that should come from me. It needs to be Houston in his own words. Please give him a chance to tell you how he feels for himself."

"I don't think I can. I was hoping I could face him tomorrow. I don't think I can do that tonight, though."

"I know my son. I think you should by now too."

"I thought I did. I can't be humiliated any more than I am for one day, Grace."

"What makes you believe you will be? Have you ever known Houston to do that to you?"

"You didn't see the look on his face."

"No, I didn't. Are you sure you properly interpreted what you saw?"

"If I misunderstood, he could have corrected me. He didn't. He may have felt regret afterward and came to you to get him a chance to talk his way out of it. What I do believe is he doesn't feel the same way I do. I'm glad to know this now before I allowed myself to fall any harder for him."

"You're both so young. You can't really know what love is yet. I believe Houston loves you the best he can for his young age. He does know how to love, but he's just learning about romantic love. You both need to learn. I'm not really sure if that's something you'll learn together. That remains to be seen. But you can't just run away when things get difficult. Maturity is facing whatever it is head-on. Remember, men develop a lot slower than women. All I'm asking is you talk with him. Work it out together. You each owe each other that." She hugged Sandi. As she stood, she drew Sandi's hands with her.

Sandi stood up reluctantly. She didn't know what it was about this woman. She seemed to easily bend everyone in this house to her will. Sandi couldn't help but adore her. She was the calm in their storms.

"He's waiting for you on the front porch," Grace said.

Sandi took a deep cleansing breath and went out the door.

When she stepped out on the porch, Houston was on the swing and looked up. "Oh, good. You're here. Come sit with me."

"I'd rather stand."

Houston started to stand up.

"You stay where you are," Sandi instructed.

"I don't want to be this far away from you."

"I can just as easily go back to my room."

He sat back down. "At least come closer."

Sandi closed the distance between them by half. "What is it you have to say that escaped you before?"

"Please don't be like this. I didn't mean to hurt you."

"But you did."

"You have to understand, of all the things I could have guessed you were going to say, that wasn't one of them."

"Are you kidding me? You really didn't know how I felt?"

"Don't you mean how you feel?"

"No. I said what I mean. How I *felt*."

"So, you don't love me?"

"No. I was being a foolish girl with a crush. Your mother set me straight: apparently, I'm too young to know what love is. Now, I put the fear of God in you with three little words. I get it. You're biding your time with me. Well, I'm making this easy for you. We're through. We don't have a choice. Now that our parents will be married, we have to live under the same roof. I won't make it awkward for you. You live your life, I'll live mine. Find a new girlfriend, and I'll give you your privacy. We just have to make it through the rest of the school year, and I'll be gone anyway. I have never intended to return once I leave for college, so you'll be free to come and go as you please."

"You're being ridiculous."

"Oh! Not only am I foolish, I don't know what and how to feel, but I'm ridiculous too. Glad we had this talk." Sandi turned on her heels, heading toward the door.

Houston, with his long legs, was on her in a moment. "Stop!" he said as he grabbed her arm. "Stop right there. That's not fair."

Sandi stood frozen in place. She refused to turn to face him. He came around to stand in front of her.

"You can be the most maddening, stubborn person I have ever known. You coming out here dictating to me what I think and feel and how it *will* be is not giving me a chance. It's not giving us a chance."

"There is no *us*. You made that clear."

"I couldn't have. You won't let me set the record straight. How about you listen to me?"

Sandi crossed her arms over her chest in a defensive stance. "Then be my guest. Talk all you want."

"Come sit with me."

"No. Say what you have to say so I can go."

"For someone who's supposed to be so open-minded, you're looking pretty closed off to me."

"I guess it is what it is. Speak your piece, MacAvoy."

"Look, I had no idea this is how you felt. I was just caught off guard. Before I could wrap my head around what you'd just said, you ran and wouldn't let me in. You are still not giving me a chance to tell you what *I* feel. Nice of you to put words in my mouth, but they are not *my* words. How about you let me tell you in my own words and don't run away from me."

"Fine."

Houston took a step toward Sandi. Sandi took a step back.

"You have something to say, say it!" Sandi snapped.

"I can't touch you?"

"No, you can't. I think you've been stringing me along by touching me, making me think one way when you feel another. You don't need me as your girlfriend. You stir my emotions and play me. This is obviously a game for you. Now, I know how you really feel. I'm not a willing participant anymore."

"I'm glad you know it all!" Houston bellowed in an angry tone.

It shook Sandi to her core. She had never heard him raise his voice. It scared her.

"You listen to me, Sandi Powell! You throw your mouth around all the time. You have a sharp tongue that rips people apart because you're smarter than everyone around you. I knew it was simply protection for yourself. Well, you don't need protection from me. What you never give me is the benefit of the doubt. You don't give me space to think about things. You just make assumptions, and you've been wrong. So wrong. You're wrong now, but you're too stubborn to let your guard down— with me, of all people—and just listen."

Sandi's mouth opened. He gave her a look that said he meant business. She closed her lips.

He continued. "I told you I've never known anyone like you. You're the most intelligent girl I've ever encountered. You're witty and fun to be around. There's never a dull moment with you. You've got a big, generous heart. You're beautiful, and yes, you are sexy as hell! I don't know how many times or how many ways I have to tell you, I have wanted to make love to you since the first time I kissed you. You think you have the monopoly on cold showers? Not on your life. Your father's water bill has got to be astronomical.

"You want honesty? Here it is: I do love you. I love you so much it scares me. It just surprised me that you felt the same way I do. You're so independent. I never quite know what's going on in that head of yours. I have dreamed you will one day be my wife. I know we're young, but I can't and don't want to imagine any other woman by my side for the rest of my days but you. My dad used to say you never really know someone until you live with them. He was right. We've been lucky to see that we can live together when that day comes. Living with you, I *do* know you now. It makes me a very happy man."

Sandi let her arms drop to her sides.

He went on. "We have another year of high school and many years of college and graduate school to get through. I love you so much, I'm just sad I will have to wait so long to make you my wife."

Sandi's jaw dropped. Houston stepped closer. She remained. He closed the distance between them and crushed her mouth with his. She wrapped her arms around him and allowed him to deepen the kiss.

"Yes, I want you, Sandi Powell. In the worst way, I want you. Every minute of every day. You are the only woman I will ever want. Please don't break up with me just because my brain froze in shock for a moment. Stay with me."

"Yes, I will stay with you. I do love you. I know your mother thinks we're too young. I'm sure my father believes that too. I know how I feel. I don't ever want anyone but you."

"Will you continue to be my girlfriend? Remain by my side? Even when I do stupid stuff?"

Sandi hugged him tightly. "I will. Even when you do stupid stuff. And you'll love me when I do stupid stuff?"

Houston nodded, leaned down, and kissed her softly, sensually this time. He then led her to the porch swing, sat down, and pulled her onto his lap. "Don't ever do that to me again."

"Do what?" Sandi asked.

"Walk away from me without giving me a chance to explain."

Sandi agreed.

Thirty-Eight

The new school year had begun again.

Houston always drove the two of them to school. Max usually picked Jana up. Everyone wanted to hang out with Max. The more he was around Jana, Sandi noticed, the meaner he became to Sandi and Houston. When he did speak to her, some of his words really hurt, regardless of the language he used.

It was Friday night, and Max was going out with Jana. Sandi figured they wouldn't see him until Monday morning, as usual.

Sandi stopped him in the upstairs hall. "Date?"

"So?"

"So, is there any reason you can never be nice to me anymore?"

"Hey! This was your doing."

"No. This was *your* doing. You're the one who cheated on me with someone you knew I couldn't stand. I moved past it. You can't even be cordial to me at home?

"She's fun. She doesn't have a problem having sex with me. You did. I moved on. Get over it."

"I did get over it. You could at least act like you even know me."

"Why should I? You're nothing but pond scum."

Sandi felt like she'd been slapped. "Now you sound like Jana."

341

"And what's wrong with that?"

"That's beneath you. She's beneath you."

He gave her an irritating smirk and said, "Not yet, but she will be before the night is over."

With that, he walked out.

Ooh, he made her so mad! She went to the lab and started banging things around.

"Who stomped on your toes?" Houston said, startling her.

"Max has become disgusting the longer he's with Jana. Do you know he called me pond scum just now?"

"Yikes. Sounds like Jana. Just ignore him."

"I can't. I brought him into this world, I could take him out!"

"Now you sound like a sitcom. Just let it go. You don't travel in the same circles. You don't have to cross paths with him. We'll be gone soon enough."

He was right. She needed to let it go. She just didn't know how.

~

SANDI WALKED into her first block class to be verbally assaulted by Jana. "You need to leave my boyfriend alone, Messy!"

"Shut up, Jana," Sandi said.

"No! You shut up." Jana shot back. "I know when Houston wises up, he'll drop you like a hot potato. I don't know what he sees in you to make it worth slumming. But you have no control over Max, so leave him alone. You're disgusting, and he is some kind of fine, just like Houston. It's just that Max figured out the truth about you. Houston will. And I'll be there to gloat."

"I said shut it, Jana!"

"Or what? You'll break my nose again?"

Sandi stopped talking. Jana continued, but Houston had taught her it took two to fight. She wasn't going to do it.

~

SANDI WAS STILL in the lab, fuming over Max and Jana's ugly words. She'd had enough. She hated the way he treated her now and wasn't going to be made to feel like an outcast in her own home. Max was done with her? Fine. She was most certainly done with him.

Thinking through everything, she contemplated just ending Max's life. That wasn't who she was. She couldn't just kill him. With her luck, she'd end up in prison, and she didn't look good in orange. She might not be one of the beautiful people he associated with, but she was the one who'd given him life. He could at least be nice to her.

He was getting more arrogant every day. He needed to be put in his place. She had made him so she would no longer be looked at as lower than the Kristys and Janas of the world, and instead, he had become just like them. She would love nothing more than to rip their beautiful hair from their mindless heads and make them bald. They wouldn't act so arrogantly then. If there were some way to strip them of their beauty and make them humble. She'd love to.

Ooh, she thought. There wasn't anything she could do to them, but she could to Max. *Think, Sandi.* There must be some way to knock Max off his high horse. She didn't like the thought of hurting him. She just knew she couldn't keep being treated like this at school and then at home where she should be safe.

She paced the lab trying to think. What did Max have that Sandi could use against him? She thought about giving him a communicable disease, but she wouldn't be surprised if he didn't already have one of those. He had too many friends to turn all of them against him. Then it came to her. His looks. Without his good looks, he'd no longer be one of the popular people. Jana wouldn't have anything to do with him anymore. Sandi would always love him as her creation. He'd see that and return his loyalty to her. But how would she accomplish that?

She thought about the makeup of a body. It was a delicate balance. When something went out of balance, any number of things could happen. What to do to throw his body out of balance? That was the dilemma. Oh! She had it. It wouldn't be that hard to do, either. She went to work.

THE NEXT MORNING, Sandi was waiting in the hall for Max when he came out of his room. He looked at her with disdain. "What is it you want, maggot?" He turned to go down the stairs.

That was her last straw. She no longer regretted her decision. She walked up behind him and jabbed the syringe she held in her hand into his left butt cheek and emptied the contents into him.

He jumped and yelled, "What'd you do? What was that? Get away from me, you freak."

She turned and walked back to her room. There. Now they'd see who the freak was.

~

FOR A WEEK, Sandi kept watching Max for any changes. Nothing. She was certain an addition of stem cells would have some adverse effects. She had used some of the female bone marrow on him. She didn't understand. How was there no change?

When she got to the breakfast table, everyone was somber.

"What's up?" Sandi asked.

"Something's wrong with Max," Grace said.

"Really? What? Catch something from your tramp?"

When he spoke to her, his voice cracked. "What'd you do to me?"

"Me? You have nothing to do with me. What'd she do to you is more like it."

"No. That day in the hall, you poked me with something. What was it?"

"Are you losing your mind? Are you sure you don't have HIV? I've heard it can create neurocognitive disorders."

"Did you infect me with HIV?"

"I've never slept with you, or did you forget—that would be Jana. There's no telling what she's infected you with."

"You stabbed me with something. I know you did something."

"Sure, I did, Delusional. Now, you're making me wonder what communicable disease causes paranoia." Sandi walked to the coffee pot. She wasn't about to look at anyone and have them give credence to what Max was saying right now.

She went to the sink, looking out the kitchen window to get her composure and not give anything away with her face.

"Well, something is happening, so we need to do an examination," her father said. "After breakfast, let's go to the lab, Max. Do you want to join us, Sandi?"

"Nope. He wants nothing to do with me anymore. You examine him. I'm done," Sandi stated coolly.

Houston walked in. "Morning, everybody. What's up?"

"Something's wrong with Max," Grace said.

"Like what?" he asked, coming up behind Sandi and kissing her cheek.

"We're not really sure. Al is going to check him over after breakfast," Grace stated.

"You are, Mr. Powell? Why not you, Sandi?"

"I'm through with him. Let my father handle it."

"Ah. Hope you're okay, buddy. What are we going to do today, my love?" He wrapped his arms around her.

His touch eased her guilty soul. "I don't know. Anything come to mind?"

"I'm dying over here, and you're making plans?" Max said. Houston's head whipped toward him.

"Whoa! What happened to your voice, dude?"

"That's what I'm talking about," Max said. "I don't know. Sandi did something to me. She won't tell me what."

Houston turned her toward him. "You did something to him? What?"

Sandi shook her head. "I think he caught something from his skank and he's trying to blame it on me."

"Okay, enough with the name-calling and blame games," Sandi's dad said.

"I'll stop when he does," Sandi said.

"What are you, two years old?" her father asked.

"Fine. I'm out of here," Sandi said.

"Juice first," he called after her, but she was halfway up the stairs.

She was shaking all over. That was too close to being busted. At least

345

she knew her plan was set in motion. He wouldn't be so high and mighty for long. He was about to eat a slice of humble pie.

TWO DAYS LATER, Jana stopped Sandi in the hallway at school. "Where's Max? What'd you do to him?"

"Get away from me. I didn't do anything to him. What disease did you pass onto him, since you're the one who spreads her legs for anyone who will lie down?"

Sandi walked away.

Jana ran after her. "He won't talk to me. He's not in school. He texted me and said you did something to him."

"I'm thinking you passed him HIV, and now he's delusional. I said, leave me alone."

"You really are a freak," Jana said to Sandi's retreating back.

Sandi was starting to worry. If Max told enough people, they might start to believe him. He would be fine. She just wanted him to get a grip.

~

BY THE END of the week, Max had developed all sorts of bumps and growths all over his body. That's what Sandi had anticipated would happen. He wasn't so attractive now, was he? Jana would drop him as soon as she laid eyes on him. He would come crawling back to Sandi as his only friend.

Her father came into her room. "What did you inject Max with?"

She looked at him for a moment, then down at the floor.

"That's what I thought. Why?"

"You have no idea what he's put me through! He has become just like his tormenting girlfriend and all her mean friends. I couldn't live with him being awful to me in my own home. You should hear the horrible things he's been saying and doing to me. It was time he learned some humility and stopped treating me like I'm the one who hurt him. He was the one who cheated on me with a known arch-nemesis."

"What did you do? If I have any hope of helping him, I need to know what I'm dealing with."

"Then don't help him."

"Sandi, that's not who I am. It's not who you are. What did you inject him with?"

"Female bone marrow."

"What?" The shock in his voice shook her.

"Oh, he'll be fine. He just won't be such a pretty boy anymore."

"How much?"

"He'll be fine, Dad."

"How much?" he said sternly.

"Just 30 ccs."

"Just? Sandi, how am I supposed to undo that damage?"

"You're not meant to. It will certainly humble him."

"It sounds to me like you're the one who needs some humility. I've told you not to play God. Do you have any idea what you have done?"

"Yeah, I do. I've thrown off his hormones."

"No. You may have just created a monster."

"Oh, please don't be so melodramatic. He's been incorrigible. I couldn't take anymore."

"You talk it out. You don't destroy a life."

"He's trying to destroy mine."

"Now who's being melodramatic? You'd better hope there's something I can do to reverse these effects." He walked out and slammed her door.

Oh boy. That didn't go well.

Sandi sat thinking about what her father had said. Was there something she could do to reverse what was taking place in Max? She hadn't meant to do serious damage, she just couldn't be treated like that any longer.

Houston walked in and sat on the side of her bed. "Boy, your father's pretty mad right now. What's going on?"

Sandi looked at her hands in her lap.

"Hey. What happened? Talk to me. You know you can tell me anything."

Sandi simply shook her head.

"What? Can I help?"

She started to cry.

He pulled her to him. "Hey. What is it? Is it Max? Are you worried? Your father is brilliant. I'm sure he'll figure out what's going on and fix it."

She shook her head and sobbed. "No. He can't."

"Of course he can. It'll be okay."

"You don't understand."

"Then tell me."

"I can't. You'll hate me."

"I could never hate you. I love you, remember."

"You couldn't love me if you knew."

"Just tell me. I thought we didn't keep secrets from each other."

"Max is telling the truth."

"About?"

"I injected him with something."

Oh! What?"

"Female bone marrow."

Houston sat back, put his hands on her shoulders, and held her at arm's length, looking at her.

"Why? What'll that do?"

"I just wanted him to come down off his high horse and stop treating me like the pond scum he kept saying I was. I thought if I put some extra stem cells in him, he might not be so attractive to all the pretty people in school anymore."

Houston dropped his hands and stared at her. "You cannot be serious."

He started to walk away. She said, "That's why I didn't want to tell you. I knew you would hate me. You said you wouldn't. Please don't leave me."

"I can't even be in the same room with you right now. If you ever needed to give me space, now is that time."

He walked out, leaving Sandi to feel alone and isolated. What *had* she done?

Epilogue

⌒⟋⟍⌒

S andi went through her last year of classes ostracized and alone. She was treated as a stranger in her own home. No one, even her father, ever talked to her anymore. Houston avoided her like the plague. She stopped even going near Grace. She couldn't take the way the woman looked at her with disdain.

Max passed in his sleep that spring after his heart finally gave out. Her father came to her room to inform her, but she was so numb by now, she couldn't bring herself to feel anything. She had thought that if Max ever left this world, a piece of her would go with him, but she believed there was nothing left of her anymore. Every bit of her being had been stripped from her soul. Piece by piece, stolen by those she thought had loved her. It had begun so many years before when the mean girls chipped away at her self-esteem. She believed she had created someone who would love her unconditionally. She was wrong. She had felt restored by Houston's attention and love. Now she realized there never had been any restoration; the damage had only been masked momentarily. Her true undoing came that fateful day when Houston walked out of her room and out of her life. Her finality came when the one person she believed would love her forever turned his back on her:

her father. Now, she had no one and was totally and utterly alone. It wasn't supposed to be like this.

As soon as she had finished high school, she requested that her diploma be mailed to her new address in California. She wanted to be as far away from where she was raised as possible. She rented an apartment on the Stanford University campus where she would attend college in the fall. They were the leading university in stem cell research. She would just start all over with a clean slate. No one here knew her. She could assume whatever identity she wanted.

Maybe it was wrong to have a God complex. We weren't gods, just human. He had worked everything out much better than we ever could. Her first thought was maybe she should stop what she had spent her whole life learning, and let God make the humans. Her follow-up thought was that God gifted her with the intelligence she had to better the world. She would use it to do just that.

She thought, in the end, it was all about loving and being loved. So, she would find someone to really love her and not judge her. Not having a past would help. She would reinvent herself.

Sandi was in her kitchen making her dinner when her doorbell rang. She grabbed the towel from over her shoulder to dry her hands on the way to the door. She swung it open and froze.

"Sandi."

"Granddad. What are you doing here? How'd you find me?"

"It wasn't that hard."

"I'm sure, with all your money."

"It's not like you tried to hide."

"It's not like anyone cares."

"Are you going to invite me in?"

She stepped to the side and spread her arm out.

He stepped past her. "Cozy."

"Yeah. What are you doing here?"

"Your father filled me in."

"I see."

"No. I don't think you do."

"I really have listened to a lifetime of lectures."

"I'm not here to lecture you. I'm here to offer you a job."

"You're what? Why?"

"Because you have what I've never been able to find. You're a lot like me."

"I'm nothing like you."

"Oh, but you are. You have a brilliant mind, you're innovative, industrious, and a bit ruthless when necessary."

"Those are not all good traits, Grandfather."

"But in our line of work, at the level I need you for, they are all important. Come work with me."

"I have college."

"Oh, please. You could probably teach most of your classes. This is a waste of your time and talent. Come work with me, and together we will change the world."

"Why can't you do that on your own?"

"I'm sure eventually I can. However, together, we can dominate. You're who I've searched my whole life for. Your father was always too soft, too touchy-feely. I need someone who's not afraid to try, fail, and try again. What do you say?"

"I've signed a year's lease here."

"That my attorneys can break by morning. Come home with me. My plane is waiting at the airport."

Sandi stood studying her grandfather's eyes. She did see herself in them. She turned off the oven, tossed the hand towel on the counter, picked up her purse, and followed him out.

About Laura Ranger

Laura Ranger is a natural storyteller who has been turning life's moments into tales since childhood. A mother of one and grandmother of four, Laura began writing down her fictional stories to the delight of family and friends. With over thirty years of storytelling experience, her passion for writing has only grown stronger over time.

Her publishing journey began with a short story featured in the Christmas anthology *Eight 'Til Christmas*, a project supporting the fight against child hunger. Seeing her story in print lit a creative fire she describes as unstoppable.

Laura is the author of *Deception* and *Royalty*, and she co-authored the novel *Rogue*. In 2025, she will release two new titles: *Made for Me*, and *Taken: The Complete Carl Higdon Story*, a non-fiction work. Her novel *Royalty* has blossomed into a four-book series, with *Heirs* (Book Two), *Chosen* (Book Three), and *United* (Book Four) all slated for release in 2026.

She is also developing a thoughtful new series called *Lessons*, which she envisions as a shared reading experience between parents and children. While originally written for young readers, Laura discovered that the meaningful themes resonate with readers of all ages.

A prolific writer with countless ideas in the works, Laura continues to bring her stories to life, one book at a time. "God blessed me with a natural gift of storytelling," she says. "It's up to me to use that gift to the best of my ability."

Beyond her work as an author, Laura is also the owner of *Foundations Book Publishing Company*, where she helps others share their stories with the world.

Girl on a Swing, Wounded Bird, Book 1

Get it Here: https://www.amazon.com/Girl-Swing-Friends-Romance-Wounded-ebook/dp/B0DXDFCJV3

An award-winning series!

On the "Best Friends to Lovers Contemporary Romance" list on Goodreads.

"Made me laugh out loud, gasp and cry. I find this modern-day love story to be an affirmation of life, love, strength and determination." – **Abbie, Goodreads**

Sometimes the road to love takes an unexpected turn...

For the past ten years, Wren has been trapped in the wreckage of her past. Ever since her parents were killed in a car accident, her life has spiraled out of control. Stuck in a crumbling marriage, her dreams of becoming an artist have withered, and the last flicker of hope is slipping through her fingers. If she doesn't break free now, she may never escape.

Desperate for a way out, she turns to the one person who's always been there—Maddox, her lifelong best friend. With his unwavering support, Wren begins to reclaim her strength and rebuild her life. But falling in love with him was never part of the plan.

When their undeniable connection threatens everything Wren has fought for, she's forced to make an impossible choice. Love just might be the lifeline that saves her—

or it could shatter her for good.

Perfect for fans of Colleen Hoover and Lucy Score, *Girl on a Swing* is an emotional rollercoaster that will keep you hooked until the very last page. It's a story that will break and heal you.

Foundations Book Publishing

Our mission is to exceed the expectations of our authors and the reading community with an uncompromising commitment to quality, individualism and personal pride. We measure our success one book at a time.

You can find more great works in multiple genres including Romance, Literary Fictions, Thrillers, Suspense, Young Adult, and more!

Visit us at FoundationsBooks.net